THE ROMANOV STONE

Robert C. Yeager

Gail —

It's been great to see you
Again and to feel that connection
to Anne. I'm so glad you enjoyed
The Romanov Stone.

abbott press
A DIVISION OF WRITER'S DIGEST

Bob Yeager
5-27-13

The Romanov Stone

Abbott Press books may be ordered through booksellers or by contacting:

Abbott Press
1663 Liberty Drive
Bloomington, IN 47403
www.abbottpress.com
Phone: 1-866-697-5310

ISBN: 978-1-4582-0156-0 (sc)
ISBN: 978-1-4582-0157-7 (hc)
ISBN: 978-1-4582-0155-3 (e)

Library of Congress Control Number: 2011962575

Printed in the United States of America

Abbott Press rev. date: 1/10/2013

For Judi

PEPE LE MOKO (admiring her necklace): What did you do before?

GABY: Before what?

PEPE: Before the jewels.

GABY: I wanted them.

—*Charles Boyer and Hedy Lamarr in*
"Algiers," Wanger Productions, (1938).

On the eve of World War I, estimates put the wealth of the Romanovs at beyond fifty billion dollars—as great in real terms as the combined fortunes of Bill Gates, Warren Buffett, and the Sultan of Brunei today. In power for three hundred years, the tsars controlled the world's fourth-largest economy and held its most sizeable store of gold. Their jewelry included the Imperial Crown, encrusted with nearly five thousand diamonds weighing 2,858 carats; the Imperial Scepter, which contained the 194.5-carat Orlov diamond, said to have been pried from the eye of a Hindu idol; the fabulous Moon of the Mountain diamond of 120 carats; and the Polar Star, a breathtaking 40-carat ruby. The Romanovs had imperial trains and yachts, seven palaces, and five theaters. They directly employed more than fifteen thousand servants and officials.

June, 1831

THE GEMSTONE lay on a small, plump cushion of white silk. In the private chambers of the Tsar of all Russia, it glittered darkly, like wet winter grass.

"It is an especially large emerald," Nicholas I observed. His tone seemed distant. He walked across the room and gazed out a window. In the summer of 1831, with revolutionary fervor sweeping Western Europe, the state of his empire's armies was of greater concern to the tsar than his lapidaries.

"That is precisely what is so unusual, sire. It is not an emerald."

Eight months earlier, a charcoal peddler had been making his way along the banks of the Tokovaya River in western Siberia. Slogging through the snow, his shoes wrapped in rags for warmth, the man came upon a large tree, upturned by a storm the night before. In the exposed roots, the peasant found a cluster of stones he believed were emeralds.

A few weeks later, he took them to Ekaterinburg, center of the tsar's cutting and polishing operations.

The emissary from the emperor's jewel works cleared his throat. "It was under illumination," he recounted, "that the lapidists first saw the extraordinary properties of these stones. A small party journeyed to Tokovaya and more were found. This was the largest."

Nicholas returned to the small table. His towering figure made the cushion and its contents seem tiny and insignificant. He would not have added this meeting to an eleven-hour day had not the Urals mining operations grown steadily more important to the Romanov purse.

"Notice please, Your Highness," his visitor said, "size is not what distinguishes this stone. *This* is what sets it apart from all others."

The visitor lit a small kerosene lamp with a polished reflector and a brass-ringed focusing lens. He aimed its beam directly into the stone.

In an instant, the gem that had appeared to be an emerald flared into a ruby. Its purplish fire rose from the cushion like a vermilion sunrise.

"Astonishing!" Nicholas exclaimed.

The man from Ekaterinburg put down the lamp and moved around the table to stand daringly close to his liege. "Your Highness," he gushed, "consider the colors. Green and red—the imperial colors! There is something else, sire, if you will permit me."

The emperor some called the handsomest nobleman in Europe nodded.

"The gem's discovery was confirmed on April 30 of this year, the same date as the eighteenth birthday of his young Highness, Alexander. Indeed, Majesty, the lapidists call this the Tsarevitch stone."

Part I

Chapter 1: The Present

"THEY HAVE found us."

Shaking, Irina Gavrill lifted herself on one elbow in the hospital bed. Muffled by the oxygen mask, her voice sounded fearful and weak.

"Who has found us, Mom?" Kate's stomach lurched at the sight of her mother's tubes and bandages. She'd not seen her parent in nearly eight years, and during that time they'd barely spoken. Looking at her now, like this, was unnerving. The room's white curtains glared from the walls like an overexposed photograph. Outside the door, a steady stream of intercom announcements droned down the corridor. Despite the sticky June heat, Kate's fingers shivered as she gripped the bed's metal side rails.

Less than an hour ago, in rural central Pennsylvania, Irina had been struck by a pickup truck as she crossed a street. Now she whispered between gasps.

"We haven't had a real talk for a long time, Katya, not since your troubles. But there are certain things I must tell you now, things that should have been said long ago."

Irina's use of her birth name—the name she'd hated as a teenager—conveyed an urgency Kate Gavrill recognized from childhood. She pulled a chair closer to the bed and looked into her mother's eyes. They were her own glacier-blue eyes—"wolf eyes," Kate's students at Marion State called them—but they lacked luster, as if, quite abruptly, Irina's inner source of energy had been unplugged.

Leaning forward, Kate caught her own reflection in the room's aluminum-framed window. With shoulder-length, black hair and lean muscled limbs, she knew she sometimes appeared almost as young as her students.

Fortunately, her professorial bearing and focus were as sharply defined as her East European cheekbones—almost feline in their angularity. Often, just in the way Kate Gavrill lifted her chin, her pupils sensed their separateness. Kate's typical outfit for work, a tweed blazer, penny loafers, and white oxford cloth shirt underscored her buttoned-down style. A widening at the bridge of her nose, a somewhat broad forehead, and a slight fullness in her lips softened her appearance, but not enough to encourage any youthful inclinations to depart from academic decorum.

Irina pulled Kate back into the moment, back into the white room and the terrible, inexplicable events that had transpired only a short time before. "There has been a long coldness between us, Katya," her mother said, "and a time when I swore I could never forgive you. But you are my daughter and you must know everything now. All of it. Everything we kept from you for so long."

"Please, don't talk." Kate's voice caught. She felt an internal dam crumbling. How many times in the last few years had she yearned to talk, really talk, to the injured woman before her?

Wincing, Irina continued. "Hush, girl, and listen. I have little strength and less time. On your mantle, in the frame behind Anya's picture, you will find my tape recording and her letter. You are in great danger."

"Mother, what *are* you saying?"

The older woman's head dropped back to the pillow. She did not answer.

★   ★   ★

Six Hours earlier, Irina Gavrill had pulled her shawl closer and brushed at a spill of white hair. She stood before a booth of antique farm implements, admiring their rough-hewn, wooden handles and worn wrought iron. For the eleventh year, she'd attended the opening day of the annual Pennsylvania Dutch Festival in Kutztown. What a contrast, she thought, between the fairgrounds scenes of peaceful Amish farm life, and the tumult of her own and her family's lives. Her palms moistened and the muscles in her arms grew taut. With age, she thought, emotions grow as brittle as bones.

She remembered the expression on her grandmother's face, years before, when Anya spoke of the night that meant they could never be safe again, not even in Paris, not even in 1933, more than sixteen years after they'd fled Russia. Irina had been a small child, but she still remembered the terror, the night of shouting and screams, and Anya, her beautiful, lithe granmama, pulling her across the slippery rooftop tiles in the dark.

Shaken by the memory, Irina stumbled on a paving stone as she walked toward the exit. Her legs, however, moved lightly and instinctively, and she steadied herself with deceptive grace.

She sighed and twisted a square of brightly colored quilting between her fingers. Clouds were gathering over the fairgrounds. Suddenly, Irina wanted more than anything to see her daughter. The time had come to put their differences aside, if for no other reason than their own mutual safety.

In a deserted field a few miles away, two men stepped from a Mercedes sedan they'd driven under a stand of covering trees. Beside the big German vehicle sat an ancient Ford pickup, dented and dull. The truck was black, the same color as the men's suits and flat-brimmed hats.

The smaller of the pair, pudgy, with a soft face and hard, dark eyes, entered on the passenger side, the old door clanging shut behind him. The other man slid behind the wheel. When he turned the key, the engine—a high-performance motor installed just two weeks before—started without hesitation.

Moments later, they parked the truck in Kutztown. A thin scribble of smoke slipped from the driver's partially opened window.

They sat for nearly an hour.

Abruptly, the men spotted a slender, gray-haired woman striding across the fairgrounds at a surprising pace. They stared at a photograph the driver had balanced on the dashboard, then back at the woman.

Beneath the ancient Ford's rusty hood, the transmission made a grinding sound as the driver shifted into gear.

The tires squealed, pluming blue, acrid smoke. The photo slid off the dashboard.

From the opposite side of the street, a brightly colored ball slowly rolled across the pavement. Five-year-old legs churned close behind.

★   ★   ★

FIFTEEN MINUTES later, the old pickup, with its bloodied front fender, shrank in the departing Mercedes' rearview mirror.

Tartov, the shorter, fleshier man, pressed a button on his cell phone and, quite suddenly, the old vehicle burst into flames. His companion fished in a pocket to retrieve his own ringing mobile. "Yes, Excellence," he said, then listened wordlessly to the caller. He handed the phone to Tartov. "It's for you," he said.

"Yes, Excellence," repeated Tartov, who listened, then closed the phone. He shifted in his seat.

"Stop the car," Tartov ordered.

The Michelins ground into a patch of gravel on the edge of the road. In the adjacent field, rows of corn gleamed in the fading sun. "You swerved," Tartov said, staring straight ahead. "She might not even be dead."

"If not, she will die soon."

Tartov twisted his short body fully around to confront the driver. "You swerved," he said again. "Your job was to hit her full on. Did you think Excellence wouldn't find out?"

The driver's lips firmed into a straight line. "You saw the boy, Tartov. Why kill him too? That's all. It won't happen again." His voice had a high, pleading tone.

"No, it won't," his passenger replied.

The little fat man slipped a hand inside his jacket. It emerged holding a German-made Walther automatic. "Get out," he ordered. "Walk."

Descending an embankment, the pair disappeared into the corn stalks. Only the smaller man returned.

December, 1911

SEATED AGAINST the carriage window, knowing precisely how brightly the moon would flash in her chestnut hair, Anya Putyatin tossed her head. Outside, the night's otherwise peaceful silence was shattered by the clatter of sixteen hooves—the drumbeat of a prancing quartet of horses drawn from the Cossack Imperial Guard.

The white-haired man opposite her seemed to sink into the ostrich hide upholstery. Hidden in shadows, his face effectively disguised any expression. He'd scarcely spoken since arriving for her at the comfortable flat she shared with her parents on Strastnoy Bulvar. Now he stared beyond her to the dark streets. Grand Duke Alexander did not approve, Anya sensed, of a 16-year-old ballerina, most especially the Imperial Ballet's prima ballerina, visiting Russia's Tsar aboard his private train.

Moments later, however, that is exactly where she stood. Alone in the elegant saloon car, with its gracefully curved silk and leather armchairs and polished oak paneling, Anya felt suddenly plain and inconsequential. The train itself stood motionless on a heavily guarded siding just outside Kursky, the main Moscow rail station to St. Petersburg. Leaning forward, she parted a window curtain. Outside, puffing tiny clouds of cold air, two dozen soldiers in heavy woolen coats formed a single line parallel to the train.

Boots thumped on metal steps, a door swung open and Nicholas II strode into the railcar, bringing with him a gust of frozen air and the pungent smell of cigar smoke and locomotive fumes. He clapped his gloves against the cold and bowed slightly, waving an apologetic hand over his green and red military tunic with its heavy epaulets, light blue sash and campaign ribbons.

"Please forgive my over-dress," Nicholas said, smiling. "I'm afraid I had to attend a regimental banquet." He took Anya's hand, bowed slightly and looked directly into her eyes. "I'm so glad you could come."

Lifting her dark lashes, Anya took him in. He was short, though at five feet-seven inches still two inches taller than she. Somehow, however, his uniform, the room and, yes, the unmistakable aura of power, endowed him with impressive apparent height. His light brown hair was—as it had been since he was a boy—parted to the left side. His blue eyes were simultaneously intense and gentle. He touched her elbow, leading her to a deep maroon setee.

"I know you are wondering why I sent for you," he began. "The answer is quite simple."

Anya lowered her eyes again and smiled nervously. She'd wound many a *danseur* around her finger, and even traded mash notes with a young Prussian baron until his wife discovered one of the missives in his jacket. This, however, was no junior member of the German aristocracy. This was the most powerful man in Russia, and one of the most powerful men in the world. Anya lifted her gaze, awaiting his explanation.

"My dear Anya Putyatin," he began, "surely you know of my love for ballet. I have seen you perform now half a dozen times. It may not be prudent to say this to one so young, but truth is truth and not served in the denying. You are simply the greatest dancer there has ever been."

"Excellency, your Highness, please—"

He closed her lips with his forefinger. "You needn't take the word of your besotted tsar," he said, smiling. Slipping a hand in his pocket, Nicholas withdrew a crumpled wad of news clippings. He plucked out the first, and read: "'The whole of her person, marvelously slim and elusive, moves with perfectly coordinated harmony.'" He cast it aside and snatched another: "'Never have such complicated *pirouettes* been executed so impeccably.'

"Please, Anya," he said, leaning forward. "No false modesty. You are the first woman to master forty *fouettes*. They call you 'toes of steel' because of your impossibly long pauses *en pointe*."

In spite of herself, Anya shrieked with laughter. "So," she said, feigning insult, "you brought me here to examine my feet!"

Impulsively, she leapt up. "Sire, if it is my feet you wish, you shall have them!" Anya stood on her tiptoes, and boldly lifted her skirt to her calves. The daringly risqué gesture exposed the soles of her dress slippers as they rose in perfect parallel vertical lines from the floor.

Now it was the tsar's turn to laugh. "No, no, I brought you here to talk about your art." He stood, crossed the car to the window and momentarily parted the curtain as she had. Frowning, he opened a burled walnut cabinet, poured two glasses of red wine, and turned back to her. His tone abruptly shifted to one he might have used at a state dinner or even, perhaps, the banquet he'd just attended.

"We live in a time of great turmoil," Nicholas said, "a time of erratic, wanton behavior. Your dancing is visual evidence of the rewards of order and discipline. It reassures the masses. It says to them, 'Do not pull down the past, it is the foundation for the future.'"

Anya remained silent for a moment, then spoke hesitatingly, uncomfortable to counter her country's head of state. "But sire," she said, "I am only a dancer, and dancing is inherently impulsive and intuitive."

His eyes sparkled; he was clearly enjoying the give-and-take. "Au contraire, Anya," Nicholas replied. "Art is evolution, not revolution. Think of the discipline required to perfect your movements. No, my dear, however avante their creators may think them, all forms of art conform to the laws of succession. They build on what went before. Today, no other dancer is capable of your *pizzicati*, so clear-cut, so elegant, so flowing. In a generation, however, it will be altogether another thing: Every ballerina will be held to your standard."

They began a long discussion about art. Anya marveled at how intently he listened to her views. At one point she realized she was expressing herself more freely with the tsar than she ever had with someone outside dance. As their talk rambled, Nicholas spoke fondly of his youthful love for a ballerina—though he was too discrete to use names, Anya knew her as the famous Kshessinska—and a world cruise he'd taken years before with youthful male companions. Today, he was obviously a man burdened by a position he never sought and, she intuited, a marriage increasingly distracted by his son's health.

One week later, Grand Duke Alexander again called at the Putyatin flat. Two weeks hence, he called again. At this third meeting, Anya and Nicholas II, Tsar of all Russia, did not discuss art. And Anya did not return home until the following morning.

Chapter 2

———————◦《◎》◦———————

DAZED, KATE stood in the drab hospital hallway. She'd always taken pride in her ability to keep her emotions in check. An important part of her competitive armor, she'd told herself. Now, however, tears welled at the corner of her eyes. Somehow she knew she would never forget this moment—or the changes in her life that it would set in motion.

"We did all we could," the doctor said with a look of futility. He twisted his hands together and stood awkwardly a few feet away. Massive internal bleeding, a broken leg and a severe concussion had claimed Irina Viktoria Gavrill, aged 69. "I only hope they catch the bastards."

The grim-faced physician touched her arm, then faded down the hospital corridor, white tails billowing.

Kate pressed a hand to her lips. Not even a year past 30 and she'd lost her mother, her only remaining blood relative and her last link to a history she scarcely knew. As a teenager, Kate had rejected all things Russian, most especially the ballet, opting instead for the uniquely New World sport of high-board diving. Only as a maturing young woman, had she begun to appreciate the grace and beauty of her heritage, as well as the parallels between the sport she'd chosen and the art form she'd rejected. That grace, beauty and heritage would be much diminished in a world without Irina, a world she must now face alone.

The only offspring of older émigré parents, Kate had been pushed from childhood to excel. Her mother earned a modest income as a ballet instructor and, after her husband's untimely death, she and her young daughter shuffled through a series of small towns in the northeastern U.S. Kate's was a rootless, financially strapped childhood, lived in a series of apartments, unmemorable except for the antique furniture and icons—icons Kate scorned—that Irina dragged between domiciles. After completing her Ph.D., Kate took a teaching position at Marion State, a liberal arts college. Her mother was only one state and a few hours drive away, but by then the emotional gulf between them had congealed into a bitter, impenetrable mass. Their conversations were like a bloodless vein, functional but empty.

Behind her, Kate became aware of another presence.

"Miss Gavrill?"

"Yes?" She turned back to the speaker.

"I'm Lt. Donald MacMahon, State Police." A tall man in a dark uniform and a wide-brimmed trooper's hat stood a few feet away. He showed her a badge and ID card.

"Miss—Professor Gavrill, I'm sorry to have to do this so soon after your mother's death. But we believe the perpetrators may still be in Pennsylvania. I need to ask a few questions."

"Not now. Please."

The officer had a lean-boned, western face, and warm, emotional eyes. Early forties, Kate judged.

"Miss Gavrill," he began in a quiet voice, "I realize this is a difficult time, but the quicker we move at this stage of our investigation, the better our chances of apprehending whoever's responsible."

The air had grown stuffy. Filtered through a draped window, the moon fluffed into a colorless angora ball. Kate felt dizzy; she touched the wall for support. Summer heat closed around her like a sweltering crowd. On impulse, Kate opened her mobile phone. She'd missed a call; the number was Irina's, the time less than an hour before her

13

accident. What had she wanted? Her mother hadn't called her cell in years.

MacMahon persisted. "Did she have any enemies—"

Dismissing him with her hand, Kate moved toward the exit. *Behind Anya's picture,* Irina said. She must get home. Now.

March, 1917

KEEPING LYDIA close at her side, Anya had braved Moscow's smoldering open fires and roaming bands of Reds to reach Nicholas in Pskov. It had been almost three years since they'd seen each other. Then, he'd been off to congratulate the troops on their success against the Germans and Austro-Hungarians in East Prussia and at Galicia. Now, with the Russian army defeated and dispirited, they met on the same train where they'd first shared their passion.

The fleshy bags under Nicholas's eyes made him look sad and old. He greeted her, lightly kissed her lips and then held her close. It was an embrace of affection rather than desire, but he clutched Anya so tightly she had to turn her head against his chest.

A young aide whisked Lydia out of the room. And they both sat, as they had so long ago, in the swoop-backed setee. On this occasion, however, he looked at her almost sternly.

"Anya you must never reveal what we discuss this afternoon, agreed?"

She nodded.

"All is lost," he said without emotion. "The rebels have taken Tsarkoe, and most of the villages nearby. Tomorrow, I will abdicate in favor of—"

"No, Nicky, you must not, for the good of—"

He interrupted her. "For the good of Russia I must. It is the only way to bring an end to this cycle of . . . of death and self-destruction. And to this hopeless war. You and the child must leave Russia immediately."

"But—"

"Yes, now. I am giving you these documents." He handed her a small envelope. "They will grant you access to a depository account in Lydia's name—you are the executrix—at the Bank of England. The amount is the same as I have set aside for my other children."

He handed her a heavy, tightly sealed package, smaller than a shoebox. "As proof of ownership of the account, you will also need these."

"Inside, is a valuable gemstone that has been in my family for many years, and a special Faberge piece to contain it. Per my instructions, the bank in London will require you to present both as proof of ownership of the account."

He paused and they stared at each other, mutually struck by the gravity of his words.

"I'll never see you again, will I?"

He looked beyond her to the window, whose silk curtains had been replaced by coarse military cotton. For the first time she noticed that his shirt collar was frayed against his neck and that two small stains marred the front of his tunic.

"My dearest, Anya," he said slowly, "our hours together have been few but glorious. In that brief time you helped me forget the sadness of life. For that, I am more grateful than you can ever know. My fondest hope is that you and Lydia find safety and happiness."

He drew her to her feet and again embraced her. "You must go," he said. "Now. Archbishop Chenko will be waiting for you outside with a carriage. He is a close family friend. Lydia is with him. Go."

Anya turned as she reached the door and looked at Nicholas one last time. He stood in profile, a stooped, middle-aged man who suddenly appeared quite small. She thought of a Russian proverb: Happiness is like a butterfly that briefly delights us, then flits away.

Chapter 3

———=《O》=———

S**TILL** **REELING** from Irina's death, Kate bruised her Saab's tires as she parked in front of the two-bedroom home. Built in 1875, the structure's simple, square–pillared facade belied its ornate interior.

She moved slowly up the front steps, feeling an overwhelming sense of Irina's presence. It was as if her mother's spirit occupied the house, even though Irina herself had never lived here or even been inside. Perhaps subconsciously hoping not to disturb any ethereal occupants, Kate opened the heavy front door gingerly, just enough to slide through. The foyer beckoned with a soaring cherry wood staircase and its own hand–carved fireplace.

Kate had bought the house of necessity. Marion had few apartments and its beautiful old Victorians were a bargain by big city standards. A year before, Kate's improving salary as a professor had allowed a major renovation. She'd told the architect to bring in more light. Now, however, even as the moon cast neon shafts through its windows, the place seemed gloomy and improbably dark.

What had Irina meant 'they' have found us? Her mother had been in nearby Kutztown, attending the annual Amish fair. Her brief cell phone message had sounded urgent: *I must see you right away, today.* But why? Who had found them and what were 'they' looking for?

Suddenly, Kate felt an utterly illogical yet desperate urge for a quick diving session at the university pool. The world she'd occupied since the doctor's terse pronouncement of Irina's demise seemed shapeless and terrifying. At its center lay the most troubling, incomprehensibile question of all: Why would anyone run down Irina Gavrill with a car and then just drive away?

A few quick dives would offer a chance to return, temporarily at least, to a world she understood and could control. Before her athletic and romantic life crashed around her, Kate had been an Olympic candidate. She still kept up a rigorous training regimen. Competitive diving—precise, disciplined, yet incredibly liberating—reflected the rythyms of life. When light danced on the pool's surface, *this* was Kate's symphony. She could almost feel the stiff flex of hardwood under her feet, the surge of power through her thighs, the water slipping over her body like cool hands. High-board diving had been the vehicle for her independence when she felt suffocated by her culture and Irina's unmet expectations.

Her mother had dreamed of a different path for her daughter.

Kate could still remember the glow in Irina's eyes when her seven-year-old attempted her first baby-step pirouettes. "Just watch," she told Anya excitedly, "Katya will be at least a principle dancer, perhaps even a prima ballerina."

Years of musical child labor followed. Six days a week Kate spent four to five hours at the practice bar. In the evenings, Irina and Anya played videotapes of performances by Margot Fonteyn, Svetlana Lunkina and even Pavlova in grainy black and white. Irina prayed to St. Vladimir for her offspring's success.

Alas, Kate's career *en pointe* was not to be. As happens with many a young dancer, as she reached her teens, Kate's body changed in ways that made the gods of *balleto* frown. Her arms and legs were long and shapely, but her arch lacked height and her fingers were a trifle short.

"Classical ballet is not a kind or forgiving art—as you both well know," Kate's instructor told Anya and Irina, "It makes rigid demands for a certain body type. In Katya's case, the shortness of her arch is affecting her turnout," she said, referring to the 180-degree opening of the pelvis, in which the dancer points her toes in opposite right and left directions while the rest of her body remains in vertical alignment.

"She can correct that with stretching and strengthening exercises," Irina insisted. "She musn't stop now."

Anya was more stoic.

"You know as well as I do, Irina, that dance is all about the lines of the body," she said when they talked later. "A high arch and instep are critical to their perfection. Exercises can't change the shape of the bones in her feet or lengthen her fingers. Look at Pavlova, half of her dance was in her hands."

Irina couldn't hide her disappointment from Kate, but Anya was more philosophical. "You are going to be a beautiful, healthy young woman," she said. "You must not let this discourage you. Classical dance can be a cruel master. There are many other ways to express yourself, Katya, and you will find the right one for you."

Stung to the core, young Kate retreated to her room. "Whatever I do next, I'll be the best in the world," she resolved, "and I won't pray to some dead saint to do it." Within a year, Kate was captain of the girl's diving team, and a year after that she'd won the state high school championship. Now, standing in middle of her darkened living room, Kate smiled bitterly at the memory. You almost made it, girl, she said to herself, you almost made it.

Her answering machine beeped.

Lt. MacMahon wanted Irina Gavrill's financial records. His tone sounded unofficerlike somehow, almost apologetic. She shouldn't have brushed him off before. He seemed like a nice enough guy, just doing his job. Kate pressed the stop button, and looked at her watch. A few minutes past 2:00 A.M. Cried out and wrung out, she undressed for bed and poured a glass of wine. The rest of the messages could wait; what she must do next could not.

Kate crossed the room to the fireplace.

Atop the mantle, next to a lacquered icon of the virgin—one of the few icons Kate kept in her house—sat an oversize, nickel-plated picture frame. Though nearly a century old, the photograph it contained would captivate any man in any age. Its subject wore a high-necked, snug-bodied gown that profiled her small but shapely figure. Her eyes were large and luminous above a delicate nose and full lips. Tawny hair streamed down her back in a cascade of waves and curls. She'd been born in the last years of the nineteenth century, danced as prima ballerina for the Imperial Ballet, and lived until the 1980's. This was Anya Putyatin.

As a little girl, Kate remembered sitting on the floor while her great grandmother watched her line up a set of *matryoshka* dolls she'd received for Christmas. Painted in vivid blue, red and gold lacquer, the nested dolls told the famous Pushkin fairy tale of Tsar Saltan.

"Which is your favorite, Katya?"

"This one, Granmama Anya. The Swan Princess rescued by Prince Guidon."

With surprising lightness, the old woman knelt beside her, quickly rearranging the dolls in a circle. She placed Kate's favorite in the middle, then turned back to face her.

"Katya," she instructed, "always put the things you love at the center of your life."

Despite Anya's wise words, as a teenager Kate had little use for her heritage. "I don't want to take *piroshkis* in my lunch box," she'd screamed at her mother after an argument. "I never wanted to be a ballerina anyway. And I *hate* being Russian!" Mostly, of course, she hated being different. Once, when Irina baked traditional potato dumplings for a school potluck, Kate had seen some of the other girls spit them out. "Yuk, who wants Russian food?" whined one blonde-curled princess.

Kate again thought of Granmama Anya's words. And of the parent she'd just lost. Even with their estrangement in recent years, she'd never doubted her mother's ultimate love. With Irina gone, she wondered, where was her center now?

Carefully, Kate lifted out the back of the large picture frame. From its deep velvet recess, a silver key fell into her palm. She removed a single tape cassette, and a folded, unsealed envelope.

December, 1917

WHERE *WAS* the archbishop? In the cold night air, Anya tangled her fingers in a clump of frozen curls.

For more than a month, Anya, Lydia and Archbishop Radislav Chenko had huddled in a blown out tailor's shop just off Tolstovo Street near Kiev's main rail station. The shop's Jewish owners, Herman and Yullya Meyers, were afraid to go outside. Whenever the house was empty, thieves stole bread and milk, or tore boards from the floors and walls for firewood.

Like a sea-tossed ship, Kiev rocked back-and-forth between war and revolution. Since March, the city had changed hands eleven times. Ukrainian nationalists had mobilized within days of Nicholas' fall. Now, Polish troops massed in the west and the Bolshevik Red Army prepared to invade from the north. Every night the earth rumbled with the heavy guns of the German-Austro artillery. Rumors raced of pogroms in Kharkov and other towns to the east. "The world has gone mad," Herman Meyers muttered, kicking a rusty German helmet from his doorway into the street. "The world has gone mad."

The Meyers invited them in when they saw the archbishop trying to construct a temporary shelter from empty petrol drums near Peremohy Square. "It is September," Yullya said, "soon the cold weather will come. At least with us, you will have walls—as long as they last."

Both the Meyers's sons were serving in different armies, Anatole with the nationalists, and Karl with the Bolsheviks. A German shell had obliterated the shop's upstairs apartment. Downstairs, however, a parlor, kitchen and pantry still stood and—with the exception of broken windows and a gaping roof—remained relatively intact.

A week had passed since Archbishop Chenko departed, saying he was going to Pechersky Lavra, the "Caves Monastery," to pray. The monastery was little more than two miles away; he should have returned in a few hours.

Anya pulled Lydia closer. They slept under her last good heavy coat. Through the partially collapsed ceiling, Anya could see the flare of heavy guns against the horizon. Higher in the night sky, stars gleamed in silent, incongruous, beauty. A dozen feet away, the Meyers stretched orange palms toward a small fire they'd built from splintered furniture.

Folding her arms across her chest, Yullya Meyers crossed the room to sit beside her. "We will have to leave soon," she whispered. Rural anarchists had looted the Meyers' small farm just outside Kiev. "They took all our chickens, even our cow. There won't be any food. Herman says it's all the fault of Kerensky and his damned 'Land and Freedom' speeches."

Yullya moved closer. "You wait for this archbishop because he has something that belongs to you? This is what keeps you here?"

Anya nodded. She'd never laid eyes on the treasures sewn into the prelate's frock, yet their possession obsessed her. Aside from a few broaches she'd hidden to pay for their journey, this was all that remained of Nicholas' love for her, and it was all that remained of Lydia's future.

The next morning Anya awoke with a clear sense of purpose. She could no longer wait for the archbishop, she must find him. She must go to Pechersky Lavra herself.

"When will you come back, *matryoshka*?" Lydia's dark eyes were round with concern.

"Soon, little one," Anya assured, kissing her daughter on the forehead. "It is only a short distance; I'll be back this afternoon. Granmama Yullya will look after you until I return."

She left in an icy rain, briskly walking nine blocks to Hrushevskoho Street, which paralleled the Dnieper River, rising southeast along a ridge to the monastery. Thick stands of maple, lime and oak trees covered the riverbank's steep slopes.

For some reason, except for the "shushing" sound of rain, the morning seemed eerily quiet. She passed the Mariinsky Palace, built in 1750 as the tsars' residence in Kiev. Canon shells had chipped the blue-and-cream façade, and most of the glass had been blown from the windows.

She reached the monastery's main gates. Above ground, the site consisted of a sprawling ensemble of white-walled church buildings with green and gold rooftops. Below the surface, however, the Lavra became a virtual necropolis, an underground city whose "streets" were tunnels and caverns. For centuries these same passageways had provided burial places for monks and disciples. The monastery was also a destination for tens of thousands of devoted pilgrims, though the current fighting had slowed their numbers to a trickle.

"The archbishop was here," said an elderly monk at the registration desk. "He came to pray and stayed for two days."

"Did he say where he was going when he left?"

The monk's voice was filled with sadness.

"Oh, Miss Putyatin, I thought everyone knew. The Bolsheviks. They killed him. When he first arrived, he said to give this to you if anything happened to him." He handed her an envelope.

As if struck, Anya snatched the small rectangle of paper and spun away from the counter. She stumbled back into the rain and headed down the ridge. It was so bitterly ironic: she'd just been thinking of a treasure she and Lydia hadn't seen. Now chances were they never would.

Bent against the storm, Anya almost stepped on the boy.

No more than seventeen or eighteen, he lay with his back curved against a fountain in Mariinsky palace's adjacent park. Doubtless he was one of the hundreds of Kiev youths—most of them now dead—who'd risen against the Bolsheviks.

Wet maple leaves plastered his lower legs and feet. His shabby gray uniform was torn at the armpits. A dark orange circle stained his chest; apparently he'd been killed by a single shot. His finely featured face turned upward, long strands of yellow hair wisping from beneath his cap. Birds had devoured his eyes. In the empty sockets, the flesh was black and torn.

Recoiling in horror, Anya ran until she reached Tolstovo Street. It was still quiet—the rain had lessened. People scurried now, heads down, faces cramped with worry.

Holding Lydia in his arms, Anatole—the Meyers's oldest son, who had come to visit his parents—stopped her before she could enter the house. He was sobbing.

"Both dead," he blurted. "Anarchists. I took Lydia for a walk while you were gone. When I returned . . ." His voice trailed away, then resumed. "Father tried to stop them. They killed them with pitchforks."

Anya cried out and covered her eyes. Then she peered around the weeping soldier in cracked boots. Drenched in blood, the Meyers lay across each other, just inside the doorway. Pinned to their chests were separate sheets of paper, each crudely scratched in charcoal with a six-pointed star.

Anatole wiped his eyes and put Lydia down beside her. "Anya," he said, "the Red Army is nearly here. There is a train leaving for Warsaw and you may still be able to connect to Paris. This is probably your last chance."

Anya scooped up her few belongings and hoisted Lydia onto her hip. Without saying goodbye, she began running toward the rail station. Not until they reached Poland did she open the envelope given to her at St. Sophia. It was a photograph, already worn at the edges, of a large, oval-shaped stone. On the back was scrawled a single name, "Mikhail."

Chapter 4

ONCE AGAIN, Kate felt a powerful sense of her mother's presence. How long ago, she wondered, had Irina recorded this tape? When she lifted the cassette closer to see if its label contained a date, Kate thought she smelled the passion flower notes of Irina's favorite perfume. The scent had been a gift from Nicholas to Anya, specially made for the tsar in Moscow by A. Rallet & Co., whose chief perfumer later created Chanel's famous No. 5. Anya brought seven bottles to America. Only two remained and Irina carefully meted out their last drops for special occasions. The night she made this recording must have been one.

Irina spoke slowly. "Katya, this recording is for your ears only. She paused, then continued in a slow, measured tone.

"To begin, we must go back to the early part of the century, and to Mother Russia. To the time of poor Nicky and Alexandra and their dear beautiful children.

"You recall how I told you why Grandmama Anya seldom spoke about the old days in Russia? Because it was too painful for her? Well, there was another reason, Katya. We were afraid. For ourselves. And for you."

Tears began to fall at the sound of her mother's voice. Stopping the tape, Kate nodded to herself, remembering the petite, lively great-grandmother who'd died at 85, when Kate was 12, marking another devastating family loss. She remembered, too, hurting her great grandmother when she blurted out why she did not bring school friends home. "We've got stupid icons all over the house," she said, "they'd think I'm weird." Anya turned her face away. When Irina heard of the outburst, her daughter ate dinner in her room for three days. The icons stayed.

Her name had triggered another battle.

"Who is this 'Kate,'" Irina asked sharply, holding up Kate's Ninth grade report card. "Do I know her? Does she live in this house? My daughter," she said, glaring fiercely at her teenage offspring, "is named Katya."

"But, mother, Kate means the same thing. And it doesn't sound as strange."

Irina looked at her, and Kate saw the sorrow and resignation in her eyes. "All right," her mother said, "you can call yourself this name at school, and no more will be said. But to your family who loves you, and in this house, you will always be Katya."

Those upsets, of course, were of little consequence compared to the big trouble, the trouble that spread a stain over her college career, the trouble that caused Irina to lock herself in her bedroom, where she sobbed uncontrollably for a week. Kate would never forget her mother's expression when she emerged. Pain carved her face like the sun carves lines in a desert. "Katya," she said over and over, "he was a married man. How could you? How could you shame us so?"

It was then that Kate Gavrill left home.

Now, however, Irina's disembodied voice resumed, and she spoke of another family's tragedy, one that had taken place long ago. "What happened at Ekaterinburg in the Spring of 1918 can never be forgotten," Kate's mother said on the tape. "But God knows there was more. Much more."

Kate stretched out her hand. It was as if they were still in the hospital and she were stroking Irina's pale temples. "Mom," she wanted to say, "let's talk about this when you feel better."

But Irina's voice continued.

"Anya's hair was famous," she said. "A mane fit for a lioness. Pushkin wrote about its beauty. Even Nicholas, who'd always been faithful to Alexandra, couldn't resist her. They all had their ballerinas, of course. Most of the female contingent of the Imperial Ballet served as mistresses for Russian noblemen. They kept the House of Faberge in business.

"Before he married Alexandra, Nicholas had a long affair with a ballerina, Mathilde Kschessinska. Alix knew about Mathilde, but she was also wise enough to let sleeping lovers lie. Alix was secure in Nicky's feelings for her and she was right to be. Among all of Europe's royals, theirs was the truest—perhaps the only—love match. It's really the saddest story of the last century, isn't it? Those poor people, well-meaning, but so naive in their own way. And all dying in that dirty cellar."

"Mother, I know all this," Kate interrupted the steady drone of Irina's recorded words. Before her great granddaughter grew rebellious, Anya had infused Kate with Russian culture and history, often before bedtime.

"If Alexandra hadn't begun seeing so much of that disgusting monk," Irina went on as if in answer, "Nicholas would never have strayed. The Russian people hated Rasputin—with good reason. He was a world-class debaucher, a cultist and a clerical con man. But he was also a gifted hypnotist who could control their son's bleeding.

"In any case, it had become a fragile balance. Nicholas, the Empress, and that devil—all of them devoted to the boy, but one of them also using the boy to serve himself and his dark pleasures. It was a witch's brew, and sooner or later it was bound to boil over.

"One night, in the winter of 1911, when they were to attend the ballet, Alexandra instead stayed at the palace in St. Petersburg to see Rasputin about the boy. And if Alix hadn't met with the 'mad monk,' Nicky . . . and Anya . . . well, there might never have been any need for secrets.

"Anya was just sixteen, and already the fastest-rising ballerina in Moscow. When Grand Duke Alexander introduced them, the tsar's gentle eyes immediately drew Anya. And she was no innocent—she flirted outrageously with him. From his standpoint, she was pretty, available, and a desperately needed diversion from his wife's intense involvement with Rasputin and Alexis's hemophilia. He pretended he saw Anya for her art, but the truth was he saw Anya for Anya.

"What happened physically between them didn't last long, but it burned intensely. For a brief time that winter, they were seldom out of each other's arms."

Kate couldn't believe her ears.

Again she spoke aloud: "Mother, what are you saying?"

And again Irina Gavrill's recorded voice answered. "Your great-grandmama Anya and Nicholas II had a love affair. And my mother Lydia—the grandmother you never knew—was their child. You and I, Katya, are their progeny. And when I am gone there will be only you—the last tsar's only direct heir.

"And that brings me to what I must ask of you.

"When I die, the treasure that Nicholas bequeathed my mother will rightfully be yours."

Irina's voice intensified now. Kate could feel her mother's energy lifting the barrier that death had placed between them.

"I urge you to find our fortune and use it for the good of Russia and the restoration of the Romanov name. It is our birthright. More than that, it is a chance to atone. Anya and I could do little while the Communists were in power. But things are different now. Such a treasure could help make up for the bloodshed and suffering that has gone before. Please promise you will do this, Katya. Nicholas and Alexandra made many mistakes, but their children and descendants suffered far beyond any requirements of justice. This is a chance for you too, to right the past, perhaps to make a new start."

KATE SAT in the darkened room, staring at the now silent tape player. Irina's words burned in her thoughts: *A chance for you too, to right the past, to make a new start.*

She was only six years old when Henri Gavrill disappeared, a week before her seventh birthday. Her French-born father had acted as a buffer to the Russian heritage of the household's female members. A big, lively man, with dancing brown eyes and a graceful, almost dapper, manner, he gave Kate her first swimming lessons a few days after she turned five. Years after, she would recall big palms turned upward against her belly in the public pool, holding her in place while she paddled. Perhaps that explained why, just weeks after her future as a ballerina fizzled, Kate returned to the familiar world of aquatics. In any event, for months following Henri's disappearance, Kate stood in their window, waiting for her father to come home.

Henri left behind a lonely, intense girl with only a partly formed notion of who she was. Her mother and grandmother insisted Kate remain inside the house, and offered vague replies when asked about her father's absence. Kate's early childhood companions were mostly on paper—cats, dogs and birds she created in crayon and ink and upon whom she lavished affection and attention. In the borders, she often drew the solitary figure of a man.

In providing an alternative to ballet, diving gradually assumed Henri's role of balancing the cultural intensity of Kate's home. What life experience, she often asked herself, could be more liberating? It was as if her tumbling body drew a sketch in the air. And in those few precious seconds—besides freedom—Kate felt something else: an exhilarating sense of self-control. "I loved dance," she told her mother in explaining her decision to try out for the varsity diving team in high school, "but when I dive I come alive."

Life out of water, however, was another matter. Falling for Jack Nars drove a stake in the heart of her athletic career. What once had been a clear path to All-American status and the Olympics instead became a bumptious road to shame and scandal. She'd survived, and even recovered enough to emerge with a *cum laude* economics degree from Penn State. She told herself the experience had made her stronger. But underneath it all, Kate Gavrill's brusquely capable air was mostly a self-invented mask.

She shook her shoulders, and broke her reverie. Her past was just that—her past. Whatever had happened before, somehow she knew her future lay in this tape cassette and the letter just a few inches away. Would Anya's words add to the bombshell of her mother's recording? Fingers trembling, Kate withdrew the pages inside and began to read.

Chapter 5

IN A small, dimly lit room in Moscow, the man slipped off his wireless headset and studied the young woman who lay beside him. Her long brown hair spilled over the edge of the narrow cot, almost touching the floor. Against the sheets, her shoulders were as smooth and white as soap. In the hollow of her neck, she wore the Byzantine cross.

"You've been an excellent subject," he said.

Her head rose from the pillow, then fell back. Her eyes looked glazed and vacant. The man smiled to himself. Even a concert violinist needed daily practice to stay at the top of his talent. This bodacious morsel would be his scales. He'd perform the full symphony later, in a different hall with a different subject, and before a very small, select audience. The concert would be held far away—on Threadneedle Street in London, to be exact.

"My great-grandfather Grigori Rasputin was the leading mesmerist of his time," the man mused aloud, now staring at the ceiling and speaking as if to a student. If she comprehended, the young woman gave no sign. Her fingers curled absently around his thigh.

Adriadna's parents had hoped their pretty daughter, a rosy-cheeked brunette with large eyes, long dark lashes and a lush figure, would marry a local farmer. But her mother died of tuberculosis, and a year later her father was killed fighting in Afghanistan. A month after his death, the girl, then fifteen, entered the convent of St. John the Theologian in central Russia.

"That was, of course, the secret of Grigori's success in treating the child," the man continued, as if speaking to himself. "He learned in their first meeting that Alexis was highly hypnotizable. Today some psychiatrists would label the boy an 'hypnotic virtuoso,' among that tiny percentage of the population most easily placed in a trance. He turned, and smiled at her. "Such as you, my lovely."

He touched her nose and continued. "Whenever a bleeding attack threatened, Grigori would put Alexis under. His success, especially at the beginning, was quite remarkable. I have long suspected that Empress Alexandra was a virtuoso as well. Certainly that would explain Rasputin's extraordinary hold over her. And it would follow the theory held by some that extreme hypnotizability is hereditary."

The man rose, stood next to the cot and again looked closely at his companion. Employing "shock induction," a technique used by stage hypnotists and occasionally in hospital emergency rooms to control hysterical patients, he'd needed only seconds to place her in a deep trance. Her head had dropped forward and she'd slumped defenselessly against his chest.

Now, the great-grandson of Rasputin again sat beside her. Gently, he traced a line along her cheek to her forehead. He smiled as her eyes glided high in their sockets.

The young woman moaned and turned, exposing a breast. Groggily, she pulled the straps of her chemise back over her shoulders. Unwanted thoughts flitted at the edges of her consciousness. She shuddered and clutched the gold crucifix. She felt her will slip away like surf sliding off a shore.

The man placed his hand at her waist, then shaped his palm to the roundness of her belly. He moved his hand lower, molding his palm to her warmth. His mouth covered hers, and her lips softened, surrounding him.

Her limbs felt heavy as he rolled her over. He secured her wrists and ankles to the cot's frame using four short lengths of cord he drew from his pocket. She did not resist. Her mind filled with unspeakable images of copulating satyrs draping themselves over the flanks of mares.

Feeling a surge at her own loins, she pictured the rusted icon that hung above her bed at the convent. "Oh mother of Vladimir," she prayed, "deliver me."

The man stood, and began removing his garments, stripping down to a string-tied black bikini. His body was lean and muscular.

He tugged one of the strings, and the garment fell away.

She moaned again as he pulled down her pantaloons. In the cool air, her rounded bottom flushed pink, as if her flesh were gathering the last colors of a fading sun.

Later, the man would cross the darkened room, thread a single light bulb back into its socket and open a steel door. He would speak softly into the corridor. "Guard, my visit with Sister Adriadna is over now. I feel much closer to God. Please see that sister gets home safely."

Behind him, the young woman would pull on the bulky garments that proclaimed her calling as a Rassophore, finally donning the *klobuk,* or veil, of a Russian Orthodox nun.

Chapter 6

ꞏꞏ«(●)»ꞏꞏ

"**M**Y DEAR Katya," Anya's letter began, "if you are reading this, you must be as strong as I know you can be. You will already have learned the truth about Tsar Nicholas and me, and I will almost certainly be dead. The rest of the story is this: just as Nicky established bank accounts for his children with Alexandra, he also set up an account for Lydia, our daughter."

Kate read on:

> As with the other accounts, the funds were deposited at the Bank of England. It was to be Lydia's dowry and came to five million English pounds, the same amount given to each of Nicky's other children: Tatiana, Olga, Anastasia, Marie, and Alexis. Upon Lydia's death, that money rightfully became Irina's. When she dies, it will be yours.

> Some said Nicholas repatriated all the Romanov deposits to pay for the war. Indeed, following World War I, Sir Edward Peacock, director of the Bank of England, declared there were no Romanov funds left in his or any other bank in Britain.

> Either deliberately or innocently, however, Sir Edward misspoke. In fact, in 1986—after seventy years—Baring

Brothers, a private London bank, released sixty-two million pounds of Russian bonds. The bank later insisted none of it belonged to the Romanov heirs, but who knows? Anna Anderson, who claimed to be Anastasia, produced sworn court testimony—some of it quoting Alexandra herself—that money existed in England and France. Nicky did start repatriating foreign accounts at the beginning of the war, but the fact that he was still calling in money in 1917 should tell you something: there were still funds to bring back. And there was the money in Berlin, although those funds later expired as worthless due to inflation. In any case, I will never believe that Nicholas touched the children's accounts. After all, they weren't his.

Based on the formula used to settle the Baring Brothers matter, the five million pounds Nicholas initially deposited in Lydia's name would now be worth approximately seventy million U.S. dollars. There was money all right.

As proof of Lydia's birthright, Nicholas gave me incontestable physical evidence of our daughter's bloodline—a huge alexandrite, discovered in Russia in 1831. The gem had been in the Romanov family ever since. For the sake of discretion and as a favor to the crown, Faberge himself quietly finished the stone and personally designed its container, a trademark jeweled egg. The base of the stone was etched with the Romanov "double-eagle" coat of arms. It was said to be the largest gem-quality alexandrite ever found.

Additional important materials have been secured in a safe deposit box your mother and I have at Chase Manhattan bank in New York. The number and address are taped to the key you found in my picture. You must go there and review the contents. Do not delay.

Kate turned the notepaper face down in her lap. "My God, granmama," she said aloud, "Why didn't you and mother tell me? Are there other secrets? What will I find in New York?"

Lifting her eyes from the page, she took a sip of wine. The papers dropped into her lap. Her tears came without warning and in a flood.

April, 1933

Fɪsᴛs. Fɪʀsᴛ, Anya heard the fists. Heavy fists against heavy wood—the thick oak of their entry door. Splintering sounds. Shouts. The startled voices of Lydia and Sergey, her husband.

Beside her on the floor above, Lydia's daughter still slept.

Anya clapped her left hand over Irina's mouth. With her right, she seized the seven-inch long hatpin on the nightstand beside the bed.

"In the name of the Revolution," bellowed one of the intruders in Russian. Even in Montmartre in the dead of night, even in the shadow of *Le Sacr`e Coeur,* the Basilica of the Sacred Heart, they seemed not to care about the noise they made. It was as if, Anya later thought, they wanted all the world to hear.

By now Irina was fully awake, her four-year-old eyes round with terror above her grandmother's clasped hand. On the floor below, drawers scraped open and closed as the invaders searched for valuables. They wouldn't find much. Even when she slept, Anya kept the photo of the alexandrite, along with the little money and bits of jewelry she still had, in a flat pouch tied around her waist.

Later, Anya and Irina would refer to what happened only as "that night." Nothing more. But Anya would never forget Lydia's piercing screams—as shrill as any factory whistle—as the Reds slit Sergey's throat. Nor Sergey's pitiful moans as he lost consciousness before dying. Nor the shock of hearing the single assassin's shot that killed Lydia. The police would not permit her to see the bodies, or photographs of the killings. But Anya read their reports. While still alive, Sergei had been disemboweled.

Anya grabbed Irina's arm and dragged her to the small door, partially disguised by paneling that led to the attic. She pulled the child into the narrow stairwell, then halted for fear of being heard.

Too late. Boots creaked on the stairs from the main floor.

Anya gripped the long hatpin in her right hand.

More ransacking noises. Closets thrown open, clothes and drawers flung. Footsteps. Closer. Fumbling sounds.

The door opened, framing a hulking figure in the moonlight. Anya lunged forward, arm extended like a matador's final *estoque*.

The man groaned and fell, rolling over on the floor, an open shirt flap exposing his round hairy belly. A crimson wreath bloomed below his chest.

More footsteps. Starting up the stairs.

Anya again grabbed Irina with one hand. In a single motion, they brushed past the fallen terrorist. Anya dashed a chair through their bedroom window, then pulled the girl through to the tile roof.

Momentum carried them another 50 feet. Anya dropped to her haunches and clutched Irina close. Reaching the eaves, they leaned forward like a pair of tobogganists and slid off the roof. Flexing her dancer's muscled legs, Anya managed to absorb the shock of the narrow cobblestone street below.

Then Anya Putyatin ran, dragging her precious granddaughter behind her, through the winding canyons of Montmartre.

★   ★   ★

"You cannot go back," Nina Berberova said. "They will be watching the house. My Andre knows a police officer. He will go for your clothes. You and the child must leave Paris as soon as he returns."

Like Anya, Nina, a portrait artist, had thrived thanks to *La Vogue Russe*, painting oils of local aristos and embroidering French names on wide Siberian hats. Along with thousands of other Russian refugees, they'd ridden the cultural wave that swept Paris in the early 1920s after the final defeat of the White Armies. For a bright, tinkling decade, all that was Russian was *"avant"* and the city's large expatriate colony flourished, enjoying a social and official status not afforded other immigrant groups in France.

Indeed, France had taken in her former Great War allies as if they were lost neighborhood children. Russian immigrants like Nina and Anya could expect special treatment under tsarist laws. Parisians, meanwhile, flocked to performances of *Ballets Russes*—Anya mentored several of the company's ballerinas—and worshipped displaced Russian celebrities like film star Ivan Mosjoukine, playwright Nicolai Evreinov, and artist Alexandre Iacovleff.

Everything changed on May 6, 1932, when tall, powerfully built Pavel Gorgulov, a deranged Russian émigré shouting "To die for the Fatherland!" fired his Colt into the brain of Paul Doumer, France's genial, 75-year-old President.

"We have much to lose," Nina told Anya after the shooting. "The French have been good to us. Imagine, after this, what it will be like if your name ends in '-off,' 'insky', or '-ova'?"

A year later, Nina's concern resurfaced. "Perhaps this is why your Lydia and Sergey were killed."

Anya shook her head. "No," she said, her lips quivering at the recent memory. "These animals were not avenging the memory of France. They hoped to kill the memory of Nicky and his family." She turned to glance at Irina, quietly reading a children's book near the window.

Nina patted her hand. "You know where you must go now," she said.

Anya nodded.

"Denmark," Nina said. "Grand Duchess Olga will help you. And then . . . for you and Irina . . . America."

★　　★　　★

KUNDSMINDE FARM clung to a windswept hillside a few miles outside Copenhagen. Even in spring, patches of snow splotched the frozen, sparsely grassed terrain.

About twenty yards from the main building, two women greeted each other inside a weathered shed with large glass windows and a steel-and-wire skylight.

At first, they spoke awkwardly.

"You must realize, Anya Putyatin, how very reluctant I am to see anyone who claims to be part of our Imperial Family." As if defensively, the plain, middle-aged woman circled away from her guest and sat on a simple wooden bench behind an artist's easel.

The comment did not surprise Anya. Eight years before, she'd read Paris newspaper accounts of the trip Grand Duchess Olga and her husband made to Berlin to visit Anna Anderson, who claimed to be Anastasia, the tsar's daughter. Anderson's supporters had seized upon the visit as evidence of her legitimacy.

"The woman is a fake and I renounced her," Olga said, reading Anya's thoughts. "But I felt sorry for her. She is such a pitiful creature."

In an open hearth a few feet away, burning cedar logs popped like volleying rifles. Startled, Anya jumped. But the fire's scent evoked fragrant memories of her Nicky's cigar humidor, quickly soothing her.

"You, on the other hand, come recommended," Olga continued. Then she smiled and Anya glimpsed the caring aristocrat who'd been the tsar's closest sibling, a front-line nurse in World War I, and now an increasingly successful artist.

Rising, the older woman put down her brush, walked around the easel, and took both of Anya's hands. "My Misha—Nicholas—wrote to me about you before they were sent to Ekaterinburg. He'd heard about the archbishop's gruesome death and feared very much for you and Irina. He asked if there was any way we could help."

Anya sighed at Nicky's memory—and with an audible sense of relief. As the tsar's secret mistress, and the mother of his child, she'd journeyed to see his sister in Denmark with only a vague notion of what to expect when she arrived.

"You needn't be embarrassed," Olga reassured her. "I am not easily shocked. After all, I divorced a Grand Duke to marry a commoner after a 12-year affair. We all tried to warn Misha about Alexandra's dangerous liason with Rasputin. What was that about, really? Frankly, I am not surprised—I'm delighted—that he found someone to make him happy, even briefly."

Anya knew of the narrow escape Olga and her husband Nicolai made from the Caucasus in 1918. With the help of an aide de camp, they'd barely slipped out of the grasp of the Red Army. They made their way to Copenhagen, and lived with Olga's mother, Dowager Empress Maria Feodorovna, until her death in 1928.

"In his letter, Misha asked me to save two pieces for you," Olga went on, taking a folded velvet packet from a nearby cupboard. "So I persuaded mother to hold these back from any sales."

Anya'd also been privy to the Paris gossip about Maria's jewels. Rescued by her cousin King George V from the Crimea, the Dowager Empress managed to haul millions in Romanov gems aboard the *HMS Marlborough*, then stashed them in a trunk under her bed in Copenhagen. To little avail. Britain's wily Queen Mary contracted for the desperate woman's treasure at market prices. Then, during the Depression, she cruelly delayed payment until values fell to an even smaller fraction of their former worth. Most outrageous, England's queen flaunted her spoils, delighting in publicly wearing baubles such as the Empress's prized cabochon-sapphire brooch.

Olga spread open the purple cloth. A pair of glittering virescent frogs, each about three-fourths of an inch in length, squatted in the folds as if ready to jump. "These pieces were initially made for my mother as a gift to Anastasia on her birthday. Of course, there wasn't a chance to present them. Misha must have sensed there never would be.

"They were meant to be worn as a pair," Olga continued. "The setting is pure gold and the gems are very rare green garnets. One of them should cover both your fares to America. The other you should keep in a strong box, and perhaps make it into a pendant. It will grow more valuable in years to come."

Olga looked at Anya knowingly.

"These will not replace the stone you lost," she said, sympathy in her blue eyes. "Nothing could. But they can help you and Irina start a new life. These days that is all any of us from the old world can ask."

As she departed, the gray, foreboding sky reminded Anya of Elsinore, a bare 25 miles away on the Baltic coast. There, in Kronborg Castle, had dwelled that most melancholy Danish prince of all. His mood matched hers now. "For this relief much thanks," Hamlet had said. "'Tis bitter cold, and I am sick at heart."

Chapter 7

———◦《◦》◦———

KATE'S SKIN felt cool and fresh as she stood on the high board, more than thirty feet above the water. As Kate's sanctuary of ultra-focus, diving helped her achieve a perspective and clarity she couldn't find elsewhere. Of all days, this was what she needed.

She especially loved a workout in the early morning, when no one else had been in the pool. Its surface untouched, the water lay smooth and quiet, so transparent it almost didn't exist. Breaking that surface would be like shattering a spell.

In Marion State's cavernous, Olympic-size swimming pool, Kate made a solitary figure. She had endured—and finally given up on—a restless night's sleep. Indeed, at 6:00 A.M., she'd already been awake an hour and a half. In the darkened home, the truth had come to her with full force: she didn't just feel alone, she *was* alone, totally alone, an adult orphan without a sibling or even a close friend.

Besides helping Kate see things more clearly, physical exercise had always calmed her, even when her thoughts and emotions were churning. This morning should have been no different. As she did every day except Sunday, Kate began her exercise regime by wrenching her 125-pound frame through a dozen bedside "pikes"— the classic mid-air maneuver in which a diver bends at her waist and, legs straight, touches her pointed toes. Still in her pajamas, she'd followed with knee bends and sit-ups. Finally, donning sweats and a halter, she'd jogged two-miles to the pool.

Today, however, even after a full workout, she felt overwhelmed. First, there had been Irina's terrible accident. Next, her mother's instructions about Anya's picture. Then her death, and the tape and letter—literally voices from the grave. The enormity of their secret still reverberated. Like Kate herself, her great grandmother—her granmama Anya—had been a married man's mistress. But Anya's lover had been the ruler of a nation, and she'd given birth to his child. Kate's closest relatives—most troublingly Irina—had actively concealed this from her for more than three decades. Not even at the heighth of her storm over Jack Nars had her mother breathed a word about Anya Putyatin and Tsar Nicholas II.

To some extent, Kate could understand their silence. Bolshevik assassins might seem a relic of the past, but the lust for treasure never would be. Obviously someone, probably more than one someone, had known about the fabulous gift Nicholas bestowed on his lover and their daughter. Perhaps they—or rather their descendants—still searched for it now. Yet at least so far as Anya and Irina knew, no one had ever found the Romanov Stone or tried to claim the Bank of England account.

Kate's raw emotions rippled like muscles, contracting with each doubt, expanding with a growing sense of anticipation and excitement. After all, even if Anya and Irina had deceived her, they'd also presented her with two precious gifts any competitor could only relish: a great challenge and an equally great opportunity.

Usually, Kate's Zen-like athletic concentration would blot out such globally extraneous thoughts. Today, however, mixed with anger and pain at her mother's death, she felt a surge of energy at the prospect of taking a fresh path, unlike any she'd traveled before. This was not a new lesson plan or an abstract economic theory. It was a chance to restore her family's place in history and with it, perhaps, her own soul. It was also a chance to make things right with Irina who, God surely knew, she'd put through hell. Standing on the board, Kate drummed her fingers against her belly, feeling the taut bundle of muscles just beneath the skin. A slight aroma of chlorine tinged the air.

Girl, you've still got the power, an inner voice whispered.

The diver nodded to herself. She'd always been proud of her strength. Pound-for-pound, Professor Gavrill was arguably the best-conditioned member of her faculty.

Indeed, at Kate's age, few women would dare wear her ancient, single-piece swimsuit. She loved it for its comfort. Despite its high neck and conservative leg-cut, however, when wet the material traced the lines of her body like a second skin, revealing every rise and hollow.

If she knew in advance she'd be seen, Kate usually donned a newer, neck-to-knee body suit. Its black stretch fabric, while equally form-fitting, tended to compress and therefore mask anatomical details.

Go, girl! Again, the inner voice prodded her to action. Kate took four long steps and powered off her right leg, springing into the air. Thump! She landed back on the platform with both feet, then launched herself from the end of the board. Still in an ascending arc, her body folded, fingers meeting toes. Twenty feet above the water, Kate turned on her own horizontal axis, rolling into a forward somersault. She kicked out, looking directly at the pool below. In an instant, she would drop through the surface.

At the last moment, however, her body rotated awkwardly. Rather than dropping as straight and vertically as a falling spear, her splaying feet made a soft splash.

What was that? Where was your concentration? What happened to your spotting?

The pointed questions probed Kate's major weakness as a diver. Eleven years before, poor spotting had prevented her from adding a third somersault to her repertoire and moving on and up from All-

Ivy diver to All-American and Olympic Medalist. Poor spotting had led to the worst mistake of her life: the affair with Jack Nars, her married diving coach, with whom she'd fallen in love at twenty. Poor spotting led Jack to Dr. Borschel and, eventually, damaged both their lives. And with all that, with the huge price she and Jack had paid, spotting remained the one athletic challenge she'd never fully mastered, not even with the help of Dr. Borshel's "medication."

The odd thing was she had mastered spotting as a ballet dancer, or at least she had mastered the elements of the technique that confront a beginning dancer. But spotting in ballet took place while the dancer's body remained in a level plane, her neck whipping from the spot and around again as she whirled in a pirouette.

In diving, spotting—as in dance a single visual reference point—happens while the body is tumbling in its own futile defiance of gravity. Spotting told Kate her exact position at any moment during a dive. The spot could be a reflection in the water or a mark or number on the pool itself, even a ceiling rafter. Great divers so honed this skill they could shift their gaze to different focus points during each spin or somersault—all without moving their heads. As undeniably skilled and gifted a diver as she'd become, Kate had never mastered holding that focus point—her spot—beyond a second body rotation.

In smooth, even strokes, Kate swam toward the edge of the pool.

She rested her forearms on the side, trailing her legs. She closed her eyes, flushing water from her lashes.

THE ARM that circled her shoulders came attached to a well-muscled, if stocky, masculine body. Its head contained square-cut, even features and dark blue eyes that could squint fiercely if you weren't giving everything you had; they'd soften just as quickly if their owner sensed you were. Somehow this man balanced a demanding yet protective nature better than anyone she'd ever met.

Jack Nars had been named Princeton women's diving coach two months before the start of her junior year. Almost instantly 20-year-old honors student Kate Gavrill fell under his spell. Fifteen years her senior, Jack became her mentor, guiding Kate to her first major successes as a diver.

It was late afternoon, long after the other girls had finished practice. Kate had just completed a series of disappointing dives.

"Keep at it," said Nars, his lips inches from her ear. "The spotting will come. It always does."

She'd learned the truth when a local sports show recorded her dives on videotape. "Let's look at this again, Kate," Jack had said. Leaning toward the screen, her coach slowed the tape, and zoomed-in on her face. Seen in grainy close-up, the two gray spheres above her cheekbones melted into her skin. By the time Kate hit the water, they'd vanished completely.

"My God, how could I miss it," Jack had exclaimed. "After the second spin, you're closing your eyes!" He shot the tape forward, and again pressed play. "Look, you're doing it on every dive!"

Nars tried to help, unsuccessfully. Dr. Borshel—Stefan Borshel, the sports psychologist Jack had taken her to—tested Kate for weeks at the University of Pennsylvania. The results were inconclusive. "It's clearly a concentration issue," Dr. Borshel reported, "but so far at least, we can't put our finger on why." For hours, Kate practiced holding her eyes open without blinking. She even stuck waterproof tape to her eyelids before her dives. Nothing worked.

Now Kate leaned in discouragment against his stolid frame. Seven dives, not one on the money. "I'll help you beat this, Kate," Nars assured her, hugging her closer. "We'll beat it together." His comforting arm seemed like a bulwark against her inadequacy.

Suddenly—she would never remember exactly how—she was vanishing into him, surrounded by his strong limbs.

"Oh my God," Kate gasped, "We can't do this." But do it they did. An embrace that became a long kiss became his hands touching her. Then, feeling his arousal. Flimsy swimsuits sliding from wet flesh, puddling at the side of the pool. Their bodies sagging to the damp concrete. Moans, their moans, echoing in the cavernous plunge like some erotic Gregorian chant.

It was the first time Kate had made love.

Afterwards, they would be more discrete. Their subsequent couplings were furtive and brief, usually occurring in Jack's office after practice. Their affair had begun and it would play out, chapter-by-chapter, ultimately following the only tortuous course that it could, to the end of love, mutual loathing, betrayal and ruin.

★   ★   ★

"MISS GAVRILL? Can we talk?" A different voice, booming in a different empty pool building, drew her back to the present.

Kate lifted her head to see Lt. MacMahon looking down at her intently.

He frowned. "Sorry to interrupt your workout, but the case has gotten more complicated. I needed to talk to you again. The man at the main gate said that you come here to exercise."

"Well, you found me," Kate said. Talking to MacMahon was the last thing she wanted to do but, hey, if nothing else, he deserved an "I" for intrepid. "Give me a few minutes to change. I'll meet you in the parking lot."

MacMahon nodded silently, then stood awkwardly a few feet away. Kate climbed from the pool, turning her body away from the tall policeman's gaze as she reached for her towel. His blush told her he'd gotten an eyeful.

Moments later, in a freshly starched shirt and designer jeans, Kate caught up with the officer, leaning against his state police car. She sensed he was a man who could appear infinitely relaxed one moment, then uncoil in fury the next. *I wouldn't want to be a bad guy around Donald MacMahon,* Kate thought. She reached in her purse and pulled out a legal-size envelope.

"Here's the financial stuff you wanted. Except for a savings account, my mother didn't have much beyond a couple of insurance policies. She has—had—no partners or even any real business anymore." Kate wasn't about to reveal the fortune Irina had described, at least not now. "Christ, she was just crossing the street, a dance instructor who never bothered anybody." Kate started to choke up.

MacMahon squeezed the end of his nose, looked down at his shoes and shook his head from side to side. He raised his head and smiled ruefully. A dimple creased the plane between his cheekbone and his jaw.

"Miss Gavrill," MacMahon said, "how close were you to your mother?" His eyes seemed to have a permanent squint, or perhaps that was just how they trained cops to look at people they were questioning.

Kate stared back at him. It didn't seem appropriate or necessary to go into what had happened in college and her strained relationship with Irina. "She was my mother. We had our ups and downs. Like anybody else."

MacMahon pulled at his nose again. "Well, there are a number of unusual factors in your mother's case. I'm just trying to look at all the angles."

"What do you mean 'unusual'? What 'angles'?"

He seemed to choose his words carefully, pausing for an instant between each sentence. "My investigation isn't complete, of course. But her accident doesn't appear unintentional. It looks as if either your mother wanted to be hit or somebody wanted to hit her."

"That's ridiculous—she *wanted* to be hit—how can you say that?"

"Miss Gavrill, this isn't my theory. We have at least one witness who says your mother appeared to be hurrying to meet somebody, and wasn't paying any attention to the truck, which was plainly visible, when she walked into the street. And *all* the witnesses agree there was no way the driver could have avoided seeing her."

"She could have just been distracted, by any of a thousand things." *Calling me on her cell phone, for one.* Kate's voice caught, remembering Irina's bruised face against the hospital pillow. "If you're suggesting my mother had some sort of, of death wish, that's absurd."

"That's not what I'm suggesting at all. I'm just trying to give you a sense of what we're hearing when we talk to people who were there. It's all over the map." He stepped closer, spreading his arms to emphasize the scale of their inquiry.

"The fact is we're proceeding on the assumption of deliberate intent."

"Who'd want to hurt my mother?" How many times had Kate asked the same question of herself? She still had no answer, even with the knowledge she'd gleaned in the last 24 hours. Kate's eyes began to fill, and her body shook, as much in anger as in fear. "You can't let them get away with this!"

"Miss, we're doing our best." MacMahon closed the short distance between them. He placed his hands lightly on her shoulders. Suddenly Kate sensed a quality she didn't often associate with police officers: compassion.

"I'm sorry. It was just everything coming down at once," she said. She daubed her nose. "What have you found out?"

"Well, take the truck that hit her. Witnesses say the engine sounded like some modern race car. Not the sort of vehicle you'd expect to be driven by local farmers. And then there's the two men in the truck."

"What about them?"

"They were middle-aged, dressed in traditional Amish clothing."

"So?"

"When it's accidental, people who commit this type of crime are usually young, drugged or drunk—often all three. The Amish are known to be abstainers, law-abiding. They're also deeply devout Christians. Why didn't they stop their truck and come back to help?"

"That's easy," Kate responded. "They weren't really Amish at all; they were just in costume for the fair. They might even have been wearing stage makeup to look older. Lots of participants do."

"I thought of that," MacMahon replied. "People said they were smoking and using a cell phone—one even said she heard them swear." He squinted at the ground again. "But even if you're right, it just raises more questions. Anyhow, thanks for the financial data." He opened his car door and slid behind the wheel. He lowered the driver's window and pushed an elbow over the sill.

Kate touched his arm. "Sorry about before, about brushing you off."

"No need to apologize," he said. "You'd just learned your mom was dead." He switched on the ignition. "I'll be in touch."

Kate waved and turned, heading to her Saab. She heard the sound of brakes and realized MacMahon was pulling up alongside her. He stopped and looked at her, shading his eyes with his free hand.

"One more thing," he said. "There's the direction of the truck."

Kate frowned. "I don't understand."

"After they struck your mother, they spun that old truck around like it was a Ferrari. Made a full u-turn into the other lane. Then they headed back the same way they'd come."

Kate stared at him, still uncomprehending.

"Twenty years I've been doing this and I've never seen that. Arsonists sometimes stay to watch the flames. Amateur killers—and psychopaths—return to the scene of their murders. But . . . at least when it's accidental . . . hit and runners always do the same thing."

"What?"

"They keep going."

Part II

Chapter 8

A WEEK after Irina's funeral, Kate boarded a bus to Philadelphia on her way to New York. Pennslyvania's sweltering hills, burned to the color of Russian *pakhlava* by the summer sun, rolled by her bus window.

So far, this is what Kate knew: Just as he had for his other children, Nicholas II established a Bank of England trust account for Lydia, his child with Anya. In this instance, however, he'd stipulated that no claimant could take legal possession of the bank funds without first presenting the original documents of deposit, the Romanov alexandrite, and its container, a miniature Faberge carriage.

According to Irina's tape, Sir Edward Peacock, the Bank of England's director, was fully aware of the account's discrete nature. He was dealing, after all, with a matter of utmost delicacy involving a close relative of the Royal Family. Prudence dictated complete privacy. Thus, at least to the best of Irina's and Anya's knowledge and that of their attorneys, the account had never been touched. Year after year it continued to accrue interest, sometimes at high rates.

Ironically, only a few days earlier Kate had been boxing some of her mother's bank records. They included decades of deposit books. Some of the early entries had been surprisingly small—literally five or ten dollars. Yet at the time of her death the power of compounding had boosted Irina's single savings account to more than six figures.

Kate could only imagine the size of an account, now nearly a century old, that began life worth five million British pounds.

In her checking accounts, Irina's careful notations included drafts for everything from cheese and flour to bills for household repairs. One check stub, to fix a swinging door between their kitchen and dining room, triggered a long-forgotten memory. Because the door was temporarily removed, Kate had overheard a conversation—meaningless at the time—that now seemed ripe with portent.

She'd been sitting in the living room, sketching an imaginary princess and daydreaming like any 10-year-old.

"Granmama," Irina was asking Anya, "have you ever wondered if things could have been different in Kiev?" The two women were in the kitchen, engaged in idle conversation while they washed the dishes. In the door's absence, Kate could clearly discern their words from her seat on the sofa.

"Of course," Anya replied, "Many times. But it is what it is—or was what it was. I gave everything to the archbishop," Anya said. "He was an old Romanov family friend from Irkutsk, in southern Siberia."

At the time, Kate had no idea what her great grandmother meant by "everything." Nor could she recall ever having heard of the archbishop from Irkutsk. But she knew the conversation was important, and she kept listening.

"The archbishop had a network of loyalists in Mongolia and Kazakhstan," Anya continued. "He sewed the stone into his robes, and hid the bank papers and egg in a church satchel. We got as far as the Ukraine, using his clerical status as cover.

"He went to pray at Pechersk Lavra, the Monastery of the Caves, and I never saw him again."

Kate shook her head and looked back out the bus window. Miles of going-brown cornfields stretched to a putty-gray horizon.

As Kate now knew from Irina's tape recording, the archbishop hadn't simply disappeared. He'd been killed by pagan cultists allied with the Bolsheviks. The animals cut off the prelate's head and carried it around a chapel altar, trailing a circle of blood on the floor.

Soon after, Anya and Lydia reached Paris, settling on the Left Bank for the next sixteen years. In 1928, Lydia—Kate's grandmother—married Sergey Karpov, a refugee Russian aristocrat, banker and the tsar's former financial representative in London. Five years later, Trotskyites intent on wiping out any vestiges of the tsar brutally murdered the couple.

With Grand Duchess Olga's help, Anya and Irina escaped to America. In New York, Anya rented an apartment and returned to the world of dance, using different stage names. She choreographed obscure musicals and taught ballet to rich daughters on Manhattan's upper east side. Irina became her star pupil, but never pursued a public career out of fear they'd be discovered. When Kate was born, Irina transferred her own ambitions in ballet to her new daughter. Meanwhile, until Irina married Henri Gavrill, they moved like gypsies.

This too Kate learned from Irina's recording: Her mother and Anya were secretly active in the Romanov restoration movement—they felt they owed it to all who had died, especially Nicholas and his children.

But what had they owed her? For all of Anya's and Irina's devotion to Russian tradition and culture, for all their concern about the Romanov legacy, their own flesh and blood hadn't merited a ruble's worth of honesty about her history. Kate felt a sudden surge of anger—and the need to see Irina's exact words. She reached in her briefcase to retrieve the transcript she'd made of the tape. Once again, she reread the last four paragraphs:

> Whether we were right or wrong, the reason Anya and I kept the truth from you was out of fear for your safety. I know that you and I have had a difficult time in recent years, but you must listen to what I say now. If you do as I have asked, powerful forces will conspire against you, and your life may be at risk. There are those who

will want your money, those who will want the power of your name, and those who will want both. They will stop at nothing to prevent you from gaining your birthright. Remember, they killed your grandparents, and—if you are reading this—may have killed me.

Go to my safe deposit box at Chase Manhattan on Fifth Avenue. You will find correspondence documenting my own search for the alexandrite, and the phone number and address of Mr. Peter Cushing, an attorney in New York whose firm has been very helpful. He's drawn up a charter for the charity we wish to form, if we are able to reclaim the tsar's great gift. Mr. Cushing suggested we name it the Nicholas Romanov Foundation for Peace through Music and Dance. Nicholas strongly believed in the power of art, and especially the ballet, as an antidote to strife and violence.

Someone else may help you, but proceed with caution. He is the grandson of Rasputin—Alexandra's 'special friend.' Anya said Nicholas never trusted Grigori, but this man—his name is Imre Novyck—may be useful. He is some kind of official at Lefortovo Prison in Moscow.

Despite what came between us when you were in college, Katya, I have never stopped loving you or believing in you. Fate has given you a chance to redeem yourself. I know that you will make the most of it, and again fill me with pride.

Reading her mother's words, Kate's eyes filmed with tears. *A chance to redeem yourself? Where? How? Would she have to go to Russia?* She pursed her lips, sighed and silently shook her head. Could she ever forgive herself for being so foolish? The typed lines resurrected memories that still seemed painful and fresh. They began in Dr. Borshel's office.

★　　★　　★

"CLOSING YOUR eyes isn't the issue, Kate," he'd begun. He shuffled a thick file of papers and spoke softly, with a slight European accent. "In fact, if anything, it's possibly a good sign."

Kate leaned closer to the physician's desk, holding tightly to Jack Nars' hand. For months she and Jack had been trying to get to the bottom of her spotting problems. She'd begun to suspect something might be wrong in her psychological makeup, some weak spot or rift in her will to win. But it sounded like Dr. Borshel was about to deliver good news.

"Tell me, when you are diving, when you are actually in the dive itself and before your eyes close, do things around you seem to slow down?"

Kate nodded, tightening her grip on Nars' fingers. It had been that way since she first began diving. She'd grown to see the phenomenon as another aspect of the sport's ability to transport her to a different world.

"Then I wouldn't be overly concerned." Dr. Borshel offered a professional smile. "This is something I often see in top athletes, whether their sport is football or fencing or diving. In what I call the athletic moment—the heighth of competition—you enter a self-induced trance, creating a protective shell within your consciousness. Your mind re-orders time. It shifts everything around and you go into slow motion in a way that lets you focus on one thing: performing at your absolute peak."

"But that's just the point," Kate interjected. "I'm *not* performing at my peak."

Her head spun. Just when she'd glimpsed an approaching breakthrough, she was slipping back where she started.

Dr. Borshel leaned back in his chair. "These tests," he said, tapping the thick folder on his desk; "paint a picture of an athlete with superb physical gifts, and more than enough mental acuity to know exactly how to use them." He heaved his shoulders in an exaggerated shrug, and ruffled the papers by their edges. "Whatever is stopping you from achieving your goals, Kate Gavrill, can't be found in this data."

Two weeks and six hours of additional tests later, however, Dr. Borshel had a different opinion. "The finding of self-hypnosis still stands," he said, "and it's still a big positive when it comes to your ultimate success. But there is a problem. Perhaps I missed it because I'm used to seeing it in male athletes."

He paused, and looked into her eyes. Kate glanced at Jack and slipped her arm through his.

"Kate, it may sound as if I'm describing a disease du jour, but it's now quite clear to me that you're suffering from a form of Attention Deficit Disorder, basically the co-existence of attentional problems and hyperactivity. You've probably had this since you were a small child, and in almost all areas of your life you've developed coping mechanisms—except this one, the act of diving, especially complex dives when you go beyond two rotations."

Dr. Borshel paused, and drummed his fingers on the thick stack of test results on his desk. "I'm going to prescribe what's called a cognitive awareness medication to help."

"Oh no, now just a minute—" Kate started to protest.

The physician looked at her sternly. "Kate, I'm prescribing this to help you habituate behaviors, specifically focusing behaviors. This medicine is for training purposes only. Hopefully, the effect will persist when you compete. You will, of course, need to cease its use well before any actual athletic events. But I'll leave the timing of that up to you and coach Nars."

"He's turning me into a pill-head," Kate protested when she and Jack were driving back to New Jersey.

"It's just like Adderall, for Christ's sake," Jack said when she protested. "It's the same stuff half the kids in school use to pass exams. Pilots in combat use it. Cops use it. Hell, I've even used it. You've got to give it a try. This could unlock a whole new level of performance for you."

Kate stared silently out her passenger's window. He was right. She'd been preparing for this phase of her career since she first went off a 3-meter board in high school. She glanced down at the white bottle of medication in her hand. She didn't feel good about it, but she'd go along, at least for now.

★　　★　　★

The dirty red brick buildings—blackened by years of auto exhaust and coal dust—told her they were nearing Philly. Long before the mess she got in with Jack, Irina and Anya had tried to argue her out of becoming an athlete. She had always thought it was because they still wanted her to give ballet another try. Now she suspected there had been another reason. For years the two women had succeeded in isolating Kate. How they must have worried when she showed promise—and even garnered local publicity—as a diver. After Anya died, Irina was left alone with their terrible secret. Ever since that long ago night in Paris, her mother had lived in a world inhabited by frightening strangers, each one a potential assassin. Kate's humiliation drew little public attention, even in local papers, but it could only have heightened the fearfulness of Irina's existence.

Kate's mother must have dreaded the day of truth telling, yet known that day would come. In a way, because it erected a wall of near-silence between them, what happened to Kate in college had allowed Irina to delay that reckoning for years, until she faced her own demise. She'd bequeathed her daughter an unknown history, an unfound fortune and an unmet challenge—one that could demand Kate risk her life in a country she scarcely knew.

The bus braked sharply. Under her tan linen slacks, Kate's hips tensed against the cushion. Stretching forward, she grabbed her briefcase just before it slid to the floor.

Chapter 9

FIFTH AVENUE, late afternoon. Even in suffocation, Manhattan's sidewalks hummed with human energy. The press of people generated more heat and, as she briskly trekked the dozen blocks to Tiffany & Co., Kate grew damp under her long-sleeved Oxford cloth shirt.

Her first stop had been Chase Manhattan Bank on Fifth Avenue. She opened Irina's safe deposit box and found a sheaf of papers, including one that described the alexandrite in detail, and a small gold frog, which she remembered from childhood. Kate slipped the contents into her briefcase, returned the box to its place in the vault, and walked back into the stifling air.

Tiffany's polished steel doors and rows of gleaming display cases seemed cool by comparison. She paused at a display of rings, struck by the myriad colors of diamonds and sapphires. When she asked to see an alexandrite, Kate was directed upstairs.

"Genuine examples are unusual, as I'm sure you know," said the clerk, an intimidating, overly handsome man with heavily-oiled, swept-back hair and glossy fingernails. "This isn't the largest stone we have, but it is representative."

The alexandrite was small, and surrounded by still smaller diamonds in a plain gold setting. Under the store's high ceiling lights, the gem gleamed a greenish-blue. When the clerk placed it under a display lamp, however, the same stone transformed itself, turning a dazzling, pigeon-blood red.

It's just a gimmick, Kate thought at first. The clerk moved the ring out of the light again, then back in. By the time he'd made a third pass under the lamp, she felt herself being drawn in. The alternating colors seemed to possess their own temperature and rhythm and even, in a way, separate moods. The price tag certainly wasn't a gimmick: $68,000, for a small ring. She thought of the description of the Romanov alexandrite she'd just read after opening Irina's deposit box. What would such an infinitely larger stone be worth today?

"Actually, I came about this," said Kate. "I'd like to get an idea of its value and have it repaired. It seems to need a new clasp."

She opened her briefcase and removed the frog brooch.

The clerk sighed, rolled his eyes and, after ushering her into a private consultation room, vanished.

While she waited, Kate looked closely at the brooch. She'd recognized the thumb-sized bauble at once. Anya had dangled the frog before her eyes when, as a little girl, she couldn't get to sleep. Her great-grandmother always expressed surprise at how quickly the amphibian's gleaming ruby eyes lulled Kate to slumber. "Come, look," she'd call to Irina, "Katya has already closed her eyes." Now, the creature stared up from Kate's hand, as if daring her to solve a puzzle whose secret it alone might know.

"It's an exquisite piece," Tiffany's estate jewelry manager said after quickly studying the frog under a loupe. "Very old and very rare. Genuine Faberge, I'm quite sure. But you really should show this to a specialist. I'd recommend The Vintage Russian, a few blocks north of here across from the Plaza. They've traded in the Russian aristocracy's jewels and personal artifacts since the 1920s."

Before leaving Tiffany's, Kate stepped into the women's room. She simply must do something about this heat. Besides, with her smallish figure, and under the heavy, loose-fitting shirt, who could tell the difference? Ducking into a stall, she took off her bra, and stowed the lacy white underwear in her briefcase. Slipping back into the blouse, she crossed the room to a washbasin. She wet a towel and sponged her arms, chest and neck. She re-buttoned the garment and departed.

"Lovely," said the The Vintage Russian Shop's manager. The woman slowly turned the small but dazzling gold-and-green-crusted frog between her fingers. "These are called Uraltic emeralds, after their brilliance and the area where they are found. In truth, of course, they're simply chrysoberyls, in this case very rare garnets."

The woman smiled as if Kate understood every reference, but the world she described might as well be in Katmandu. Cabochons and chrysoberyls, garnets and Uraltic emeralds, rubies, diamonds, and alexandrites—they smeared together like some sparkling lava, impenetrable in their collective mystery. How could she hope to make her way in a field whose basic elements she could barely spell, much less understand?

"It's a valuable piece and really should be appraised," the woman continued, oblivious to Kate's confusion. "I'd strongly advise that you keep it in a secure place, a safe deposit box." She leaned forward, and lowered her voice. "And do be careful carrying it in your briefcase." She slid a card over the counter-top. "Mr. Blake is just a few blocks from here. You might be surprised how much this is worth. I'm sure he can repair the clasp as well."

Kate nodded, picked up the card, and strode back into the throngs of mid-afternoon Fifth Avenue shoppers.

Chapter 10

"I DON'T see many demantoid garnets, Miss Gavrill, and especially such fine ones. Thanks for bringing this in."

And thanks, thought Kate, for expanding my glossary for gemology dummies.

Simon Blake took the damaged pendant. "I should have the appraisal for you by tomorrow afternoon," he said. "I'll have an assistant fix the clasp. It appears as if at some point it was converted to a necklace. Is that how you'll be wearing it?"

Kate nodded. She studied his features. Blake's thin, prominent nose arched just below its bridge. His brown eyes were framed by deep furrows between their brows and lines that streaked across his cheeks like creases in a canyon wall. Pewter frosted his brown hair. His clothes were rumpled in a comfortable way, and so was he: the open-neck sweater he wore had a small hole at the right elbow, and he needed a shave. He looked weary. She put him a year or so north of forty, but he could have been older.

Blake rose from his antique maple desk and crossed the room. He stood an inch or two past six feet and moved with a lean grace. A few minutes with a razor and a few hours of sleep, Kate mused, just might turn this geeky gem guy into a cool and dreamy prince. Whoa, she heard an inner alarm bell and stopped herself. Careful Kate doesn't go there.

Blake was ushering Kate out of his eighth floor office when she impulsively turned and asked, "By the way, Mr. Blake, have you ever heard of a Romanov Alexandrite?" Later, she grilled herself: Had she really believed he would know of the stone, or was she simply trying to flirt?

He scratched his forehead. "Not that I recall. Tell me more."

Without revealing her relationship to the gem, Kate briefly summarized the description she'd found in the safe deposit box.

Training his eyes on the street below, Blake stared past her through a large iron-paned window across the hall. Skepticism edged his words.

"More than 1,200 carats? I find that hard to believe, Miss Gavrill. The world's largest cut diamond—the Cullinan, part of England's crown jewels—weighs just over 530 carats. It's more than a full inch square and half an inch deep. You're talking about a gem twice that size, and alexandrites typically run smaller than diamonds. I can't believe I wouldn't know of it."

Kate searched his eyes. "Mr. Blake," she blurted, "I'd never even seen a real alexandrite until two hours ago. I don't know anything about precious stones. And I don't know where to go to find out. I need help. The Russian shop recommended you, but I need to know I can trust you." The last thing Kate wanted was to put her faith in a man she'd just met. But she really had no choice. She had to find someone who could guide her through the unknown world of precious gems.

He arched an eyebrow. Belatedly, Kate realized she'd insulted him.

"Miss Gavrille," Blake replied slowly, "trust is really the only asset someone in my business has. It's the reason, for example, that I never purchase or deal in stones I evaluate. Selling gems would inevitably compromise my impartiality. And impartiality is why my clients are willing to pay dearly for my time."

He leaned against his office door, shoved both hands deep in his pockets, and gazed down at her. To Kate, Simon Blake suddenly seemed simultaneously pompous and remote.

"As far as the alexandrite is concerned," he continued, offering little to change her impression, "don't feel embarrassed. Most people have never seen a real one. It's many times rarer than a diamond or emerald, for example.

"The alexandrite," he went on, "is the only precious gem that changes color—from green in normal light to red under illumination. Some believe the stone possesses metaphysical properties that can help balance one's emotional state. The Russians who first discovered it were convinced the stone could cure swollen lymph nodes and intensify"—his mouth curved in what Kate took as a slight smirk— "feelings of sensuality."

Self-importance seemed to drip from his words. Nonetheless, Kate chose to ignore his tone. "I'll pay you, of course," she said matter-of-factly, suppressing a practical urge to ask about his fee. She plunged her hand into her briefcase. "Let me show you this document."

She withdrew the paper in a single motion. To Kate's horror, besides pulling out the sheet of paper, she'd also launched a miniature parachute, which now floated ominously above Blake's head.

In an instant, her airborne bra settled principally in the geographic region above Blake's prominent nose. The twin white cones rose from his forehead like misplaced cartoon ears. Half-an-inch from his upper lip, the strap dangled tantalizingly. Above his single visible eye, Blake's brow again arched, this time quizzically.

Kate doubled up, her body shaking with laughter. Her breasts swung wildly beneath her blouse but she was quite certain that, with his impaired vision, the oh-so-authoritative Mr. Blake hadn't noticed.

Lifting its strap, Blake carefully undraped the flimsy garment from his face. Smiling broadly now, he handed it back to her. "Well, I must say, Miss Gavrill, you do know how to make an entrance. Or should I say, exit?"

Pink as a rose, Kate pressed a hand to her lips. She took the bra, and handed back the alexandrite's formal description. "Would you copy this," she said, briefly summoning her composure, "and tell me what you think tomorrow afternoon?"

Blake nodded. He crossed the room, made a photocopy, and returned with the original. Then, bending low at the waist in a mock bow, he held the door wide for her. Halfway down the corridor, Kate began laughing hysterically.

Chapter 11

KATE NEEDED only a few minutes to walk from Blake's office to her hotel at 37th and Park. The documents from Irina's deposit box were now spread across her bed.

The first, from the man her mother had mentioned in her tape, was a hand-written letter in an open envelope bearing Russian stamps and Lefortovo Prison, Moscow, as a return address. Hadn't Irina said he was an official there? Dated nearly three years before, it read:

> Dear Madame Gavrill:
>
> This is to inform you that I have located the file referred to in my previous correspondence. This material verifies the existence of valuable property belonging to your family, originally entrusted to Archbishop Chenko of Irkutsk. I refer specifically to the so-called Romanov Alexandrite and fitted Faberge container. While very old, the materials, which eventually were passed along to my grandfather, Ivan Novyck, are quite clear. I'm sure they will greatly assist you in locating your items. I'm also certain that we can work out a mutually beneficial arrangement for their transfer to you.
>
> Your Servant, Imre Novyck

Kate stared at the short message. What did he mean by "materials" that had been "passed along" to his grandfather. He obviously wasn't referring to the actual stone or its container. Could Anya have been wrong? What did "originally entrusted" mean? Perhaps the archbishop had never been in possession of the alexandrite and documents or had given them to someone else out of fear for his own—or the treasure's—safety. Who exactly was this Novyck? Did he know the location of the stone and the egg?

A second, partially completed note lay in the same envelope. Written in a shaky hand, it was a six-months old missive from her mother, presumably never finished or sent:

> Dear Mr. Novyck:
>   It appears that your warnings were well founded. Earlier this week, while I was shopping in Philadelphia, the same man appeared in three department stores shortly after I did. He tried to be inconspicuous, but I am certain I was being followed. I finally hid in the restroom of the last store until past closing time. I must tell Katya soon . . .

Kate held the folded note in her lap and rubbed her forehead. Just months ago, Irina had been followed! Or thought she had. Of course, it could have been sheer coincidence or paranoia, but Irina clearly believed otherwise. She'd taken the incident as evidence that her fears were warranted, that someone had learned the secret she'd shared for all those years with Anya. Still, why hadn't she sent this note to Novyck? And why hadn't she told her, Kate, about her fears? But that was one question to which Kate already knew the answer. Her mother had held off telling Kate until her final hours because the wound between them had gone too deep.

★　　★　　★

"It's NOT working." Kate's head hung to her chest as water from the pool washed off her body. Hands on hips, she stared at the floor. "When I don't take the pills, I can't hold my spots." She shook her head. "It's just no good."

"Calm down." Jack glanced around furtively. "I'll call Dr. Borshel. Meantime, go back on the meds."

"But it's only a week before the first meet." She shivered. Her swim suit felt clammy. In the big indoor pool, their whispers echoed as they might have in a subterranean tunnel.

"Don't worry about it."

"But I do worry about it. If the drugs aren't out of my system by then, they'll say I cheated."

He put both hands on her shoulders and smiled that square smile she couldn't resist, the one that made the muscles in his jaw break into taut, even planes. "Take it easy, Kate. We'll figure it out. Let's talk in my office tomorrow night after I've spoken to Dr. Borshel."

The next evening, sitting on the office sofa after they'd made love, Kate looked at him expectantly. "So what did Dr. Borshel say?"

Turning away from her, Jack crossed his arms across his chest. "Forget Borshel," he replied brusquely. Reaching into his briefcase, he withdrew a small plastic squeeze bottle and handed it to Kate. The bottle contained yellow liquid and a thermometer embedded in its side. Two wires with battery clips dangled from a metal plate at its base.

Kate held the apparatus closer for inspection. "What the hell is this?"

"It's synthetic urine," Jack said. "The liquid contains everything found in natural pee." He reached into his desk drawer and pulled out a pair of 9-volt batteries. "They'll be testing before our first event. Half an hour before you go in, attach the batteries. Once the indicator reaches 98 to 100 degrees—body temperature—it will hold for at least four hours." He lightly tweaked her cheek. "Piece of cake."

"Piece of cake?" Kate retorted. She pulled away. Perspiration still gleamed from her breasts. "You're telling me to cheat."

"You won't get caught, Kate. Hell, anybody can buy this kit on the Internet. It's called a urinator. Practically every other new hire for the government or major corporation has used one of these."

Kate stared back at him coldly. Whatever their conflicts, Irina and Anya had instilled in her a sense of ethics based on the strictest tenets of Eastern Orthodoxy. Cheating in any form simply wasn't on. She reached to her chest to fasten her bra, then slowly began buttoning her blouse. "I won't do it," she said.

"You've got to do it," Jack countered. He looked deeply into her eyes. "And it's not ethically wrong, or at least it shouldn't be. You're a great diver, Kate. You could be one of the best ever. Why should a minor mental handicap stand in your way? I'm not asking you to take something to increase your physical abilities—that would be wrong. I just want you to use a legally prescribed medication so your head can be all it can be. So you can compete on a level field."

Kate imagined her mother and Anya. What would they think? "I'm sorry, Jack. I can't do this. I just can't."

His gaze dropped to the floor. "Well, if you won't do it for yourself, do it for us. Or do it for me. Look, I'm not getting any younger. I've got to produce champions if I'm going to move up to athletic director or go on to a bigger school." Now he raised his eyes to hers. "We've talked about this before, Kate. If we're going to have a new life together, I've got to be in a position to make that life work."

"I won't," she said, her lower lip trembling. "It just isn't right." A strong odor of chlorine wafted up the concrete corridor from the pool two flights below. Kate loved Jack, but she couldn't believe he was suggesting this.

Jack put both hands on her shoulders and stared hard into her eyes. "Look, you want to get to the next level in your diving. I want to get to the next level of coaching. Don't you see, Kate? We can both win. We can get to the Olympics together."

He paused again, and his voice grew husky. "Don't take that chance away from us, Kate. Please."

Still sitting on the leather sofa, Kate nodded silently. She glanced at the large photograph above Jack's desk of the great American diver Greg Louganis. Louganis, who came back to win double Olympic gold after hitting his head on the diving board, had been her hero. He'd overcome his adversity, why couldn't she?

"Hey," Jack said abruptly, glancing at his watch. "I've gotta run. Will you lock up?"

She nodded. "Sure. It seems like you've always got to run."

He flashed that chunky grin. "Lots of balls in the air, baby, just trying to do the best for us I can." His dark blue eyes twinkled the way they did when he wanted to make love. "Think about what I said. I'll call tomorrow."

Leaving the office door partially ajar, he departed. Far down the hall, Kate heard the soft whirring of an overhead paddle fan. Across the opened door's frosted glass, Kate read her lover's name in heavy, gilt-edged black type: "*JACK NARS*." Would she take that name someday? Would she be the coach's wife?

Kate looked at her hands, still clenched in tension after their argument. She thought of *Faust*, the nineteenth century ballet she'd watched as a child with Anya and Irina. Dr. Faust traded his soul for the power of magic. Was she trading hers for an Olympic medal? Was Jack her Mephisto?

On the other hand, maybe Jack was right, and the rules were unfair. She wasn't taking drugs to bulk up her muscles, run faster or throw farther. She was just trying to get her brain and her eyes to work the way nature intended.

After failing as a ballerina, she'd resolved never again to be overcome by her physical limitations. She'd vowed to be the best at whatever she did. Through hard work and talent, she'd almost succeeded—she'd risen within reach of the top rungs of her sport. Now, however, just like years ago, her continued success wasn't being threatened by a superior competitor. The challenge came from her own body, her own physicality. Would she let those shortcomings defeat her a second time?

Kate was a grownup now and the decision she faced wasn't about some little girly ballet. It was about a chance at global competition, an Olympic medal, perhaps even a world championship.

She picked up the plastic bottle and turned it slowly in her hands. After all, didn't somebody say winning was the only thing?

★ ★ ★

HOLDING THE copy he'd made, Blake crossed the room to a cabinet behind his desk. He removed a bottle of single barrel bourbon and a cut-crystal glass. Pouring neat, he started reading.

THE ROMANOV ALEXANDRITE

Approximately two inches long and an inch wide, the stone weighs 1275 carats, or more than half of a standard Troy pound. This makes it by far the largest gem quality alexandrite known to exist. The stone is rounded in shape, containing 528 facets in 16 rows.

Under candlelight, the stone is violet-red in color. It is much closer to a true ruby red than most fine alexandrites. In natural daylight, the stone is very slightly bluish green. It is much closer to true emerald color than most fine alexandrites.

The Romanov Alexandrite is believed to be the finest example known. It has a current estimated value of no less than ten million British pounds.

Philippe Genet Lukinoff, Chief Gem Analyst, House of Faberge May 10, 1911

Blake put down the glass and lowered his head into his hands. Slowly, he rubbed his temples. As a boy, Simon Blake had collected agates in streambeds near his Indiana home. More than three decades later, he remained fascinated by the mysteries hidden inside gems— their fractures, molten traps and myriad colors. Now he imagined the stone described in the document. Using his microscope, he would probe the deepest reaches of the alexandrite's interior, entering a startling universe. The gem's crystalline inclusions would float like emerald moons; as he added illumination, its facets would radiate slender spokes of crimson. It would be a masterpiece, as surely as any Michelangelo.

Brushing aside his brief gemological fantasy, Blake returned to the far greater likelihood: that despite the paper he'd just read, neither he nor anyone else had seen such a stone precisely because no such stone existed, now or ever. And there was something else, a truth he knew very well. If somehow such a stone did exist, sooner or later its owners would confront a question that inevitably came to haunt those who held jewels of great fame and fable. Did they possess its beauty or did its beauty possess them?

Chapter 12

KATE'S GAZE rolled up the walls of her hotel room like a video camera, panning over the ceiling and back down again. The lens froze on her image in a mirror above the dresser. Despite her finely chiseled head, wideset eyes and striking cheekbones, she felt suddenly plain. She put her hand to her throat, tracing her pale, unadorned flesh.

She looked back down at the bed. Among the deposit box papers was a formal declaration, bearing the official Faberge coat of arms, and signed by the firm's designer, Henrik Wigstrom. It read:

THE BALLERINA CARRIAGE.

The carriage is on wheels so that it stands upright without a base. It is made of six layers of red and green engine-turned enamel and trimmed in solid gold. Its egg-shaped compartment opens on top and is lined in white satin. The Romanov alexandrite fits into an impression that reveals the upper portion of the stone. When the egg is closed, a scrolled gold strip conceals the opening. An image of the Romanov Double Eagle is etched in a gold plate mounted on the front of the carriage. It matches a similar etching at the base of the stone itself.

The box's final document was a tattered deposit slip carrying a Bank of England letterhead and dated June 26, 1913. It bore an official notary seal and the signature of Sir Edward Peacock. The slip contained a single entry line: "Lydia Natasha Putyatin, esq., deposit in interest bearing trust, in the amount of 5 million English pounds." Rubber-stamped diagonally across the document were the words, "Confidential Private Account." Nowhere was the funds' source identified.

On one level, it was all just too much. The most expensive jewelry Kate had ever owned was a cultured pearl necklace she'd purchased for a party after receiving her PhD. She'd found it at Saks for $700. The prospect of great wealth seemed wholly unfamiliar to her and, in its own way, profoundly unsettling. Her quest for excellence in athletics—imperfect though it surely was—had been about achieving her personal best, not about money or fame. The pieces described in these papers might have belonged to Hollywood royalty like Audrey Hepburn or Grace Kelly or, for that matter, a real queen, like England's Elizabeth. Yet not only had they been gifts to Kate's very own great grandmother from one of the world's most powerful men, but each had been individually designed and, in the case of the alexandrite, specifically cut for Anya. Nicholas must have cared for her—and their daughter—very much indeed.

Kate's gaze shifted to the window. Across 37th Street, her eighth floor room could easily be seen from other buildings. She rose, walked to the window and pulled the curtains closed. Had someone been watching her? Could the same man who'd followed Irina be following her? A chill crept from the back of Kate's neck to her shoulder blades.

Chapter 13

—————«⦿»—————

"**W**OULD YOU mind if I delivered the report over dinner? It turns out my afternoon is booked. Besides, I'd like to discuss this with you in person. We could meet at a restaurant near your hotel."

Blake's invitation took Kate by surprise. Was he trying to ingratiate himself with her for some reason? He'd seemed highly skeptical of the alexandrite. In any case, she accepted; she'd planned to leave the next day. Now, as she walked to the address of the theater district cafe he'd named, Kate's heart raced. Perhaps he'd learned something that persuaded him the stone was real. She saw her reflection in a window and smoothed her hair.

The place turned out to be a cozy below-street-level bistro with red brick walls, rough plank floors and an unlit fireplace.

Blake met her at the entrance and led the way to a table in a deserted corner of the restaurant.

Seated, Kate glanced around the room. "Nice choice."

He nodded back. "Best crab salad in Manhattan."

She looked down at her hands, feeling suddenly nervous and distinctly awkward. Why had he wanted to have dinner? It was as if they were on a first date. "Do you know the city well?"

"I suppose so. I'm an addicted Manhattan walker." He smiled, but his eyes seemed to search hers, belying the blandness of their conversation.

Enough small talk, Kate thought. Even before their wine arrived, she got to the point. "What did you think of the stone's description?"

"Well, first," he replied, dodging her question, "here's the appraisal for the frog brooch. I think you'll be pleased to see its value. You should get it insured—right away." He handed her a business envelope, closed but unsealed. "And, please, be a lot more careful about carrying it around. If you're not wearing it, it should be kept in a safe."

Kate opened the envelope and the enclosed estimate. She blinked.

"This is nearly $140,000."

He shrugged, and nodded. "Yes, well, it's genuine Faberge, beautifully crafted, and as I told you earlier the stones are rare. This is why I want you to be more careful." He cleared his throat. "As far as the alexandrite is concerned, I'm afraid I have less positive news. It's an exciting possibility, or perhaps fantasy is a better word. I think somebody's pulling your leg."

"How so?"

"I did some checking with a friend in the Russian history department at Columbia."

The waiter interrupted, fussily arranged their table, and uncorked the wine. He seemed impatient as Blake rolled the liquid in his glass before tasting it.

Kate leaned to one side to resume their conversation. "And?"

Blake ordered their entrées and the waiter melted away.

"Well, the good news is that Faberge's chief gemologist was indeed Philippe Lukinoff. He died in a Bolshevik prison camp in 1920. Henrik Wigstrom, the designer, was also a real person. He seems to have simply disappeared. Unfortunately, however, the fact they were real people is really quite irrelevant. Basically, I couldn't find a single piece of hard data that helps authenticate your report."

"Nothing?"

"Zip. There's simply no history of this stone, Miss Gavrill. And even if the other historical records and registries had somehow missed it, meticulous diaries of all the Romanov jewels were kept by Empress Alexandra. My Russian history friend had a copy of her inventory and I reviewed it line by line. I found nothing even remotely like the stone you mentioned. I don't see how a gem of such size and quality could have escaped her attention."

Kate's heart fell. Perhaps the whole thing had been Anya's personal fairytale, a story she'd invented to lend legitimacy to her affair with Nicholas, one she'd passed on to her granddaughter. But then how could she explain the documents at Chase Manhattan?

"Miss Gavrill," Blake said, leaning toward her, "I must admit I'm quite curious. Why are you so interested?"

Kate's gaze fell to her hands, then went to the room's rough-hewn rafters. She toyed with the stem of her wine glass. "Well, it appears this stone has been willed to me." Even as she uttered them, Kate had a hard time believing her own words.

"By whom? There must be some record of such a piece. Someone would have insured it, surely."

"Not likely. It's been lost for many years."

"Ummm." His grunt had that patronizing tone she'd picked up the day before. "I wish I knew more about the circumstances."

Kate stared back in silence. Despite being something of a know-it-all, he did seem to have a strong sense of integrity. Even so, she wasn't about to reveal all the details about her family's connection to the stone to someone she'd just met.

The fussy waiter returned, smoothed and resmoothed their tablecloth until Kate glared at him. He then disappeared, flinging a hand in the air in disgust.

"Anyhow," Blake said, picking up their conversation, "Be careful what you wish for. Do you realize the danger such a stone would pose to its owner?"

"How so?"

"My God, Miss Gavrill, have you any idea what the piece described in that document would be worth? I should hazard $50 million or more. Perhaps much more. And that's a very conservative guess. Every major collector and museum in the world would be in a bidding war for such a stone. It would have everything—great provenance, great rarity and unmatched quality."

The waiter brought their food, which they consumed in silence.

After the meal, Kate hunched forward. She smelled the faint spoor of wine on his breath, and detected that he wore no cologne. He still needed a shave. "What if I were to bring this stone to you, actually show it to you in person," she said, lowering her voice. "Would you be able to confirm its authenticity?"

"Of course. That's my business. I'll buy you a better dinner too, as long as you promise not to engage in any more wardrobe malfunctions." He smiled. Kate did not smile back. "But, seriously, where would you go to find it?"

"Russia."

"Alone?" There it was again, that supercilious, disempowering tone.

"Yes, alone. Guess what? I'm all grown up. I go places by myself. Unless, of course," Kate added mockingly, "you're volunteering to come along as my protector. Given what you've just said, however, anyone would be a fool to come with me, don't you think? Chasing after a non-existent treasure would be a waste of time."

"Don't joke with me, Miss Gavrill. I know something about doing business in Russia. It can be a dangerous country, even more so if you are carrying valuables. Do you really believe you could move about with such a jewel and no one would notice? International thieves operate all over the world. Their networks are as close as the nearest Internet café."

"I'll be fine," she said, her voice rising to the determined tone of a classroom declaration. "I have friends there."

"Oh yes, and when we met you were walking around Manhattan with a $140,000 Faberge brooch, which any teenage purse snatcher could have had in a split second."

"How would you have suggested I get it to you? In a Brinks truck?" In fact, she'd decided to wear the piece as a talisman. It circled her neck now, if he'd bothered to notice.

Kate stood and offered him her hand. He took it with his own palm up; in the way men had a generation earlier. There was something courtly in the gesture, and for an instant she found herself warming to him. But then, he probably had clients in Old Europe, where such mannerisms were part of business etiquette.

Kate rotated her fingers into a sideways grip. "Thank you very much for dinner, Mr. Blake." She forced a smile. "I'll call when I return."

Blake's expression changed to one of serious concern. "If you really are thinking about going to Russia alone, Miss Gavrill, please reconsider. I didn't make it up. There are criminal gangs all over Russia and they prey on people in the jewelry business. You may not be safe."

But the young woman hadn't heard him; she'd already headed for the exit.

AFTER SHE left, Blake crossed the street to a parking garage and sat silently in his car, an ancient Bentley Continental coupe. His striking dinner guest had made a greater impact than she knew, personally and professionally.

He thought of her frost blue eyes, pale as the arctic, and her rose petal skin. No question Kate Gavrill was attractive, beautiful even. Their shared humor the day before made her more so. He could still recall the scent Manhattan's heat had baked into her bra. It was an athlete's smell: fresh, scrubbed by chlorine and strong soap, without the masquerade of perfume.

But she also seemed wary, tightly wound and, in a brittle way, vulnerable. He doubted she was married. Blake's own brief marriage had broken apart over his obsession with work. He gauged Kate Gavrill's genetic imprint to be not unlike his own. A chief attribute—as his ex-wife never failed to reminded him—was an inability to open up about one's inner feelings.

Adrienne, of course, had no trouble at all getting inside him, whether he felt like being open or not. She read him like a book. Blake's current companion and occasional bedmate was, at forty-eight, seven years older than he, but looked five years younger. Theirs was a quasi-platonic relationship or, as Adrienne tartly put it, tugging on his ear, "sometimes we're just friends and sometimes we're friends with benefits." When she was in a raunchier mood, Adrienne said they were "fuck buddies."

They made an odd pair—he in his carelessly creased trousers, rustic sweaters and worn loafers, and she, a fashion editor and former model, always impeccably turned out. Perhaps, Adrienne had suggested, the arrangement worked because each was too separately committed professionally to be jointly committed personally. In any case, Adrienne would be on his arm at the theater tonight.

It's a film clip that for years will replay in her head.

At first everything seems to go exactly as planned.

It's the opening event of the season, the women's 10-meter board, and Kate appears at the examination room about an hour before competing. The scene is pure, pre-competition hubbub: divers mill about; sign forms; traipse in and out with paper cups; giggle to hide their jitters.

"Hand me your purse and fill these out," a heavyset monitor says curtly. Nearly six feet tall, with tightly bound hair, a broad, pink face and wire-framed glasses, the woman looks like a prison guard. Heart pounding, Kate signs and returns the papers. *No turning back now, girl.*

The woman hands her a paper cup and crooks her finger. Kate follows her to a restroom about 30 feet down the hall.

Once inside the dimly lit bathroom, Kate feels relieved. It was probably built before they even started giving drug tests. She'd been sure there'd be just a single stall and that she'd be accompanied. Instead, there are four toilets in a line, each separately enclosed.

The monitor takes a widespread stance near the bathroom door. Kate slips into the stall at the far end.

In the past, these same tests seemed as routine as pulling on her swim cap. Now, however, Kate's fingers tremble as she sits on the toilet seat and unbuttons her blouse. Beneath the stall's partition, a reflection from the room's single overhead light gleams up from the shiny concrete floor. She hears the muffled shouts and laughter of athletes passing in the hall.

Kate places the paper cup atop the toilet, and slides a flattened palm inside the padded, underwire bra. The plastic bottle feels warm against the outside of her right breast.

Abruptly, Kate hears the shuffle of rubber-treaded soles. The monitor's lace-up brown leather shoes pass in sight under the partition. And stop. The woman stands less than a dozen feet away.

Fingers still shaking, Kate undoes the clasp at the front of her bra. Her fingers close around the plastic container. Holding the bottle tightly—if dropped, it will be in clear view—she reads the thermometer: 98.6. Perfect.

Kate squeezes the warm yellow liquid into the cup. It even sounds like real pee.

Later, Kate will be unable to decide if jumpy nerves cause her to squeeze the bottle too tightly or whether some of the phony urine has spilled onto its sides, making it slippery.

Either way, Kate freezes in horror as, spewing yellow fluid, the vessel pops from her fingers, shooting under the stall wall and across the slick concrete floor. It skids, spins, and stops.

Between a pair of lace-up brown leather shoes.

★   ★   ★

HE TREATED you like a little girl.

While her thoughts swirled around Simon Blake, Kate slouched in her seat, waiting for the train to pull out of Penn Station.

Oh, hell, I deserved it. Besides, I'll make him eat every word. I've already bought the plane tickets.

Could he have a thing for me?

Nonsense. All he did was put me down. And how about that Eisenhower era handshake? Those sloppy, circa sixties Ivy League clothes? That cocky George Clooney eyebrow thing. He's so . . . so . . . archaic!

The train lurched forward. Kate pulled her curtain closed. Her feisty confidence dissolved.

Blake didn't need to convince her that danger might lie ahead. Her entire life had been turned upside down and her mother was dead—claimed by an accident that may well have been no accident at all.

Moreover, how could she be sure Blake's skepticism about the alexandrite wasn't justified? After all, what real proof did she have that the egg, stone and bank account even existed? Or ever had? A few measly scraps of easily forged paper?

She didn't really know anything about the note-writer Imre Novyck, or his relationship with her mother. Could he shed any light on what she'd learned? Had Irina intended to tell her anything else about him?

She'd had another cell phone message from Lt. MacMahon. No news, he said, and still no suspects. When would she learn what really happened to her mother?

Yet Blake's skepticism had also focused her determination. As a diver, Kate had learned to use her rivals' competitiveness to rev up her own. The more her opponents wanted to win, the more she strove to best them. His condescending manner seemed to release those same juices. No matter her doubts, this lady wasn't for turning. This Gavrill was moving forward.

Nothing Blake had said could dilute the potency of her mother's words, or the power of the obligation Kate felt to make things right between them. Was her Romanov fortune real? What could she lose by finding out? She knew this much: It was worth a trip to Russia, no matter how risky.

★　★　★

MORNING SUNLIGHT streamed through the high windows above Blake's desk, warming his back. He rustled through some papers and thought again about what he should have said the night before.

He should have told Kate about Bret Steiner, his former assistant and protégé. Correction, his *late* assistant and protégé. Bret had died in Russia, slain by jewel thieves.

Why hadn't he told her? She'd left before he could. But he'd seen the look in her eyes. She wouldn't have listened. Still, he could have been more forceful. Perhaps, Blake thought, he didn't want to risk driving her away.

He stewed for three days, then dialed the Pennsylvania number on her card. The phone rang four times before her answering machine picked up. Kate Gavrill, it announced, was on leave for the summer, beginning Monday, July 24. She would be traveling abroad on family business, and wouldn't be checking her messages. So that was the end of it. She'd left two days before, and there was nothing he could do. Blake wondered if he would ever again look into those mysterious eyes, or hear of the Romanov Stone.

Chapter 14

KATE'S HEAVING chest sucked Moscow's oppressive heat—and its admixture of unburned diesel fuel—to the depths of her lungs. People might think of Russia's capital as cold and snowy, but during the summer the city boasted the highest temperatures in northern Europe.

Kate's thighs shook as her feet pounded into the cinder path alongside the Yauza River. Shoving up the sleeve of her loose popover jacket, she glanced at her wrist. Out for her first two-mile run in a week, she was making good time. *Fresh legs.*

Writers often compared Moscow's circular layout to a sawn tree trunk. As Kate crossed the Garden Ring, she could see why. In its 850 years, the city had grown relentlessly and concentrically, radiating out from the Moskva River Fortress that later became The Kremlin.

She jogged to Leftortovo Park. The afternoon sun draped a sparkling tiara over tiny, breeze-blown minarets that danced on the surface of the park's ponds and streams. Couples sat on benches and kissed. Lefortovo's Dutch canals had been a favorite trysting place for three centuries, ever since the district first swelled with West European expatriates, mostly Swiss and Germans, who served the tsars. Catherine the Great built a majestic palace here, then promptly died. Her son Peter, who hated his mother, turned the spectacular structure into an army barracks.

But neither her route's history nor its unique architecture could explain Kate's presence in this Moscow district. That could only be attributed to a much more ominous edifice, the notorious Lefortovo Prison. Located just a few blocks from her hotel, it was there she would meet the next morning with one Imre Novyck, the man to whom her mother had written before her death.

★   ★   ★

THREE THINGS struck Kate about the person she'd come to see. First, contrary to Irina's belief and her own assumption, he was not a "corrections official" or "judicial officer" at Lefortovo. Imre Novyck was an inmate.

Second, he wore a white surgical mask, even during conversation, and a wireless headset that crawled around his ear and cheekbone like an annelid worm. "Tuberculosis," Novyck explained, pointing to the white material that covered his face. His hand brushed the air in a rapid gesture of dismissal. "I don't have it, but many others here do. TB pervades this hell-hole."

Kate covered her mouth with a handkerchief.

Third, was Novyck's unexpected charm. Despite the muffling mask and ever-present earpiece, his voice was soft and oddly Western European, a mix of Moscow and Oxford-BBC. Peering out from an overhang of thick, untamed eyebrows, his dark eyes glowed like embers in a cave.

Kate quickly sensed their ability to hold her attention. After a few minutes, she began to notice an odd and unsettling contradiction. Juxtaposed with Novyck's well-modulated voice, his smouldering gaze left an observer feeling peculiarly off balance, as if teetering between a sense of soothing calm and an imminent fear of being devoured.

Novyck stood near a small recessed window. The morning sun skimmed his wiry body like a stage light. Beneath his thin prison T-shirt, lean muscles rippled across a hardpan stomach. Kate took the fact they could meet alone—in an unattended guard's room—as clear evidence of his special status at the prison. In addition, the headset indicated he also possessed a smart phone, a seemingly unusual perk for the inhabitant of one of the world's most notorious dungeons.

"Please accept my apologies for the circumstances of our meeting," he said, sensing her question. "Despite what you see, I am not a criminal."

"Why are you here?" Kate remembered the cautious tone of Irina's note. How would her mother have reacted if she learned she'd been either mistaken or misled about Novyck's status at Lefortovo?

Sensing her skepticism, Novyck's voice rose behind the paper mask. "I am not a criminal," he insisted again. "I am being illegally detained for political reasons. There are many in my situation. A remnant of old Russia, I'm afraid."

"I wouldn't know one way or another," Kate replied. For some reason—jet lag, perhaps—she felt slightly woozy. "I'm here because my mother thought you could help me find some, uh, family belongings."

The eyes trained steadily on her. Obviously, he knew precisely why she'd visited and what she was talking about. "I know," he said. "I wrote your mother to offer my humble assistance. After all, my family has served yours for what amounts to a century."

Now his low voice trembled with barely contained passion. "You are the great-granddaughter of the last tsar. The closest living link to our sainted Romanovs."

Abruptly, he dropped to his knees, taking her hands in his. "From the beginning, my family recognized the Romanov's divine right to rule. We suffered, but we never wavered. It is no different now."

Astonished, Kate pulled back. Suddenly dizzy, she sought her footing on the uneven concrete floor. She sat down on one of the small room's two hardwood chairs. Kate judged Novyck to be some years older than she. He was slender-framed and stood only an inch or so taller. Yet despite his momentary kneeling position, he exuded an aura of power, mastery and dominance.

Finally, she asked, "How do you know this?"

"How could I not know? Your secret has been entrusted to my family for generations. Beyond a handful of people, however, the Romanov Stone's existence was virtually unknown. The Empress herself never catalogued it—she never even mentioned it. The reason, of course, is that Nicholas made certain she never knew of its existence. The alexandrite remained vaulted and uncut until the tsar decided to present it to your great grandmother. My own grandfather risked his life to protect her treasure."

He rose and stepped closer, glancing around to make certain no one could overhear. "Your mother was very clever in concealing your identity. But I knew as soon as I learned of your visit who you were and *exactly*"—he spoke the word as if cutting the air with a knife—"why you were here."

Kate began to feel more than slightly uncomfortable. Had Anya or Irina ever met this man? Would they have told her if they had?

"How do I know you are who you say you are?"

"You can easily verify that I am the descendant of Grigori Rasputin. Go to any library. Look me up in the *Moscow Times*. Google me if you want to. It is public record, along with the fact that I am a political prisoner. As for your family's property, I can show you something that no one else but your great grandmother's original collaborator could possess."

He reached in his pocket, and withdrew a small leather satchel. Searching inside, Novyck produced a tattered black and white photograph, yellow with age. "Your mother sent this to me. It was taken in late 1916," he said, handing it to her. "Just after the alexandrite was polished."

Though faded, the photo depicted a large, perfectly shaped gem, resting inside a half-opened, potato-sized Faberge egg. Scrawled on the back was the name, "Mikhail."

Novyck tapped his finger beneath the signature. "I believe a monk named Mikhail was the last person to possess the Romanov Stone."

A new wave of dizziness swept Kate. She stretched out her palm and touched a cold, slimy wall. Pulling her hand away, she wiped it on her trousers. Again, Kate thought of Irina's note. Her mother said Nicholas hadn't trusted this man's ancestor. The source of Novyck's knowledge—obviously extensive—had to come from someone other than Russia's last tsar. But who? And when?

"Why do you say this?" she asked.

"My great grandfather was born in Siberia in a village near Irkutsk. He knew the archbishop as a young boy and the pair saw each other in Moscow. They were close, although His Holiness knew nothing of Grigori Rasputin's excesses. In 1917, in the spring after Grigori was assassinated, the archbishop visited my family in Siberia to offer condolences. He had a young woman and her daughter with him and they were leaving for Kiev. One evening—after a bit too much sacramental wine—he confided that he'd been given a treasure for safekeeping. He showed them the photograph I just showed you. But he also told them he'd become convinced that his prominence was actually a detriment and was almost certain to lead to discovery. Anyhow, the archbishop had decided Lydia's fortune would be safer in the hands of a simple priest. He said he planned to pass it on to a monsignor he knew, a monk named Mikhail, presumably either there in Siberia or on his way through Kazakhstan."

Kate's brain stumbled as if she were in the middle of a bad dive. Novyck's story confirmed what Anya had surmised. That the archbishop had given the treasure to someone, probably a priest, named "Mikhail." But how had Novyck gained this knowledge, which she'd assumed to be known only by Irina and Anya?

"The archbishop's premonition turned out to be tragically correct," Novyck continued. "My own father tried to find the stone, as have I." Novyck paused. "To return to your mother, of course."

Briefly, Novyck sketched a history of his own quest for the alexandrite, egg and bank papers. His words seemed to drone over her, lulling Kate with their slow rhythm. They told of his journeys to Siberia and St. Petersburg, and of his fruitless search from abbey to abbey for a mysterious Father "Mikhail."

"Finally, I grew so desperate I ran an ad in the newspaper. Amazingly, a village priest came forward that said he had known this priest Mikhail in Russia. Regrettably, it was at this precise time that my life was interrupted by these unfortunate and bogus charges." He cast his eyes around the dismal cell in disgust.

"You really must let me help you," he said, again taking her hands and staring deeply into her eyes. Kate sensed a powerful pull toward this man. Was it witchery or sex? The prison's gray walls seemed to creep closer, and she felt out of breath. "I know what your mother was trying to do," he went on, "the good she was trying to bring Russia from the ashes of her own family's tragedy. The Romanov cause is my family's cause too, as it always has been."

Kate thought of her mother's note again. Clearly, she must remain cautious, but Imre Novyck just might prove useful. He certainly knew the terrain better than she.

Novyck glanced furtively around the dreary room. "Whatever you do, keep the stone's existence a secret," he warned. "You could be in great danger from criminal elements. Besides, if anyone in the Russian government should find out, your birthright will be confiscated immediately. This is what I propose: When you have located the items, return to me here. I can help arrange safe passage out of the country for you and your property."

Kate had no way of knowing that Imre Novyck had put his own counsel of secrecy to practice. He did not tell her of forging bank documents, fabricating a fake egg or manufacturing a synthetic Romanov alexandrite. The replicas had been good enough to fool a Russian geologist who worked for the Moscow *mafiya*.

Another carefully concealed detail Kate would learn later. Three years before, in a little noticed decision by its board of governors, the Bank of England had changed its rules regarding claims for dormant accounts. Henceforth, on all such holdings of more than one hundred thousand pounds, authentication would require that claimants produce, along with other proof, confirming DNA samples. This critical evidence Novyck did not possess and could not fake. Only Kate Gavrill could give it to him.

Chapter 15

⟫⟩⟨⟨⟫

THE UKRAINIAN Boeing 737 made the trip from Moscow to Kiev in just over ninety minutes. The flight included lunch, a quarter of a boiled chicken—not a breast or leg, but a sawed-off fourth portion of a whole chicken. The brutalized poultry lay under a clear plastic wrap, like a corpse.

"The food on domestic flights is to be wondered at, but never eaten," the concierge at her Moscow hotel had warned. Kate took his advice.

At Kiev's airport, peeling paint and drooping ceiling tiles testified to a public spirit grown weary and poor. Like Russia itself, Kate thought, the Ukrainian Republic seemed stuck in some economic purgatory between socialism and capitalism.

Even so, Kiev offered a friendly contrast to Moscow. Kate's taxi slowed in traffic on Kreschatik, the main thoroughfare, and she watched the sidewalks widen into a relaxed parade of fountains, street boutiques, al fresco cafes and teenagers on skate boards.

Her hotel was a former Octoberskia, or October Hotel, built for Communist Party members in most Soviet cities. Her room's furnishings were comfortable enough, but the carpet had been sewn unevenly. She found an empty toilet paper dispenser in the bathroom, but for this emergency Kate had come prepared. Remembering childhood tales of Russian toilet paper as stiff as twenty-pound writing bond, she'd stuffed three rolls in her suitcase before leaving New York.

Nonetheless, the place had its charms. From her balcony, Kate could see the Dneiper River, a broad blue band that wound through the city under ornate pre-1917 bridges.

Kate sat on the narrow bed's hard, horse hair-stuffed mattress. Taking Imre's photograph from her briefcase, she placed it face up on the spread.

Even in an ancient, tattered rendering, the alexandrite was captivating.

Kate slipped out of her clothes and into bed. As her eyes closed, she pictured Blake when he saw the stone. His reaction would be measured and restrained—that of a connoisseur in the presence of a masterwork.

In sleep, Kate tossed and turned. Again and again, she made the same high-board dive. On the bottom of the pool, she saw the face of Simon Blake. His lips were moving—he was calling to her—but his words were unintelligible, muffled as if they were being uttered underwater. Then Blake's face dissolved into that of Imre Novyck. They both seemed to want to help her. But why?

Once before, Kate had trusted a man. She wouldn't make the same mistake again.

★   ★   ★

"EXPULSION, MISS GAVRILL, and banned from sports competition— that is your well-deserved punishment." His office's book-lined walls seemed to slow the frowning, white-haired dean's cadence, magnifying the gravity of his words. His lips turned down in disgust and he stared at her feet as if fervently hoping they would remove an unclean presence as quickly as possible.

Kate hung her head and sobbed.

Dr. Borshel came to her defense, pleading before conference authorities that she'd used a legally prescribed, cognitive enhancing medication unrelated to physical performance. The panel peppered him with skeptical questions, but the physician did succeed in getting Kate's ban limited to a single season.

That, however, was only the beginning.

Just as school and athletic officials had wished, the doping inquiry, held in a university library conference room, drew light attendance and little media interest. Sitting in a sparsely populated gallery of journalists, interested parties and potential witnesses, Kate mused that if she'd been a football player, the New York Times would have sent a reporter. As it was, only two local weeklies and a single country radio station showed up.

Taylor Mathews, a willowy blonde, was the first of Kate's teammates to testify.

Interrogator: "And, Miss Mathews, how long did your, er, romantic relationship with coach Nars continue?"

Kate's head snapped back as if she'd been stung by an insect. A low murmur swept the audience. A dozing, heavy-set reporter for the *Germantown Gazette* blinked, his pencil moving rapidly over a pad of yellow notepaper. Jack Nars' attorney was on his feet.

"Objection your honor, move to strike. Miss Mathews' testimony has no bearing on the case."

"Over-ruled. First, this panel is not a court of law. Second, the university has strict rules governing faculty-student relationships. This goes to the heart of the question of character, and to a pattern of behavior by Coach Nars that is central to the matter before us."

Kate sat forward, her lips trembling.

Interrogator: "Will the witness please answer the question."

"Well, it was–is still continuing," Taylor replied, blushing. "As of last week, anyway."

Around her, Kate heard uncomfortable laughter.

Interrogator: "Where did your, er, liasons, take place?"

Taylor Mathews: "I live off campus, so in my apartment, usually. Or his car."

Again, muted chuckles.

Interrogator: "Were you aware of Coach Nars' marital status?"

Taylor Mathews: "No sir."

Kate's stomach churned and stomach acid flooded her saliva. The room seemed to wobble, like a top ending its spin.

Interrogator: "At no time did Coach Nars inform you that he had a wife and children?"

Before Taylor could answer, Kate bolted from her wooden chair, brushed past two other potential witnesses, and headed for the chamber door. Outside, she paced back and forth. An all-enveloping anger surged up from the center of her being.

The door opened and Jack emerged, followed by his attorney.

"Married? Taylor Mathews?" Kate screamed. "You lying scum!" Her voice echoed shrilly in the high-ceilinged hall. Carrying a stack of books, a passing library clerk lowered her head, her feet making soft padding sounds as she scurried by.

"You had balls in the air alright!" Kate yelled. "Your own damn balls!" Bent at the waist, she hurled the invectives as if shooting arrows into a target. "How many of us did you fuck, Jack? Besides me, and Taylor, and the whole damn diving team, I suppose? And, of course, the little Mrs. Nars. So we were going to build a life together? All you were building were conquests in the sack!"

Head down, looking neither right nor left, Jack kept walking.

Kate never took the stand. After the devastating testimony by Mathews—who also admitted drug use—the investigators rested their case. Barred from coaching at the college level, Jack Nars eventually found a job in another state, teaching gymnastics at a private junior high. Kate never saw or spoke to him again. The only thing that survived was her love of diving; she continued to practice, though she did not return to active competition.

The most severe damage was to her relationship with Irina. Although local coverage of the scandal had been mercifully brief, Kate found an open newspaper beside her coffee on her first morning home. SCANDAL ENGULFS COLLEGE DIVERS, read the local sports page headline. The story quoted Taylor's testimony, and Kate was included in a list of named divers.

"It's bad enough that you cheat in your sport," Irina shouted, slamming a kitchen cupboard with her small fist. "Now you also cheat with a man against his wife. So you reject your heritage, you reject our art, and now you reject our morality too?"

"I didn't know he was married, mother. I thought I loved him."

"You foolish, foolish girl. What do you know about love? You have destroyed our future as a family, Katya. And your behavior has endangered both of us in ways you do not even know. Thank the Holy Father that Henri and Anya aren't here to see this."

Their estrangement left deep scars. Kate transferred to Penn State, a huge school where she could vanish in an anonymous sea of undergraduates. With quiet determination, she rebuilt her academic standing, graduated with honors, and even returned to Princeton for her Phd. Although Irina still fretted over Kate's safety, contact between the two women remained stilted and infrequent.

Kate strove sporadically to repair their relationship; her attempts were uniformly rebuffed. "You are still my daughter, Katya, but you have dishonored your family and yourself."

Her emotions seared, Kate shrank from further romantic involvement, steadfastly avoiding risks in her personal life. She might have been guilty of making poor choices, but Jack had coldly manipulated and deceived her. Could she trust another man? Now— nearly a decade later—the question still festered. Irina's deathbed revelations and her desperate plea to find and reclaim their mutual birthright had given Kate more than a last chance to make amends to her mother. Besides absolving years of guilt, and restoring her own and her family's name, the Romanov Stone also held the key to restoring Kate's inner courage and sense of self-respect. All she had to do was find it.

Chapter 16

————— ◆ —————

KIEV'S MONASTERY of the Caves, a centuries-old compound of churches, libraries, bell towers, fortified walls and underground Catacombs, stood outside the city on the banks of the Dneiper River, not far from Kate's hotel.

Kate had agreed to Novyck's plan because she had little choice, but also because she believed she knew at least one important fact he didn't. When the archbishop transferred the stone, egg and documents to Father Mikhail, neither man was in Siberia or Kazakhstan. Both had been here in Kiev, hundreds of miles away. At least that was the gist of Anya's letter, and the conversation Kate overheard as a girl between Irina and her great grandmother. A priest named Mikhail, in fact, served at St. Sophia's Cathedral, part of the Monastery's ensemble of structures. This information Kate had not shared with Novyck, nor had she mentioned her plans to fly to the Ukrainian Republic.

At first, finding Father Mikhail had seemed easy. Kate simply went to the Hall of Records in Kiev and asked for him by name and order. Unfortunately, Father Mikhail had died nearly twenty years before.

"In the old times, he might have been buried right here," a kindly monk reported in broken English as they stood near the Bell Tower. At three hundred eighteen feet, the tower was the monastery's most famous structure. The diminutive old prelate angled his head in the afternoon sun. In his spectacles, Kate saw a reflected blackbird cross from one lens to another in flight.

"The most saintly monks went into the caves," the priest said. "It was a high honor. They also buried some notable lay people here."

His white goatee bobbed with each word.

Occupying some fifty acres and including more than 80 buildings, the Caves Monastery had served for centuries as a spiritual and intellectual center for the Orthodox Church. The earliest monks held services in the caves, which later became a burial grounds. Due to a fortuitous combination of temperature and humidity, bodies in the caves became naturally mummified and did not decay.

Not all of St. Sophia's corpses were so fortunate. "Peter Arkadievich was shot in 1911," the monk related. "It happened right before the tsar and tsarina's eyes at the Kiev Opera House, only a short distance from here. But you can't see him. They buried him and then disguised the grave, so the Bolsheviks wouldn't find the body. Even then, they were desecrating Romanov cadavers."

As the monastery developed, the Catacombs closest to the surface became known as the "Near Caves," those at deeper elevation the "Far Caves." Contained in glass-covered coffins, the monks' well-preserved remains clustered in groups of two and three in alcoves hewn from the walls.

The old cleric shook his head when Kate asked about Father Mikhail. "So many from that time are gone now. Even I am too young to have known the period as an adult. You should talk to Father Timothy. He's younger than I am, but Mikhail was his—as the Italians say—*mentore*."

He led her to an office in a small out building that served as a museum. A monk with a smooth-shaven, round face and short-cropped black hair glanced up from behind a large, cluttered desk. He was in his early seventies and looked like a corporate human resources manager who just happened to be wearing a soft brown robe rather than a suit and tie.

"I met Father Mikhail as a novitiate," said the businesslike monk. "He was very elderly, in his early nineties, I think." But the cleric shook his head when Kate vaguely described a valuable gemstone that had passed from her family to a priest at the monastery.

"Father Mikhail was perhaps the most selfless human being I've ever known. Years ago, one of his uncles died, leaving him a large amount of money and an estate in Sardinia. He simply signed the deed over to the church and dropped it, with all the cash, in the offering box."

He leaned back, smoothing both hands over his chest. "In my position, at the time of his passing, I make an accounting for each priest's belongings.

"When Father Mikhail died, everything he owned could be put in a shoebox. I remember thinking how much of the spirit and how little of the world he left behind."

His mouth quavered and he turned briefly away.

"There is no way he died with anything of value," he said, turning back to her with moist eyes. "If he had, Father Mikhail would simply have left it here, with us, in the Monastery of the Caves."

Chapter 17

———➤❮◉❯◀———

Flicking on the lights as she entered, Kate gasped. A burly, black-haired man stood in the middle of her hotel room holding a flashlight and a silky scrap of lingerie.

"Very nice, Miss Gavrill," he said in English, twisting a silk thong in his fingers and smiling in a way that reminded her of an oil slick. "On the outside, you dress very conservatively. Tweed coats, heavy slacks. On the inside, however, we find something else, something very different." He had heavy brows and a wet, fleshy smear of a mouth. "Our women would do almost anything for such delicacies." He gazed at her boldly. "So would our men."

"Put those down!" she demanded, flushing. Her penchant for thongs had been Kate's sensual secret, something she wore on special occasions when she wanted to feel sexy, or to hide panty lines. They were also cooler, and the high-waisted, "control" model she favored featured a wide crotch that didn't cut in. "Why are you here?"

Behind him, Kate could see her clothing and papers scattered across the hotel bed. From the balcony and bathroom, two men in gray suits drifted toward her. One slid between her and the door. Kate pointed a shaking finger at the big man. "Who are you?"

"Kiev Police. We're here to ask you the same question, Miss Gavrill." He reached in a navy sports jacket and briefly flashed an identification badge bearing his picture and a row of numbers. "I'm

Detective Lieutenant Vulcan Krasky." In one gesture, he motioned
her to sit on the bed and for the other men to leave.

Kate sidestepped to avoid being brushed by the departing officers,
but remained standing. She crossed her arms, gripping herself just
above the elbows. She tried to stop shaking.

Krasky rose and slowly walked around her, stopping behind her
and closing the distance between them to a few inches. His breath
felt hot against her neck. It smelled of garlic and onions.

"Why, Miss Gavrill, do you go around Kiev asking questions
about dead priests?" He spoke the words softly, almost caressingly,
into her left ear.

She stared straight ahead. Her heart rate climbed. "I can talk to
anyone about anything I choose. I'm an American tourist."

"Indeed you are, Miss Gavrill. From Pennsylvania, I believe. But
your field is economics, not religion, no? So why do you want to
know so much about holy men and their churches?"

"I'm surprised you can't answer that yourself. Especially after
illegally rummaging through my personal belongings."

"I will decide questions of legality here, dear lady." Krasky slid
his hand under her left elbow, pinching his fingers into a claw. "You
are trembling, Miss Gavrill. It would be much easier for us both if
you would cooperate." He applied light pressure.

"There's nothing—"

"Are you looking for something, Miss Gavrill? Something
valuable?" Grasping her shoulders, he pulled Kate back toward him,
then twirled her around and pushed her into the chair. Resting both
hands on the arms, he bent over her.

Her superior conditioning would have given her a chance in
the open, but in leaning over her Krasky deployed his sheer bulk to
overwhelming advantage. Used to confidence in her own strength,
Kate was angered at its sudden absence. "How *dare* you touch me?"

"We don't fear your popes and presidents here, Miss Gavrill,"
Krasky said in the same soft tone. "And just so you know, in the

Ukrainian Republic it is a high crime to remove religious icons, artifacts or other objects of historic importance. Unless, of course, you have prior official permission."

He rapped once on the door and the two goons reappeared on her threshold.

"I hope we meet again under more pleasant circumstances, Miss Gavrill," Krasky said, slowly moving out of the room. From his left sleeve, he pulled an embroidered handkerchief, which he used to dab the perspiration on his forehead. "For now, however, I strongly suggest that you leave Kiev." On reaching the door, he turned and tossed her underwear back to her.

★ ★ ★

VULCAN KRASKY had been a mob soldier for years. When he shook down Kiev businesses, Krasky rationalized that he was providing a service. The *mafiya* held to a code of conduct not yet offered by official police or government agencies. If a business had a labor dispute with another business, the owner contacted his local *capo;* the difficulty would be quickly, quietly and efficiently resolved. In many rural parts of the country, the *mafiya* presence was like that of a patronly local government, woven into family life and traditional holidays. It supplied stability and services, such as food for the poor, which were once the sole purview of the church.

As in Russia, the Ukrainian *mafiya* determined who opened a business, stayed in business or went out of business. Punishment for flaunting that authority—punishment that Krasky occasionally meted out—included brutal beatings or death by briefcase bombings or machine gun bullets.

In compensation, Krasky's lifestyle stood several clicks higher than that of more honest colleagues. He took his children to puppet theater shows, enjoyed a glass of *Miskhako* with most meals and was a heavy spender at the Sarochin Market every August. Like other corrupt cops, Krasky made a good side living turning over apartments and cars seized from middle-class citizens who had the bad fortune to get in traffic accidents. Wearing his uniform, Krasky would show up at the scene to warn victims to settle quickly with the *mafiya*. The hapless motorists would sign over their property, which Krasky would then sell on, splitting the take with his capo, Boris Lada.

Chapter 18

KATE RUBBED her shoulders and, with trembling hands, tried to sort through the clumps of clothing and paper on her bed. She could still feel Krasky's fingers around her arm.

There isn't any stone here. The insistent voice of doubt grated in her head. *What real evidence did you have that the stone was in Kiev anyhow? Memories of memories by Anya and Irina? Did you really think the Romanov Stone—if there were such a thing—would just be sitting here, waiting for you to drop by and pick it up?*

Kate had no ready answers. In retrospect, it seemed utterly foolish to have believed that, in the space of a few days, she could locate a long-dead, impoverished monk who—nearly a century ago— had secretly been given a super-precious gem. In the chaos and desperation of post-Revolutionary Russia, wouldn't anyone, even a holy man, simply have kept such a jewel for himself? Why hadn't Blake, an internationally known gemologist, ever heard of the stone? Or found it listed in even a single standard reference? And, of course, there was what amounted to an official Bank of England denial that a Romanov account ever existed.

Now, a sadistic big-as-a-bear cop was sniffing around. Who knew what Krasky's real motives were? Maybe he had a side business shaking down tourists.

The photograph! Sudden fear choked Kate's throat. She plunged both hands into her suitcase, between the folded t-shirts where she'd slipped the fragile image in its brown manila envelope.

It wasn't there! She turned her luggage upside down on the floor and rifled through its contents.

Unless she'd simply misplaced it, the picture was gone. By now Krasky and his thugs had almost certainly seen it. Which meant they'd be back, either to collect a bribe or to arrest her.

Simon Blake warned you this would be dangerous.

"Dammit! He *won't* be right! I won't let him!"

Kate clapped a hand to her mouth. She'd shouted the words so loudly they rang in her ears.

★　★　★

An Hour later Kate's resolve had melted. Face it, she told herself as she stood in front of her hotel bathroom mirror, Blake was right. This *is* stupid. And dangerous.

Kate picked up the phone, changed her airplane reservations and ordered a taxi.

It was almost 11:00 P.M., but she'd have time to catch a 1:00 A.M. flight to Moscow.

Maybe she was being a coward, but right now leaving seemed the prudent path. She'd run into a dead end, and finding Krasky in her room had unnerved her—and fully verified Blake's warnings. Especially now, with the photograph missing. Or perhaps the enormity of what she was attempting had finally sunk in. The former Soviet Union, she'd concluded and as Blake had warned, could be a scary place.

Even so, Kate made a fervent pledge: what she was doing would be a strategic retreat, not a surrender. She'd head back to Moscow and regroup, rethink her options. She wasn't about to walk away from

Irina's challenge. After all, it wasn't just about finding the Romanov Stone. It was about finding herself.

Kate was on her way to the airport when it struck her. Or rather, when the words of the priest replayed in her head. *Father Mikhail would simply have left the treasure here, the old monk said.*

Sitting in the taxi, Kate put her face in her hands, and shut her eyes. She pictured herself climbing the high board above an Olympic-size swimming pool.

She looked down. The water appeared calm and unbroken. Think, she commanded. THINK.

What if, before he was assassinated all those decades ago, the archbishop had made the same decision when he arrived in Kiev, but with a twist? What if, although he knew he couldn't safely keep the stone himself, he also feared entrusting his precious cargo to another living soul, even an ordained priest? After all, being found by the Bolsheviks with the Romanov Stone would mean death, no matter what one's clerical rank. Or, perhaps, he'd merely wanted to retain his options, including the option to be greedy.

He would also have had completely legitimate reasons to delay a choice between keeping his promise to Nicholas II and keeping the stone himself. After all, Anya and her little girl might die in flight, or simply never show up. In that case, the dowry should rightfully go to the next closest members of the Tsar's family.

Kate stepped up on the imaginary board and prepared to dive. Focus, she whispered to herself. Focus.

Weighing such possible outcomes, the prelate might not have given the Romanov treasure to a living person at all. Once in Kiev, he might have decided to hide it with someone else, someone whose silence and honesty could be assured—for all time. Moreover, to better ensure it would be found if something happened to him, he might logically have written that priest's name on the photograph he left for Anya. And, when the archbishop perished, the stone, egg and documents would have remained exactly where he left them—with a now mummified monk named Father Mikhail, dead for nearly a century, in the Monastery of the Caves.

Again, Kate thought of her mother's death and her last words, the fervor of Irina's hopes for her family and her people. Suddenly Kate's courage flamed like fire under a kettle. She squeezed her eyes tight and leaned forward. *Don't be afraid, girl. You've still got the power.*

She was off the board now, floating in a perfect, slow-motion arc toward the surface below.

She slipped silently into the water.

Kate slid open the driver's window, keeping her face slightly behind and to one side of the opening.

"Please turn around," she said, "I've changed my mind. I'm going back to Kiev." Kate sat deep in the rear seat, using the shadows to conceal her features. By morning, she knew, Krasky would be questioning every cabbie in the city.

"Take me to a quiet hotel," she told the driver. "Something small, without any foreigners." Kate would have to wake somebody up, but so be it. She wasn't quitting yet.

Chapter 19

SHORTLY AFTER midnight the following day, Kate stood before the Monastery's wide, high-arched entry which, as custom decreed, stood open. The heavy, carved door to the Near Caves appeared formidable, but its simple pot-metal bolt proved no match for Kate's arm strength—and a pry bar she'd purchased earlier that same day at a local ironmonger's, along with a flashlight and other tools. Beneath skintight rubber gloves, her fingers tingled. Kate jimmied the lock, then rested her hand on the heavy rope handrail at the cave's entrance.

That morning, at the Monastery registration desk, she'd thumbed through an ancient, leather-bound ledger which revealed the location of each of the interred monks, with separate rosters for the Near and Far Caves. While some of the saints had died a thousand years before, their bodies were still perfectly preserved. None had ever been treated with formaldahyde or other chemicals. Earlier generations and today's pilgrims believed this to be a miracle, but Soviet-era scientists attributed the phenomenon to the caves' absence of moisture, which prevented organic decay. The biggest miracle may have been that the monastery itself still stood after seventy years of atheist rule. One tale, perhaps apocryphal, claimed that, under orders from Moscow, Soviet trucks arrived to haul away the cadavers but were forced to abandon their mission when the vehicles refused to start. Stalin did succeed, however, in ending use of the caverns for any new burials.

Kate theorized that the archbishop had hidden his secret treasure with a monk's cadaver during the actual process of internment, perhaps even using his office to officiate at the burial. So she focused on "Mikhails" who died during the years 1917 and 1918, when the prelate might still have been alive.

Her heart jumped when she found a "Father Mikhail," deceased in 1918, in the Near Caves. But a moment later, she came upon a second Mikhail corpse, dead a month earlier, located in the Far Caves. There were a dozen more Mikhails, but each had died before 1917 or after 1920, when the archbishop himself was already dead.

Signing up for one of the monastery tours, Kate resolved to locate both remains, but to start with the Near Caves, where the bodies were reputed to be better preserved. In the Near Caves, each monk's brass name was buffed to a high polish. But when her group reached the Far Caves, she'd needed to rub the dust off six coffin plates—she could make out the capital "M," but little else—before finding the second Father Mikhail. Once, the monk leading the tour turned around, frowned when he saw what she was doing, but said nothing. As soon as she'd located the second coffin, Kate slipped away from the group and out of the monastery.

Now, only hours later, Kate took 110 carefully counted steps down a long narrow passageway. She'd already determined that no electricity—and hence, in all likelihood, no alarm systems—existed in the caves themselves. On the tour, they'd carried twelve-inch candles. Her flashlight's strong beam played against the shadows of the rough-hewn walls.

Save for that solitary cone of light, her surroundings were black as coal. The only sounds were her own footsteps and breathing. The air stank of dried clay and death.

She reached the Near Caves, and the first coffin. Kate was bending over to examine the top when she saw the date written on a yellowing card taped to the lower right hand corner. *March 12, 1937*. She stood upright, breathing deeply in the darkness. The registry must have been mistaken. She was certain the recorded date was 1917. In any case, this priest was still alive, or perhaps even a child, when Anya and Lydia fled their homeland.

That left just one chance.

Kate walked deeper, into the Far Caves, arriving at the second and, she fervently hoped, *correct* coffin. It offered no outward clue as to when its occupant had died.

Like the other monks-under-glass, this Father Mikhail resembled a life-size leather doll. The flashlight cast every shadow into relief, making his features seem oddly incongruous. Above the flat plane of his face, a finely chiseled nose and chin jutted eerily, like mountains on the moon. His skin was the color of undyed candles.

Kate slipped off her raincoat. Against the black spandex body suit and navy tennis shoes, her hands and ankles seemed to float in the darkness, like ghostly appendages. She took a breath and ran her hands over her invisible body.

Was she absolutely mad? Who did she think she was—Angela Jolie in "Tomb Raiders"? A month ago she was standing in her classroom in rural Pennsylvania, teaching economics. Now she was standing in a medieval cave looking for dead bodies.

Insane or not, however, Kate had gone too far to turn back. She shivered once and went to work.

The top of the coffin came to her waist, allowing good leverage. She clamped the flashlight under her left arm. Removing a can of penetrating oil from the bag and fitting its plastic nozzle, she squirted a drop of the liquid around each of the lid's twelve screws. She paused then, and in clockwise order, began removing them—they came out surprisingly easily.

Kate placed the screws in her bag, then wedged the pry bar under the coffin's heavy glass lid.

Sliding the lid half open, Kate felt around the open side from the priest's head to his toes. Nothing. Again using the pry bar as a lever, she slid the glass cover to the other half of the coffin. She made the same quick inspection, and came up with the same negative results.

Kate paused a second time. She crouched, crossing her arms over her chest and hugging her shoulders. Looking up, she gazed at the blackness around her. Damp, fetid air brushed her cheeks.

Standing, Kate shrugged and rotated her head to relieve the tension in her back and shoulders. Then she reached across the coffin and, grasping the thick glass, turned it on its axis so that it rested crossways, fully exposing the dead priest's upper and lower body.

Kate searched again, this time reaching under Father Mikhail's form. Beneath his right shoulder, her fingers touched something firm and round. Frantically, her hands dug at the rotting cloth beneath the body. Whatever she'd felt, she couldn't budge it.

If only she could shift the cadaver out of the way. Kate walked to the casket's head. Leaning over, she tried not to look at the priest's closed, sunken eyes. Inserting both hands just below the neck, she flattened her palms against his shoulder blades. His corpse felt like a hard leather husk.

Tightening her knees and belly for greater power, Kate lifted her body straight up.

Crack! A dry, splintering sound ruptured the silence.

The mummy's head had broken off at the neck, and now lolled awkwardly back from its desiccated body. The priest's upside-down, pie-shaped face blindly ogled her, his trunk gaping open toward the ceiling. From his now mutilated form, the stench of trapped, dead air and rotting clothes escaped like a volatile gas, enveloping her.

Kate stifled a scream and dropped the flashlight, fighting nausea.

Get hold of yourself! Pick up the flashlight and get on with it.

Kate slid her hands beneath the ruined cadaver until she again felt the object. It seemed surrounded by material, as if in a satchel or purse. Kate tugged the container and it started to move.

In an instant it lay in her hands, heavy, about the size of a pear, in a gathered velvet pouch.

In the darkness, the thirty-one-year-old professor sank to the floor and splayed her legs like a little girl. She clutched the pouch to her chest with both hands. *You've found it! My God, you've actually found it!*

She loosened the drawstring and drew out a pocketsize book bearing the inscription, in faded gold, "Bank of England, Private Account." Next, she withdrew what could have been a large potato.

Without her flashlight, the miniature Faberge carriage would have been almost impossible to see.

Reverently, Kate placed the piece on the floor. She shined the beam directly upon it. The egg-shaped container's glistening enamel surface gleamed like colored vapors. She touched the top with her finger and heard a solid click.

Slowly, Kate partially opened the egg. As she did so, her flashlight bathed the stone, causing it to emit a bright crimson glow. Kate's heart pounded.

Suddenly, she was seized by panic. What if the authorities found her? She'd heard of old Soviet prisons, where inmates' leg irons were removed only upon death. What if she were caught stealing, as both Ukrainian and Russian law would surely define it, a state treasure? She imagined Krasky's face, saw him sneering.

Abruptly, she closed the Faberge container and jumped up, brushing the casket.

The glass cover momentarily teetered, then slid to the hard floor.

It shattered in a dozen sections, clattering into a jagged, crystalline heap.

Kate froze, paralyzed by the cacophony that echoed through the cavern. She had to get herself under control, think through her options. What options? She had zero time. She had to get out of here. Slinging her tool bag over her shoulder, she grabbed the pouch with her free hand, then bolted back toward the stairs.

She pulled open the heavy door to the caves and an instant later was outside, sprinting free.

Behind her, a window being raised creaked in its jamb. Kate heard muffled shouts. Lights blinked on in the cathedral. She dumped her burglar's bag in a trash can and kept running.

Only a trained athlete could catch Kate Gavrill in full flight. By the time the curious few had convinced themselves they'd only heard an animal, she'd reached the edge of the city. The Monastery of the Caves again lay shrouded in darkness.

★   ★   ★

Temporarily safe in the bed and breakfast where she'd checked in the night before, Kate slowly and delicately, undid the ancient cloth wrapping. She eased the alexandrite out of the egg. Heavy and surprisingly cool to the touch, in the dim light, the gem glowed a dark, sparkling green. She flicked on the lamp next to her bed. Magically, the jewel blazed back at her, flaring into a pool of fire.

Kate contemplated the stone. She'd never cared a whit about jewelry, but this incredible gem seduced her. She felt a deep, visceral bond with the alexandrite's history, so much of which was interwoven with her own. But something more held her: the stone's fundamental mystery. Beneath its glistening surface, nature had captured the essence of ambivalence. Was it an emerald or a ruby? What, Kate asked herself, was its true identity? What, indeed, was her own?

Chapter 20

——⊫◀◉▶⊫——

VULCAN KRASKY's monthly meeting with Boris Lada had not gone well. As was their custom, the two men sat together in the back room of a Kiev strip club. With the door open, they could watch the girls walking to and from the stage, naked breasts jiggling, faces shiny with makeup, thighs quivering under net stockings. Sometimes, Lada would order one of the dancers to come into the room and service his companion with oral sex.

Today, however, no such favors would be granted. The door remained closed. Lada knew, as boss of the local *mafiya*, they would not be disturbed. His hired cop could speak freely, after which Boris would slip him a 100 *hrivnya* note. Even allowing for rampant inflation, the money was worth less than one hundred dollars. The arrangement had made Boris a rich man. Krasky the mule owned an apartment and a shiny used car.

"You fool!" Red islands blotched Lada's pale neck. He stared at the ancient photograph of a large alexandrite. The tangy odor of female sweat, 10-*kopek* vodka and dense tobacco smoke hung over the room, creating a scent as pungent as a barnyard in the steppes.

"The woman didn't have the stone," Krasky protested. "Just the picture."

"Of course she didn't have it *then*," Lada said. He rose and circled Krasky, seated at a small wooden table, before returning to glare into

116

his eyes. The Slovenian-born criminal was nearly two feet shorter than his gunsel. Standing, his eyes were on a plane only slightly higher than Krasky's, yet the feeling of relative dominance was unmistakable. "Admittedly, I'm no *detective*"—Lada drew out the word with scorn— "but isn't it *possible* that the break-in at the monastery was carried out by this Gavrill woman or her accomplice? And isn't it *possible* that they made off with this, this treasure?" His voice rose and he flung the picture down on the table between them.

"We don't know that," Krasky responded, finding his spine. "We aren't sure if there is such a treasure. It's an old photo; it could just be a piece of costume jewelry, a family remembrance of some kind. And we don't know if Miss Gavrill broke into the monastery, or even if anything was taken. A coffin lid was broken, but nothing was reported stolen."

"You idiot!" Lada shouted. "Of course nothing was reported stolen! No one knew it was there." He sat down in one of the room's two wooden chairs and, resting his elbows on the table, buried his face in his hands.

When he'd looked up, his eyes were glacial.

"Hear this," Lada said. "I am not going to be the one to tell our superiors in Moscow that we let this slip away. Today is Monday, July 31st. You will find this woman and the stone by our next meeting. Either that"—he paused—"or we will find a new Vulcan."

EARLY THE next morning, Kate sat in a restroom stall at Kiev's airport.

She balanced her suitcase on her knees. She'd repacked her belongings to render the pouch's contents as invisible as possible. She was certain the Faberge Egg contained no ferrous metal, so she didn't have to worry about detectors. They had x-ray machines in Kiev, but nothing resembled a weapon in her belongings. Still, she couldn't be too careful. She decided to leave the pouch and egg in the suitcase and keep the jewel and bank documents in her purse.

Setting the suitcase down, Kate rested her elbows on her knees, and put her head in her hands.

Her mother's disclosures, and their implications, tumbled in her head like nested Russian boxes. Irina had insisted the lies she and Anya told were for Kate's own good. But if there were a real threat, how could it have been safer to keep that knowledge secret? Confusion, loss and anger mingled uncomfortably in Kate's mind, like immiscible liquids.

None of the questions she faced appeared straightforward. Even if rampaging Bolsheviks seemed faintly antiquarian, her mother's death was not. It remained a raw wound, open and, for now at least, unexplained. There was also the matter of justice. Kate couldn't let Irina's killers get away with their crime—that she knew with burning certainty. What if she had children of her own some day? Choosing not to act could condemn them to a life of fear or, worse, the same cycle of self-deception begun by Anya and Irina decades before.

Shaking her head, Kate stood, shut the snaps on her purse and suitcase and left the stall. In passing, she briefly paused to check her appearance in the faded restroom mirror, then stepped out onto the concourse. She gasped, and immediately turned toward the nearest wall.

A man stood thirty yards away.

Even at a distance, and even with his back turned, Kate recognized him. A coil of flesh rolled above his collar, and his coat rode high at the left shoulder, probably from the bulge of a chest-holstered automatic. The man was Detective Lt. Vulcan Krasky.

Chapter 21

KRASKY MOVED the weight of his large frame from one foot to another, eyeing the Aeroflot ticket desk. His upper body was still strong, but at forty-three, his arches had fallen and standing for long periods was a misery. Nonetheless, he had to stick it out. His membership in Kiev's petite bourgeoisie depended on keeping Boris happy and the *hrivnya* flowing.

It was a tricky situation. He had no warrant, and despite his network of corrupt judges, no Ukrainian court would certify a search for items never reported stolen. When the Gavrill woman showed up, he'd have to bluff his way through. Head her off before she got to the ticket counter, then escort her into a customs inspection room. Flash the badge and tell her he was seizing the stone under the republic's contraband art treasures law. Hell, he'd strip her to her knickers if he had to.

Krasky glanced at his watch. Allowing for bathroom breaks and a stroll to the coffee counter, he'd been standing here for nearly four hours. Where the fuck was she? He'd pressed an informant into service to watch her hotel entrance, but she hadn't been there either.

The woman at the ticket counter didn't mask her annoyance when he approached for the fourth time. Resting both elbows on the counter, she leaned forward and smiled stiffly.

"As I told you before, Lt. Krasky, the Miss Gavrill you are looking for did not change planes or cancel her reservation. She simply never showed up."

★   ★   ★

KATE SLIPPED out of the airport when KRASKY went to the men's room and—at the rail terminal where she caught the Bulgaria Express for Moscow—evaded two of the thugs who'd been with him in her hotel room.

Arriving in Moscow, Kate called Simon Blake's number from the train station. He didn't answer and she left a voice mail message. Before she exited the phone booth, Simon called back on the international cell phone she'd leased.

"I warned you this was hazardous," Blake said. His voice carried an equal mix of irritation and concern. "I've said this before: Even if the stone isn't real—and I very much doubt it is—you may be in serious danger simply because others think it's valuable.

"You must understand," he went on, "that today's Russia is filled with desperate, not particularly sophisticated, characters. Chechen terrorists. Gangsters. Corrupt cops. People who've been cut off from the old state but aren't a part of the new one either. That's why the Russian mafia is among the strongest in the world.

"Please, Miss Gavrill—Kate, take the next plane home."

Fiddling with a pencil and small spiral notepad from her portfolio, she ignored his plea. "Simon, Mr. Blake, assuming the stone is real, how do I get it—and the egg and bank papers—to New York?"

He sighed in exasperation. "Well, if they were mine, I'd have them shipped by Brinks Overseas. But you don't have that option."

"Why not?"

"Because without the proper documentation, receipts and so on, Customs officials would take these pieces away from an official courier, just the same as they'd take them away from you. Besides, Brinks would never accept it under those conditions."

"So what's your answer?"

"You'd have to conceal them. And that's so risky I don't even want to think about it. You could wind up in a Russian jail. Are a fake stone and Faberge container worth that? Frankly, my advice is go to a public library, find a quiet room and leave the stone and egg on a reading table. Somebody will pick them up and have the gem made into costume jewelry, which is all it is or ever was. I'm sure the egg is a copy. And you can toss the bank documents in a trash can."

"You're not taking me seriously. You may be the world authority on precious gems, but you haven't seen what I've seen."

His voice took on a cajoling, almost flirty tone. "Look, Kate, you've won our little bet. You *found* the stone. I'll buy you dinner at your favorite restaurant in New York. Just get rid of those ticking time bombs you're carrying and come home. Now. Please." The last word was uttered softly, as if he were begging.

Kate twisted her lower lip between her thumb and forefinger. Outside the phone booth, hundreds of dark-suited evening commuters rushed for their trains home. The faces of working Moscovites looked utterly fatigued and emotionally drained. Much as Irina's had on a Pennsylvania hospital pillow.

You've gone through too much to slink back with your tail between your legs. Call Novyck; he said he would help.

"Kate? *Please.*"

Kate pressed the receiver into her ear, fingers clutching the device with a fierce grip. "You're wrong," she said, "I've seen it. I *know* it's real."

Hanging up, she immediately began searching her bag for Imre Novyck's mobile number.

#

Chapter 22

—◦—

"YOU WERE wise to call me." Imre Novyck's soothing tone seemed disconnected from the bustling world outside Kate's telephone booth. "I told you earlier, I can get you out of the country, no trouble. But I'll need a few hours to arrange things. Phone me back tomorrow morning. By the way, use your mobile; I'm not certain these public telephones are secure.

"Come to the prison at exactly noon," he instructed the next day, "and say you are my niece. I have friends here; I need to time your arrival with the guards' shift change so they will be on duty."

The following day, Kate's pulse raced as she entered Leftortovo's small, shabby waiting room. She identified herself as Novyck's relative and was escorted to his cell. She wasn't searched or even asked to sign in. She thought again about how differently he lived than most of the prison's miserable souls.

"We won't be disturbed," Novyck said, closing the door and removing his paper mask. Viewing his unobstructed features for the first time, Kate saw a striking if narrow East European face—a straight, slender jaw with a short, thin nose and heavy brows. The Bluetooth headset still crept around his ear and along his cheekbone, and he wore a full beard, which heightened the intensity of his dark eyes.

For some reason, his uncovered visage unnerved her. Kate felt jittery, as if she were attempting a dive she'd never practiced.

Novyck, by comparison, remained smoothly in control. His room—in contrast to the dim, stone-floored corridors, which stank of mildew, sweat and urine—was freshly painted and brightly lit, and even boasted a single screw-in ceiling light. "Unlike most of our residents," he noted, "my cell is fully enclosed. And I have a purifier to cleanse the air."

Besides Novyck's bunk, the room contained a worn but comfortable looking sofa, a painted chest of drawers and a small wooden table with two chairs. It was the sort of room, Kate thought, that might suit a priest or university student.

"For being in prison," she said, hoping to nudge him off balance, "you seem to live well."

He shrugged. "My friends know that I am here as the result of injustice, so they try to make me as comfortable as possible."

He looked at her closely, dark eyes piercing. "You're very tense, my dear."

"I think it's this place." She shuddered, sensing that the two of them were somehow struggling for control. "And I've never possessed anything this valuable before. I must have been crazy to bring it here."

Novyck laughed. "Just the opposite is true, Katya," he said, using her given first name.

She sat still. The last person to call her Katya had been her mother.

"This den of thieves is the safest place in Moscow for your treasure," he went on. "Most inmates want to get out of here so badly they wouldn't take the stone if you gave it to them. You really do need to relax. In any case, I am going to make your alexandrite appear so dull and dowdy that even you will no longer believe it is valuable."

As he always did when a young woman visited his cell, Novyck propped a chair against the doorknob, insuring their privacy. The guards would think Kate was just another of his "nieces."

Like a priest arranging a sacramental table, Novyck turned away and lifted his bed covering, then carefully withdrew a long strip of electrical cord from an opening in the mattress. The cord had a male plug at one end, and a primitive heating element at the other. From beneath the bed, he pulled out a large coffee can, and a smaller mate, with a crude soldered-on coat-hanger handle.

"Kate Gavrill," Novyck said with a wink, "I've been preparing for your visit. I'm going to show you how we prisoners can make anything from a gourmet meal to boiled borscht. This time, of course, I'll be cooking up a special broth for your gem."

In rapid steps, he crossed the room to a metal sink and filled the larger can with water. After pulling on a pair of skin-tight rubber gloves, he stood on one of the room's two chairs and inserted the plug end of the wire into an outlet on the side of the light bulb socket. Novyck placed the can on the table and plunged the heating element into the water.

Kate heard a pop, then a sizzling sound as the water heated up. Next, Novyck produced a block of yellow tallow. Glancing around furtively, he slipped a knife from beneath his mattress and cut off a chunk about the size of a cube of butter.

"Now," he said, clicking his tongue with satisfaction, "We will transform the spectacular into the ordinary."

Novyck dropped the tallow shavings in the smaller can and dipped it into the now bubbling water. A heavy odor of melting wax filled the room, as if a bank of candles had been lit.

From a cardboard box beneath his bed, Novyck took a small bottle filled with black liquid. "India ink," he announced, as if speaking to himself. He poured a few drops over the tallow.

"Please, the stone." His voice sounded like a physician instructing a nurse during an operation. Heart pounding, Kate hesitated. For the first time since she'd found it—actually for the first time in nearly a century—someone other than she was about to touch the alexandrite.

He looked closely at her again. "Relax, Kate. Try this: without moving your head, look up at the icon on the ceiling, slowly shut your eyes, and draw a deep breath."

"What icon? Why?" Instantly bristling at his direction, Kate nonetheless momentarily glanced up. She gasped.

To her astonishment, framed in heavy dark wood, was an icon identical to the one that stood next to Anya's portrait on her mother's mantle in Marion. In gold leaf and heavy lacquer, it portrayed Mary, the Mother of God, reclining before a cave in a hill.

"Where did you get this?"

"It was a favorite of both our families. This, however, is a very special rendition. Take a deep breath, Kate. Observe the fine gold leaf and lacquer work in the manger."

On the ceiling, the newborn Christ radiated back at her upturned face. The infant lay with Mary outside the cave, watched by an ox and an ass. Angels, their gilt wings gleaming, hovered at the upper corners. At the lower left, a rosy-cheeked Joseph listened to an old shepherd.

"Look up, Kate, look at the child's pink fingers," Novyck said.

As her eyes rolled toward the ceiling, Kate felt her lids grow leaden.

"Good, very good." Novyck said. "Take the icon's spirit inside you,"

Suddenly obedient, Kate drew in her breath.

"May I?" Novyck asked. Through half-closed eyes, Kate saw his hand stretch toward her.

She removed the gem from her portfolio and placed it on the table. Even in the bulb's low wattage light, it glowed a muted red.

Kate tried to follow Novyck's movements, but she seemed oddly out of her own skin. She felt alert, but her eyes trailed his motions by a beat, like a camera falling behind the action at a sports event. His gloved hand picked up the stone and floated toward the can.

She shook her head, hard, and her vision seemed to sync up. Dipping the gem into the now bubbling wax, Imre Novyck turned it delicately, lifting it out and gingerly shifting it in his fingers. He did this for several minutes and then held it out to her. The once-glittering stone now looked lifeless, its brilliance obscurred by the coating.

"Paraffin, ink and a touch of bunker oil," he said. "Works every time."

Turning, he again lifted the mattress and pulled out a gaudy breastplate necklace. "I had this made out of plated tin by one of the inmates," he said. "I thought we might need it."

He clicked the stone into the centerpiece. One at a time, he bent eight crudely made prongs around the gem to hold it in place. He looked at her closely. "Would you mind slowly counting those off to make sure I've got them all? From highest to lowest."

Kate acquiesced, methodically verbalizing the numbers, "Eight, seven, six, five, four, three, two, one."

"Good," he said, smiling. He tested the large piece of jewelry with his fingers, but his gaze was on Kate. "You should be fine, now. You're ready for the world to see."

He leaned toward her. "You do look better. How do you feel?"

Kate squirmed. Her head seemed suddenly clear, but the question was too personal. His eyes roved over her. She shrugged and avoided his gaze, hoping to shift his focus away from her, to take back control.

"Why are you doing all this?" She blurted the question. "Why have you gone to all this trouble?"

He paused before replying, and smiled. His teeth were beautifully white against his dark beard. His penetrating eyes were fully upon her, bright with passion. His face looked innocent and open. "I knew your mother, Kate, if only by correspondence. I share her dreams. It is my Mother Russia too."

She swayed slightly, realizing that in the time she'd been in his cell she'd never sat down.

"Display this prominently," Novyck said, his tone becoming matter-of-fact. He gently lowered the big necklace, wrapped in wax paper, into a dirty paper bag. "And dress to match. Wear something flamboyant, revealing. We seek to simultaneously distract and conceal. So make the jewelry seem like a flashy accessory worn by someone who always dresses that way. Look like a gangster's girlfriend, hmmm?" His eyes traced her body again.

"And remember," he said. "The coating on the stone is still soft. Try not to touch it for a day or so. When you reach America, use hot water followed by fingernail polish remover. It will peel off like an eggshell.

"For now, go to GUM—the department store—and buy a cheap Faberge knockoff for the egg. Throw it away in a public waste bin, but save the empty box and receipt. Use this one for the stone." He handed her a forged GUM invoice for jewelry showing 6,000 rubles, or about $200.

Novyck rose abruptly. "You must leave now. My people will go off shift soon and their replacements would find it highly irregular for you to be in my cell." He stood close to her and placed his hand high on her waist, almost touching her breast. Kate did not pull away.

"Go home and follow your heart, and your mother's wishes," he urged in soft, rhythmic tones. "I will be free soon, and when you return to Russia I will help you more."

Again donning the paper mask, he opened the door. As he turned away, he touched the device at his ear, apparently to take a call.

Walking down the corridor, Kate felt strangely uneasy. *What just happened in there? Did I miss something? Why would I return to Russia?*

★ ★ ★

Nᴇʀᴠᴏᴜs Sᴡᴇᴀᴛ slickened the telephone receiver against Vulcan Krasky's ear.

"What do you mean you *lost* her?" screamed Boris Lada "I don't care if you have to permanently live, eat and sleep at Sheremetyevo. She can't be allowed to leave the country with the stone, and if she does, you better be on the next plane."

Chapter 23

THE WOMAN in the mirror at Moscow's Sheremetyevo Airport was not Kate Gavrill, college professor, of Marion, PA.

Gone were her signature loafers, tweed jacket, Oxford cloth shirt and wide-wale cord trousers. In their place were stiletto-heeled black boots, tight lambskin pants and a matching top—with a mandarin collar and plunging, zippered front. Kate drew the zipper down to expose her braless cleavage. Soft hills of ivory danced under shiny leather. Turning for an over-the-shoulder assessment, she almost blushed. Poured into the black leather trousers, her rear glistened like a pair of ebony moons.

Although used to donning brief swimsuits as an athlete, Kate had never worn such an outfit in public. Sensing her discomfort, the saleswoman in GUM had tried to reassure her. "With your figure, madame, he will love it, trust me. Nothing brings out the primitive, sensual side of a woman like the hide of an animal next to her skin. It is as if she is back in the cave, no?"

They both laughed. What would the salesgirl say if she knew the man Kate was dressing for literally lived in a cave, as an inmate at Lefortovo Prison?

On impulse, Kate redid her hair too, trimming it to a length somewhere north of Sinead O'Connor and south of Winona Ryder. Still in the GUM salon, she smooched up her mouth and applied a thick coat of Testa Rossa—the lipstick of Ferrari wives, according to the text on the box.

Only now, waiting for her plane, did she open her bag and remove Novyck's oversize necklace. Securing the heavy clasp, she draped the gaudy jewelry around her neck and marveled at how clever he'd been. Overwhelmed by its gold-painted, ornamental-tin surroundings, the Romanov stone sat as lifeless as paste at the piece's center, seeming almost to disappear—precisely the effect Imre Novyck intended.

Though not without risk, his plan seemed solid.

Kate was almost swaggering by the time she boarded a nonstop flight to New York. Not a single security official had even noticed her existence, let alone asked to examine her belongings. She was starting to enjoy the charade. By contrast, the passenger ahead of her, a burly Italian from New Jersey, had been forced to open three pieces of luggage when an agent became suspicious.

Kate settled into her seat and dozed.

The intensity of her seatmate's stare awakened her.

"How unusual," the female voice beside her said as Kate's eyes fluttered open. "It's almost as if there's a ruby under the surface."

Kate felt a flash of panic. Glancing up, she realized she'd fallen asleep with the reading light on. When she slumped over in her seat, the small but brilliant beam effectively pierced Novyck's disguise. In a small spot on its otherwise dull surface, the stone was behaving exactly like an alexandrite—and glowing a deep purplish red!

The woman extended her index finger to touch the spot. Kate reached up and flicked off the light, capturing the woman's hand with her own. "Really, it's just a fake," she said, her lips turning down in a sign of disdain. Her fellow passenger smiled, and feeling the strength in Kate's hand, quickly gave up her quest. Nonetheless, the incident unnerved Kate. She remained awake for the rest of the trip.

In New York, a U.S. customs inspector, a small red-faced man with baggy blue eyes, took a close interest in the Faberge egg. The

GUM receipt satisfied his initial curiosity, until his eyes fell upon her necklace.

Boldly reaching toward her, the inspector tapped the heavy jewelry on her chest.

"Remove this please," he said. She handed him the heavy adornment, hoping he did not see her fingers tremble.

As Kate's heart pounded, he looked the piece over.

Act as natural as you can. We're almost home free.

Finally, the man handed Kate's treasure back to her, sympathy softening his words. "I hope you didn't pay too much for this," he said.

Chapter 24

GETTING OFF the airport bus at the New York Port Authority, Kate at last felt safe; she was home. She'd take a cab to Penn Station, then head for Marion and regroup before returning to gloat over her success with Simon Blake.

Rolling her bag through the terminal corridors, Kate suddenly felt slightly ridiculous and very, very tired. The long flight was finally taking its toll. Glimpsing her own reflection in a polished metal door, Kate thought how foolish she must look: a wiggly-butted bimbo in a slinky black leather package—a mobster's moll, just as Novyck ordered. On the other hand, the simple ruse had worked, and she now stood on American soil, the key to her family fortune intact and in her possession. It seemed impossible that only two days before she'd been sitting in one of the world's rankest prisons in Moscow.

But the bodice jiggle had to go; she tugged the form-fitting top's zipper up under her chin. Even so, Kate heard a low whistle as she lengthened her stride, exiting the Port Authority.

Parking her heavy suitcase on the sidewalk, she queued up for a cab. She stood with her back to the head of the line, watching the taxis drive in. As each cab picked up its fares and the line moved ahead, Kate inched along with it, dragging her suitcase, still facing backward. She turned suddenly when she reached the front and inadvertently struck a wall.

Or a slab of human flesh she thought was a wall. Tall and stolid, the man she'd bumped into instinctively backed away and mumbled an apology in a thick foreign accent.

Kate gasped.

Shrugging off his confusion, Vulcan Krasky moved toward her, reaching for her shoulders.

But his hands closed on empty air.

Reflexively, Kate executed a half side step, a diving board maneuver she'd done a hundred times. Off-balance, Krasky stumbled over her suitcase and fell heavily, scraping his head against the pavement.

Kate shot down the sidewalk, clutching her portfolio tight to her body. She twisted her head once to see Krasky, head bloodied, slowly getting to his feet.

A cab pulled to the curb. Pushing past the departing fare, Kate flung herself across the back seat, thrusting two twenty dollar bills at the surprised cabby.

"Go!" she shouted. Her original plan had been to take a cab to Penn Station and then the bus to Marion. But that would lead Krasky straight to her door! There was only one place she could turn.

"I'm staying on Fifth Avenue," Kate said, hastily giving him Simon Blake's address.

She was swept by a sudden wave of depression. Just when she'd been giddy with success, she'd almost lost everything. She couldn't let that happen again.

On his knees, Vulcan Krasky rifled through the suitcase, flinging clothes on the sidewalk. He found nothing of value except a torn business card showing an American name but no street or telephone number.

A Port Authority policeman approached. Slipping the card into his pocket, Krasky rose and quickly walked away, dabbing his forehead with an embroidered handkerchief. The disguise had fooled him momentarily, but the good news was that he'd followed his instincts and boarded a plane to New York. The American woman had gotten out of Russia. She would not get away again.

Chapter 25

---•◦•---

GREEN EYES swept Kate from her toes to her scalp. "Is Simon Blake here?" she asked.

"You've got a girlfriend here in panther skin," Adrienne Lane announced over an arched shoulder. She flipped back an auburn bang, and swung open the door to Blake's home-office. "But if we're going to make the curtain, sweet, she'll have to settle for a peck on the cheek."

There hadn't been time to call. Kate hadn't even been sure that he'd still be in his office-apartment. Now she stood in the doorway, feeling desperate and embarrassed.

With its dark brown leather furniture, flat gray carpets and steel-framed windows, the room exuded a masculine presence that somehow seemed an unnatural habitat for two females.

Blake appeared, black tie dangling.

"I'm really sorry," Kate said, her heart pounding in her throat, "I had nowhere else to go. I've got the stone. And you were right. Someone's following me."

"Please come in," Blake said. He took her hand. Ignoring his companion's remark, he introduced their visitor: "Adrienne: "Miss Kate Gavrill. A client with a very interesting story." Kate detected a hint of rebuke in his last sentence.

"Miss Gavrille, this is my friend Adrienne Lane."

135

Blake gestured toward the small living room and the women settled in two pleated chairs; he centered himself between them on a tufted leather sofa.

"By all means, *do* tell," urged Adrienne from her corner of the triangle. Though Kate judged her to be well into her forties, the woman had a model's lean body and, clearly, an editor's dagger wit. Adrienne darted a glance at Simon and ignored Kate. "But try to make it quick. I really don't want to miss the curtain, dear boy. It's opening night. And by the way, please do shave."

Kate sensed Simon bridle at Adrienne's possessiveness, but it was also clear the pair had a long-term relationship. She felt as if she'd stumbled into their bedroom.

"Really, I shouldn't have barged in—" she began.

Blake touched her hand again. "Nonsense. Don't apologize. We want to hear what happened, don't we Adrienne?"

"I'm sure it's a wonderful story," Adrienne replied, "but *I'm* going to the theater." She addressed Simon directly. "It's now or never, dearest. And if you don't get a razor on that face I'm going to disown you." She rose, resting her palm on a slender, satined hip.

Blake stood and turned to face his date. He cleared his throat.

"I'm going to stay, Adrienne. Miss Gavrill is here to show me a very special stone, and I want to conduct some tests tonight."

"Suit yourself. Just make sure you don't conduct any tests on Miss Gavrill. She looks like she could win a hard body contest." Adrienne walked toward him. Under her sheath, her lean frame moved like liquid. She circled a slender arm around Simon's neck and pulled his face down to hers for a long sensuous kiss. "Remember the song," she said softly, patting his butt: "'*Don't Go to Strangers.*'"

She slid through the door with a mocking wink. Kate felt the blood crawl up her neck. She'd always hated the way she blushed.

Blake stood in the center of the room looking simultaneously foolish and irritated.

"I better start from the beginning," Kate said. She briefly recounted her mother's accident, bedside confession and death. She summarized the story of her lineage and Anya Putyatin's perilous escapes from Russia, Kiev and Paris.

"Why didn't you tell me this earlier?" he asked.

"I wasn't sure I could trust you," Kate said. Her eyes locked on his. "I realize now I was wrong. You were right to warn me about how dangerous this could be."

Kate also related her recent experience, book-ending the tale between her meeting with Imre and her surprise encounter with Vulcan Krasky at Penn Station.

Blake hung on her words, shaking his head like a worried relative, leaning forward when she talked of the alexandrite and its retrieval. Oddly, he seemed not to take in her changed appearance, offering no comment when she told how she came to purchase the all-leather outfit. For some reason, his lack of reaction left Kate feeling deflated—was she jealous of the woman who'd just departed? In any case, so much for being a guy-magnet in these clothes. Or maybe it was just their fundamental lack of chemistry. When Blake did ask questions, his manner was methodical and cautious. Compared to Imre's seething energy, he appeared bland and analytical.

"Your fiancée is striking," Kate observed.

Blake shook his head. "Adrienne and I are just friends," he said. "Look, Kate, I've got several tests to do on your stone. I'd like to get started."

"Of course." Taking off the necklace, she said, "Imre coated it with something. He said it would come off, I think with fingernail polish."

"That's fine. It will also come off with ultrasound, which is what I use to clean gems."

He resumed a formal tone. "There's one thing I should mention: The terms of my insurance don't allow me to assume liability for a stone of this potential—and I emphasize the word potential—value.

I'll need you to sign a waiver, and I'm afraid you're going to have to stay until I finish the tests, which could take a while."

Kate looked at her watch. It was nearly 10:00 P.M.

Following her glance, Blake said, "Look, it's too late to find a hotel room, and that goon is still out there. You can sleep in my bedroom."

"I left all my clothes at the station. Does Adrienne keep a nightie here I can use?"

His irritation was visible. "Adrienne does not sleep here." He left for a moment and returned with a blue-and-white-striped Ralph Lauren dress shirt. "You're welcome to this."

"Thanks." Retreating to the bedroom, Kate slipped out of her clothes and into the oversize shirt. The garment hung on her like a produce bag.

Getting out of the tight leather was like being liberated from a stiff corset. Emotionally drained and physically exhausted, she shuffled wearily to the lab where Simon sat hunched over a draughtsman's table, wearing a pair of special magnifiers.

"I've got to get some sleep," she said in the doorway, "I'm about to crash."

"Of course."

Blake pushed up the magnifiers on his forehead. At last he seemed to look at her.

"You cut your hair," he said.

Chapter 26

STANDING AT a metal workbench in one of his suite's two small lab rooms, Blake used a rubber spatula to scrape as much loose wax from the alexandrite as possible. Then he slipped on a pair of white cotton gloves and placed the stone in a wire basket. Carefully, he lowered the gem into a cleaning machine that transmitted sound waves through a liquid mixture of ammonia and detergent. Thirty minutes later, he raised the basket out of the solution.

Wiping the last drops of cleaning solution away, Blake nearly lost his breath. Like any crystalline gem, even through his gloves the stone felt cool to the touch—cooler than the room around him. But this alexandrite, deep green and nearly the size of a tea bag, was larger and more beautiful than any specimen he'd ever seen.

Blake began his examination by using a special measuring instrument called a micrometer. He placed the stone in the device's "jaws," then read its dimensions by rotating a calibrated shaft which accurately gauged the gem's length, width and depth. The result: 65.08 mm in length, 63.62 mm in width and 42.18 mm in height—the metric equivalent of 2.5 x 2.5 x 1.6 inches. Blake smiled and nodded to himself. He'd been so skeptical of this stone, and any possibility that it might be real. Now, he had to admit, the young woman who'd seemed so very naïve just might be right: the dimensions indicated by the micrometer were precisely those in Kate's document.

His excitement mounting, Blake opened a plastic-windowed electronic scale and placed the stone inside. The digital read-out flashed a number: 1,244.37 carats.

Blake frowned. His second test had turned up a discrepancy. According to the document Kate had given him, the stone should weigh 1275 carats.

In ancient times, jewelers used carrow seeds, known for their consistent size and weight, as scale-balancers. Today's digital scales, however, were so sensitive that even the motion of human breath could alter their readings. For this reason, modern scales were enclosed in glass or Lucite. But Blake shook his head: even if trace air currents were present, they'd hardly account for a difference of about 30 carats.

He turned to the credenza behind his desk, and opened an old but extremely accurate mechanical balance. Electronic instruments had let him down before, but this trusted scale, with its glass case, hand-rubbed mahogany base and brass armature and weights, had never erred.

Blake placed the stone in the device's right tray and filled the opposite tray with nineteen 64-carat weights. Atop the scale, a needle connected to the balancing beam moved toward dead center. But when he added a 32-carat weight, bringing the total to 1248 carats, the pointer swung past the median-line. Only by removing the 32 carats, then successively adding smaller weights, could he get the scale to balance.

Blake swore. The weights added up to 1244.37 carats. He'd confirmed the initial digital finding.

Assuming Kate Gavrill hadn't risked her life for a fake, only two circumstances could explain these results. Either the original stone had been re-cut after the documents were written, or this gem—magnificent though it might be—was not the original stone.

Blake rubbed his chin, lifted his eyes from the ancient weighing instrument and stared into the distance. Original or not, as a genuine alexandrite the stone would still represent an historic and spectacularly valuable discovery.

He must continue the tests.

After dropping the gem into a vial of heavy liquid to confirm its specific gravity, Blake crossed the room to a high maple table and stool. Kneeling down, he unlocked a cupboard and withdrew a large, binocular microscope with a heavy illuminated base. He attached the instrument, specifically designed for probing the interior of gems, to a flat-panel computer screen. This would be his hardest work; if successful, it would enable him to declare with certainty whether the Romanov Stone was a natural wonder or a man-made counterfeit.

Before starting his task, Blake stood up from the stool and stretched. He crossed the small, windowless room to a book shelf, then paused. He thought again of Kate. Because of her, a beautiful, self-assured woman whom he'd known for years and with whom he'd shared passion if not love was sitting alone in a Broadway show next to his empty seat. What seemed to be pulling him toward the other female, someone he knew so little about? Was it lust for a stone or for a younger woman?

Shrugging off the questions, Blake bent over the microscope, lowering his eyes to its twin viewing lenses. He might be as fumble-headed as any man in trying to probe the mysteries of human attraction, but using this instrument he could peel away the external layers of an otherwise impenetrable geological substance, peer deep inside its interior, and ascertain the origins of its creation. Was it natural or synthetic? He chuckled to himself: Was it real or was it Memorex? Steadily increasing the microscope's magnification, he would employ the device like a physician might employ a CAT-scan, and find out.

This most critical and complex part of Blake's work was as much art as science, and it was the part Blake loved most—when his mind

141

joined his eyes in soaring through the inner space that gave each gem its unique character.

For the next several hours he would examine minute traces of material, trapped within the crystal, that, he hoped, would yield the truth. The inclusions in a natural alexandrite revealed the environment of the stone's origins—the surrounding earth and rock where it had been created by centuries of heat and pressure. A synthetic, however, nearly always contained telltale residues of the metal crucible in which the stones were artificially grown.

First, Blake studied the gem's surface. He flipped on an external fluorescent light mounted on the miscroscope's specimen stage. Slowly, he turned the alexandrite so that the soft beam skimmed its facets. Considering its age, the jewel was remarkably free of even superficial mars and scratches—the happy result, he presumed, of being stored in a monk's coffin for most of a century.

Now Blake turned off the fluorescent and examined the stone using an incandescent ring light that encircled its sides. Against a dark background, the gem glowed a candy red.

Cranking up the microscope's power, Blake saw the crimson, fingerprint-like inclusions that signaled the stone's genuineness. Then, adjusting the fine focus, he spotted something else. Almost at the gem's exact center was a small oval-shaped cavity filled with liquid and, inside, a tiny air bubble. When he turned the jewel, the bubble floated to top center, like a carpenter's level. This was a three-phase inclusion, rarely found in alexandrites, and nature's signature of authentication.

Tired as he was, Blake's heart skipped.

Invisible to the naked eye, the evidence he'd seen proved what the stone was not: a well-executed imitation worth a few thousand dollars. Instead, it was a genuine alexandrite worth uncounted millions.

But he still could not say whether it was *the* Romanov alexandrite.

Working with both scales, Blake re-weighed the stone a half dozen times. Each exercise produced the same result: 1244.37 carats. Finally, still clutching the weights needed to balance the stone at 1275, he slumped over the table asleep. The brass cylinders scattered out of his hands and across the credenza like tiny barrels.

When he awoke, Blake rubbed his eyes. He'd slept for three hours: It was 5:00 a.m.

Propping up his head, Blake made a tripod with his elbows. He gazed around the room. The first thing he saw was a 60-year-old magnifying glass at the corner of his desktop. It was then he remembered.

The international standard for carats wasn't adopted until the early part of the twentieth century. He'd been forced to recalculate the weight of antique jewels before.

Blake again crossed the room to his bookcase and removed the aging leather volume he referred to when handling estate jewelry. Flipping to the index, then back to the text, he found the section containing conversion tables.

Prior to 1913, the Russian carat had been 2.24 percent lighter than the current international standard. The math was straightforward: 1275 X 97.56 % = 1243.89. So adjusted, the weight listed in Kate's papers almost perfectly matched the results from his scales.

He walked to a small, stainless steel basin and splashed his face with cold water. Despite his weariness after hours of work, an almost giddy elation swept Blake from his toes to his scalp. He felt like Gallileo discovering the moon. In the world of gems, Simon Blake had just confirmed a specimen of towering significance. Suddenly, however, Blake felt a bolt of fear. His warnings to Kate echoed in his head: 'Do you realize the danger to someone who possessed such a stone?' he'd asked. Then, the question was rhetorical. Now, it was real and imminent. He rose, strode quickly to the office condo's front door, and re-latched its three deadbolt locks.

Returning to the table, Blake scrawled his conclusion across the bottom of a notepad, musing at his earlier skepticism. He was sure of it now: the jewel described in the documents and the specimen on his desk were one and the same. Kate's gem was *the* Romanov Stone—the largest and most exquisite natural alexandrite he or anyone else had ever seen.

★   ★   ★

STREAMING IN from the high windows, morning light silhouetted a slumped form in a chair at the end of her bed. Kate opened her eyes to see Simon Blake sitting less than three feet away, his gaze locked on the large stone he held in his hand.

"It's real," he said, as if to himself. "All the tests were positive. I've also verified that it is the Romanov alexandrite, the stone described in your document." He looked at her, moving the chair closer. "I've been in this business more than twenty years," he said, "and I've never seen anything like it."

Kate's pulse quickened as his words sunk in. The terror she'd experienced only a few hours ago at the Port Authority seemed far away.

Her eyes narrowed. "How much do you think it's worth?"

He shrugged, still gazing at the stone. "To the one who wants it, who must have it, whatever is asked. On the open market, $40 or $50 million, perhaps more. Perhaps much more. There's really no way to put a ceiling on the price. It's unique in all the world; there's simply nothing else like it."

Pulling a small but powerful light from his pocket, Blake probed the now crystal-clear gem. As if electrified, the alexandrite flared with a raspberry glow.

Their eyes met above the stone.

"Can you believe the beauty?" His voice was low, husky, breathless. His excitement infected her. Her own breathing became shallow, more rapid.

Kate rose to a sitting position. The bedspread she'd slept under slipped to the floor. Instinctively, she drew her knees up, and pulled down the shirt, making a tent around her body.

"Touch it," he said, moving to sit beside her. She caught the scent of him. "Hold it."

She reached out to take the stone and her fingers brushed his. Energy hummed beneath his flesh.

Again, their eyes locked. This time they both drank more deeply.

Impulsively, with surprising quickness and strength, he pulled her toward him.

As Blake bent to her lips, Kate averted her head. She moved her head to one side, then the other, then yielded. Her arms collapsed against her chest. The stone dropped into her lap. His lips touched hers, pressing against her mouth with a fierce hunger.

Abruptly, he pulled away, turned his back to her.

"I'm sorry," he said hoarsely. "That was way, way out of line. It was the stone. I was just so excited about the stone."

Kate rubbed the back of her hand across her chin. How long had it been since she'd been kissed like that?

"Are you sure?" she asked.

She touched his shoulder, then slid her hand up to his neck. Gently, she drew him back to her. As he turned, he looked at her intently. His eyes seemed warm and dark and fathomless.

His hands slid down to her waist, then up to her arms, grazing the sides of her unconfined breasts.

Blake dropped his lips to hers again, and she did not resist. He opened her top and cupped her.

Kate arched against him. The Romanov Stone rolled out of her lap, down the length of her thigh and off the bed. Without breaking their kiss, Simon Blake shifted above her. He dropped his hand over the mattress and, like an infielder trapping a baseball, caught the gem before it struck the floor.

#

Part III

Chapter 27

—⟫⟨◍⟩⟪—

BAREFOOT AND wearing a black silk kimono, the slender dark-skinned Latino stood in the living room of his luxury condominium. Twenty-seven floors below, a drenching, mid-afternoon rain steamed from the sidewalks of Bogota. Before him, in a semicircle, sat seven young adults—six men and a slender, shy-looking woman.

"*Es impossible*," said one young man in Spanish.

"Not only can it be done, but you will do it," their teacher countered in the same tongue. "You have been chosen by the cartel for this training. You will not only undertake the exercises I am going to show you, you will excel at them."

"By the time you are finished," Hector Molina continued, "you will know your body more intimately than you ever thought possible. You will be able to control the tiniest movements of your muscles and to interpret each flutter of your nerves.

"Thus . . ."

Turning away in a single dramatic motion, Molina let the robe slowly slip from his shoulders. Seen from the back, his well-proportioned body, clothed only in a black athletic supporter, was almost nubile in its beauty. A slim waist, rounded hips and thighs, and a soft-swelling musculature echoed the gentle contours of his face. A sheen of oil gleamed on his dark skin.

Tied to his ankles, wrists, elbows and neck were seven sterling silver bells.

Still facing away from the class, the instructor opened his hips; his feet were in perfect alignment with his pelvis. Heels touching, back straight, he gracefully bent his knees. Slowly, he moved from the second through fifth positions of a ballet dancer's basic exercises, beginning with his feet wide apart, and ending with his heel against his big toe. Arching both hands above his head, he executed a slow-motion *glissade*, sliding until his feet were fully stretched. Rising in a flowing motion, he leapt, then dropped back to the floor, rotating in a full pirouette.

During the entire exhibition, his students had heard not a single sound. Not a jingle, not a tinkle. He slipped on the robe and turned to face them.

"Bien venidos, mis banditos," the man said, his voice morphing seamlessly into a perfectly cadenced, English-Spanish imitation of actor Cary Grant. "Welcome to La Escuella de las Siete Campanillas— the School of The Seven Bells."

★   ★   ★

MUTUAL AWKWARDNESS and embarrassment marked their first encounter the following afternoon.

"I did as you suggested," Kate reported. She noticed that, for the first time since they'd met, Blake was clean-shaven. The lack of fuzz emphasized the clean line of his jaw; he looked years younger. "I took the stone, the egg and the documents back to Irina's safe deposit box at Rockefeller Center."

"Good God," Blake responded. "Next time take me—or somebody—with you."

"It was on my way to the lawyers," Kate said. She dropped her gaze. "Besides, you were still sleeping."

Struggling to regain a professional footing, Kate spoke in a bright, impersonal way about her morning meeting with the law firm of

Kidder, Cushing and Wakefield. Blake seemed as uncomfortable as she about what had happened the night before.

"Five hundred thousand dollars!" Kate repeated the lawyer's retainer, still in disbelief.

"Legal work on missing estate property is always high," Blake countered, "and in the UK especially so. There are no contingency fees in English courts, and this matter is apt to be complicated."

"I suppose you're right," said Kate, still avoiding his eyes. "Of course, I have no idea where I will find it."

Kate paused, hearing her own words. Money had moved to the center of her life.

"We also have a deadline, one I didn't know about," she went on. "It turns out there are many old accounts in England, and the banking industry succeeded in getting a law passed that reverts all deposits dormant for fifty years or more to the bank of record. It takes effect on the First of September, this year. That date falls in precisely twenty-one days."

"So? You've got the stone, the egg and copies of the documents. What's to worry about?"

"You're right," she said. "There shouldn't be a problem. But, as Mr. Cushing pointed out, I'm claiming an account that's almost a century old. With interest, it could easily be worth more than $100 million. The Bank of England won't simply hand me a check. I'll have to meet their deadline, and prove our case to their satisfaction, under their laws. Oh, and there's one more thing. Proof of ownership now includes DNA evidence."

"DNA evidence?"

"'Whatever additional proof meets the highest prevailing technical standards at the time'"—she emphasized the words, reading from a copy the Cushing firm had received from the Bank of England. A successful claimant must 'establish with certainty that she is, in fact, Anya Putyatin or her heirs, directly descended from Nicolai Romanov II, tsar of all Russia.'"

Years before, under retainer to Kate's mother and Anya, Cushing and Wakefield had documented the secret Romanov account's existence. In fact, one of the firm's attorneys had become obsessed with the case, eventually retiring from the firm to work for the two women on a contingency basis. Before dying, he'd identified a numbered account at the Bank of England in the name Lydia Putyatin and had a letter from the bank's director attesting to its validity.

Lacking both the stone and the egg, however, Kate's relatives had been stymied. Now, thanks to Kate's trip to Russia, that obstacle had been swept aside. The lawyers possessed copies of the actual bank documents. The originals, together with the alexandrite and Faberge egg, were safely locked away in Kate's bank just blocks from their offices.

Blake listened carefully, then spoke.

"One exposure still troubles me," he said, "and it's a big one. You're telling me that your personal biological sample will be needed to certify this bank account claim in England?"

Kate nodded.

"That takes us back to personal risk," he said. "Do you realize how much this multiplies the danger you are in? Good God, it's bad enough that you've been walking around with a stone worth perhaps tens of millions. Now there may even be a price on your body parts.

"I know one thing," he continued. "You can never go back to Russia. Never. They wouldn't even need the stone. They could just hold you—dead or alive—for ransom."

"That's nonsense. Of course I can go back, and whenever I wish." Kate thought about Vulcan Krasky and knew her words had the unmistakable ring of false bravado.

He paused. "Let me tell you about the world I know."

In short narrative strokes, Blake recounted the fate of Bret Steiner.

"I sent Bret to look for a source for Russian synthetic diamonds, and to do some general research about business conditions there," he recalled. "The Russian mafia murdered him, brutally, left him in his hotel bathtub to bleed to death. He was about your age—twenty-eight, I think."

Kate ignored his flattering chronological error as Blake looked at her closely.

"Bret," he went on, "was killed for a pile of synthetic stones worth less than $30,000. If you went back, a woman alone, whose hair clippings might be worth $100 million, how long do you think you'd last? To someone desperate enough, even a a scrape of your skin could be worth a fortune."

Kate stood and walked toward the window. In her thin summer dress, the late morning sun flared around her, silhouetting her shape. Blake suppressed a surge of desire.

"I know people who would help," Kate said. "People my mother knew, who felt as she and Anya did about redeeming the Romanov legacy."

"By 'friends,' do you mean people like that inmate at Lefortovo Prison?" Blake's tone barely concealed his sarcasm.

"Him, yes. And others I am sure will come to my side." Kate felt a flash of resentment. Why should she have to defend herself?

"Ah, others," he echoed in the same skeptical tone. "Others like the good Lt. Krasky. The only reason you're still alive is that he doesn't know where you are."

Blake sneered in disgust. His sense of protectiveness was clearly misguided, if not wasted altogether on a woman like Kate Gavrill. She seemed so foolishly headstrong. Just like Bret.

Now she looked directly at him, her ice blue eyes wide and intense, her tone crisp. "I need your help."

"Where to get the $500,000?" Blake said, returning her gaze and again feeling a powerful pull. So much for disengaging.

"Yes."

"I know someone," Blake said, reaching out. For the first time since they'd made love, he touched her hand.

Chapter 28

"WHY ARE you showing me this?" Jacob Massad's eyes narrowed as Blake withdrew the glittering Faberge carriage from Kate's brief case. Then Blake opened the top. Massad sighed. In the subdued evening light, the stone glowed intensely, as green as the center of the sea. Massad knew at a glance it was the finest alexandrite he'd ever seen.

"Of course, you must keep this in strictest confidence," Blake said. "Miss Gavrill has removed the stone from her safe deposit box only long enough for you to see it." Kate sat silently beside him. The Persian jew was Blake's friend; she'd never even met a Persian jew.

Massad's full lips pursed in injury. "How long have we known each other, Simon? Twenty years? How can you make such a comment? After all this time, do you doubt my discretion?"

Blake's eyes softened. After all, it was Massad who'd initially recognized his passion for stones, and helped him establish his business. Apologizing, he quickly summarized the alexandrite's history and its key role in establishing Kate's right to the Romanov account in England.

"She needs $500,000 for legal representation?" Massad sounded incredulous.

Blake nodded. "You know the drill. It's a retainer against costs. Foreign courts are complicated and expensive. The bank may still try to deny her claim. Also, there's a fuse running—if the claim isn't settled by September, the money reverts to the bank."

"So the stone would be collateral, but I wouldn't have it." Massad's eyes kept drifting back to the alexandrite. The gem emitted a soft red–green light as a slanting ray of sun brushed its surface. "Wouldn't things be better all around if I just held it here in my safe?"

"Miss Gavrill can't allow that; anything that might cloud the chain of custody could undermine her claim on the bank account. She must retain possession so that it can be presented as evidence to the bank. In effect, you will have a lien on the stone."

"Are you vouching for its authenticity?" Massad's gaze remained locked on the gem, as if no-one else were in the room.

"I've examined the stone," Blake replied, "and my analysis verifies its authenticity. As a precaution, I plan to have Alen Bertram at MGI take a look at it, using an infrared spectrophotometer. We both know how tricky alexandrites can be. But I've run all my standard tests. I'm certain it's genuine."

Kate looked sharply at Simon. He'd never mentioned showing the alexandrite to someone else or further tests. She wasn't sure she liked the idea. Perhaps he was getting too involved in this project. On the other hand, she desperately needed his assistance. She kept quiet.

At last, Massad pulled his eyes back to the two people in his small, simply furnished office. "I'm not a pawnbroker, Simon. Besides the lien, I'd want a right of first refusal on any subsequent sale of the stone, signed and notarized."

"And the striking price?"

"Say $3 million."

"Wait a minute," Kate broke in. "What is he saying?"

"If you should sell the stone, he would have the right to purchase it for $3 million."

"No way," Kate said angrily. "We all know the stone is worth millions more than that. Don't we?" she added, looking at Blake.

The friendly tone left Massad's voice. "If you want my $500,000, Miss Gavrill," he said, addressing her directly for the first time, "it will be worth $3 million."

Kate rose. "Mr. Blake, I think it's time for us to say our goodbyes." She extended her hand. "Thank you, Mr. Massad, we will go elsewhere."

Not taking her hand, Massad turned to Blake as if Kate didn't exist. "Is she talking or are you talking?"

Kate put both hands on Massad's desk, leaning forward so that she came between the two men. "I'm handling this. Mr. Blake is my consultant."

For the first time, Massad fully focused on her. He suddenly smiled broadly. "Very well," he said in a charming voice. "Simon is an old, old friend, and you are obviously his friend. His very beautiful friend, I might add."

"The answer is still no, Mr. Massad. As I said, Mr. Blake and I have a professiona—"

Massad broke in, patting her forearm, and speaking in a low, confidential tone. "Dear woman, I am nearly seventy years old. I have known Simon since he was very young. I have seen him grow in knowledge and experience. My advice to you, Miss Gavrill, is to listen carefully to the gentleman seated next to you."

Kate squirmed. "Mr. Blake has already been very helpful," she replied. She blushed, thinking how her words must sound to Simon after the previous night.

Massad turned back to Blake, his tone again businesslike. "If Miss Gavrill can't pay me, how do I get possession of the stone?"

"You have my word. If any thing interferes with your repayment—Miss Gavrill and I will personally deliver the alexandrite to you."

Massad looked at them both, shifting his eyes from one to the other. A dreamy expression crossed his face, as if he were savoring a romantic memory. "I'm sure we can work this out," he said, "but let me sleep on it. We'll meet again day after tomorrow."

"Is he really your friend?" Kate asked when they were outside. "I didn't like how he looked at me. Like I was a rock under his microscope."

Blake shrugged, mumbling a vague reply. They left, and returned the stone and its container to Kate's safe deposit box at Chase Manhattan. He drove silently back to Penn Station, where Kate bought a ticket for the next train to Philadelphia.

Alone in the station, Kate felt an overwhelming sense of uncertainty. From the moment Irina uttered the words, "They have found us," everything in her life had changed. It was as if she'd washed ashore on an uncharted island. To survive, she must endlessly press ahead, push on through a jungle of doubt. Meanwhile, the future seemed formless, shifting as quickly and easily as the imaginary sand beneath her feet.

Before boarding, Kate glanced up and down the platform. Her eyes searched for a thick-shouldered Slav.

"**You've learned** nothing new?" Kate couldn't hide her disappointment. She'd called MacMahon for a meeting as soon as she got home. Now they sat across from each other at a small desk in a spare office at the Marion police department.

"I'm sorry, Miss Gavrill, sometimes this work is slow. We've checked out the few leads we have. We've now got sworn witnesses who say those two men were smoking, and didn't appear to be Amish." MacMahon's eyes reflected compassion and concern. "Your mother's death was no accident, I'm sure of that."

"You were sure of that weeks ago!" The emotions she'd kept in check since Irina's death started to slip out of control. A trembling began in Kate's abdomen and spread to her shoulders.

MacMahon moved to the edge of his chair and stretched a hand toward her. He thought of his younger sister, about Kate's age. "Miss Gavrill," he said, "Please be careful. I'm concerned about you. I don't have all the answers yet, but from the beginning I've suspected these people killed your mother deliberately, for a reason. We found the car. They burned it up to destroy the evidence. But we found enough to know the engine had been modified by pros. It's tough. We know there were two men, everything points to them being gunsels for hire, but it's as if they vanished from the face of the earth. There's no reason to think you are in danger, but it is possible. We don't know what they were after, so it's hard to be sure."

Kate bit her tongue. Should she blurt out that she knew exactly what the men were after and why? That she bloody well knew she was in danger? Somehow, she sensed that the backstory—including her escape from Russia and the business about Krasky following her to Penn Station—should stay under wraps, at least for now. The first questions out of any law officer's mouth would be how had she obtained the stone, and why, in both Russia and America, had she worked outside official channels with private citizens rather than authorities.

She shook her head. She'd gone so far beyond anything she would have wildly considered doing just a few short weeks ago—so far beyond anything even faintly resembling safe boundaries.

Kate stood, turning to face the wall, out of MacMahon's direct line of sight. Her sobs came in a rush. The law officer rose, and walked behind the small desk. He touched Kate's shoulder, then circled his arm around her. She leaned into him, feeling suddenly small and more than a little afraid.

PROPPING HIS elbows on the high countertop, Jacob Massad braced his forehead against the heels of both hands. He peered into the fiery planes of a five-carat, pigeon-blood ruby. He'd owned this, the centerpiece of his very private gem collection, for more than a decade. He still marveled at the stone's purity of color and brilliance.

It was a fine ruby, rivaling even the best museum specimens in every way but size.

Massad's was an eccentric, costly, clandestine and sometimes illegal hobby. His private collection was housed in a safe within a safe. To view Massad's commercial inventory, customers entered the room-size chamber in which he stood, a cinder block fortress and his main business vault. But Massad kept his special stones in a separate dual-combination tool-and-torch-proof floor safe. No one else had ever seen its contents.

Painstakingly acquired over many years, all the gems were world-class, the best specimens privately available. Resting regally on a six-inch square of black velvet, this blazing carmine stone had only become his after lengthy and bizarre negotiations.

As always, he'd been careful not to insult either the jewel or its seller. But with his Middle Eastern bargaining skills and almost unlimited cash resources, Massad nearly always got the piece he wanted.

Massad shifted his 5'-6" frame and patted the white curls at the base of his neck. He looked longingly again at the ruby.

Ten years before, the stone had been a consolation gift to himself. At age fifty-nine and as an eight-year widower, Massad had finally acknowledged that he would never remarry.

His feelings for women, he found, had reached a kind of equilibrium with his appreciation for gems, growing at once more refined and more superficial. In both cases, it was the surface physical appearance that drew him. What was visible was honest. What you saw, you could trust. The rest—the subtleties of character, personality and emotion—remained infinitely variable and always subject to interpretation. Young women lured him with charms as clear-edged and directly apparent as a jewel's facets, undiminished by age or guile.

Regrettably, the most attractive younger Persian Jewish women were already the captives of arranged marriages. Thus, when Jacob

Massad sought female companionship, he purchased it. Similarly, to meet his exacting standards for gemstones, at times Jacob Massad had been forced to make acquisitions through extralegal channels. He didn't try to excuse this behavior, any more than he apologized for his occasional calls to escort services.

Carefully, lovingly, Massad refolded the velvet around the ruby. Returning it to the safe, he pulled the heavy door shut, and spun the dials. His thoughts were already elsewhere—on what could be a last chance to possess the gem of a lifetime.

Chapter 29

———————⸺«◎»⸺———————

Two days later, Kate and Blake again sat in Massad's office. Their host went straight to the point.

"I will lend you the money," Massad said, handing Kate a typed agreement. His tone sounded as if he were making a pronouncement. "You will pay me back in twelve months, in cash, at fourteen percent interest. The interest portion will be paid every month, also in cash."

Blake nodded. "Tough terms. But fair. What are the penalties?"

"If Miss Gavrill doesn't pay me in full in twelve months, the stone is mine. As we agreed earlier, if she sells the stone within two years, I have first right of refusal. If she loses the stone, she owes me $3 million."

Blake and Kate looked at each other. Hardball the offer might be, but even these terms amounted to an act of kindness. No ordinary bank would make such a loan. Financial institutions rarely lent money on jewels, which were dead assets to a banker. And sharks would have charged far more, especially without the physical stone as collateral. Kate quickly signed the paper and they left.

After they'd gone, Massad stood near his small office window and tugged on an earlobe. Reaching into his lowest desk drawer, Massad drew out the old-fashioned black telephone he sometimes used when expanding his private collection. Its private line was still registered in his late wife's maiden name. The billing address was an anonymous post office box.

First, he called Larry Halset, a local private investigator.

His second call went to Colombia, to someone he'd known for years.

★　　★　　★

As PART of their training, Hector Molina explained, the students would be taught the seven bells exercise.

"You must practice as I do, each day," Molina said, his teeth flashing in a wickedly white smile. "It is the only way to achieve complete control of every part of your body."

Contained in a soft oval, Molina's dusky features—a delicate nose, large brown-black eyes and full, romantic lips—could almost be described as angelic. Despite his 39 years, at 5'-10" and 165 pounds, he was as slender and agile as a boy, attributes basic to the master thief he'd become as an adult.

Thievery of jewels had lifted Hector Molina from Bogota's hardscrabble slums to luxury. Now he served as mentor emeritus to a new generation of picaroons. The cartel saw to it that, in return for polishing the skills of their best and brightest *estudiantes*, he lived very well indeed.

No longer, however, did he live happily. Staying at the top of his profession meant trusting no one. His life lacked a lover, a caring relative or even a close friend. Suddenly, desperately, Molina wanted to end his loneliness. At an age when many Latin men were counting their grandchildren, Molina craved a family.

The need to be free clawed inside him, like a ferret in a bag. Hector Molina wanted out of the cartel.

Separation would not be easy, but that he already knew. Once "made," a cartel member's only severance from his employers came with death. But some—admittedly few, but some—had disappeared. If he moved across the world, assumed a new identity, perhaps changed his appearance—who could say? Was he not, after all, a master of diguise as well as imitation? His work had created a global network of trusted contacts and colleagues who could help.

Now, tapping a pencil against his lower lip, Molina paced in a small circle before his class. "As a philosopher said," he intoned rhetorically, repeating a phrase he'd used many times, "discipline is the ancestor of excellence. It is the predecessor of precision and the precursor of progress."

To graduate, each student would be required to pass two tests. The first: a simple but real-life pickpocket theft wearing two of the bells. Next, working as a team, they must steal an item of high value from a specific victim. One would be the pickpocket or grab man, one the driver, one the technician—usually a specialist in electronics, especially alarms—and, finally, a fourth, the group's leader and planner. Hector made the assignments based on his personal assessments of the students. Only after successfully completing both capers would they graduate.

Molina was interrupted by the telephone. The call came from his superiors, speaking on a secure line from across town.

"It is time for the return of 'El Mimico'," the voice said, using Molina's former nickname as a thief. He'd become renowned for his proficiency at imitating voices familiar to his victims. Besides serving as a valuable tool for gathering pre-theft intelligence, his ruses drew owners away from their gems, minimizing the likelihood of gunplay. As a result, Molina had never felt the need or any desire for a weapon. In fact, as the years passed and his professional confidence grew, Molina became outright disdainful of violence and its instruments. He forbade his students to carry so much as a knife.

"I am inactive," Molina said, "you know that." His last theft for the cartel had been nearly two years ago.

"We have a special challenge, one that requires your skills," came the retort. "Our intelligence sources have detected the movement of a large emerald—or ruby—through Moscow, destined for America.

The stone was successfully disguised to pass through customs. There already have been two Russian mafia attempts to steal it, both unsuccessful."

Molina protested, "You don't even know what kind of gem it is"—but his superior would not be dissuaded. "This may be the biggest single-stone opportunity in many years," the voice said, "and you are the best thief in a nation of thieves. You must leave for New York at once. Your first class tickets will be in the usual place."

Hanging up the phone, Molina felt a twinge of excitement. In a twenty-five-year career, this sounded like a worthy challenge.

But it also meant backpedaling from his dream. Molina wanted out, not deeper in. Even one arrest would make escape infinitely more difficult, reduce his chances of ever moving in "normal" social circles, and again put him firmly under the cartel's thumb. Skilled thieves could count on at least three significant prison terms during their careers. He'd never served a single day. How much longer could he expect to stay lucky?

Molina crossed the room and stared at the sidewalks far below. None of his arguments mattered. He simply wasn't prepared to break away. Not yet. He hadn't made the necessary arrangements. He wasn't rich enough. He must accept the assignment. Dismissing his class early, Molina rode the elevator downstairs and entered a dark bar on the ground floor. Molina rarely drank, but on this late afternoon he needed a mood chaser. He drank enough wine to get sleepy, then took the elevator back up to his condo and fell into bed.

The next morning the telephone rang again, with a call from New York City. And on this occasion, when Hector Molina replaced the receiver, he was smiling.

Chapter 30

FOR KATE, the past few hours had been a blur. She'd met for a second time with the attorneys, given them Massad's $500,000 as a retainer and authorized the Cushing firm to access her safe deposit box in case they needed to ship the documents, gem and egg to London. Such a shipment, they stipulated, would only occur via armed courier.

Now, rushing to get ready for dinner with Simon Blake, she brushed on her lipstick. So much had been crammed into the weeks since her mother died that sometimes it seemed as if Irina the person was being pushed out of her consciousness. Steadily, the grief, anger, and guilt that Kate felt at Irina's loss was giving way to the day-to-day business of making her mother's dreams come true. It was as if the older woman were urging, *Don't memorialize me. Make my life count by what you do.*

Her cell phone rang.

"Kate, this is Dr. Borshel. I realize it's been years since we talked, but I felt I should call. I got your phone number from the college. As a matter of fact, I'm calling all my former patients as a courtesy. There's been a break-in at my home office."

"I'm sorry to hear that," Kate replied. She knew the psychiatrist had moved to New York, but she hadn't spoken to him in more than a decade, and couldn't stay on the phone long. "I guess crime even comes to Park Avenue. It's terrible, but how does this affect me?"

"The break-in apparently happened two weeks ago. The funny thing is I didn't notice at first. I'm semi-retired now and it took me that long to realize one of the file cabinets had been jimmied. Very carefully. The cops say they were probably looking for laptop computers—I don't even own one."

"So?"

"As far as I can tell all the files are intact, except yours. Some of the tests you took back in college and a videotape are missing. The police think they were interrupted and just ran with whatever they were holding."

"Well I don't know what that stuff would be worth to anybody." Kate got a mental picture of Simon Blake pulling up his sleeve to peer at his watch.

"Kate, they also took newspaper clips about coach Nars and the diving mess. I think your name is mentioned in some of the articles."

"Is my file the only one missing?"

"No. They also took two of my papers based on government research I conducted years ago. About hypnosis. The hypnotic virtuoso phenomenon, actually. I meant to speak to you about it when you came to see me. Funny, it's been on my mind—"

"Dr. Borshel, I'm late for an appointment. I'd like to catch up, but can we talk some other time?"

They said good-byes, but the call was more than a little troubling. Had it been a random break-in as the police suggested, or were her files targeted? And if so, why?

BLAKE WAS already seated. But he stood when Kate arrived and as she hurriedly explained she'd been delayed by a call from her doctor.

"I'm sorry." His face reflected concern. "I didn't know you were ill."

"Uh, I'm not," she said, feeling awkward. "I saw him when I was in college."

"What for?"

"Nothing. I-I hadn't been to him for years." Why had she brought it up?

Blake frowned. "Well, what kind of a doctor is he?"

Kate looked away. The restaurant was brightly lit and noisy, with shiny floors and hard surfaces. Everyone, including Blake, seemed to be talking in a loud voice. Their meeting tonight should be all—and only—about business. "He was my sports psychiatrist," she finally replied. "I went to him for some problems I was having diving."

Blake's eyes narrowed. "Your psychiatrist?"

Kate regarded him cooly. "*Sports* psychiatrist. I thought we agreed to keep our relationship on a professional basis. Anyhow, his call didn't have anything to do with my treatment." She quickly sketched Dr. Borshel's account of the break-in, omitting any mention of the missing news clips. Her story only intensified Blake's concern.

"Think about it, Kate," he said, touching her right hand. She pulled it back and put it in her lap. Blake went on: "Thieves looking for laptops don't break into file cabinets. Nobody even has file cabinets anymore. They took personal records from your folder. Was anything else missing?"

"Something, some work he'd done for the government a long time ago."

Blake scrunched his lips. "Somebody could be looking for an address, trying to find you. What if it's that Russian cop?"

"Ukrainian, actually. Anyhow, I've moved a bunch of times since then. I saw Dr. Borshel when I was in college, in New Jersey." Kate gazed at the ceiling. Oh, why did I say anything?

"Look, I know about this," Blake said. "In my business, I have to. No professional thief would break into a retired doctor's office to steal a couple of paper files and an old video tape."

Kate turned away to look at the other diners. She was sick of his prying. She was even more weary of the you're-just-a-foolish-girl-who-needs-me-to-protect-her routine.

"Frankly, I don't want to talk about it anymore. I'm 31-years-old—not 28—and I can take care of myself. Let's order dinner."

Blake glanced around the room and then at her. "Listen," he said in a hushed voice, "I'm concerned about you. I don't want to see you get hurt. And we can dance around it all you want, but the fact is there are feelings between us. We both know it. I want to talk about it."

Kate stared at her wine glass. That sounds like the woman's line, she thought, just before she asks why the guy isn't ready to make a commitment. Where was he coming from?

"I thought," she said, "that we agreed to forget the other night. We were just two people, maybe a little lonely, thrown together in the big city, both excited about the stone. Okay, so we lost our heads. Anyhow, what happened happened. Right now we both need to keep our focus on professional, not personal, objectives."

She knew in a way it was a dodge. Clearly, strong emotions *were* simmering between them. But she hadn't expected—or wanted—to confront the subject so directly. Keeping her voice low and her eyes on her plate, she went on. "In any case, I can't afford to deal with this now."

"If not now, when?"

She lifted her gaze to meet his. "Certainly not until I file my claim with the bank of England or, God forbid, until after the first of September."

"You have to face life, Kate," he said. "You can only run from feelings so long." For the second time, he reached across the table for her hand. Again, she pulled away. They finished their meal in silence.

Blake rose to help her with her chair, but Kate pushed back from the table on her own. She'd probably said more than she should. And the truth was, aside from the personal issues he'd thrust into their meeting, she had the same frustrating questions Simon Blake did. Could it really be mere coincidence that someone had broken into Dr. Borshel's office? Who would want to pore over research he'd conducted back in the sixties? Or, for that matter, to pry into her own musty records of a decade earlier?

Kate opened the restaurant door and stepped out into the humid Manhattan evening. Reaching in her skirt pocket, she touched a piece of folded paper. It was from the notepad she'd absently written on while phoning Simon from Moscow. Unfolding the scrap, Kate saw her own given name—Katya—scrawled over and over again.

#

Chapter 31

HECTOR MOLINA's rented black Lincoln Town Car was waiting at the curb when he walked out of the St. Pierre Hotel on Fifth Avenue. He immediately recognized the driver as a "wheelman" he'd worked with in the past.

"Buenas dias, *El Mimico*," greeted Ricardo Mondalvo, "It's been too long." He handed a small snapshot over his shoulder. "This is Kate Gavrill," he said, continuing in Spanish. "Too skinny for me, but a looker, yes?" He chuckled. "Perhaps this time you will get a bigger reward for your services than a cold gem."

Molina smiled but did not respond. He held the photograph gently, as if it were a rare watercolor. Taken with a long lens, the photo showed Kate, in tight leather pants and bustier, as she had appeared during her first two days back from Russia. If Molina found her attractive, it was not evident: His expression remained impassive. His only comment was a terse question: "What kind of stone?"

"We still aren't sure. Somehow she coated the gem with wax or grease before bringing it through. We think it's an emerald or ruby. There's an odd thing though." He paused.

Molina leaned forward.

"We've been watching her since she arrived. But she is also being followed by someone else." Mondalvo handed Molina a second photograph. "This one you better be careful of, amigo."

Molina shrugged. The image depicted a large Slavic man aiming a camera with a telephoto lens. "He looks Russian. They are all stupid. What is he photographing?"

"He seems to be interested in the man Miss Gavrill has been seeing lately."

Hector's mobile phone rang. *"Hola,"* he said into the phone.

The caller was a real estate agent in Bogota, informing him that—as he requested—his condo had been privately listed for sale.

"Gracias," he said to the caller, smiling to himself. He'd taken the first step toward a new life.

Turning back to Mondalvo, he picked up their conversation.

"And who would that be?"

"A prominent gemologist named Simon Blake. The gem could be in his office safe."

"Has the Russian tried to steal it?"

"Not that we know of. But he met with some other Russians who broke into an apartment on Fifth Avenue a few nights ago. So far as I can tell, the two events aren't related. You know these *Mafiya*. They're all just common criminals."

"Does this Russian have a rented car?"

"A Towncar. Just like this one. It's parked in the garage of his hotel, the main Hilton on Sixth Avenue."

Molina paused for a moment, weighing the information.

The driver broke the silence. "You want me to punch it?" he asked, referring to a favorite ploy among Colombian jewel thieves. The technique called for drilling a small hole in the red lens of a prospective victim's taillight. Barely visible during the day, at night the opening emitted a brilliant white glow, making a car easier to identify and follow.

Hector Molina stared out the window. A sourness low in his stomach told him how badly he wanted this to be his last job. His head dropped in a nod. "Do it tonight," he said. "And put taps on both men's phone lines. I want studio quality recordings of their voices."

"Done, said the driver, smiling and speaking in a mix of English and Spanish. "*El Mimico* returns, *si, jefe?*"

Molina's face was somber. "Let's try and get there first. Sooner or later this big Russian will succeed. I don't relish having to steal the stone from him."

Chapter 32

"**I** GUESS I don't understand why we even need these new tests," Kate said. An hour after their dinner, she was still feeling combative as they left the city. Nestled in the big Bentley cosseting passenger's seat, Kate studied the outline of Blake's profile against the dark window, now spattered with summer rain. He looked almost belligerent. Kate sensed he was a man who, once he'd made up his mind, rarely changed course.

"My tests indicate with extremely high probability that the stone is genuine," Blake replied. "But nobody's perfect; there's always the small chance that I'm wrong. And meeting the deadline won't do us any good if we don't meet the conditions. We can't afford that risk."

"But I'm running out of time," Kate protested. "The bank deadline is just two weeks away. Besides, I thought your analysis proved the stone was genuine."

"This is just one more way of being absolutely certain," he said. "If we went in with only my analysis, the Bank of England is bound to require a backup certification. This way we're doing that step for them." He smiled and patted her arm. "But not to worry—your alexandrite is real."

Scattered, stop-start small talk made up their conversation during the rest of the drive from Manhattan.

While they chatted, Kate found her thoughts returning to the man beside her. Only last week, she'd melted in his arms. Now, they seemed like distant business partners, plotting their next moves. Mostly, what they shared was silence.

Condensation fogged the inside of the old car's windows. Blake reached across to crack the passenger's wing, lightly grazing her thigh. His touch recalled the fierceness of their hunger a week ago, and Kate's heart briefly raced. She turned away.

Behind them, the road stretched into the night, deserted except for a pair of headlights trailing far in the distance. Farther back, a second pair of lights escaped both Kate's and Simon's notice.

★   ★   ★

PROFESSOR ALAN Bertram's thatched brown hair fell over a nose that hooked as sharply as a parrot's bill and, magnified behind thick glasses, eyes that seemed as large as eggs. Lit by his desk lamp, the alexandrite sat between Bertram's hands, flaring crimson sparks. Turning the gem over in his hands, the scientist looked at Blake and Kate, his oversize orbs as sad as a Bassett hound's.

"I'm truly sorry," Bertram said, "but your stone is not natural."

Blake's stunned expression was only matched by his incredulity. "You must be mistaken," he said. After spending the night in separate rooms at a nearby motel, they'd delivered the stone as soon as Bertram's office opened, then waited in the hallway. The tests had taken less than ninety minutes. "Are you absolutely certain? I found no platinum residues of any kind in my tests."

"What does he mean?" Kate couldn't believe her ears.

"Synthetic stones are basically cooked in metal containers," Dr. Bertram explained. "Usually platinum. The process almost always leaves traces of the metal in the gem."

"But I specifically looked for that, and ruled it out," Blake protested.

"You shouldn't feel bad," Bertram said. "The Russians have come up with a new synthetic alexandrite that can only be detected at the molecular level. They're virtually impossible to identify without extremely sophisticated digital instruments. Actually, this is only the second one I've seen."

"I can't believe this. You must be mistaken." Blake felt as if he'd been kicked in the stomach.

"Well, of course you are free to seek a second opinion, but, unfortunately, there's little chance I'm wrong—I wish I were." Bertram replied. His eyes looked even sadder as he pushed a sheet of paper toward them. "The new Russian process is apparently used by criminal elements there. The police in Brighton Beach sent us one to test a few months ago. Completely mimics the natural in almost every way. In fact, I re-ran the entire suite of tests just to be sure. I've written you a certification memo reporting my findings. It's a great fake, it's a beautiful fake, but it *is* a fake. I am sorry."

Stifling a sob, Kate snatched up the alexandrite—and the report—and bolted for the door.

★   ★   ★

TWISTING SLIGHTLY, Blake hit the exit door's release bar in full stride, half-stumbling into the Institute's parking lot.

Still spattered by rain, the burgundy Bentley gleamed like a wet plum in the early morning sun. Beside it, Kate sprawled on the damp pavement, facing away from him. Moving rapidly, a hulking figure widened the distance between them. Kate heard the door open, lifted herself on one arm and turned back to Blake. Her eyes were wild.

"Forget me!" she screamed. "Get *him*! He's got the stone!"

A few feet beyond, Vulcan Krasky lumbered across the parking area toward his auto. Blake sprinted past Kate, cut him off, and dove straight into the slav's expansive but surprisingly well-toned waist.

175

Like wrestling bears, the men tumbled across the asphalt. Blake sprang up, sucker-punching Krasky with a solid shot across his cheekbone. The heavier man shook his large head and, from a half-crouch, launched a devastating uppercut toward Blake's chin.

Blake landed heavily on his back, out cold.

#

Chapter 33

Some 150 yards to the east, screened by a row of bushes, a black Lincoln sat on a small overlook. Soft eyes followed the action below through binoculars.

"He's knocked the gemologist down," Hector Molina said, "and he's not getting up."

Mondalvo was already turning the ignition key. Below, the big man had reached his car and was pulling away.

★   ★   ★

Sitting in the Bentley in the Institute parking lot, Kate's emotions swung between anger and despair. "That stone has to be real," she said. "I took it from a cadaver that hadn't been touched for eighty years. You told me they weren't even making synthetics then."

Blake rubbed his chin. Blood smeared his gums. "You've got to retrace every moment that the stone's been out of your sight."

"That's easy," Kate replied, her voice crisp. "Never. Not once. Except this morning with the professor. And then last week, when it was with you." Her left brow arched and her next sentence dripped with sarcasm. "You *do* remember that night, I hope."

"Are you suggesting *I* stole your stone?"

"I'm not suggesting anything. I'm merely stating the facts. The stone has been out of my sight exactly twice. One of those times the professor was testing it. The other time, you were."

"Do you think I would have taken that beating . . . that I would have chased that gorilla . . . if I had stolen your goddamned alexandrite?" Blake's voice rose. "You'd think I've never handled precious stones before. I'll tell you this: never have I been accused of being a thief." Through Blake's swollen lips, the last word came out as "teef."

Kate's gaze returned his heat. She knew she'd dug a hole with her words, but she had to vent at someone and Blake was the only person handy.

"All I know," she said, "is that my entire future collapsed this morning, and not through my doing. And, frankly, I wonder if you're being completely candid. Why did you want to come here in the first place? Was it because you were unsure of your own findings?"

"I'm not going to apologize to you," Blake replied archly. "I made an honest mistake. Not more than one person in ten thousand has ever even seen a real Russian alexandrite. In a twenty year professional career, I've seen perhaps fifty. Besides, as I told you before: Anybody in the business would have expected this test. And by the way, dear lady, the results saddle me with a problem every bit as big as yours.

"Jeeeezus," he said, and stopped talking.

"Look," he finally continued, "It took at least a year to grow a synthetic stone of that size and quality. So neither the professor nor I could have done it—we wouldn't have had the time. Either the stone was a fake from the beginning, or it was switched in Russia. And that leads us straight to your friend Novyck."

"The stone was only in his cell for an hour. And I was watching every minute."

"Did he see the original descriptions or a photo of the alexandrite?"

"I told you, he *had* a photograph. He gave it to me. Krasky got the picture in Kiev. Why?"

"Because *if* there is an original genuine stone, whoever made the fake had to have its specs. How big it was, its dimensions, how much it weighed. The one I tested matched the stone in the document you gave me—exactly."

"Imre Novyck had a photograph, and I showed him the stone's original documents when I visited him in Lefortovo. But he also may have had the stone's measurements earlier, through correspondence with my mother."

Fresh waves of regret swept over Kate. The stone she'd risked so much for wasn't real. Or it had been real, and one of two men she'd thought she could trust may have stolen it. Or the thief might be a harmless old professor. If MacMahon had only found the monsters who'd run down Irina everything might be clearer by now.

For the moment at least, she saw only a single course: Trust no-one.

"So, basically," Blake summed up, "We have two questions. Assuming a genuine stone exists, how was the synthetic made and how and when was the genuine stone switched?"

Kate rubbed her chin. Her anger ebbed, giving way to a sense of descending gloom. "Logically, I can see what you are saying, but it just can't be him. I have met this man. I know him. It just couldn't be him. His family has been serving mine for nearly a century."

Blake spoke to the windshield. "Yes, and see the result. After nearly a century, your ancestors are finally found, shot and scattered in a field." He paused. "What about the original stone? Could it have been switched? So that the stone you gave Imre wasn't real to begin with?"

"Not likely. Those coffins were sealed in the twenties."

Blake shook his head. "Well, at least we can forget the idea the original was a fake. The technology to create an imitation of this quality simply didn't exist then."

Kate clucked her tongue. "Which takes us back to Imre. I can't believe it. But you're right, I have to start there. Which means I have to go back."

Blake shifted toward her. "Not *you*, Kate, not alone. Not again. You must allow me to go with you. You could be risking your life, and I'm not sending a second person to Russia to die. As soon as you set foot in that country, there will be people quite willing and anxious to kill you. And once the thieves who struck us just now discover the stone they have isn't real, they may seek revenge.

"And there's something else too, something you need to know going in."

Kate waited expectantly.

"Even if it exists, you may never find the real stone. Many important collectors keep their gems secret. They simply aren't inclined to share their treasures, especially if they were obtained illegally. For them, the lure of owning such a stone is all about capturing its beauty for themselves."

Blake turned toward her, his voice becoming quiet. "Kate, the wisest course might be to give up now. Let it pass and move on with your life." His eyes measured her intently.

Kate stiffened. Was this just a ruse to throw her off the—perhaps his—trail? It didn't matter. She felt the same competitive impulse that swept her when she stepped out on the board before a dive. *Don't give up now, girl, not now. Think of us—your family who went before.*

To Blake, she said, "Don't you see? I don't have a choice. I *must* find it. I've got $500,000 riding on this. And a pile of my money—my family's money, Russia's money—is sitting in the Bank of England, soon to be escheated. Many people could benefit from those funds. Besides, I'll be damned if I'll let them get away with killing my mother." She brushed her palms across her thighs, then stared straight out the old car's windshield. "I'm a competitor, not a quitter."

Nodding, Blake shrugged. Kate couldn't tell whether the gesture was a sign of acceptance or resignation.

"I have a lot at stake too," he said. "As you point out so eloquently, my reputation is on the line." He briefly fell silent, then spoke again.

"All right, we'll go for it. But I've got to tell Massad."

Reflexively, Kate extended her hand, touching his forearm. "Please, don't. You can't tell him. What will we say? Sorry, I don't have the collateral for your loan anymore? Sorry, the stone's a fake? What good would that do?"

"I have to tell him. It's a matter of ethics and a twenty-year relationship."

At that moment, Blake's cell phone buzzed in the Bentley's glove box. He pulled the car over, opened the clamshell case and spoke.

"Yes, Jacob," Blake said, swiveling slightly away from her.

Kate sensed Massad was asking Simon whether she could hear.

"No," she heard Blake say, confirming her suspicion. "But go ahead, I'll just listen."

Blake's mentor spoke quickly and in a hushed voice. "I've learned something I thought you should know. Are you aware that Miss Gavrill has been treated for mental illness? Has she shown any signs of being unstable?"

Blake masked his surprise with a brusque tone. "Of course not," he replied.

"A source tells me she regularly saw a psychiatrist in college."

With Kate sitting so near, Blake opted to remain silent. Massad's informant was making a mountain out of a 10-year-old molehill. Probably just some p.i. running the meter on his day rate.

"There's something more," Massad's muted voice spoke into his ear again. "Some sort of scandal. I don't have details, but it was serious enough that she left Princeton and finished her degree at Penn State."

"Well, Miss Gavrill and I are going ahead with our plans," Blake said aloud. "I'll be in touch with you soon."

Returning the phone to the glove box, Blake gazed at the striking woman who sat next to him, her profile etched against the passenger window. Despite the stressful morning, her skin looked fresh and luminescent. Her lips, scarlet and succulent, curled in a mysterious smile. Turning the ignition key, he realized how very little he knew about her.

Chapter 34

———— ⫸⫷ ————

HECTOR MOLINA stood in the shadows cast by a collapsed pier, his form concealed by scattered pilings and debris. A parking lot and a stretch of sand separated him from a cheap oceanfront motel in Brighton Beach. As darkness fell, he grew more relaxed. During the day, his olive skin, dark eyes and Spanish accent made him uncomfortably obvious in this community of mostly pale, blue-eyed Russians and Ukrainians.

It was called "Little Odessa by the Sea" for a reason. Long home to the nation's largest population of Russian Jews, over the past decade Brighton Beach had become home to something else: the tentacles of the Russian mafia. Though much of the seaside town remained a pastiche of trash-littered lots, mob cash had built strip malls, flashy nightclubs and restaurants.

It was here Vulcan Krasky had come, seeking a safety zone until his return flight to Russia.

And it was here that Hector Molina had followed him.

Molina knew the chances of Krasky leaving the stone in his room were small. But he'd been watching the motel since early afternoon, hoping the other man would come out. Even the slimmest chance that the Ukrainian might leave the gem behind would make the time he'd invested worthwhile.

If Krasky were to leave the alexandrite in his room, its theft could still be relatively safe. Carefully executed, there'd be little risk of physical confrontation and—for a while at least—no one would know who'd taken the gem. He'd be gone, really gone. With plenty of time for a Spanish plastic surgeon to do his or her work, and for Hector Molina to become someone else.

Over the last few days, Molina had followed the same disciplined approach that had earned him an international reputation. He'd listened to Russian language recordings, eaten in Russian restaurants, and scanned quickie Russian language books. But mostly *El Mimico* had listened to recorded taps of Krasky's telephone conversations. Within a few days, to all but the most critical listener, Molina's voice became that of one of Krasky's local contacts. The vocal replica wasn't perfect—no mimic's ever is. But he'd mastered the vowel inflections and "tells"—breath patterns and favorite phrases that amounted to an auditory signature. For example, Krasky's most frequent Brighton Beach contact habitually snorted between sentences. And almost always began any new thought with the heavily accented English phrase, "that is to say."

Leaving his observation post, Molina walked from the motel parking lot to a phone booth across the street. His finger rested on a small tape recorder. Molina had electronically removed the voice from one of the tapes so that only the background noise of the Brighton Beach's busy Boardwalk could be heard. When Molina called now, Krasky would hear the authentic background of shouting shopkeepers, people talking and honking horns.

Minutes later, Molina "invited" Krasky to join him and couple of local "ladies" at a local Russian restaurant. Having heard his compatriot's voice only a few times, the big man easily fell for the ruse.

Molina crossed the street to the motel. He knew the deception would only hold briefly. When no one showed up, Krasky would begin fidgeting at the restaurant. Within half an hour, he'd be bound to call and discover he'd been duped. And never again would the big man be so easily fooled.

Using a lock pick that retracted like a fountain pen, Molina entered the motel room. Moving rapidly, he turned the mattress, checked the toilet tank and hacked the stuffing out of the room's single upholstered chair. Pulling open the nightstand drawer, he discovered a single one-way air ticket to Moscow, booked for that coming Sunday. Not until he fell to his hands and knees for a second look beneath the bed, did Molina glimpse the briefcase.

A bungee cord held the elegant container tight against the bottom of the mattress. Concealed by the valance and the dark shadows under the bed, the maroon calfskin case would have gone unnoticed by all but the most determined searcher. Molina's temples pounded as he freed the case and laid it down on the bed. His pick made quick work of the brass lock and in an instant the top flipped open.

Molina inhaled sharply. He'd not expected the contents, whose sight made him instantly nauseous. Polished brass knuckles with flesh-tearing spikes, a seven-inch switchblade knife, a nine-millimeter machine pistol and—in two sections—a sniper's high-power polycarbonate rifle and scope. All were nestled snugly into a fitted, Styrofoam lining. On top, lay a coiled wire garrote, its ends wrapped with non-slip tape.

Krasky had obviously secured his working tools for pick-up by a stateside "associate." The fact that to get past airport inspectors Krasky must dispose of these deadly implements did not keep Molina from feeling a twinge of fear mingled with his disgust. These were the tools of a killer, not a thief.

As he slipped out the door, Molina knew three truths he hadn't known before. First, Vulcan Krasky must be carrying the stone. Second, his own success—perhaps his survival—would now depend upon his skills as a pickpocket, skills he'd not actually plied in several years. Third, he must steal the alexandrite in the next thirty-six hours or be forced to follow Krasky to Russia. If Hector Molina were seeking a farewell challenge, he'd clearly found it.

★   ★   ★

Exhausted and cold, Molina resumed his watch from the shadows. It had taken longer than he expected for Krasky to return to the motel. The big Slav entered his room, then burst out again, pistol in hand. He paced up and down the length of the building in the vain hope of spotting the room's ransackers. Molina waited thirty minutes, then walked back to the street where he'd made the phone call. A few more blocks and he reached the darkened lot where his driver had parked the Town Car hours before. Moments later, the two men checked into the same motel where Krasky now slept unevenly only ten rooms away. Before turning in, Molina placed a small, folded piece of paper on the floor directly in front of Krasky's door. When he returned to the room, Molina picked up the telephone. While Ricardo Mondalvo snored, he booked three flights, the first for one-way first class accomodations to Barcelona, Spain; and then—the tickets he hoped not to use—for round-trip coach fare between New York and Moscow.

#

Chapter 35

"**W**HAT ARE we going to do?" As she sat beside him on the airplane, Kate's ice blue eyes fixed on Simon Blake's battered features.

He stared ahead, swollen lips pressed together like strips of uncooked meat. The rush to get to the airport had exhausted his last reserves. And he was still trying to assess Massad's disturbing news. Could it be true? She'd seemed tightly wound since the first day they met, but he'd never suspected that Kate might be mentally ill. Next to him, she sat stiffly, twisting her fingers together, occasionally chewing at her mouth. Wearing a set of loose-fitting exercise sweats, she seemed somehow smaller in the airline seat.

"At least you could have thought to send the stone by armored carrier," she said at last. Disdain edged her voice.

Simon suppressed an unaccustomed urge to smack Kate across her spoiled mouth. Who did this Russian princess think she was? Then his anger crumbled into guilt: He'd asked himself the same question. For three hundred and change he could have hired a security guard for a few hours.

And why hadn't he picked up that they were being followed out of New York? Truth be told, he'd been too distracted by the stone and the physical nearness of Kate. He still remembered brushing her thigh when he'd reached over to close her window in the rain.

Now, of course, that glow was gone, smashed into oblivion by the professor's finding, the theft of the stone and Massad's revelations. Before, he'd been drifting in a romantic haze with a woman he might love. Now, Blake found himself on a needle-in-a-hay-stack mission to a country he feared, accompanied by a woman who might not be stable.

Beside him, Kate looked away. Her thoughts also centered on their fateful drive to Massachussetts. Her mood, however, was even less romantic. She needed his help, but that didn't mean she had to trust him, or even like him. She kept recalling a pair of distant headlights in a sideview mirror. Had she missed a warning? How had Krasky known to follow them to Massachusetts?

KATE AWOKE to the steady roar of the aircraft engine—and to find Blake studying her closely. Moments after they'd changed planes in Paris following a long layover, she'd curled into her seat and fallen into a deep sleep. Now, somewhere over Poland, she'd reawakened. As an intensely physical person, Kate hated long-distance flying. Now, instinctively, she stood beside Blake's aisle seat and groggily began a series of deep knee bends.

"Look, I realize we've talked about this before," Blake began as soon as she sat down again. His voice, irritating in its intensity, cut through her comfortable drowsiness. "But if you've been treated for mental illness, I need to know."

Kate rolled her eyes. Even in first class, the cabin smelled of stale coffee, hours-old air and slept-in clothes. Clearly, he'd been simmering since their last discussion. "Why are you bringing this up again?"

Blake kept his voice low. "Before, you told me that years ago you saw a sports psychiatrist for a minor neurosis. Now I'm asking you directly, was it more than that? Do you have a history of mental illness? I'm not trying to pry. I need to know. It could be a safety issue for both of us."

"Whom have you been talking to?" She asked. "Have you had me investigated?"

"Massad mentioned something."

"*Mentioned* something," she mocked. "Lovely. Really lovely. So your best friend had me investigated?"

"I think he may have hired a detective." Blake paused, feeling cornered. "Do you think it's that unusual, to try and learn something about someone you loaned $500,000 to, and don't know much about?"

Kate hunched down in her window seat, forcing Blake to turn back to see her. She shoved up the shade, blasting his eyes with sunlight.

She brought her face close to his.

"He lent that money because of *you*, because of *your* relationship. And if he's sicced an investigator on me that's because of you too."

Abruptly, Kate's eyes grew moist.

"Since you think you know everything about me," she continued, "there are things you don't know. Some traumatic things happened in my life, beginning with the death of my father when I was a little girl. Later—years later, when I was in college—I made a bad decision. I hurt myself and my family. Mostly, I picked the wrong guy to fall in love with. But of course no emotionally healthy woman has ever done that. And that, Dr. Freud, is my extensive history of mental illness. Are you satisfied? Are you proud you and your friend invaded my privacy? For all I know that's who broke into Dr. Borshel's files." Kate glared at him through flooded eyes.

Blake devoutly wished he'd never brought up the subject.

But Kate had a head of steam. "What I've told you is part of me. I carry my own water and deal with my own problems, just like any other functioning adult. Why am I risking my life to find this damn stone? A big part of it is to make up for the pain I caused my mother. If you don't like it, that's too damn bad. And, no, I am *not* crazy." Though whispered, the vehemence of her words turned fellow passengers' heads.

Her shoulders shook. "I thought I could trust you," she said, inwardly cursing her unaccustomed fragility.

Stop your sniveling, she commanded herself. *He's not worth it.*

Blake stretched out a hand; she brushed it away.

"You *can* trust me," he insisted. "*I* didn't investigate anybody. And nothing has changed."

Kate turned away, feeling violated. She pushed her hands under her; the seat's slick leather chilled her palms.

KATE STRETCHED her arms as their plane approached Moscow. Blake's behavior troubled her on more than one level. From the outset, she'd known that her attraction to him bore a singular resemblance to the pull she'd felt toward Nars. Both were older, both secure in their professions, both seemingly emotionally strong. Blake was about the same age her father had been when he died—he even had grayish hair.

Imre, too, was older, and in many ways more intriguing. Here was a man whose family had earned the trust of hers for generations. He had history on his side, especially compared to Simon Blake, whom she'd known—what?—barely a month.

She dismissed Blake's suspicions of Imre. Someone else had switched the stone. In any case, of one thing she was certain: No matter what anyone said, the gem that blazed like blood in the catacombs of Kiev had been real.

Chapter 36

THE SOUND of a bell ringing softly at his elbow caused Molina to abruptly halt his morning exercises. Enraged, he ripped the bells from his naked body and flung them across the room, startling the snoring driver out of his sleep. Damn it to hell! He knew his body was getting older, but he also knew two hours of daily exercise kept it sound. Something—some frustration—must have broken his concentration.

Molina dressed and went outside. He crossed the street and entered a grimy corner diner, where he ordered breakfast. On the way back, he sidled by Krasky's room. The folded paper sat in front of the door, exactly where he'd placed it. That meant Krasky was still inside. Again, Molina retreated into the shadows of the piers.

For the next eight hours, Molina kept his vigil, alternately sitting, standing, squatting. Despite the soothing salt air, his entire body ached. At one point, he removed his shoes and rehearsed the opening moments of Swan Lake in the sand, his finely muscled legs kicking out in perfect arcs. He rested, leaning against the piers, his eyelids sliding to halfmast.

Mostly, he worried: Had Krasky somehow disposed of the stone during the previous evening?

Shortly before 7:00 P.M., the Ukrainian emerged, his dark hair slicked back, his heft draped gracefully by an elegant Italian suit. He pulled a white handkerchief from his sleeve, looking almost foppish as he blotted his brow.

Molina quick-stepped across the sand, slipping into the Lincoln's front passenger seat. "Vamanos compadre," he ordered Mondalvo. They followed the bright spot in the other man's taillight as Krasky drove out. Approaching an upscale seafood restaurant, Krasky pulled over. Two fleshy blondes and a short, swarthy man approached his car. After introductions, the foursome entered the building.

After Mondalvo parked the car, Molina waited several minutes, then followed the foursome inside. He found a table on the opposite side of the room, where he could study his prey at a safe distance. Molina saw no evidence Krasky was carrying the stone—no bulge in his coat, no fanny pack or brief case, and he wore no vest.

The Latin felt apprehensive again. Could the stone be in an inconspicuous parcel on its way to Moscow? Not a chance, he answered himself. No thief would trust that stone to a courier. Perhaps, through accomplices, he'd secured it someplace locally, say in a bank safe deposit box. Molina stared across the room again, his eyes raking the Slav's bulky form. Krasky rose, started walking, and for a moment seemed headed straight toward him. Molina's heart leapt. Then the big man veered to his left, making for the bar.

Standing, Krasky leaned forward, and hooked his shoe on the bar rail. When he reached down and rubbed his right leg, Molina spotted the small lump below his calf.

Of course. How had he missed it? An ankle pouch. Usually supported by straps that looped below the heel and around the lower leg, the pouches were often used by couriers and jewelry salesmen to conceal their precious cargo. The container rode just above the ankle, large enough to carry a bracelet or necklace, a man's watch or—as in this case—even an outsized jewel.

Molina left the restaurant. He'd located his target now, and he knew precisely where and when he and Vulcan Krasky would meet.

★　　★　　★

EARLY MORNING. A brightly lit corridor at Kennedy International Airport. Vulcan Krasky felt the merest brush of air against the left side of his coat. He noticed an Hispanic-looking man passed him as they both approached the KLA check-in area. But in that fleeting moment, Krasky failed to see or sense the shiny metal disc Hector Molina slipped into his pocket.

A green cylinder rolled slowly past Krasky's foot. The Ukranian blinked. It was a tightly wound wad of $100 bills.

The Hispanic man knelt beside him, but Krasky got there first, stooping from his waist to retrieve the money.

Fingers light as breezes touched Krasky's ankle.

Awkwardly, both men rose at the same time, nearly colliding.

"Pardon me," Krasky said politely, almost as if he were speaking to a stylish woman. He handed over the roll. "Is this your money?"

Murmuring thanks, the man with curved lips and soft eyes turned away. Moments later, a security guard glared at Krasky as the metal detector buzzed.

"I'm sorry, sir," said the guard, "you'll have to step over here." When he triggered the buzzer for the third time, Krasky was motioned to one side, where another guard held an electronic wand.

Krasky's blunt features bore a puzzled frown. He'd been careful to remove any traces of ferrous metal before approaching airport security. Of course, he'd returned the borrowed suitcase of weapons to his Brighton Beach colleagues. He'd emptied his pockets of coins and keys. He'd even thrown out a package of chewing gum and taken off his belt.

The guard traced the wand over his large upper frame. Krasky's eyes followed the device down to his own waistline.

"I believe it's something in your pants pocket, sir," said the officer triumphantly. Krasky reached into his pocket, and pulled out a foil strip about the size of a stick of gum. He must have missed it when—

He felt a sudden nakedness at the end of his leg. The pouch—and the treasure it contained—had been cut away clean.

Krasky started screaming.

"You fools," he yelled in Russian. Two security guards quickly seized both arms. "That man—that faggot Mexican—stop him! He's a thief!"

Jerking an arm free, Krasky gestured frantically down JFK's huge polished corridor. But there was no one to be seen.

UNTIL HE stepped into the Boeing's tiny john, Hector Molina's flight to Barcelona had been uneventful. Now, as he sat on the commode, the severed pouch seemed heavy in his hand. He'd cut it clean, bringing a single-edge razor within a fraction of an inch of Krasky's skin. Now the leather straps dangled like fringe from their container.

The stone slipped into his fingers and with it a scrap of paper. In the low fluorescent lighting, the gem gleamed a deep green.

Molina unfolded the paper and his world changed.

"MASSACHUSETTS GEOLOGICAL INSTITUTE," the letterhead read, and in smaller type, "Official Analysis."

The document bore a date only a few days old. Under the heading "Certification," it listed a series of tests, culminating with the label, "SPECTROPHOTO ANALYSIS" typed in capital letters across the middle of the page. It went on: "This stone is certified as synthetic chrysoberyl, species hydrothermal alexandrite, probably Russian in origin. Test performed using two-stage, infrared Spectrophotometer." The document was signed, "Alan Bertram, Phd."

Molina groaned. The big Russian could not have avoided seeing the paper, but his lack of technical knowledge about gems—and his poor English—had combined to make the report indecipherable. Molina, by contrast, instantly recognized its significance.

The Latin rose, stared into the mirror and rubbed his chin. His skin felt suddenly clammy, as if he were coming down with a cold.

What had happened? Clearly, the young woman who brought the alexandrite into the U.S. believed it was real. A corrupt customs agent might have switched it. Another possibility would be that someone in Russia made the switch, so perhaps the real stone had never left that country. Or, of course, it could have been a fake all along.

There was a good chance he'd never know the answers to these questions. But this Molina *did* know: His dream of stealing the alexandrite, changing his identity and disappearing in Europe lay in ruins. He could no longer afford the plastic surgery, let alone the purchase of an annuity to fund his hoped-for retirement. And if he tried to pawn off the synthetic as genuine, he'd either be killed or arrested.

Arriving in Barcelona, Molina immediately booked a return flight to New York.

Arriving at JFK International in Manhattan, he stepped into the first class lounge, called his real estate agent in Bogotá and cancelled the listing. If his superiors found out about his trip to Barcelona, he'd pass it off as a vacation gone awry.

He faxed his contact in Colombia a copy of Prof. Robertson's report, then called on a voice line.

"Tell our friends in Bogotá to be more careful when they send me on an assignment," Molina said. "El Mimico does not like to waste his time, or to take great risks for nonexistent rewards."

"I'm going to remain here for a few days," he continued. "I intend to enjoy myself at the cartel's expense. Do not disturb me unless it is for a very good reason."

Reaching his room, Molina made another call. "I'm afraid our arrangement is cancelled," he said. "The stone is a synthetic. I'm mailing you a photocopy of the certification report." He heard an oath as he returned the receiver to its cradle.

For a moment, Molina had a mental picture that made him cringe. It was an image of the container he'd opened at the motel: Vulcan Krasky's weapon-crammed suitcase of horrors.

Chapter 37

SIMON BLAKE spoke to the curator of the Catacombs through a translator, turning to Kate to relay what he was saying. While Blake stood inside the monk's tiny office, the cramped space forced Kate to linger in the doorway, just out of earshot. Directly across a small courtyard was the entrance to the caves.

The old monk's answers were less than satisfying.

"He says the glass covers were actually installed over the coffins in the late 1940s," Simon said. "Each lid was sealed with wax, and none of the seals were broken until recently."

For a moment, Kate relived her terror when the coffin lid slipped from its resting place and shattered on the Catacombs' stone floor. She'd never actually seen the wax, but it might explain why she'd lost her grip.

Blake spoke to the monk, and the old man began thumbing backwards through an oversize guest registry on the counter.

"*Julio* 30!" he abruptly cried. Blake relayed the man's chatter in sound bites—"lid shattered . . . broken glass . . . only break-in in fifty years"—but the additional words were needless. Kate instantly understood; he was describing the night she'd reclaimed the Romanov Stone.

Two hours later, they sipped aperitifs on Kate's hotel balcony. Kate watched distant lights sparkle on the Denier River and realized

197

she'd been standing in the same spot little more than a month ago. But there was an important difference: That night she'd believed the stone would soon be in her possession.

She still resented Simon's insinuations about her mental health. He couldn't escape responsibility for a serious professional lapse, but he seemed to have concluded that endlessly beating up on Imre was a no-win strategy. She sensed, on his part, a slight move toward accommodation.

"Maybe he can help us," Simon proffered, referring to Novyck without using his name.

Kate nodded, sipping the cool, slightly acidic drink.

"Imre obviously wields power within the walls of Lefortovo," she said. "If the real stone wound up in some criminal underground in Russia or the Ukraine, who would have a better chance of tracing it?"

Stepping closer to the balcony's edge, Kate looked over the city. She could see the less than pristine district where she'd spent the night after finding the Romanov stone. Memories of that evening drifted back to her. She saw herself walking down the inn's narrow corridor, carrying a bathrobe and a towel. She'd desperately needed to get out of her sweaty clothes and out of that tiny, dingy room. At one point, she'd taken a shower. Could she have left the stone unattended, even briefly?

"Who am I kidding?" she said aloud. "Maybe I lost it. Maybe they switched it while I was in the toilet." By now, the damn stone could be anywhere.

"Well, we know Krasky didn't switch it," Blake said. "Otherwise, why would he have followed us all the way to Massachussetts? To steal a fake?"

Kate shrugged. Someone at Lefortovo other than Imre might have substituted the fake stone. But how and who? It could have happened at the inn where she spent her last night in Kiev. But she'd slept with the gem under the covers. Perhaps the woman who sat beside her on the plane swapped it while she was sleeping. Or the customs inspector when he asked her to remove the stone and necklace. Unlikely on both counts, but who knew? One person increasingly seemed a less likely suspect if, indeed, he had ever been one at all: Simon Blake. She'd lashed out at him in anger after Professor Bertram's proclamation that the alexandrite wasn't genuine. But Blake had too much to lose—and had already risked a great deal—to benefit from a forgery.

Dropping her chin in her hands, Kate emitted a weary sigh. She wore a thin short-sleeved blouse. The cool, humid air chaffed her skin into goose bumps.

"It's all about the chain of custody," Kate said finally. She dropped into a metal chair. "And we've got some very weak links."

Blake chewed his lip. "Right. The best course is to take this a day at a time. It could easily have been someone other than Imre Novyck." He stepped behind her, and his large hand fell protectively on her shoulder.

"But I can't take it a day at a time—there are only 10 days left."

"All we can do is what we can do," Blake replied. His hands began a gentle massaging motion. "Even if Novyck can't locate the stone himself, he may know who can."

Blake moved down her arms, kneading her biceps. His fingers seemed to pluck each tendon individually, like chords on a cello. Kate's head lolled back, and she looked at him through half-closed, unfocused eyes.

Still standing behind Kate, Blake leaned forward and outlined her forearms with his palms, which came to rest in her hands.

Careful! A warning voice grated in her head. *You've been down this path before.*

"I'm just so damned tired," Kate said aloud.

Blake peered at her, but did not reply. His hands resumed their work.

Kate grew limp as she gave in to Simon's strength. Under her blouse, her breasts swayed in cadence to the movement of his hands.

Abruptly, Blake halted the massage and stepped around the chair. He traced his left forefinger along the side of her neck.

"You know what Mae West said," he joked. "Give a man a free hand and he'll run it all over you.

"Kate," he said, making a quick turn to seriousness, "I'm beginning to realize that, since we met, everything I've done—and not done—has driven us apart. It's not what I want, and I'm sorry."

The sincerity of his apology—coupled with her utter relaxation—seemed to rupture an inner dam. Kate moved imperceptibly closer to him, her lips parting as if to speak.

"Listen," she said finally. She took a deep breath. "There are some things I should tell you. About the trouble I got into in college."

"Not now," he said smiling. "Whatever happened, it was a long time ago. I care about the beautiful grown woman here beside me. Tell me when we're old and gray."

He knelt and kissed her, slipping his hand around her waist and pulling her toward him.

"No," she said weakly. But Blake's fingers twisted a button and moved inside her blouse. She hooked her right arm around his neck and crushed his lips to hers.

You can't let this happen again!

Kate gently pushed him away. But their fingers remained tangled and she squeezed his hand tightly before letting go.

Chapter 38

VULCAN KRASKY'S Brighton Beach buddies caught up with Hector Molina as he crossed Fifth Avenue into Central Park.

An hour later, they were alone in Molina's St. Pierre Hotel room, the smaller man gagged and bound by duct tape to a silk-cushioned Chippendale chair.

Krasky quickly got to the point.

"Pretty little man," he said, "you may have made a fool of me once, but you are not the only one with friends in Colombia. Perhaps it would have been wise to be less famous. Your reputation, as they say, preceded you."

Molina fastened terrified eyes on the case Krasky had been carrying when he broke in. It lay, ominous and unopened, on the bed.

As Molina looked on mutely, Krasky methodically tore apart the room, ripping out drawers, spilling the contents of the Latin's luggage across the floor, upending mattresses and cushions.

After fifteen futile minutes, the big man collapsed beside his prey.

Sweating profusely, Krasky swabbed a sleeve across his dripping brow. "You will tell me where it is," he grunted. Krasky rose and walked to the other side of the bed. Popping the case's latches, he raised the lid and studied its contents.

After giving Molina a long look, Krasky walked slowly into the bathroom. Minutes later, he reappeared carrying one of the hotel's large white terry cloth towels—dripping wet—and an ice bucket filled with water. Pulling the gag—a wadded embroidered handkerchief—from Molina's mouth, he wound the towel around the man's head.

Molina could barely breathe.

Krasky loosened the towel, and it fell around the Latin's shoulders.

"Didn't you understand the certification report?" Molina said, choking out the words. "The stone I took from you was a synthetic. But the real stone must exist. Blake and the woman would not have taken the fake for testing unless they thought it was real. So there is only one place the genuine alexandrite can be—still somewhere in Russia or the Ukraine, probably still in possession of whoever made the switch."

Krasky grunted skeptically. "They could have already sold it."

"Not likely, not a stone of that significance and value. It would be too hot. There isn't a fence in the world who would touch it yet. Believe me. I know them all." Molina knew this was a lie, but he hoped Krasky would buy it.

"Look, the point is we should be working together. I know a way we can both win."

Krasky moved back toward the suitcase. Molina took a deep breath, for the first time spotting a way out of this. The Slav pulled on a single heavily weighted black glove. Such devices were the *mafiya* executioner's coup de grace, used to pound the recipient's insides. The victim suffered massive internal bleeding and, often, an agonizing death.

Instead, however, Krasky appeared to change his mind. He pulled off the glove, turned back to Molina, and picked up the half-full ice bucket.

"Suppose everything you say is true, pretty little one," he said, sneering. "For what does Vulcan Krasky need you?"

"You need me because I am the best thief in the world. I stole the stone from you and you didn't even know it, right?"

Krasky backhanded Molina across the face. "Don't remind me!" The blow left Molina with a bleeding nose.

The violent act seemed to calm the Ukrainian. He knew his own career and life might also be in jeopardy—not from his captive, certainly not from Blake and the Gavrill woman, but from Boris Lada. Yet if the stone Molina took was a fake, and the real gem was still in Russia, why hadn't his capos known that beforehand? Why had they sent him on a wild goose chase? Or, a darker possibility: One of his own men in Kiev had stolen the alexandrite and was setting him up.

Sensing the other man's hesitation, Molina moved in.

"Imagine what a team we'd make," he said, "with my stealth and your strength. And, of course, courage."

Krasky faced him again, but this time he was listening.

"Think of this," Molina went on. "If a real stone exists, there's never been anything like it. It's worth millions. Tens of millions. It could set us both up for life—if we so choose."

"Pretty talk from the pretty man."

Molina lowered his voice, trying to sound confident. "No, this is real talk," he said. "I have a buyer, on the black market. He will pay $40 million in U.S. dollars on delivery."

Krasky looked at him. Molina could sense the other man teetering.

"Why should I trust you?"

When Krasky uttered the question, Molina knew he'd won. Even before the big man finished pulling off the duct tape, they'd agreed to the rough outlines of a deal: Krasky would stall his bosses, and they'd steal the stone back for themselves. A 50–50 split.

"What of the girl and her jeweler boyfriend?" Krasky asked.

"My people followed them to the JFK airport," Molina replied, "they were heading to Moscow." Standing at the bathroom sink, he moistened one corner of his St. Pierre bathrobe and gently daubed the blood at his nose. The swelling looked less serious than he'd expected.

"Ummmmm. So they will be on—how do you say—my turf," Krasky said. "We can let them lead us to the stone. I like this plan already."

Rubbing his throbbing nose, Molina shot Krasky a reflected glance in the mirror. "I'll call my travel agent and book the tickets on my card," he said. "Consider it an investment in our collective future."

Chapter 39

THEIR CAB smelled stuffy, but Kate didn't notice. She sat close to Simon Blake, her head brushing his shoulder, her body crooked into the long gully of his arm stretching across the back seat. Still in the glow of their last evening in Kiev, she felt closer to him than since they'd met.

Blake gazed out at Moscow's drab tapestry of gray concrete, soot-stained masonry and black business suits. He glanced down at Kate. Afternoon sun glossed the top of her hair. With her boyish cut, ebony strands parted around her ears, making her seem waifish and innocent.

But Blake's mood was anything but protective. His mind spun in spirals over the mess he was in, mostly the implications of deceiving Massad. He knew that, despite their past relationship, Massad would give no quarter when it came to getting his money back. Unless they could retrieve the stone, Blake faced ruin.

Kate stirred, turning to look up at him. "When you meet him, you'll see," she said, completing a lengthy verbal dissertation of which Blake hadn't heard a single word. He correctly surmised she was discussing Imre Novyck.

"He really was helpful," she said.

Blake grunted. Her blithe optimism abraded his nerves.

"There's something almost charismatic about him," Kate went on. "It's as if he has a special energy."

Blake looked away, rolling his eyes. "Ummm, right."

Kate pulled back and frowned.

"I thought we were finally on the same page about Imre," she said, suddenly unsmiling. "I don't think you've heard a word I've uttered."

Blake bristled and turned back to her. "I've tried to stay open-minded," he said. "But how can you be so sure about him? I say if he is useful, fine. But I don't have to be in love with him." He paused, then dug in the knife. "The way you rhapsodize about Imre Novyck, somebody might think you are."

Kate eyes flared. "Is that what *you* think?"

"I didn't mean that the way it sounded."

"Really? Just *how* did you mean it?"

Blake reached for her, pulling her toward him. "Look, this is stupid," he said. "I'm tired and I misspoke. I'm sorry."

Glancing in the mirror, the cab driver shook his head and slid the divider closed.

Kate turned her face to the side, put both hands on Blake's chest and pushed.

"You're not sorry," she said, sliding further away. "And I don't see how we're ever going to work together. One minute we seem to be in sync, growing close even. Then the next you're full of suspicion again. Meanwhile, you and your friend have pegged me as some kind of psycho. And now you sound jealous of Imre. You're pathetic."

"Am I?" Blake asked, his voice rising. "Do you realize the jam I'm in? My 'friend,' as you call him, will demand that loan the instant he learns the truth. Don't you realize what this could do to my business, to my reputation?"

"Oh, stop playing to the back row," Kate sneered.

With Blake's face less than three feet away, Kate could see droplets of sweat in the stubble on his upper lip. He looked exhausted and desperate. "It was your idea to go to Massad in the first place."

"Why do we keep covering the same ground?" Blake asked. Their relataionship seemed so volatile, soaring to fuzzy pink highs, then just as quickly, crashing to darkly desperate lows. "Where would you have gotten $500,000 if I hadn't contacted Massad? And why is it always me who screwed everything up? What about your record? After all, *I'm* not the one who found a fake stone."

Blake peered at her: the beguiling waif had disappeared. Kate's lipstick smeared into one corner of her mouth, the tip of her nose blushed like a small rose, and her cheeks were blotched.

"And thanks," he added, "for acknowledging the help I've tried to give you." Where, Blake wondered, was the cuddly kitten with whom he'd entered the cab?

Now, scrunched into the crevice of the seat, the feline hissed like a snake. "Well, thank you very much, *Mister* Blake, but I'm not going to need your 'help' anymore. I'll be handling the rest of this project on my own."

The cab drew up in front of their hotel and she exited, slamming the door behind her. Blake stalked up the stairs in silence.

He approached the desk. "You have reservations for Mr. Simon Blake and Miss Kate Gavrill?"

Kate stood several feet away, staring in the opposite direction.

"Yes, sir. Regrettably, we have only two single rooms left, and they are on separate floors."

"That arrangement couldn't be better," Blake said.

He disappeared, trailed by the lobby's only visible bellman.

Fuming, Kate stood alone, still holding her bags. The bellman returned and, without offering to relieve her of her suitcases, led the way to the seventh floor. Her room offered a view of the building next door, a mere two feet from her window.

Kate flopped on the bed. Switching off the lamp, she glared at the ceiling, picturing Blake four floors below. Thank God she wasn't in the same room—let alone the same bed—with that man.

Kate rolled onto her side. What had she ever seen in him?

Chapter 40

ON THE large television screen, the young woman on the diving board drew a deep breath, bounced twice, then took four evenly spaced steps before hurdling straight up, bringing her knees to her waist and unfolding in a vertical line. Her body twisted downward through a series of tight spirals, breaking the water with barely a ripple.

"Ladies and gentlemen," the off-screen sports reporter said, "you have just seen a perfect dive. If Kate Gavrill can repeat that performance next month in Barcelona, she just might come home with Olympic Gold."

In the rear of the room, Imre Novyck, wearing black slacks and a matching turtleneck sweater, rose, pressed "Stop" on the TV remote, and flicked on a light switch.

Released the day before, Novyck had been met at Lefortovo by a conveyance most of the prison's inhabitants had only seen in magazines—a newly delivered green Maserati sedan with cream-colored leather interior. In less than twelve minutes, the big car had whisked him to his Moscow home.

As plain as a police barracks on the outside, the three-story stone and mortar structure was spacious and luxurious within. The elegantly appointed rooms and central courtyard garden testified to its owner's success in Russia's leading growth industry—crime.

Two men sat on finely sculpted wooden chairs, waiting for their leader to speak. Their faces tilted toward him like pale plates.

"Where is she now?"

The shorter man, the same round-bellied Kazakh named Tartov who'd been a passenger in the car that struck Irina Gavrill, replied.

"She and the American gemologist took the stone to be examined at a university," he said. A wide, sloping nose rose from the flat surroundings of his face. He had dark, violent eyes. "They are both here in Russia—"

"Thanks, Tartov," Novyck said. Beside him, the reflection of a glass chandelier glittered on the polished tabletop. A few inches from his fingers stood a small photograph of Kate Gavrill in a swimsuit.

"Yes, Excellency," Tartov replied. His gaze smoldered, even in ordinary conversation. "They went to Kiev and are now heading here, to Moscow. We've prepared for her arrival as you instructed."

Novyck nodded. "And the $50,000 I gave you to open the trust account?" This account would eventually serve as the repository for the Bank of England funds.

"It will be handled by our associates in New York."

Novyck took a few steps and turned back to them. "Tell them good work on getting the video out of her doctor's office." He tapped his left thumbnail with a yellow pencil.

"What about the newspaper articles, excellency?"

Novyck shrugged. "I'm not sure. The events happened many years ago, and were complicated by romantic involvement. Perhaps another lever to control her? Who knows? But her eyes, her eyes are important. Get me sequential still enlargements of the eyes," he said. "Big. At least three-feet square. Right away." Tartov scurried to the television, removed the tape, and left the room.

An hour later, three large black-and-white photographs were displayed on the wall. Grainy and abstract in severe enlargement, they might have been sequential images of a planet. On closer inspection, however, each depicted a vastly enlarged human eye making a northward journey in its socket.

Lounging back in his leather chair, Novyck studied the pictures, his left hand cupping his right elbow and his right cupping his chin. He sat apart from his associates, emphasizing the hierarchical gulf between them.

Novyck spoke like a schoolteacher. "Modern science has taken hypnosis to another level," he said. He stood, sighed and placed his fingertips together, as if the explanation wearied him. "Today, thanks largely to the pioneering work of the American psychiatrist Dr. Herbert Spiegel, we know that eye-roll is the single most telling biomarker of hypnotizability, an indicator almost as certain as freckles are to fair skin. We measure this on a zero-to-five scale based on the amount of visible sclera—or 'white'—when the subject looks upward. The higher the eye roll, the higher the number. Show me a 'four,'" he said, "and I'll show you a candidate for instant trance."

Andre, the third man in the room, spoke up. "So, Excellency, where would you place this subject?" Andre had full, fleshy lips and inch-high, stiff-bristled black hair that rose in a "V" from his forehead. He possessed the kind of thick, powerful body that hovered near exits at loud Moscow nightclubs.

"If we're talking about the photo on the right," Novyck said, "We're easily looking at a category three, perhaps well beyond. But I'm not surprised. I suspected when I first met her at Lefortovo that she was highly hypnotizable."

"In the photographs here, she has, in effect, hypnotized herself, either shortly before or during her dive. I don't believe I've seen another image quite like this—focusing on an athlete's eyes during competition. Remarkable." He glanced across the room. "Good work, Tartov."

The small, violent man smiled, and bowed his head like a schoolboy.

Novyck paused, absently rubbing his chin. Again he spoke as if to himself. "Of course, we'd have to conduct further tests to develop a full profile . . . but there is a distinct possibility that she could be a Grade five. Western therapists like Dr. Spiegel classify those subjects as hypnotic virtuosos."

"Hypnotic virtuosos?" Andre and Tartov chorused the question.

Novyck's features lifted in a cold smile. "The most highly hypnotizable subjects, those who can be placed in a deep trance, not necessarily with their acquiescence. The experience is profound and typically includes a global, post-trance amnesia that obliterates the entire hypnotic episode.

"Back in the Sixties," he continued, "the American CIA documented the phenomenon in a mind control project they called MK Ultra. It's quite possible Miss Gavrill's psychiatrist knew of this research. It caused quite a scandal at the time. They even made a film about it with Frank Sinatra."

A sudden growl from Vandal briefly distracted him. Novyck owned several attack-trained mastiffs. Except for his favorite, the Alpha male, the dogs were kenneled when not on guard duty. Novyck crossed the room to a small refrigerator, opened a drawer and threw the beast a chunk of meat. Calmed, Vandal placed the morsel between his paws and began to gnaw.

Still standing, Novyck went on, "As with most virtuosos—if, indeed, she is one—Miss Gavrill's hypnotizability is not something that has been projected upon her by a therapist. It exists within her. The therapist merely taps into this naturally occurring capacity. With the virtuoso, it happens very, very easily. For us, it is a gift."

Novyck lifted the photograph from the table, peering closely at its subject.

"Miss Gavrill is the key to all our plans," he said. He spoke the words softly, but with great intensity. "We have the stone, of course, but only she can deliver the ultimate verification needed to legally claim the rest of the Romanov fortune. Miss Gavrill must be alive to appear physically at the bank and undergo DNA testing. And she must seem willing."

Andre's forehead knotted in concentration, drawing the prow of his hair closer to his eyebrows. "You mentioned a profile?"

"Yes, we'd have to test Miss Gavrill directly to develop one for her. The true virtuoso is capable of intense focus, with a rigid personality core and a trusting nature to the point of naiveté. Her actions—and reactions—are more driven by her heart than her head. In Miss Gavrill's case, her long training in economics—a highly disciplined science—tends to offset this trait.

"The analytical strand at the center of her psyche may erect an internal barrier we will need to overcome. If so, I am confident it will only provide a momentary obstacle. Besides, there are always other ways to bend a will, if need be. We will see."

Novyck drew a hand along his lean jaw. "One last thing," he said. "For some reason, perhaps because of their larger reservoirs of fantasy and association, some virtuosos exhibit tendencies toward multiple personality. Some are actually clinically mentally ill."

Andre chewed his voluptuous lower lip. "Could this have implications for our project?"

"Good question. A virtuoso with a strong alter ego can sometimes be controlled through that alter. In other words, if you can split the alter off, you can actually put the alter into the trance. The result can be far more control over the main personality."

Novyck strutted before the table in a small circle. "All this takes a master hypnotist, of course," he said. "But then, I *am* a master hypnotist.

211

Chapter 41

SIMON BLAKE shook his head, but still felt groggy. The room's green curtains hung in tiered scallops that made him think of pools swirling at the bottom of a waterfall. Accommodations at the Imperial Hotel tended to shrink in size as they rose in elevation. His larger, lower floor room, on the other hand, boasted high ceilings, antique furniture and polished wooden floors. For Blake, however, jet lag and too much brandy effectively nullified the luxuriousness of his surroundings.

After his bitter exchange with Kate the night before, Blake had repaired to the ornate ground floor bar, a glass-enclosed conservatory populated by lush, leafy plants. But even twenty-year-old Courvoisier failed to assuage his gloom.

Like a competing suitor, Novyck stood between them. Kate seemed to trust the Russian more than she trusted him. Blake sighed and punched a fist into the pillow. He was tired of being drained by their relationship. He always seemed to be circling her, and she always seemed to be backing away. He was running out of patience—and energy.

He threw off the covers and crossed the room.

Standing in the window, Blake squeezed his eyes against the morning sun. Below, shoppers bustled along Tverskaya Ulitsa, the first street in Moscow to have electric lights. Originally a processional route for the tsars, the thoroughfare had been widened by Stalin in the 1930s and now housed the city's most fashionable emporia. A favorite spot was Yeliseev's Food Hall—Gastronome No. 1 under the Communists.

Blake shaved and took the stairs down for coffee and breakfast. By the time he reached the chilly dining room he was alert.

Thin turquoise curtains screened the windows, and linen-covered tables were scattered over the dark carpet. The room's blue-tinted light reminded him of Adrienne and her cool, elegant manner. In the entire time he'd known her, they'd never quarreled. With Kate, on the other hand, he seemed to be in a perpetual war zone. He dug a fork into the tablecloth, pressing the instrument hard against its own prongs. Should he just get out of here? He thought about buying a ticket back to the U.S., then as quickly dropped the idea.

The real cause of his intense argument with Kate, Blake knew, was mutual attraction. All the thrashing about came from colliding chemistry. Natural forces pulled them toward each other, but the two of them, modern adults, each struggling to retain his or her intellectual and emotional independence, pushed back.

Absently, Blake thought about the fact that he and Kate could still have a child, no longer a realistic possibility with Adrienne.

He chided himself at his own Darwinian notions. He should be helping Kate, not complicating her life even more. Suddenly, desperately, Blake wanted to make amends, to take her in his arms or simply talk to her.

He decided on a peace offering. He signaled the waiter and ordered a tray with coffee, fruit and warm breads. When the man returned, in addition to the food, the tray held a small vase of fresh flowers. Perfect. She would melt. He paid his chit, picked up the tray and headed toward the elevator.

"Sir, excuse me, sir." The hotel clerk called out as he passed the front desk. "You have an urgent call from a Mr. Jacob Massad in New York."

Blake half-stumbled, almost spilling the tray.

"Uh, I can't take his call right now. If he rings again, tell him that I've left for the day."

Making his way to Kate's room—he'd had to ask the clerk for the number, he'd been so angry he hadn't gotten it the night before—Blake's thoughts raced ahead. How had Massad learned they were in Russia? And where they were staying? And what would he tell Massad when they talked as, sooner rather than later, they must? Had Massad learned about the fake stone? If so, he must have guessed they'd go to Russia. Or he could have discerned their whereabouts in other ways. Massad's sources of information were usually reliable, even if they occasionally skirted legality.

Blake reached Kate's room and pressed the buzzer. No answer. He pressed again, harder. Still nothing. Exasperated, Blake hammered with his fist until his hand throbbed. Silence. He put the tray down, rode the elevator back to the main floor, and strode briskly to the front desk.

"Has Miss Gavrill left the hotel?"

"Not that we know, sir."

"Has she left any messages? She doesn't appear to be in her room."

"No, we haven't heard from Miss Gavrill, Mr. Blake. Could she be in another part of the hotel? Perhaps she is having breakfast and you missed her on the elevator?"

Blake turned and half-trotted to the dining room, scanning the surroundings for a closely clipped ebony head.

He returned to the desk and asked for the manager.

"Perhaps I can help you, Mr. Blake?" A small, dark man stepped from an alcove behind the desk. "Alexander Martine, assistant manager. I was on duty and booked you in last night. If I may say so, sir, I believe there was some, ah, tension between yourself and Miss Gavrill." He placed both hands together and lifted his lips in a practiced smile. "It is a beautiful morning. Perhaps the young lady is out taking a walk."

Blake gritted his teeth at the man's officiousness. A bureaucratic remnant from the previous political system, he told himself. "I want you to accompany me to her room," he said brusquely. "And I want you to bring a key."

Martine bowed. "Of course, Mr. Blake. At once."

Minutes later, the door swung open on Kate's room. Empty. Blake rapidly covered the space to the closet. Neither Kate nor any of her belongings remained.

On the other side of the room, Mr. Martine slid his fingers along the underside of an open window. Directly opposite, the window in the building next to the hotel was also open. "These windows are always locked, Mr. Blake. Unless, of course, a guest specifically requests they be opened for fresh air." A tiny, it's-all-a-lover's-quarrel smirk danced at the corners of his mouth. "Forgive me, but was there a reason Miss Gavrill might wish to leave without your knowledge?"

Part IV

Chapter 42

COLD, UNFINISHED floorboards scuffed Kate's bare feet. The edge of the cushionless seat dug into the backs of her knees. Telephone cord looped high on her waist and wound tightly around her wrists, pinning her torso to the chair. Kate still wore the cotton pajamas she'd had on at the hotel. But her cheeks were swollen and bruised. Dried blood crusted her lips. Her nostrils recoiled at a heavy medicinal scent—the remnants of whatever had drugged her.

Hinges squealed as the door opened and a slight man with darting blue eyes walked quickly toward her. Earlier, he'd slapped her hard, at least half a dozen times. Now, however, the man carried a small steel bowl in one hand and a large spoon in the other.

"I've brought you something to e-eat," he said. His words jittered out in uneven cadence. She pulled her head back. He forced the thick wooden spoon and its hot contents—a thick porridge—between her clamped lips. He twisted the spoon roughly in her mouth, then yanked it out.

"We k-know who you are," he said. Again, the words fluttered nervously from his lips. "W-we w-want the s-stone and the egg."

Kate's toned muscles strained against their restraints. She'd spent a lifetime dominating her physical space. Now, in a matter of hours, that confident sense of control had been torn away. She'd never known such apprehension. She summoned a last sputter of courage.

"Then you also know that the egg is in New York."

He struck her full across the face with an open hand. The sound rang in the small room like a shot. "Don't lie to m-me," he said. "Not if you hope to get out of here a-a-alive. You will t-tell us the exact location of the gem and its c-container."

"You fool." Anger leapfrogged fear. "The stone is a fake. And the Faberge isn't even in this country."

He hit her again, harder this time, then strode to the other side of the room. He glared back at her. "Then I s-suppose we r-really don't n-n-need you, do we?" He paused, his chest heaving in anger. "D-do you know . . . d-do you r-realize w-who you're dealing with?"

"How would I know? Why should I care?" She spat rose-colored saliva on the floor.

He returned in quick steps, then reached down to cup her jaw. He tilted her head back and looked boldly into her eyes.

"You are a b-beautiful w-woman, K-katya Gavrill. It would be . . . a pi-p-pity to deny the world such a f-flower." He wheeled and departed.

Kate's strength ebbed. Her chin touched her chest as the enormity of her predicament washed over her. In just a week the Bank of England deadline would expire and with it the largest portion of her birthright would be lost. Her grandmother had been murdered. By all accounts, her mother had been murdered. Now she was being held prisoner by Russian mobsters who knew her birth name. Was she next?

*   *   *

KATE STARED across the room. Her carelessly packed suitcase and garment bag stood in the corner. They'd cleverly emptied her hotel room. Clearly, they wanted Simon to think she'd left in a huff with no intention of returning—he'd be less likely to follow. She'd had no indication they were seeking ransom. So who would look for her?

Behind her, Kate heard the doorknob turning. Then a rattling against the lock and the wrenching sound of metal screws being yanked from wood. Finally, a loud concussion as the door collapsed on the floor.

Kate braced herself for her captor's violent assault. Cold sweat washed her cheeks.

Instead, she saw Imre Novyck, wearing a long, flowing black cloak, and a purple priest's collar. Novyck made a complete circle around her chair and stood before her. His right hand clutched her jailer by the collar—*his* hands now bound behind him.

Novyck roughly pushed the man to the floor, kicking him in the ribs as he went down. He then turned to Kate and began loosening her bonds.

"I regret, my dear, that you had to endure this." His dark eyes filled with concern. "Are you injured?"

"I think I'm okay," she replied, rubbing her wrists and jaw. "Thank God you found me. I didn't realize you were out of prison—I was planning to visit Lefortovo. How did you know where I was?"

"This one," Novyck paused, again kicking the man in the stomach, "was not very wise about who he talked to. We learned of your location from some of my, uh, former associates at the prison."

Novyck motioned to two other men, both wearing tailored, dark blue suits. They picked up her bags and returned to drag away her jailer.

Moments later, Kate settled into the rear seat of Novyck's sumptuous sedan, sipping a warm sherry. Imre would take her to his residence in Moscow—she could recuperate there. She'd connect with Simon later and let him know she was safe. Right now, though, she was exhausted. She sank back into the cushions and closed her eyes.

Chapter 43

SIMON BLAKE picked up the phone message for Kate at the Imperial Hotel. It was from a Lt. MacMahon in Pennslyvania.

He walked over to a house phone and punched in his calling card. The connection with the state police office was amazingly clear—the miracle of satellite communications, Blake assumed.

"Miss Gavrill left a message saying she could be reached at this hotel," explained an officer who introduced himself as Lt. Donald MacMahon. "I wanted her to know we've made some progress in her case."

"Ms. Gavrill is not here at the moment. May I help?" Blake wondered whether the call was legitimate, but the man's tone sounded genuine.

"Do you know Ms. Gavrill? May I ask your name?" MacMahon seemed hesitant, almost protective.

"I've been traveling with her and she's disappeared. She told me you were investigating her mother's death." Blake quickly explained his professional connection to Kate, leaving out any personal details.

"That's true, and thanks to a local farmer who spotted the perpetrators getting out of the truck used in the hit and run, we know a little more about what happened," Lt. MacMahon went on, "They got into a large Mercedes, and a neighboring farmer managed to get most of the license plate, enough for us to trace the car to a rental company in Manhattan. Brooklyn, actually. Anyhow, the company turned out to be a shell. The real owner is a nightclub in Brighton Beach. We have a description of the two men who drove the vehicle. But it won't do much good."

"Why not?"

"We're quite certain they were in the U.S. temporarily—and illegally. They apparently split up, and at least one left the country the same day."

"Did you learn *anything* about these men?" Blake was beginning to wonder why MacMahon had called.

"They're Russian nationals," Lt. MacMahon replied. "And they're almost certainly in Moscow right now. Tell Miss Gavrill to be very careful."

★   ★   ★

KATE STEPPED out of the deep, octagonal-shaped bathtub and walked into the adjoining bedroom.

The heavy drapes and thick Persian carpet sharply contrasted with her most recent surroundings. She shrugged off the terry cloth robe she'd been given and rolled into bed, luxuriating in silk sheets and a down-filled mattress. Weariness washed over her like a soft sea.

She touched the small gold frog that hung from her neck and thought of Simon Blake. For most of their time together, she'd been a bitch. Some of it reflected her own frustration after learning the stone was a fake. But some of her reaction, Kate knew, was self-protective. Fearing her attraction to him, she'd pushed away, repeating her post Jack Nars pattern of choosing to repress signals, however strong, from her own emotions. Kate's skin tingled against the sheer, slippery bedclothes. She rolled over, languidly scissoring her naked legs.

Through barely open eyes, Kate saw a familiar icon hanging between a set of bookshelves. It was The Holy Face: a copy of an image allegedly made by Christ when he pressed a piece of cloth to his features. The face Kate saw was masculine, with a long nose and surprisingly red lips. The head was surrounded by a gilt halo. Christ's brown hair fell in even lengths, and his beard cleaved into sharp, Muslim-like points. His eyes seemed infinitely kind.

She wondered: *Is this what sustained Irina and Anya through a lifetime of fear?*

Apprehension had honed Irina's maternal instincts. But she'd had another source of strength: her Orthodox faith. As a young woman, Kate remembered feeling embarrassed the few times schoolage friends came to visit. The icons' heavy metallic lacquering and flat perspectives had seemed foolish and hopelessly irrelevant at the time.

Irina insisted otherwise. "Don't you see?" she'd asked rhetorically, "The gilding holds the eye just long enough to let God enter the soul. The two-dimensional image does not require interpretation, and therefore doesn't stand between you and God the way it does in three-dimensional western art." To Irina, the power of an icon lay not in its self-reflected meaning to a viewer, but rather in the shared understanding of a precise truth, defined and conveyed by a supreme being.

"Think of icons as sacred doors," her mother said, "between this world and a world of spiritual perfection—a place of peace, love, and holiness."

Privately, Kate scoffed at her mother's provincial religiosity. An Old World relic, she said to herself. She'd always been an atheist, at least since college. She could not deny, however, that religion had served her mother well. She hoped it was giving her peace now.

Kate rolled over. Another icon hung on the opposite wall. A hooved jet-black figure with leathery wings sat on a throne fashioned from a seven-headed serpent. Behind it rose a wall of flames. Rarely depicted in Eastern Orthodoxy, the icon portrayed an eleventh century rendering of *The Last Judgment*. The figure was that of Beelzebub, the Great Satan.

★   ★   ★

BEFORE RETURNING to his hotel room, Blake detoured to an increasingly familiar haunt: the Imperial's atrium-style fern bar. He'd spent the day running back and forth between the Moscow Police department and the airport. An interview with an inspector from the city's missing persons bureau had taken hours. People disappeared every day in Moscow, he was told—women especially. Most were surreptitiously leaving the country for prospective husbands they'd found on the Internet. Or they were going to Italy to work as whores. In any case, so far, Blake had learned nothing; it was as if Kate had dematerialized. Now Lt. MacMahon warned she was in grave danger.

Is that why she'd left so suddenly? Her empty hotel room was his only clue. It suggested an angry woman turning a page. She'd swept up her belongings and—like the old show tune—washed that man right out of her hair.

One thing was certain: Kate had shaken his life. His stable existence, his predictable relationship with Adrienne, his secure professional standing—all trembled on their foundations in the wake of Hurricane Kate.

But she'd also brought something that had been missing in his life, a heady mix of passion and excitement he hadn't known since his twenties. Sweetness too. On a warm evening a week ago, the woman who now apparently hated him, had slipped her arm through his as they strolled along Park Avenue. He could still recall the soft nudge of her breast above his elbow.

Damn! *Where was she?*

Blake saw his own reflection in the long mirror behind the bar. The gray streaks in his brown hair seemed more pronounced, the ravine between his eyebrows deeper, than a few days ago. His dog-tired bones seemed every bit as old as the man who stared back at him.

Chapter 44

———⟨◎⟩———

ON CHRISTOPRUDNY Bulvar, the eighth of ten consecutive avenues that make up Moscow's horseshoe-shaped Boulevard Ring, two men—one large and pale, the other small and dark—sat on a bench. They stared across the wide tree-lined street at a large late nineteenth-century mansion. The home's pillared, brick-and-plaster edifice extended to the edge of the sidewalk.

Hector Molina sipped coffee. Vulcan Krasky turned a rolled copy of the *Moscow Times* in his hands.

"She's been in there for six hours," Molina said, twirling a miniature plastic spoon in the dark liquid. "In the home of a priest who also happens to be one of the biggest *capos* in Eastern Europe. What do you suppose is going on?"

Krasky frowned, stroking his heavy jaw. "Follow the money," he grunted. "They abducted her from the Imperial. Then they took her to that dump. Now here. They must think she knows where to find the real stone."

"That priest cannot be taken lightly," Molina said. "We must proceed with extreme caution." Standing, he walked to the curb, poured his cup's dregs onto the pavement, then crushed the stiff paper container in his fist. He stared at the spreading stain of liquid. Even in the heat, steam rose from the concrete.

"Our plan is still valid," Molina declared. "Together or separately, the woman and Blake will lead us to the stone. In the end, if we have to steal it from this Novyck, so be it. I doubt his vaults are more secure than those at Harry Winston's or Harrods—and I've been inside both."

He turned back, lowering his head to look at Krasky, still seated on the bench. "In any case, we need to track both Blake and Novyck and his entourage."

Vulcan Krasky did not reply. He gripped the newspaper in both hands, twisting the ends into a tight tourniquet. His dark, unblinking eyes focused straight ahead. He thought of what Boris Lada would say. To Krasky, the woman across the street had become an ogress. One who had tormented his life long enough.

Chapter 45

Bᴏᴜɴᴅ ɪɴ blue leather and about the size of a catechism, the small ledger contained columns of financial data. Its tables, which reported the annual interest rates paid by leading European banks during the Twentieth Century, would be of little interest to anyone other than an economist. At this moment however, to Simon Blake the little book was as precious as a Gutenberg Bible.

"Where did you find this?" he asked. He turned the small volume over in his hand, staring at the bookplate on its inside cover: "From the Library of Professor Kate Gavrill, Marion State University." Blake's tone was sharp. He'd played the "Where's Kate" game long enough.

"Actually, it was turned in this morning," replied the same Imperial Hotel manager who'd helped him enter Kate's room. Moments before, the man had called Blake's room to announce the find. "An employee of—shall we say—a lesser hotel brought it by. Apparently, Miss Gavrill used one of our business cards as a bookmark. They found this under her bed. Miss Gavrill, I'm sorry to say, had already checked out."

Blake's irritation gave way to muted elation. Kate must have taken the ledger with her on their trip, apparently to estimate the cumulative value of her account at the Bank of England. At least she might still be in Moscow. But why would she seek out a second-rate hotel? Was she that determined he not find her?

A short cab ride later, he stood at the desk of The Khrushchev Arms, which appeared to have gone unpainted since its eponymously honored government.

The hotel's manager, a small bald man with a thick black mustache, had no memory of a female American guest. When Blake pressed a few rubles into his palm, however, his recall powers improved markedly. Two days before, he had registered a sleepy "Russian Princess" with short black hair and snow-white skin.

"Her eyes were like Siberian ice," the man said in surprisingly clear English. Momentarily turning away, he picked at a piece of curling wallpaper. "They made a mess I'm afraid."

He led Blake to a room where workmen had just finishing rehanging a battered-looking door on rusty hinges. They stood in the corridor and peered inside. The air smelled of stale bedclothes and sweat; the furnishings were sparse and worn. On the floor lay a long piece of telephone cord and an upturned chair.

What had gone on here? Blake wondered. He'd spent most of the previous night without sleep. His eyelids seemed to burn whenever he shifted his gaze.

"She arrived in a party of five men, but then all of the men left but one," the manager said. He pulled at his moustache as if adjusting it. "The little book apparently fell out of either a suitcase or garment bag."

Blake shook his head, more puzzled than ever. He looked at the dark unpainted floors and imagined Kate's smooth feet against their splinter-riddled surface. Other than the little book, there was no evidence she had ever been here.

One thing was certain. It wasn't a place Kate would choose freely, unless she was trying to conceal her location.

His concern was rapidly deepening into fear. Blake glanced again at the room's door. Kate was physically strong, amazingly so for her size. But she was no match for five men.

At least he knew where to look next. The first place, assuming she was free, that Kate herself would go: Lefortovo Prison. And her only reason for going there would have been to see a man he had never met or trusted: Imre Novyck.

#

Chapter 46

—————— ·((◉))· ——————

LEFORTOVO'S RIM of coiled barbed wire underscored its official description as a "prison and investigation complex." Blake remembered seeing a list of some of its past occupants, nearly all arrested on false political charges. They included Raoul Wallenberg, the Swedish businessman and savior of Jews during the Holocaust; Alexander Solzhenitsyn, the writer; Larissa Shiptsova, an environmental activist; and Rusian Alikhadzhiyev, speaker of the separatist Chechen parliament.

Indeed, it was entirely possible, Blake thought, that, just as he'd claimed, Novyck had also been jailed on trumped-up charges. After all, the former Communist regime had been expert at applying a veneer of legality to cases against its political foes. Sometimes a dubious psychiatric diagnosis would be excuse enough to confine political prisoners. Any of these could explain Novyck's incarceration. Or he could just be a crook.

A black Volga taxi took Blake to the prison. At the main visitors' entrance, he was met by a guard who ushered him through a narrow, low-ceilinged passage into a small office on the first floor.

Within a few minutes a prison officer appeared. From the three stripes on his sleeve Blake judged him to be a sergeant. The officer was noncommittal when asked to name Novyck's offense. "A political

231

transgression," he replied, cocking an eyebrow. "Like everyone else here."

Inside, Lefortovo seemed as hostile and remorseless as it did on the outside. It took 200,000 rubles—better than a month's pay for a prison guard—for Blake to learn that Novyck had been abruptly released much earlier than expected. Fifty thousand more yielded his address.

His meeting with the prison officer ended abruptly at 5:00 P.M., when the guards began dispensing teapots through the small access doors in each of Lefortovo's cells. Even through the prison's thick walls, Blake could hear clanging sounds as he made his way outside.

He left the facility in a state of depressed confusion. Why had Novyck really been imprisoned? Was he innocent, as he insisted and Kate apparently believed? Had the former Soviets regarded him as an enemy of the state, perhaps for good reason? Why had he put himself at risk to help Kate in what—at least to official eyes—could have been considered a crime? Was the true reason old family ties? And why was he suddenly and unexpectedly released?

He couldn't answer even one of these questions. But he did know what to do next.

BLAKE ENTERED Boulevard Ring at Old Arbat Road, once home to the country's most revered writers and artists. Strolling through the tree-lined park at the boulevard's center, he joined a stream of humanity—mothers with baby carriages, couples strolling arm in arm, boys chasing each other around benches and shinnying up lamp posts. He passed squares and playgrounds, leafy clearings where old men sat at tables playing chess, and street sellers hawked ice cream and *kvas*, a Russian wine made from bread.

For generations, Moscow's illuminati populated the city's "rings" and their "crookedly" side streets. The signature pink, green and yellow pastels, the high, airy windows and delicate friezes—all the characteristic features of the city's most treasured eighteenth and nineteenth century buildings—were found, distilled, within these former fortifications.

Blake's walk canted down at Rozhdestvensky Bulvar, sloping off one of the city's few hills. To his right and a mile away, crowds were already lining up outside the Bolshoi for tickets to that evening's performance. He quickly strolled the length of Stretensky, the shortest of the ring's boulevards.

Blake pulled a square linen handkerchief from his pocket, shaking it out as he brought the cloth to his forehead. The sun had dropped, but the July humidity was at its stifling worst, rising up from the Moskva River like a suffocating blanket.

A glossy-black, fortress-like wooden door, opening directly onto the sidewalk, served as entry to Novyck's mansion on Christoprudny. Two stories above the street and supported by white pillars as tall as three men, the facing wall extended sixty feet. A small, colonnaded balcony jutted out to the curb.

Blake lifted and dropped the large iron knocker. On the sidewalk, a woman in a red jacket dragged a small dog with sad eyes at the end of a leash.

A heavy-shouldered man wearing a black Armani suit opened the door, which swung soundlessly on its massive hinges. Moments later, Blake sat in Imre Novyck's study.

"So!" Novyck clapped his hands as he entered the room from a side door. "You are searching for our mutual friend, Miss Gavrill?"

Despite Blake's earlier suspicions, in person Novyck seemed gracious and concerned. Yet his opening gambit, which implied their equal standing in Kate's eyes, triggered a flash of jealousy. About his own age, the man moved with assurance. And although Blake found his electronic earpiece disconcerting, he dressed simply but elegantly, much like his subordinate at the door, in Armani black.

Novyck offered him a cognac, which Blake accepted. His host poured himself a glass of Pellegrino, shifted his weight to one leg, and braced an elbow against the bookcase. As Novyck leaned forward, a gap opened in his silk shirt. From a thin silver necklace, swung a small, finely made Eastern Orthodox crucifix. It included two additional crossbars, a shorter nameplate above the head position and, below, an angled bar for the feet.

Blake let the slithery liquid heat his throat. "I had reason to believe," he began, "that she would contact you."

"Yes, exactly so," replied Novyck, still standing. "But that was some time ago. I have not seen her recently."

"Didn't you help her get the alexandrite to America?"

"Ah, so, you know about Katya's treasure? Yes, she seemed frightened. We both worried she might be set upon by villains, either in this country or yours. I helped her disguise the stone so she could transport it safely. As you may know, my family has a history of service to hers." Novyck's shoulders dipped in a near bow. "I was relieved," he said, "to learn that Katya arrived safely in New York, with her health and dowry intact."

Again, Blake noted Novyck's obvious familiarity with Kate. He was clearly aware of her quest and all that it implied. And there was the hint of a relationship that went deeper—calling her *Katya*, something Simon himself had never done. "We *both* worried," had the clear ring of *they as a couple worried*. Of the two of them, after all, Novyck obviously had a deeper knowledge of Kate's family and background. Perhaps his, Blake's, best tack would be to exploit that knowledge.

Blake rubbed his forehead, bunching the flesh between his eyes into a small ridge. "Do you have any idea why she would check into a cheap hotel, with an entourage of men, in the middle of the night?"

Novyck blinked, momentarily surprised by the bluntness of Blake's question. "None at all. Not unless they were all part of some celebratory revelry. Miss Gavrill, however, doesn't strike me as the sort of woman who engages in such bacchanal frivolity."

Blake rose, facing Novyck. "Nor does she me." A chiming clock drew Blake's eyes to the bookshelf; he was swept by an overwhelming sense of urgency. "How can I find her?"

Novyck smiled, but without humor. "If one wishes to, it is easy to lose oneself in Russia. It sounds as if Kate may not wish to be found, at least by you."

Blake felt his blood rise. Who was this faux priest to presume to know Kate's wishes?

Novyck pulled a green velvet chair from beneath an ornate writing desk, and sat down. "I have many questions of my own", the prelate continued. "Why did Kate return to Russia? Why did she want to see me? Why are you two here?"

Without warning, the conversational tables had turned. Now he and Kate were paired. Blake's mind seemed sluggish, but he sensed a risk in specificity. "We both had personal business in Russia," he replied vaguely, "so we decided to come together."

Novyck settled back in the chair. He clearly felt more comfortable directing their exchange. "I'm sure I can help," he said expansively, as if bestowing a gift. "What is your business, Mr. Blake?"

"Right now, my business is secondary," said Blake, hearing the evasive tone in his own words. He must keep the spotlight on the missing woman. "I want to find Miss Gavrill."

"And, of course, I will do anything I can to assist you." Novyck stood, and took Blake's hand.

For the first time, Blake felt the full power of Novyck's eyes. Set deeply in his skull, they were dark brown and incredibly bright. They seemed rarely to shift position. The effect gave the man's gaze an uncommon intensity, quite unlike anything Blake had encountered.

"If you learn anything," Novyck continued, handing him his card, "please contact me. The chances are Miss Gavrill is simply behaving in the inexplicable way women often do, and you, or I, will hear from her soon. Nonetheless, I am concerned."

"Know that I am your blood brother in this mission," he continued, rising. He smiled and pressed Blake's hand tightly between both of his own. "No-one has a greater concern for Miss Gavrill's safety than I." He bowed his head slightly.

"Thanks," Blake replied, his focus seeming to return. "For now at least, I will look for Miss Gavrill on my own. If I need your help I'll call."

"As you wish." Novyck again offered a slight bow of his head.

Outside, the air felt closer than before. To cool off, Blake decided to walk toward the river before returning to his hotel. He passed the three-tier Menshikov Tower, built by an apparatchik to Peter the Great. The egomaniacal adviser had grown wealthy, and constructed the wedding cake-edifice as part of a church, crowned by Moscow's highest spire, on the grounds of his own estate. The edifice had later been consumed in a fire and then partially rebuilt.

Blake looked at the lavishly decorated tower and wondered: was his own ego charting a course for disaster? Was it vainglorious to believe that, by himself, he could find one woman in a city of eight million people?

A better approach might be to accept Novyck's help, but covertly. If he retraced his steps, he could watch the one place where, sooner or later, he was convinced Kate would appear: before the same black door where he had stood a short time ago, and which was clearly visible from across Christoprudny.

Blake re-crossed the wide street. Reaching the curb, he walked in long strides until dense foliage swallowed him from view. He stopped when he stood in a stand of tall bushes directly across from Novyck's residence. He was unaware of the parked taxi that had trailed his movements since early afternoon.

Chapter 47

FROM AN upstairs window, Imre Novyck watched Blake leave. Then, crossing a hallway, he slowly opened the door to the bedroom in which Kate Gavrill slept. He walked to a small locked cabinet, inserted a key and—stooping—withdrew an empty hospital syringe, sealed in a sterilized plastic bag. He would use this to withdraw a small sample of Kate's blood, and with it, her DNA.

Novyck recrossed the room and stood at the foot of her bed. She looked utterly relaxed; the powerful sedative he'd slipped into her sherry appeared to have done its work. Soon, he mused, he would no longer need or want drugs to control this subject. Heavy medication would be unseemly—and sure to draw attention—in the patrician world of Threadneedle Street.

The ebony silk sheets clung to Kate's form. The outline of her body against the thin fabric made it obvious that, in the summer heat, she'd slipped under the covers without any clothing.

Kate's body shifted and desire rose in Novyck like a hot wind. Her white skin seemed almost newborn in its purity. Damp from her bath, her short black hair curled in a fringe of small ringlets. Thick dark lashes touched her cheeks.

Setting the syringe on a small table near the wall, Novyck eased onto the bed. He brought his right forefinger to his lips, wetting the end with his tongue. He touched Kate for the first time then, through the fabric, making feather-light circles at the apex of her left breast.

He imagined placing his hands on her knees and opening her, suffocating in the heavy mists of her.

He would feel remorse later, and flagellation would lift his soul to the highest joy of all, cleansing his spirit, purging the foul vessel of his body. First would come the colonics, until his excrement ran clear as a stream. Then he would beat himself, especially about his genitals and buttocks, using the knotted leather lashes he kept in a locked cabinet. The whipping would continue until blood spattered his legs in a gentle rain.

His penance would be conducted entirely in private.

Novyck had gone into seclusion after his recent debauchery with the young nun. When it was over, he threw open the windows, rubbed his wounds with salve and prayed.

Beneath the sheets, Kate's hips stirred slightly.

Novyck jerked his hand back. He felt suddenly and outrageously stupid, as if his intellect were an elephant, backed into a corner by a herd of lecherous mice. You utter fool, he remonstrated himself. Are you ruled by your phallus? Is one fling with her worth billions of rubles and all the power they could bring? You'll have her, your way, later.

Novyck walked to the table and picked up the syringe. Recrossing the room, he drew back the sheet. Gently, he slid the needle into her upper arm.

★   ★   ★

A SHARP tingle awakened her. Kate rubbed her arm above the elbow. Her eyes opened slowly.

Abruptly, they opened wide—a man sat on the side of the bed. She pulled the bedclothes to her collar bone.

Imre Novyck's voice came to her, calmly, reassuringly.

"You've been out for hours, Katya. It's still early evening. Go back to sleep."

"Wha—what day is this?"

"Saturday, my dear."

He took her hand, which lay limp in his. Drowsiness settled back around her. *But she couldn't sleep; she had to get back to the hotel.* It was August 26th, Simon must be looking all over Moscow for her.

Novyck crossed the room. Standing at a side table, he turned his back to her. When he returned, he held two glasses.

"Try this, my dear. A little sherry to send you back to dream land."

Sitting on the bed, he took her hand again. Kate sipped the drink, and her head spun. Her hand curled into his. This time she sensed his flesh, and her fingers crawled slightly in his palm.

Behind Novyck's professional detachment, Kate sensed a smoldering hunger. He caught her recognition and, pulling back his hand, rose quickly from the bed in a smooth motion. After making a slight bow, he turned off the main ceiling light. Now the only source of illumination was a small lamp on the table where he'd momentarily laid the syringe. He tucked the device beneath his coat and quietly closed the door.

Kate turned her face into the pillow. Like the Romanov Stone, her nature seemed to swing from fire to ice. Blake had risked his professional future for her, yet an instant ago she'd sparked, however briefly, to the touch of another man—and that man was Imre Novyck.

Chapter 48

KATE'S EYES opened. After hours of sleep, she felt refreshed and strong. Cool air touched her skin as, nude, she crossed the room to her garment bag, hanging in an open closet. Rummaging through its contents, she found underwear, shoes, a pair of jeans and a faded "Marion Athletic Dept." tank top.

As she dressed, she noted a curious salmon–colored spot on her arm. She'd obviously been given an injection, but what? And when?

She *had* to call Simon and let him know she was all right.

Finding no telephone, she walked to the door, turned the knob and stepped into the hallway.

A large man wearing a black turtleneck and a putty-colored suit sat in a wooden chair directly opposite her door. Earlier, Novyck had introduced him as a valet.

"*Tyeh-lyeh-FAW-nah?*" She asked him, trying to sound out the Russian word for telephone.

"So sorry, Madame, no *puh-AHN-GLEE-ski,*" he replied

"*Yah khah-CHOO V'EE-dyet* Comrade Novyck?" She had no idea why she used the Communist era relic, 'comrade,' in stating her desire to see Imre.

A few minutes later, Imre Novyck stood beside her in the hallway. "I really must go," Kate said. "There are people who are anxious for me. I don't want to worry them needlessly."

"Of course, my dear," he replied, taking her hand. "But in good time. You are simply not well enough at the moment." His demeanor of overt concern, Kate sensed, barely concealed impatience.

"Yes, but these people will be frantically trying to find me," Kate responded. Never mind that the "people" she referred to came down to one lanky gemologist from Indiana with impossibly brown eyes. "Let me at least call them."

He patted her hand, leading her to the door. "Certainly," he said. His lips lifted in a soft smile. "I know that you want to contact Mr. Blake. There will be time for that later in the day."

"But—"

"No buts." He continued holding the fixed smile. "Right now Dr. Imre prescribes a little more rest." His palm slid upwards and closed lightly around Kate's wrist. He led her back into her room, then stepped back out into the hall.

The door clicked as it was locked from outside. Kate's neck muscles jumped at the sound.

She paced the room in a wide circle, stopping beside the double window she'd noticed earlier. It was really two windows, one on each side of a typically massive Russian wall—she guessed the width at eighteen inches. Flush with the wall in the room, and framed by an iron sash, the inner casement window opened and closed by a single hook. The fixed outer window offered a glimpse of the building's cobbled brick exterior and the sidewalk two stories below.

The curtains were still drawn. Below, on the sidewalk near the house's entrance, she could see two men talking. The room's warm air had frosted the panes of the outer window with condensation, obscuring their images. Pulling aside the curtain and opening the latch on the inner window, she leaned across the wide sill. Like a child peering out from a school bus, Kate rubbed a clear circle in the glass.

She gasped and jumped back. Her stomach bunched.

The man facing the house was the same captor who'd tormented her at the hotel. He was chatting and laughing with the Armani-clad butler who'd greeted her earlier at Imre's door. These people weren't servants, any more than the man outside her door was a valet. They were thugs, some of Novyck's "associates" from Lefortovo, no doubt.

In an instant, her plight had become all too clear.

Kate Gavrill, great granddaughter of the tsar of all Russia, was not a guest of her family's protector. She was his prisoner.

Chapter 49

———◦(◦)◦———

THE KNOB turned before she touched it. Kate drew back, and Novyck entered.

He carried a small black leather case.

"I brought something to help you sleep."

"I don't need anything. And I don't need to sleep."

"Well, you may think not. But I'm worried about you. Why don't you just sit down here on the side of the bed? Your face is flushed, and your eyes seem cloudy. Please sit so I can look at them."

Kate reluctantly complied. She now knew Imre was a fraud. Even so, the only sensible course was to play dumb and search for a way out.

Novyck sat close to her and opened the case. Inside, she could see an optical instrument with a flashlight-like base and reverse teardrop lens—the kind used for eye examinations. Beside it lay a syringe.

He lifted out the eye magnifier and switched it on.

"Are you a doctor?" She asked the question directly, but in a tone that hid her hostility.

"Of course not, Katya. But I have studied the human eye extensively. You might call me something of an amateur optometrist. A person's eyes can tell us much about his overall health. The retina, for example, can reveal early warning signs of heart disease."

"I don't have heart disease."

"Please, stare straight ahead."

She did so.

He brought the instrument to his eye and switched on the light. A white circle crawled across her cornea.

"Now, turn toward me if you will, so I can check the other eye."

Imre sat so close she could hear him breathing. The light's glaring beam seemed to bounce along the edges of her consciousness, lulling her. As Novyck moved the light over her face, his elbow brushed her breasts. Somehow, the intimacy of his touch calmed her.

Kate again felt herself being drawn to him. How could he have such sway over her?

"Your eyes look very, very tired, Kate." His voice was low and the words were uttered in a slow, deliberate cadence. "Remember, you spent hours in that miserable hotel room with no rest."

"But I've just slept." Despite her protestations, Kate's muscles relaxed; the tension seemed to flow from her body.

"Yes, but you were restless." His voice was smooth, insistent. "You kept tossing about and talking to someone the entire time. Andre heard you through the door."

Kate's pulse quickened. *Whom had she been talking to? Simon? Herself? Had she been dreaming? What did Imre know?* She shivered, imagining the henchman with v-shaped hair pressing his ear to the door.

Novyck placed the device back in the case, his hands returning with the syringe.

His deep gaze pulled her in. She became aware of the lack of separation between his eyes' pupils and irises. Each concentric orb appeared black and borderless, a seamless void, like outer space.

Around them, the room's walls faded to a soft gray and seemed to lose their edges at the ceiling and floor.

A white piece of paper was being pushed toward her. None of it made sense to her. Novyck lifted her hand and closed her fingers around a pen.

"Sign this, Katya dear. That's it. No bother."

She saw the words "*POWERS OF ATTORNEY,*" but they appeared as meaningless individual letters, strung together in bold script at the top of the page.

She signed the document.

Then, in a single, sure motion, he took her right wrist in his left hand, rolling her arm so that the underside lay open and exposed against his knee. The hypodermic painlessly pierced her skin. Her eyes grew slippery in their sockets. The room and Novyck swam together in a slow-turning whirlpool.

"Sleep well, Katya."

Like a leaf swept into a vortex, Novyck made a wide circle as he backed out of the room. The door opened, sucking him away.

Kate pulled herself up on one elbow, trying to focus. In Novyck's absence, her vision lacked a benchmark. She swung her gaze around the room. Her surroundings seemed wavy and fluid. When she blinked, the walls shuddered.

★   ★   ★

AWAKENING GROGGILY hours later, Kate confronted the question that would trouble her for years: *HOW COULD she have been so wrong about Imre Novyck?*

With her head beginning to clear, the pieces were starting to fall into place. Perhaps she would never know exactly how or when, but Imre must have switched the stones when she'd seen him in prison the second time. Locked away, he'd known he couldn't control her visit to the Bank of England. But he'd also known his release was approaching, and that sooner or later she'd discover the gem was synthetic and return. The kidnapping and rescue were faked, too, designed to get her away from Simon Blake and under his, Imre's, control.

Suddenly energized, Kate rolled to a sitting position, her legs dangling over the bed's edge.

The room rocked like a ship in heavy seas.

Kate gripped the mattress to steady herself. What a fool she'd been! If she didn't get out of here she'd suffer the same fate as Irina and lose any hope of attaining her birthright or fulfilling her mother's dreams. Simon couldn't help. She had to cope on her own. And—with September 1 looming—she must act now.

But before Kate could function, she'd need to get these drugs out of her system. Flush them out. She remembered her mother's old Russian remedy for a sour stomach: a purge of warm salt water.

Rolling off the bed, she crawled across the heavily carpeted floor to the bathroom. With any luck, she'd find what she needed under the counter.

Chapter 50

THE ALARM sounded a split second after Kate kicked out the glass.

Now she hung twenty feet above the sidewalk, clinging with her running gloves to an outcropping in the brick walls.

A block away, a transmission whined in downshift. Brakes screeched. A mix of diesel smoke and scorched tires reached her nose. It was dawn, and the city's trucks were starting their runs.

She'd risen less than an hour ago, pulling on her black spandex. Kate's lips still tasted of the salt she'd found in the bathroom. She felt tired, but an up-and-down night of the heaves, and an icy shower, had done their work: Her mind was clear.

Opening the interior window latch, she'd crawled onto the wide stone sill and rolled onto the small of her back, knees drawn flat against her belly. Then, gathering all her strength, she kicked straight out, shattering the outside window.

Now, with the alarm screaming, she heard a door slam. Someone yelled.

Kate crab-legged down the side of the building, using the jutting bricks as handholds. Her tenuous grip slipped, her cheek scraped the wall, and with a yell she dropped most of the distance from the first story to the sidewalk below.

She collapsed into a sprinter's crouch, instinctively thrusting her right leg forward. Kate wasn't a runner, but she'd often trained with them. She knew that in a good start the athlete uncoiled from the blocks in an explosion that flung her down the track. In three or four strides—about two seconds—she'd hit top speed.

Kate's lungs pulled in air and the muscles tightened above her knees. She mashed the pads of her feet into the earth.

She launched.

In an instant, she hit full stride.

"Drive with your arms and your legs will follow," a running coach once told her.

But Kate was aware of only one part of her body: the soles of her feet. They slapped the pavement like hammers hitting nails. The key to speed was this: pushing each foot down with maximum force and minimum strike, so that it touched the ground as briefly as possible.

Kate's heart pounded. The cool morning breeze brushed her face. Exhilaration blew against her back like a strong wind. She was breaking free. A mile and a half away, the Yauza River wound west through the city. After a short swim to the Moscow River, she'd hide along the banks of an adjacent canal.

Her eyes cleared a path before her. The world shrank to the drumbeat of her feet.

Slap! slap! slap!

Kate closed out the sound of dogs barking behind her. The universe became her churning glutes, quads, knees and calves.

Her feet came off the ground as if it were ten thousand degrees hot.

Slap, slap, slap.

As animals, humans possess few weapons—no fangs, claws or horns. But they are relatively fast and durable; over long distances, a man can outrun a horse. This is how homo sapiens survived centuries of pursuit by predators, and why, in primitive societies, running remains highly prized today.

Slap, slap, slap.

As her twelve-block dash faded behind her, Kate passed through Chistiye Prudy (or "Clean Pond"), the city's oldest neighborhood, still marked by narrow, quiet streets and mostly pre-Revolution buildings. Chistoprudny Bulvar itself, however, was the widest of the Ring roads, dominated by the body of water in its center that had once been called "Foul Pond" for its stinking collection of sewage and slaughterhouse waste.

SLAP, SLAP, SLAP.

Kate passed the main Moscow Post Office—a poor place to leave a letter if one ever hoped to have it delivered. Next came the gray slab of the Procurement Ministry, then the Sovremenik Theater. She ran by three churches—two of them topped with Orthodox spires—and, respectively, the Swiss, Kazakh and Iranian embassies.

SLAP, SLAP, SLAP.

Passing the Indian Embassy, Kate entered Yauzsky Bulvar, the last and skinniest of the Ring boulevards. Lined with trees, the street became even narrower as she approached the Church of Saints Peter and Paul. Heading left, she saw one of Stalin's "wedding cake" skyscrapers, the imposing Kotelniki Apartments on the opposite side of the Yauza River. She'd almost made it: The Yauza's juncture with the Moscow River lay less than 100 yards away.

VANDAL, THE 140-pound alpha male, raced at the head of a pack of four attack dogs. So far, the fierce mastiffs had been unable to close the gap with the fleet woman. Weighing a collective 590 pounds— roughly 465 pounds more than their prey—the canines had been trained as pups to leap from behind and take down their target with a blow to the back.

Despite the large leather muzzle covering his snout, from the moment the woman began running, Vandal had locked in on trace scents of her urine. Nostrils flaring, his powerful body veered in a turn, huge haunches gathering and releasing beneath him.

Suddenly, at the boulevard's end, the woman vanished.

★　　★　　★

The trees that shrouded Kate's escape stood at the foot of the Bolshoy Ustinski Bridge, built in 1938 as a link to the district that had once served as an outpost against the Mongols. For Kate Gavrill, the gently-arching bridge was a gateway to freedom—*if* she could execute a perfect, *soundless* dive. Kate pulled herself up on the ironwork guardrail. For an instant, she paused. Her hand touched her neck; a thin strand of gold floated in the air, high and away from the river below. Then she dove.

SPLASH!

Vandal and his mates swung their heads.

Saliva foamed over Vandal's incisors, flecking his ears and chest. In seconds, his pack reached the bridge.

Below, still distant from the river's edge, the woman swam. Sensing they would gain by staying on the bridge, the dogs roared along the pedestrian walkway. Then at the last moment, Vandal vaulted over the same guardrail Kate had used to launch herself moments before. As he hurled toward the water, the beast saw his prey. His timing had been perfect: He would surface between her and the riverbank. She would be his now.

Chapter 51

Sɪᴍᴏɴ Bʟᴀᴋᴇ stood on the bridge, lungs heaving. A golden frog and a sheared necklace lay in his upturned right palm.

Moments before, Kate's scream had merged into a single, shrill alarm. Blake had watched her drop a full story to the sidewalk, crouch, then leap out in a runner's sprint. Close behind her were a pack of panting dogs and Novyck's henchmen.

Jumping to his feet, Blake had raced after Kate's pursuers, but too late. He'd watched helplessly from the bridge as Novyck's dogs herded her to the riverbank. The Russian's goons then hauled her into their waiting Maserati.

Blake turned the jewelry over in his hand. The little frog measured mere millimeters in length, but its meaning far exceeded its size. What could be a clearer message than this piece of jewelry?

Blake spotted one of Moscow's ubiquitous telephone boxes. Quickly crossing the street, he called the police. He knew the truth now: Kate hadn't gone to visit Novyck. She was his captive. At least, however, he'd found her.

★   ★   ★

Hᴜɴᴄʜᴇᴅ ᴏᴜᴛ of view in the back seat of their *chastniki,* Vulcan Krasky and Hector Molina had also witnessed the taking of Kate

251

Gavrill. Their cab followed Novyck's sedan to his residence. Then, believing the cleric's entourage to be temporarily settling in, Krasky ordered their driver to take them to a smallish rock club about a mile away. The drinks were cheap and—when bands weren't playing—the place was quiet.

"I have associates," said Krasky, swizzling a jigger of vodka. "We could take Novyck now."

Molina shook his head. "Patience, *mi amigo*, patience. There is no need for violence. Besides, bringing in your heavy-handed colleagues would only mean more knives to cut our pie. Remember, we don't want Novyck, we want the stone and the egg. What does Miss Gavrill want—that is the real question."

"What do you mean?"

"I think something else is involved. If there weren't, why wouldn't she simply turn over the stone in exchange for her freedom?"

"Yes, but then they would kill her."

"Not likely. Too much fuss. But consider another possibility. What if they already have the stone and the egg? We both believe that she smuggled what she thought was a genuine gem and its Faberge container to New York. Someone clearly switched at least the stone before she left, and fooled her—and, for a time, Blake—with a fake. Who else would be more likely to have done that than Novyck?"

"But why?" Krasky rubbed his chin. He pulled the handkerchief out of his sleeve and mopped his forehead. Embroidered and monogramed, the flimsy bit of cloth managed to be simultaneously delicate and ostentatious. At the moment, however, its main function was as a nervous diversion. As Krasky was becoming painfully aware, even at full-race, his brain simply couldn't keep pace with Hector Molina's.

"At the moment I don't know" Molina replied. "But if, as I suspect, Novyck does possess the stone and egg, there has to be another reason they are keeping the woman alive."

Vulcan Krasky looked admiringly at his new friend. He had been fortunate to find such a wise partner. In his own way, he deeply regretted that soon he would be forced to dispose of the discerning Latin.

"So," Molina went on, "my take is this: We want the stone and, if we can get it, the Faberge egg. Novyck wants the stone, the egg, and perhaps something else. Blake wants the most: the stone, the egg, the perhaps something else, *and* the woman."

Molina paused, sucking on a piece of ice. "In my experience in life," he said, "no-one ever gets everything he wants."

He put both hands on the table and coughed, as if clearing his mind.

"One of us needs to stake out the Novyck house," Molina said, "and to follow them wherever they take Miss Gavrill. The other needs to follow Blake. Eventually, the two will come together, and so will we. And when that happens, what we have been searching for will be close at hand."

"And the perhaps something else?" Krasky offered the Latin a rare, thick-lipped smile.

"That too. Perhaps."

They lifted their glasses and clicked rims. "A drop," toasted a suddenly patient Krasky, recalling a Russian adage, "hollows out a stone."

Chapter 52

"**B**UT COMRADE, there is no broken window, no woman matching Miss Gavrill's description, and no sign anyone has been staying there."

It had taken more than four hours for the *militsiya* to search Novyck's mansion and return. They'd found nothing.

Now Simon sat in a smoky room at Tsvetnoy Bulvar metro station, about two miles from where Kate disappeared and less than two blocks from the Novyck residence. Arlen Mozhaev, head of detectives, was an egg-shaped man in a black suit whose too-large coat artfully draped his paunch but whose sleeves were frayed at the cuffs.

Despite the lack of evidence and his own weariness, Mozhaev— who'd spent most of the night filling out reports—seemed sympathetic. Blake had recently read in the *Moscow Times* that the *militsiya*, notoriously corrupt, had hired a western image consultant for a public relations makeover. Mozhaev must have gotten the word. "We are the good guys," the police officer protested in heavily accented English, hands upturned and outstretched. "Guys like Imre Novyck, they are the very, very bad guys. But does anyone know? Does anyone care?" He and his colleagues were well aware, the officer continued, of Novyck's criminal connections; they would keep the house under surveillance. But when the detective turned to him and asked why he and Kate had come to Russia, and why Novyck would want to kidnap her, Blake felt uneasy. He gave an evasive reply and found an excuse to leave.

Back at the Imperial Hotel, Blake reviewed his options. With the Bank of England's deadline just four days away, Novyck must intend to take Kate to London very soon, perhaps within hours. Blake made a brief call to Lt. MacMahon in Marion.

"I can't help with an investigation in Russia," Lt. MacMahon replied after Blake filled him in on the situation. "But I do have police contacts in London. I'll call there and tell them to expect you." After jotting down a few names and numbers, Blake rang off and dialed the UK.

A few minutes later, Blake found himself talking to Detective Robert Hudson, MacMahon's Scotland Yard connection. Hudson agreed that officers would intercept Kate at Heathrow Airport. They would also look into Novyck's background through Interpol. Blake sighed with momentary relief. He could think of many reasons he'd rather take on Imre Novyck in London than in Moscow.

#

Chapter 53

HECTOR MOLINA concealed his slender form behind a light pole. It had been a humid day and, even in the dark night sky, Molina could see clouds gathering for one of Moscow's frequent summer showers.

Across the street, emerging from the Hotel Rachka, one of the men who'd abducted Kate Gavrill—Molina had seen him behind the wheel—stepped out for a cigarette. The man stood under a street lamp on Trubnaya Street, about a dozen steps from the hotel entrance.

Molina had watched Imre's house but not seen any sign of Kate Gavrill. He'd seen this same man leave and return to the house twice. The second time he'd followed him to the Rachka.

"I suppose there's still a chance they were successful in Kiev," Molina told Krasky as the latter dropped him off and ordered their taxi to take him to Simon Blake's hotel. "If so, Blake may also know where the jewel is."

Molina concentrated on the sidewalk outside the Rachka. Far more likely, he told himself, was that the secret of the gem's location—perhaps even the stone itself—currently resided directly across the street. Otherwise, why had they taken the trouble to move the woman here?

The man Molina was watching crushed out his cigarette and walked back toward the hotel.

Rain pelted Molina's forehead. Should he follow him? The Colombian thought about the prize of freedom the stone offered and crossed the pavement, circling to avoid the cones of light painted by street lamps.

Slipping inside the hotel, Molina followed his prey past the dingy elevator; for a smoker, the driver climbed the staircase rapidly. Molina trailed behind. In the stairwell, he slipped off his shoes, hooking them in his fingers until the man turned off at the third floor. Then, in stocking feet, Molina sprinted, catching the door before it closed. He cracked it wide enough to see the man open the door to Room 33. He also heard the lock click behind him.

Molina waited five minutes, then entered the empty corridor.

Something in his own nature, something beyond the stone, propelled him now. Perhaps it was a latent addiction to risk. Perhaps the sheer professional challenge of scaling this castle of cutthroats. His nerves hummed, and an intense focus melded his muscles and mind with a singularity of purpose.

Stepping directly in front of the door, Molina drew a stethoscope from his coat pocket. He placed its rubber cup just below the numerals "33." Inside, he could hear the steady drone of someone snoring.

Repocketing the stethoscope, he walked to an overstuffed chair opposite the elevator bank. He took off his coat, belt and watch, and stacked them neatly on the chair with his shoes.

Emptying his pants pockets, Molina drew out a tiny Allen wrench, what appeared to be a clasp knife and a silk cord, the latter knotted at each end and about three feet long. He draped the cord over his neck like a loose tie. It was his only weapon. Molina's artistry allowed him to induce unconsciousness rather than death.

Molina crossed the hall and stretched to reach the nearest wall sconce, unscrewing the bulb inside. He retraced his steps, quickly extinguishing the opposite light. In the now darkened corridor, Molina removed his shirt and trousers, stripping to his last garment, a skin-tight nylon body stocking that allowed complete freedom of movement.

The sheer black hosiery clung to his form, as close as Molina could come to the nude state in which he exercised with the bells. It was more than a quirky habit of dress: for what he was about to do, he would need to sense—and control—his body at a near-molecular level.

Molina's heart raced. It had been a long time since he'd chased a world-class gem. He could almost feel the oxygen rush through his veins. He faced a huge danger. If they awoke, the people inside would kill him. If, on the other hand, the stone were in their possession, it was possible he could snatch the gem in a single stroke. It would mark a great finish, a memorable cap to a memorable career.

From the knife-like clasp, he unfolded a case-hardened, stainless steel pick. It looked like a tapered swizzle stick with a squiggly end. In his other hand, Molina held a small L-shaped hexagonal wrench.

He moved to face the door. If he still had his touch, he'd be inside in less than thirty seconds.

The lock itself was a simple pins-and-tumbler design. Before most luxury hotels switched to plastic cards, Molina had picked hundreds of similar devices. The main components were a series of small pins of varying lengths and a central cylinder slotted with a keyway.

Molina's nose told him this lock had recently been lubricated—a plus because the oil would serve the dual purpose of quieting the pins and making them more slippery.

He inserted the tiny wrench in the keyway, gently turning the cylinder clockwise until it jammed in the surrounding housing. This meant some of the pins had already cleared the cylinder, but others, still protruding into the keyway, were binding.

Molina inserted the pick all the way into the keyway. Long ago he'd learned to tune his ears and fingers to the slightest changes in sound and touch as the pick passed over the pins. He projected his mind into the lock, reconstructing an image of how it responded to his manipulations.

Varying the tension on the wrench, he pulled the pick out quickly so that it bounced the remaining protruding pins up and above the cylinder—blocking them out of the cylinder's path as it turned.

The door opened soundlessly. Molina knelt to place his tools on the floor, lightly holding one end of the silk cord.

In a single movement, he slipped inside.

The man who'd smoked on the sidewalk now slumped in a chair to the door's right, head lolled, eyes glazed in near-sleep. Behind a half-opened door, Imre Novyck snored in the room just beyond. The entry to the remaining bedroom was closed.

Molina pirouetted as he moved to face the sleeping driver. His hands flew up, and the cord looped gracefully in the air, like a cowboy's lariat. By the time the Russian's eyes fully opened, his carotid artery had been sealed for nearly ten seconds. His mouth emitted a silent rush of air. His saliva rustled softly, like a dry summer wind. His chin touched his chest. He had not made a sound.

Molina stepped in long strides toward the closed door.

The woman, gagged and bound by plastic ties to her bed, lifted her head. Molina put a finger to her lips.

Don't speak or make a sound, he mouthed.

Bound and gagged, she lay on top of the bedclothes. A small nightstand lamp revealed that she still wore the same black body suit in which he'd seen her captured.

Against the room's dingy green wallpaper, Kate's albescent skin looked like fallen fruit. A crimson bruise blotched her right cheek. Blood crawled from a slash on her forehead. A purple scab clotted her lower lip. Her fall, Molina wondered, or a subsequent beating by Novyck's thugs?

Her eyes moved frantically in their sockets, from his face to the door and back again. Molina read their jittered calculus. Was he an ally? A police detective perhaps? Did his wordless warning mean he was someone who might help her?

But Molina didn't try to loosen her bindings. He dropped to his knees and looked under the bed. He crossed the room and opened a tiny closet. He went to a chest and pulled out each of its drawers. He recrossed the room and opened the nightstand.

Molina met her eyes again, and saw her dawning realization. He wasn't there to rescue her—*he was looking for the stone.*

Molina backed out of the room, closing the door behind him.

As he passed, he glanced into Novyck's room. Next to his bed was a matched set of leather luggage. The set's smallest case lay on the covers, inches from its possessor's hand. Molina now knew the gem's location.

For a moment, he paused, bringing his hands together in a steeple in front of his nose. For his task in the next few seconds, he must summon everything he'd learned and been trained for.

In quick, catlike steps, he entered Novyck's room, soundlessly moving to the side of the bed.

Novyck lay on his side, one arm draped over the leather briefcase that Molina was certain contained the alexandrite. The other circled a young woman, her voluptuous form outlined under the sheets.

Then Molina saw the blue-steel link between the briefcase and its possessor's wrist.

There'd be no taking the gem now. A bedmate and handcuffs were too big a risk, even for *El Mimico.*

Outside the room, Molina grabbed his belongings. At the stairwell, he slipped back into his clothes.

Back on the sidewalk, he flipped open his mobile.

"The stone and egg are in the hotel, in Novyck's possession," Molina told the Slav. "The woman is alive."

"What about Blake?"

"Forget Blake. Meet me here, at the Ratchka Hotel."

"I don't understand."

"Their luggage is packed. They're leaving, and we must follow. Whatever else they are after has to be where they are going. Come now."

Chapter 54

—◦◉◦—

UNABLE TO sleep, Simon Blake sat at the Imperial bar, nursing his second scotch. He'd brought the frog pendant with him after having it repaired by a jeweler in the hotel. Now he hung the necklace from his fingers, watching the glittering amphibian twist above his drink.

His other hand tightened on the glass, and his lips firmed into a thin line. Kate, he vowed to himself, would again wear this piece. In the meantime, however, there was still the significant matter of her whereabouts. Blake knew she was Imre Novyck's prisoner, but where was she being held?

Then it hit him: What if they'd taken Kate back to the Kruschev Arms, the cheap hotel where she'd dropped the ledger book? It was obvious Novyck had corrupted someone at the establishment, a night clerk or perhaps the owner. Could Novyck be keeping her there before heading to London? They had to leave soon. The Bank of England deadline was just three days away. Blake had nothing to lose: The hotel was in Old Arbat, only a brief walk from the Imperial.

Slipping the necklace into a zippered pocket, Blake headed out the door. The first rays of sun splintered between buildings as, in ones and twos, the city's earliest risers trickled across the streets. As Blake knew from previous visits, Moscow slowed perceptibly in August.

Some businesses closed down or followed reduced schedules. Wealthy residents departed for their country *dachas*.

Blake was waiting to cross Nikitskiy Bulvar—one of the southern links in the Boulevard Ring—when he saw the big man, or rather saw his reflection. The image bounced back at Blake from the side of a yellow-and-white Moscow "A" tram. In the shiny, wavy metal, the figure moved like a rubber toy. The man tried to conceal his ripply form behind a street vendor. When the sidewalk seller moved his cart, he stood exposed. But Blake had already recognized him—it was the man who'd jumped them in Massachusetts. Blake judged him to be about twenty feet away.

About a hundred steps into Nikitskiy Bulvar's park-like central mall, Blake stopped at a bench. The Slav was still behind him, but he too had halted, and was talking into his mobile. Then he wheeled away from Blake and, cell still clamped to his ear, headed in the opposite direction—back toward the Imperial Hotel.

Reversing roles, Blake now stalked the bigger man. His prey put a lot of weight and hurry on the hoof. The Slav hurled himself forward, extending his stride, his feet hitting the sidewalk on the backs of their heels. While one hand held the cell phone to his ear, his free arm flung forward in loose, akimbo arcs. To Blake, the man's hurried movements, his full-stride conversations with whomever was on the other end of the mobile, and his obliviousness to the fact that he was now the one being followed, evidenced urgency.

Was the Slav working for Novyck? Blake had no idea. Perhaps he'd concluded that Kate had the original alexandrite, or correctly deduced that she'd come to Russia in search of it. In either case, he'd followed Blake in hopes of being led to Kate. So there could have been only one reason he'd abruptly changed direction: The cell phone call must have told him where she was.

His heart beating faster, Blake walked back through the trees on Nikitskiy Bulvar. Krasky moved ahead, limbs still pumping, laddering in and out of view behind large shrubs. Remnants of

Moscow's "summer snows"—the feathery fluff that fell from the city's 350,000 poplars in June and July, still swirled in street gutters, and collected against the windward side of hedges and curbs.

Blake made his way along Gazetny Street, now trailing Krasky by about half a block. The big Slav dodged and weaved through a short line—short only because of the early hour—outside the door at McDonald's. The giant American chain had proven the truth of the Russian saying, "eating increases the appetite." More than five thousand Moscovites, working at some fifty-odd locations throughout the city, now flipped the firm's patties.

They passed the turnoff for the Imperial. Where the hell was the big man headed?

Blake looked right, past the foreboding walls of the Kremlin. Like bright, upended turnips, St. Basil Cathedral's blue, red and gold spheres poked their striped tips into the morning sky.

Its scattered onion domes kept Moscow from looking like a dozen other megalopolises. Without them, the city's glass-and-steel office buildings, and its traffic-jammed streets, differed little from similar structures and surroundings in London, Paris or New York. "Moscow," a concierge had told Blake on his first visit, "is not Russia." Indeed, take away its Eastern Orthodoxy and its Mongol heritage, and Moscow could be Any City, Anywhere.

Krasky passed the Moldavian Embassy. He turned left, his steps slowing as the elevation rose. Behind him, Blake saw the Cathedral of Nativity of our Lady, built as a novitiate in the fourteenth century but home for a commune of squatters by the twentieth. He followed Krasky as he doubled-back over Boulevard Ring.

Crossing Trubnaya Street, the Ukrainian walked about a block and a half and then stopped. On the opposite side of the street stood the Hotel Rachka, whose facade was dominated by a single row of square, one-story colonnades and a modestly appointed lobby with large plate-glass windows. Blake sidled off to a side street, eyeing the hotel from around the corner.

They were less than three blocks from Imre Novyck's mansion. Blake's pulse quickened. *Kate had to be inside that hotel.*

Another man, dark, much smaller, joined the big Slav on the sidewalk. The two came together, chatting animatedly, but in low voices. Then the smaller man walked away, turning a corner out of view.

Blake backtracked to a phone booth, grateful that a half dozen plastic *kopeks* clacked in his pocket. He slipped a token into the slot and a moment later was talking to Lt. Boris Mozhaev on the latter's mobile.

"Look, Mr. Blake," the detective said through a sleep-thickened accent, "purely on circumstantial evidence you suspect Miss Gavrill may be in the hotel. But I've already sent my men on one wild birdy chase. And some of us were up very late last night. What do you expect us to do when we get there?"

"Enter the hotel and rescue her, of course." Blake was surprised. Earlier, the officer had seemed so concerned with his department's public image. Now he seemed more interested in getting his beauty sleep, and more than a little irritated by a straightforward request for help.

"Quite impossible," came the officer's abrupt reply. "And as an American, Mr. Blake, you of all people should appreciate why. We can't simply enter private hotels, barge into their rooms and remove guests. Perhaps under Kruschev, but no more."

"You could at least go in and question the clerk." Had Mozhaev been visited by the *mafiya*?

"And what would that accomplish? If you are wrong, Miss Gavrill is not there and we have wasted our time. If you are correct, Novyck has either bribed the clerk or he owns the hotel and we have wasted our time. Moscow's crime problems, Mr. Blake, are far too serious for us to waste our time."

"But can't you see—"

"No, Mr. Blake, I *can't* see. Goodbye."

The chief detective clicked off his cell, detonating an explosion of anger in Blake. He didn't know which made him more furious: Mozhaev's apparent change in attitude or his own sense of powerlessness.

While hot rage pounded in his temples, cold fear clutched his gut. What about Kate? They had to keep her alive—at least until they'd drawn the Romanov funds out of the Bank of England—but what ordeals might she be enduring in the meantime? Were they turning Kate into a drug-addicted zombie? Were Novyck's thugs abusing her in other ways, perhaps for their own sadistic or sexual pleasure?

Worst of all, time was running out. In three days, barring an act of Parliament, the deadline for claiming dormant accounts would expire. The Bank of England funds that Nicholas had established for Lydia—now rightfully Kate's—would be lost forever. At that point, assuming he was correct that Novyck possessed the real stone and egg, her life would be of little value to them.

He had to get into that hotel.

He stuck his head around the corner. Vulcan Krasky had disappeared.

Blake darted across the street, his fear-tautened muscles welcoming the release.

The clerk was a well-shaped brunette in her late forties with tightly bound hair and lips that flattened against her teeth in a thin line. Her manner was perfunctory and unhelpful. Her heavily accented English, Blake thought, could serve as a perfect cover for deliberate misinterpretation. She wore round glasses whose lenses reflected the lobby's fluorescent ceiling lights.

"No sir, no one matching that description has left the hotel."

A 1950's cartoonist could have drawn her mouth; her straight lips moved, but the rest of her face remained immobile.

"No, no. I asked whether anyone like that is *staying* at the hotel."

"I really wouldn't know sir. I only just came on duty."

"You don't get many guests from the U.S. here," he asserted, leaning toward her on the counter. Perhaps minor flirtation would help. The woman stepped back and stared blankly at him.

The Rachka, Blake was certain, had never seen the inside of a Western travel guide. Its clientele had to be limited to nationals and Eastern Europeans.

"How many rooms are in this hotel?" he asked rhetorically. "Twenty-five? Thirty? Wouldn't the clerk you relieved have noticed that an American woman arrived in the company of several Russian men? Wouldn't they have mentioned it to you?" He was getting nowhere; Blake realized he'd asked almost the same questions in the hotel where he'd looked for Kate earlier.

"Sir," she replied stiffly, as if reciting from memory, "no one told me about an American woman. Or Russian men." She patted her hair, lifting her bust. "And my hours are quite full enough, thank you, without time to study each and every guest who signs our registry. Now"—her lips curled firmly against her teeth—"would you like to leave a number where you can be reached should your friends arrive?"

Blake shook his head. The clerk's performance had done its work. His emotional energy vanished like a volatile gas, leaving in its place a heavy cloud of depression. He turned away, and walked back outside.

Unknown to Blake, his movements were again being tracked by Vulcan Krasky. On the rooftop of a small apartment building across the street, the big Ukrainian watched him through a pair of high-powered binoculars. He saw Blake walk out of the Rachka's lobby, step into a narrow walkway between two buildings, then turn back to face the hotel.

They'd switched roles for a second time, but now stalker and prey shared the same fate. They could only watch and wait.

Chapter 55

THE FULL-throated rumble of a race-tuned, four-hundred-horsepower
Italian V-8 opened Simon Blake's eyes. He'd concealed himself by
leaning against an alley wall alongside a trio of dumpsters across from
the Rachka. In the shadows, drowsiness settled over him like a hood.
Now, he felt a rush of adrenaline as the sleek Maserati pulled in front
of the hotel. He wondered again why Novyck, a furtive denizen of
the nether world, would choose such a singularly distinctive car.

Then he saw the answer.

A woman, more buxom than Kate but about the same height
and with an identical crop of short dark hair—almost certainly, he
guessed, the unhelpful desk clerk in a wig—came down the stairs,
accompanied by a man of about the same build as Novyck and
wearing the latter's trademark Armani suit. The couple got into the
car, which drove slowly away.

About half a block down, the big Maser passed the first cross
street. A taxi pulled out and followed. Two men sat as passengers in
the cab and, an instant before it drove out of view, Blake recognized
the large Slav sitting on the right.

There could be little doubt: Clearly, the big man—and perhaps
the smaller companion Blake had seen him with earlier—planned
to trail Kate to London as well. So now, besides himself, there were

at least three underworld competitors pursuing the alexandrite and egg.

A battered, Soviet-era Lada sedan drew up in front of the hotel.

Moments later, Kate, supported on either side by Novyck's men, haltingly descended the Rachka's front steps. Dressed in a Navy pinstripe suit as if she were a businesswoman on a trip, Kate looked groggy. Her leg gave way when she reached the sidewalk, and only the arms gripping her elbows saved her from a fall. Even from Blake's distant vantage point, it seemed obvious she'd been drugged.

Novyck walked behind them, carrying a small case. A subordinate reached out to take it, but Novyck brushed him aside and entered the car, taking a seat beside Kate. His two henchmen sat together in the front seat.

They sped away.

Blake urgently needed his own *chastniki*, and—especially at this hour—it wouldn't be easy. Airport-bound drivers who hadn't paid the mafia for protection risked violent consequences; many now routinely refused fares to that destination. Blake reached inside his jacket for the zippered pocket that contained his wallet. He'd need bribe money, both for the cab and for a plane ticket. Undiscounted, a coach flight to London could cost $1,500. He'd probably need $500 more to "tip" the ticket agent.

Counting more than twenty-two $100 bills and three $500 travelers' checks, Blake sighed with relief.

He stepped out into Trubnaya Street and began waving his arms.

Chapter 56

K̲ATE'S̲ ̲BODY̲ seemed separated from her consciousness, as if transformed into something other than flesh and bone. Her spine furrowed like a stiff pole into the soft leather of the First Class Aeroflot seat. Her eyes felt sticky in their sockets, shifting almost as slowly as her thoughts.

He'd drugged her. But then—as she now realized—he'd been drugging her from the beginning, initially with his eyes.

Despite her daze, Kate became aware of a looming presence in the cabin.

Police Lt. Vulcan Krasky entered, daubing his forehead with a now sweat-stained kerchief.

He saw her and smiled slowly, just as he had when he first walked into her hotel room in Kiev. Another man, much smaller, took the seat beside Krasky. Kate recognized him too: the silent interloper who'd stood at the foot of her bed the night before, then left without helping her.

Kate looked at the passing parade as if they were figures in a slow-motion movie reel.

One man had chased her and beaten Simon; another had seen her desperation and turned away; a third was trying to steal her brain as well as her inheritance—each wanted what was hers and would do anything to get it.

Furthermore, each had reasons of his own for craving her birthright. And each, she knew even in her fog, would unhesitatingly kill her or anyone else who stood in his way.

Of the three, she judged Novyck the most dangerous. Krasky was a big, brutal thug, but clumsy of foot and mind. The smaller, handsome man seemed ambivalent and inherently less violent. But Novyck was evil incarnate. The direct descendant of the mesmerizing madman Rasputin, he was cut from the same twisted clerical cloth.

Somewhere in the laudanum mist of her night at the Ratchka, Kate had a chilling thought. She recalled Imre's passing remark. *You were talking to someone, he'd said.*

Had Imre gotten inside her head? *Was he trying to control her through someone else—an inner self?* Had he found a vulnerability, a weak point, that allowed him to enter her psyche? She'd defeated herself at Bolshoy Ustinski Bridge, partly by failing at the last instant to execute a perfect dive. Flawed spotting had been the likely culprit, but was that merely a metaphor for something she alone could control by tapping deeper into her conscious? And did that something exist in the same part of her brain where Novyck now probed? The idea was frightening, but it held a glimmer of hope, and even the prospect of power.

If she could find a way to turn Imre's schemes against him.

Chapter 57

"You have five minutes to get to the gate," the Aeroflot ticket agent said, covertly glancing at the five $100 bills Blake had pressed into his palm.

Blake had asked for a fifteen-minute delay of the flight and a First Class berth. The clerk shook his head and laughed out loud. "You must be yoking," he said in a heavy East European accent. "There are only a few bags left to check, and I just sold the last two First Class tickets. I simply can't hold the flight that long."

Blake charged down the long corridor to the departure gate.

"*Excusez-moi.*"

He'd bumped into a crowd of French college students.

"*Merci*," he said, jostling his way past them.

He jogged again, slowing when he saw the familiar airport security conveyor belts.

He showed his tickets and—without luggage—moved quickly to the boarding area.

"Wait!" Blake yelled. The flight attendant was about to close the aircraft door.

Boarding amidships, Blake squeezed into his aisle seat.

Was he a fool? Counting "tips," he'd paid more than $2,000 for a one-way fare to London, and he wasn't even certain Kate was on board.

As soon as they were airborne and the seat belt light blinked out, Blake strode to the First Class curtain. Parting it, he peered inside.

A woman with short-cropped black hair nestled against the white vinyl-covered porthole next to her window seat. Even with her face turned away, he instantly recognized Kate.

His emotions shifted from elation to fear.

Beside Kate sat Imre Novyck. And behind them two men, Novyck's thugs, faced each other, talking quietly.

Across the aisle and two rows back sat the big man and his companion—they'd obviously gotten the last two First Class tickets. Back at the Rachka, they'd fallen for the Maserati ploy—or so it seemed. Obviously, they'd quickly deduced that the couple entering the first car were decoys.

Krasky spotted him.

Too late, Simon snatched the curtain closed. He quickly reurned to his seat.

Kate was on this plane! And there was nothing either he or his antagonists could do until the aircraft landed.

Or was there?

An international pay telephone beckoned from its crevice in the seat back next to him.

He removed the receiver, tapped a string of numbers and the ring-ring of a London telephone buzzed in his ear.

"Metropolitan Police."

"May I speak to Detective Hudson, please."

Brief silence. "Sorry, Sir. Detective Hudson won't arrive on duty for an hour."

Blake pressed the flight attendant button and moments later a stewardess, wearing Aeroflot's signature starched white collar, stood by his seat. He asked for copies of the International Herald Tribune and the Financial Times, fitfully perused both papers for the next sixty minutes, and again placed the call.

This time Hudson was in.

"Unfortunately, Mr. Blake," the detective said, in a partially smoothed cockney accent, "we have been unable to locate Miss Gavrill on any incoming flights."

"I know that, Detective Hudson, because she is on the plane with me. But I can't make contact, and she appears to be drugged."

"What's your flight number? When is it due to arrive at Heathrow? I'll have my men there. We can take Miss Gavrill into protective custody, so long as she requests it, or obviously appears under duress."

"And don't worry about Imre Novyck," the detective said, "or the men with him. We can at least detain them for questioning. We'll need a court order to search their luggage for the stone you describe, but Interpol has already turned up an impressive criminal dossier on Novyck. If it comes to it, we can deny them entry. Be assured, Mr. Blake, we'll give this Novyck gent a royal welcome."

Chapter 58

———∎«(◦)»∎———

"Ladies and gentlemen," the pilot began in stilted, Russian-tinged English, "I regret to inform you that, due to an emergency at Heathrow, we will be landing at Gatwick Airport."

Blake yanked the in-seat telephone out of its niche almost as quickly as he heard the news. While Aeroflot flew regularly scheduled flights from St. Petersburg into Gatwick, most flights from Moscow went into Heathrow's Terminal Two. He had to get word to Hudson that they'd been diverted.

From the corner of his eye, he glimpsed a dark sleeve. It belonged to the same Aeroflot stewardess who'd earlier brought him newspapers.

"I'm sorry sir," she said, "you can't use the telephone during this phase of flight."

"But this is an urgent matter. I'm trying to reach Scotland Yard."

The flight attendant's brusque manner, thought Blake, would have fit in perfectly with the Aeroflot of the eighties and nineties.

For years, jokes about "Aeroflop" had been a staple among air passengers. Tupolev jets with hand-painted interiors, service-with-a-snarl stewardesses and engines that vibrated like washing machines became the stuff of Aeroflot legend.

"I'm sorry, sir, we can't allow exceptions. International terrorism regulations, you know."

"I'm going to use this phone, or I am going to the captain." Replacing the phone in its receiver, Blake unlatched his safety belt and started to rise.

The attendant put a firm hand on his shoulder. "And if you approach the pilot area, sir, you will be restrained. Please sit down."

Biting his lip in anger, he complied. He had to remember there were two other thugs on board besides Imre and his crew—and all of them were desperate. Disrupting the flight could trigger violence and put Kate in even greater danger.

As part of training Aeroflot personnel to US/UK standards—and upgrading its fleet to include new Boeings and Airbuses—a new color scheme had been chosen to reflect "professionalism, technology and warmth." Aeroflot's staff had supposedly morphed into "people-focused ambassadors" who purveyed Russian hospitality.

Blake looked a few rows up, at the navy, silver and orange "iron curtain" separating coach from First Class—and his seat from Kate's. No amount of professionalism, technology or warmth could inform Scotland Yard's finest that there'd been a last-minute change in their destination. The switch in airports would be announced at Heathrow, but the possibilities were slim that police on the other side of London could reach Gatwick before touchdown. Once in country, Imre Novyck and the others would have, temporarily at least, a clear path. Physically, they could be intercepted at the Bank of England, but, Blake knew, lacking additional evidence, there was little chance a magistrate would intervene with Bank officials. In the meantime, there'd be no way of knowing where Novyck and Kate actually were.

KATE HEARD the pilot's announcement clearly, as if someone had turned off a fuzzy filter that for days muffled every human voice in her ears. She was still groggy, but during the long flight some of the effects of Imre's opiates must have worn off.

The big jet bounced hard, then settled down on the runway.

Kate's hopes rose in direct counterpoint to the speed of the aircraft: as it slowed, her spirits lifted. She was, after all, back in familiar, freedom-loving western Europe, and at one of the most security-conscious airports in the world. They still had nearly 40 hours before the deadline—it was at least a fighting chance.

Despite a frown from their flight attendant, Novyck and his "colleagues" sprang from their seats and started pulling their luggage from the overhead compartments.

As First Class passengers, they were off the plane minutes after it landed.

In Moscow, Novyck had ordered a wheelchair to take her to the plane, and now he did so again to disembark, draping her with a shawl and pushing the device himself. She wasn't feeling well, he'd told airport authorities. Beneath the shawl, with coolness and efficiency, he lashed her forearms to the chair with plastic ties.

Though smaller than Heathrow, Gatwick had been one of the first airports to test technology—Iris-reading detectors and the like—as a means of increasing security. After the 9-11 tragedy, the airfield had confiscated as many as two thousand pairs of scissors a day. Kate wondered: Couldn't its immigration officers and security guards round up a few middle-aged thugs and thieves?

She felt Novyck's controlling palm on her shoulder. It had been there since they'd left the plane. Now, as they entered the baggage area, his hand tensed; Kate glanced up and watched his head turn. She followed the direction of his chin to a man standing on the other side of the room, nearly thirty yards away.

Simon Blake!

Novyck bent to whisper in her ear. "One sound," he said, "and your friend is a dead man." He'd obviously recognized Simon, Kate surmised, unaware the two had previously met.

Friend? The word seemed wholly inadequate. As much as they'd quarreled, no one could have been more steadfast. It was the first time in days she'd seen someone she could count as an ally.

Simon, look at me! Help me!

Kate thought the words, imagined screaming the words, but didn't utter the words. Not a sound, Imre said. She wasn't about to put Simon in further jeopardy.

His eyes met hers. Her heart pounded like a base drum. For one fleeting moment, the gray airport was transformed into a shimmering temple.

The wheelchair picked up speed.

"Leave the bags, leave everything," Novyck ordered his men, waving his hand dismissively over their luggage. "We'll get them later."

"But our suitcases are right there—on the carousel," the taller man protested.

"Forget it," Novyck barked. "I'll buy you batches of new suits on Saville Row. For now, let's just head straight to Immigration."

Simon was moving away from her now, talking into his mobile near a bank of telephones opposite the immigration checkpoint. He was calling for help! But an instant after he opened the cell Novyck's goon Andre confronted him.

From her vantage point, Kate saw the man's back. He faced Simon, who half-turned as he opened the receiver. The other man's flattened hand shot toward his windpipe.

Blake crumpled to the ground. Kate heard him groan.

"Heart attack!" Novyck's goon yelled. "Heart attack!"

Kate tried to stand up in her wheel chair. "It's not a heart attack," she yelled. "They're trying to kill him."

Novyck shoved her back down. "I meant what I said," he growled, bending closer to her ear. Novyck's hands moved from her shoulders to the grips of the wheel chair and he pushed hard toward the Immigration desk. As he picked up speed, Kate saw Krasky and the man who had been in her hotel room turn away from the Customs officer as he checked them through.

Novyck kept pushing. Clasping both their passports, he nodded perfunctorily as the Immigration Officer waved them on. No Iris-detectors here, thought Kate, of course these passengers are leaving the airport, not entering it. Her hopes of being saved by technology dissolved.

As they passed, she saw Simon getting to his feet. "I did not have a heart attack," she heard him insist to the small crowd that shuffled into a silent circle. "That man judo-chopped me! Stop him. Stop the others!"

Kate's entourage rushed toward the elevators that would take them to the trains below and from there to Victoria Station. By delaying Simon at the airport, she realized, Novyck had made it highly unlikely that the authorities—or anyone else—would find her. If she ever hoped to be free, she'd have to defeat Imre Novyck on her own.

Chapter 59

THAT REALIZATION nagged at Kate all during the cab ride to their hotel.

Since her escape attempt, the attitude of the man who sat next to her had shifted from a veneer of saccharine solicitousness to unmasked control. He barely spoke to her. He or his goons were always watching her. Her only time alone was in a locked room.

Yet there had to be something she could do.

A century ago, assassins felled Novyck's progenitor, Grigori Rasputin. They succeeded despite his power and influence, and even though he knew he was going to be killed.

In December, 1916, Rasputin had written a "prophecy" letter to Czar Nicholas. It contained a deadly curse. "I feel that I shall leave life before January 1," the monk wrote, then continued:

> Tsar of the land of Russia, if you hear the sound of the bell which will tell you that Gregory has been killed, you must know this: if it was your relations who have wrought my death then no one of your family, that is to say, none of your children or relations, will remain alive for more than two years. They will be killed by the Russian people. I am no longer among the living.

Days later he was dead, slain by assassins led by Prince Felix Yussoupov, the tsar's cousin, who poisoned, shot and clubbed Rasputin, then finally pushed him through a hole in the ice. The *starets* had been difficult to kill. When the bullet-riddled body was found, it was determined he had actually died by drowning.

Kate gazed out of the taxi at the early morning traffic, dredging her memory of Russian history. Given such a strong premonition—so strong that he'd stopped going outside his house—why had Rasputin accepted Yussoupov's invitation to spend an evening with him? After all, rumors that he would be done away with were even circulating in the Duma. And Yussoupov was a member of the nobility, the very class Rasputin had warned Nicholas against.

Then she remembered. She could almost hear Anya's voice telling the story. Yussoupov lured Rasputin by playing to his weakness, by offering the one thing that would draw him out of his well-protected shell: the promise of meeting a beautiful woman. In fact, she was, by most accounts, Moscow's greatest beauty, none other than Yussoupov's dazzling brunette wife, Princess Irina, for whom Kate's own mother had been named.

And suddenly Kate knew. Her best—her only—chance of breaking free of Rasputin's descendant would be to overcome him mentally as well as physically, using his ego and her own femaleness to lower his defenses.

Intellectually, the idea went against her every instinct. Kate had been anything but romantically precocious as a girl. As a young woman, her sense of sexuality emerged painfully, hesitatingly, and as part of an intricate architecture of ethics. Sex was not a tool to be used; it was a profoundly intimate gift, one that left her soul naked. To deliberately offer herself to another would betray those feelings. Could she pull it off?

If she were successful, sex would only serve as bait for a fish Imre would never land. After all, on the fatal night Grigori Rasputin came to call, Princess Irina wasn't even home.

Their cab wound through London's oldest section, its financial hub, known as The City, home to the Stock Exchange and Lloyds. From Monday to Friday, a million commuting workers would crowd into this single-square-mile.

Hundreds of them worked at the Bank of England where, tomorrow, Novyck would attempt to falsely claim her inheritance. "Just what is your plan?" she asked Novyck.

She spoke the words slowly and in a low voice. She hoped to disguise the fact that the drugs she'd been given prior to their airport arrival had largely worn off.

Novyck turned and smiled. For a moment the sugary veneer returned. "I'm glad you are interested in our little family enterprise, my dear. First, I'll show them copies of the papers. We'll unveil the originals in a second meeting, and, of course, yourself."

Kate looked away.

Yes, she thought, she would be the final prize, the ultimate evidence of authenticity. Or rather a husk of herself, hypnotically programmed to follow his every lead. Just as certainly Kate knew that, as soon as Novyck had deposited the Tsar's dowry in his account, the husk would be discarded.

They turned right and pulled up in front of the Langley, one of London's most elegant hotels.

Their taxi stopped and was immediately surrounded by top-hatted doormen and bell hops. As they entered the sumptuous lobby, Kate marveled at the soft fabrics, delicate furniture and gold, yellow, ochre and black color scheme. Scents of jasmine and chamomile drifted in from the dining room. Far from a hole-up for international gangsters, she thought, it was the sort of place where, in a different, better, time, one might have met Anna Neagle for tea.

The Romans had chosen this part of London for its two defensible promontories, Ludgate and Cornhill. But outside invaders hadn't brought The City down. In 1665, a virulent resurgence of the Black Death swept the area. Thousands of Londoners perished. Their clothes were burned and their naked bodies piled high on plague carts for the ride to burial mounds that could still be seen.

Novyck pushed her wheelchair into a gilt-lined elevator. Kate momentarily shuddered. It was here in London, too, that she would make her last stand.

Chapter 60

HECTOR MOLINA smiled in surprise and delight as their cab, which had followed the Novyck party from Victoria Station, slipped under the ornate entrance to London's Langley Hotel. Molina had been a guest at the hotel before—several times, in fact—both on pleasure and business.

Ahead of them, Novyck, Kate Gavrill, and Novyck's men had just disembarked and were moving—the young woman in a wheelchair—through the lobby. London's original "grand" hotel when it opened in 1865, the Langley was the first city hostelry to offer elevators—"ascending rooms" as they were called—and hot and cold running water.

"You'll like the Tsar's Bar," Molina told his companion as they got out of their cab. "They have caviar, borscht, Russian *Zakusis* and a hundred kinds of vodka."

Krasky grunted. He didn't need a tour guide to tell him about Russian bars. And relieving his frustration would take more than a few swills of grain alcohol.

Seven stories and just fifty paces north of Oxford Circus, the hotel couldn't have been more quintessentially British. A long line of Anglo-Saxon intellectual and artistic aristocracy and a smattering of royalty had signed its registry. A brass plate identified the rooms favored by Sir Arthur Conan Doyle. Another announced the "Wallis

Simpson" suite—the trysting spot used by the American divorcee and King Edward VIII before he renounced his throne for love.

Clipping two one-hundred pound notes to the registration form, Molina bluffed their way past the desk.

"We're with the Novyck party, but we don't have reservations," he said. "We need to be on the same floor."

The clerk happily obliged. Though its standard rooms were fully booked at this time of year, space could sometimes be found in the hotel's handful of ultra-luxury suites.

Moments later, Molina stuck their keycard in a door. It opened onto a curved staircase. Climbing up, he and Krasky found a large room. In its center was a king-size bed with large silk pillows, a soft duvet which matched the pastel wall decorations and Roman blinds. There were two armchairs, a table, a fruit bowl and an alcove with a lighted wardrobe. A corner window offered dramatic views of London.

Additional stairs led to a private drawing room with settee, table, another minibar and a color TV with SKY channels.

Molina put his bags down in the drawing room.

"I'll sleep in here," he said, graciously allowing his large companion the comfort of the bed.

Molina reached into a small briefcase and removed a pea-sized device. He unpeeled its backing to reveal a gummed surface. With Krasky trotting behind him, he walked a few feet down the hall and attached the pea near the floor on the door to Novyck's suite.

"It's a small transponder, powered by a wristwatch battery," Molina explained after they returned to their room. "When the door moves, it sends a signal. The range is only about a hundred yards, but that's enough to tell us when anyone enters or exits."

"How?"

"A soft buzz on this mobile." Molina held up his own cell phone, handing it to Krasky.

"So what good does it do us to know they've left? Our guns are in Russia—and Brighton Beach."

"Don't you see? We don't *want* guns," Molina said. "Nobody in London has them anyway. This"—he drew the short silk garrote from his pants pocket—"is all we'll need."

Molina's cell alarm sounded. He cracked their suite's front door, then turned and whispered hoarsely to Krasky.

"He's going. I'll follow."

A short time later, the Latin watched from a cab window as Novyck headed up a flight of stairs on Threadneedle Street and into the Bank of England. Molina was no financier, but he knew the bank hadn't held private accounts for a century or more. Why had Novcyk gone there?

He'd have to deduce the answer later. He—Molina—couldn't just walk into the Bank of England. Novyck must have official business there, but what? He'd left the two goons to guard the woman at the hotel and, unless he was fool enough to carry it, the stone as well. Molina knew those rooms, and he knew each one contained a safe. He leaned forward in his seat.

"Driver, back to the Langley, please," he said.

\#

Chapter 61

WHEN IMRE Novyck ascended the steep flight of stairs to the "Old Lady of Threadneedle Street," he was entering more than a savings depository. The Bank of England symbolized Britain's enduring role as a global financial center and, indeed, as a bedrock of civilization itself.

Greeting Novyck in the outer lobby were Peter Cushing, partner of the New York law firm Kate had retained, and Hillyer Walker-Smith, from Cushing and Wakeman's affiliate firm in London.

"Miss Gavrill isn't joining us?" Cushing asked. "This is a bit irregular. I thought we would be meeting with her. My office, however, did receive your faxed copy of her Power of Attorney."

"We will only be dealing with photocopies today," Novyck said. "We thought it would be more appropriate for her to appear after our preliminary discussions, at which time we will present the original documents and, of course, the stone and its Faberge egg container. I know Miss Gavrill left the Faberge piece with you for safekeeping—I trust you have it with you."

"Of course," Cushing replied. "It's locked in the vault at our London office. As far as our meeting with Miss Gavrill, Mister, ah,"—he glanced at the card in his hand—"Novyck, this is cutting our timetable much closer than I would like. Tomorrow, as you may be aware, is the last day we can file such claims."

"Let's proceed, shall we?" interjected Walker-Smith, an elderly but authoritative-sounding attorney of slight stature who carried Cushing's briefcase.

A few minutes later, the three sat in a room decorated with duck egg blue walls, gilded chair rails, white lampshades and heavy gold-framed oils. Facing them across a conference table were Sir Reginald Wilcox, president of the Bank, and Frederick Carlyle, representing the Bank's solicitors.

Cushing leaned forward in his leather-upholstered armchair, his face reflected in the burled walnut.

"I thought it might be helpful to open with a summary," he began, "just to be sure we are all starting from the same page."

Wilcox and Carlyle stared back woodenly.

"As you know, at the beginning of World War I, Tsar Nicholas II was acknowledged to be one of the world's wealthiest individuals.

"In 1906," Cushing continued, "Nicholas secured for his children five dowry accounts at this bank, each for approximately five million pounds, or twenty million U.S. dollars, based on exchange rates at that time.

"We are not here," he added quickly, seeing the stricken looks on the faces of the bank executives, "to address the whereabouts of those multiple funds and accounts, which were never claimed."

"*Or* proven to exist," interjected Sir Reginald, his voice dripping with sarcasm.

Cushing remained unperturbed. "We are here today to claim a *sixth* dowry account, established in equal amount by Nicholas Romanov in 1913, for his daughter with Anya Putyatin. Our claimant, Miss Kate Gavrill, is their direct descendant and heir."

Cushing now leaned back in his seat. Wilcox bent forward, and spoke.

"You are aware, Mr. Cushing, that the Bank of England functions as the central bank for the United Kingdom. It has not offered private banking services for more than a century."

Cushing now tilted forward again. The two men faced each other at eye level across the table.

"Yes, yes," Cushing said, "and I know that you, Sir Reginald, are aware that private accounts *were* historically maintained for European nobility. This is such an account, and at the cumulative interest rates prevailing over those many intervening years, today stands at a value in excess of $90 million U.S. dollars. That is the amount we are seeking."

Wilcox glared at his opponent.

"Mr. Cushing, the American imposter Anna Anderson, the most recent such claimant—whom I should like to point out no member of this bank ever actually *saw*—was in recent years revealed to the world to be a fake by DNA analysis. We will expect that your Miss Gavrill prove her claim using similar evidence.

"We are indeed, prepared to satisfy that requirement. In fact, Mr. Novyck is carrying such evidence in his briefcase."

Cushing paused, then spoke slowly to emphasize his words. "I further wish, gentlemen, to draw your attention to the following facts:

"In 1959, *The Observor* of London reported on Baring Brothers Bank. 'The Romanovs were among their distinguished clients,' the newspaper declared, adding, and I quote, 'Barings still holds a deposit of more than 40 million pounds that was left with them by the Romanovs.'

"In 1987, the British Government established a Russian Compensation Fund, administered by the accounting firm of Price Waterhouse, to compensate holders of pre-revolutionary tsarist bonds. London newspapers quoted a Fund spokesman indicating that the money had come from Tsar Nicholas II's multi-million dollar London bank account, whose existence had been denied for more than sixty years.

"Our own firm's research shows that Romanov assets included money deposited by the tsar and his family in British bank accounts—mainly this bank and Barings—and that the money was surreptitiously transferred to King George V and Queen Mary with the connivance of the British Treasury and the banks concerned. In fact, the man at the center of these dealings—one Peter Bark—had been the tsar's last finance minister. He was hired by King George to manage the sale of Romanov jewels—those that had been slipped out of Russia—at scandalously low prices to Queen Mary. Many of the most fabulous of these same gems can currently be seen on the necks of Queen Elizabeth and Princess Anne. The King, I might add, later knighted Peter Bark in recognition of his, ahem, services."

Tension lines etched the slopes of the nobleman's nose. "Now see here, Cushing, are you implying—"

"Sir Reginald, Mr. Carlyle," Cushing said, "I am *implying* very little. What I have just stated is a matter of historical record. And I am sure this information could be amplified if one were to seek legal access to the Windsor Archives."

The faces of both Englishmen turned lobster red.

"My clients and I are perfectly willing to seek such access," Cushing went on, fixing the two British hosts with a firm gaze, "and, if necessary, to press our case in the public prints. But we think you'll agree that would be unfortunate for all concerned, and, in any event, there should be no need to do so. We seek no funds the tsar may have deposited in separate accounts for his legitimate children. We seek no further compensation for the valuable—and scandalously acquired— jewels that are in possession of your own House of Windsor. Finally, we seek no accounting of the transfers of Romanov funds that may have taken place in the years after the Great War.

"We seek only those monies—with interest—due our single client as a direct heir," Cushing said. "And we will present full proof of our claims. Mr. Novyck, will you share with us the photocopies of the Bank of England documents? We, of course, retain the originals, which we will turn over to you for authentication, in the presence of our representative."

Novyck handed Sir Reginald the leather briefcase containing copies of the papers Irina had left for Kate.

"Please, allow us a few minutes to review these," Carlyle murmured, a troubled expression replacing his bulldog's anger of a few moments before. Novyck, Walker-Smith and Cushing rose and repaired to the outer office. They could hear the Brits' voices, but could not make out what they were saying. At one point, a small elderly man wearing glasses entered the room, stayed briefly, and then left. When Wilcox and Carlyle emerged, they were smiling and notably more relaxed.

"Gentlemen, we agree there is no need to make these proceedings contentious or for the subject of our discussions to leave the confines of this room. Our archivist has determined that the papers you have given us are almost certainly copies of authentic documents. We will simply ask that you present the originals, together with the so-called Romanov alexandrite and the Faberge container, for our experts to inspect—in the presence of your representative, of course.

"We would also ask that you obtain a Court of Chancery order that your client is indeed a Romanov—the DNA evidence you've gathered should suffice for that purpose."

"Time is of the essence," said Novyck. "May we meet again this afternoon?"

"Yes, Mr. Novyck, and be certain to bring Miss Gavrill," said Carlyle, still smiling. "By law, tomorrow is the absolute deadline to reclaim assets of this type. The bank will insist that you honor it."

Moments later, Novyck was back in his cab. Only a single hurdle remained: preparing Kate for her final appearance. To succeed, her submission to him must be complete—mentally, emotionally and physically.

At the last thought, he smiled, imagining the pleasures he would enjoy administering her final exam.

He tapped the window. "Driver, the Langley, please. And hurry."

The cab pulled away. Novyck did not notice a pair of Metropolitan Police cars arrive at the Bank's entrance. Nor did he see the tall American—whom he would have instantly recognized—emerge from one of them.

#

Chapter 62

—◦«(◉)»◦—

KATE STOOD before the mirror in her locked hotel room, clothed only in a black thong.

Although her mind was fixed with purpose, Kate struggled with the task of trying to look sexy for a man she despised. Moreover, her weapons of attraction were limited.

She slipped on the silk jacket from the only outfit she had—the snug but tasteful Gianfranco Ferre suit Novyck had given her to wear on the plane. Now, worn without a blouse and bra, the garment's jacket molded to her body in soft folds. With its wide lapels, saddle shoulders, and gangsta rap length, the coat teased in movement. She pulled on the lined skirt.

Considering that Novyck's decision to abandon their bags had left her without lingerie, this wasn't a bad get-up. The suit coat fully draped her, but allowed glimpses of flesh. Irina always said a man's imagination was a woman's most powerful ally.

"Tartov! My Comrade! To our mutual great fortune!" Through her door, Kate heard the clink of the Langley's best crystal. Novyck's thugs had decided to throw themselves a party.

Announced by the clatter of a serving cart, their meal had begun shortly after Novyck left. "Your beef and vodka, gentlemen," she heard the waiter say. Now, after a multitude of crystalline clashes, the formerly scary pair sounded more like the bumbling Bolsheviks in *Ninotchka.*

"Not long we get rich," Andre slurred in broken English.

"Yah," replied Tartov, "Like Imre say. Shoppink for suits on Saville Row."

Bang! The room reverberated with a loud explosion, then shouts and curses. Furniture collided against the walls and a table tipped over. A lamp crashed to the floor; its bulb popped like a toy gun.

Kate heard a fearsome voice—thick, Slavic, brutal.

"Kill them?" Vulcan Krasky asked.

"No. Please, no. There's no need." The second man's voice was cultured, assured, softer. "Use this tape around their hands," he said with a slight Spanish accent, "and across their mouths."

Someone turned the key to her room from the other side. The door opened—Kate quickly ducked behind it. A man entered.

As he passed, she saw him through the hinges. It was same man from the Ratchka Hotel who'd left without helping. His back turned to her, he headed for the closet and dropped to his knees.

Kate silently slipped around the door, making a beeline for the room's still gaping main entry.

At that moment, Krasky rose from Andre's legs, having finished taping up her guards. In full flight, Kate hurled straight into his ample mid-section.

Rough hands grabbed her shoulders. Her jacket slid to one side and her blouse opened, baring her right breast.

"So, my tasty little professor, Krasky finally gets his hands on you. And it looks like you are ready for pleasure, yes?"

Kate kneed him. Krasky groaned and folded at the center. She pulled out of his grasp, dashing for the door.

With amazing speed for his size, Krasky spun and clasped her trailing arm.

Like a dancer, he twirled her back into his grasp. Her coat opened, and he slipped both hands around her waist, drawing her against him.

His face dropped to hers. Saliva and sweat dripped from his chin. His eyes were wild with desire and rage.

She bit his lip with all her strength. Krasky flung her across the room. She crashed into the luncheon cart, scattering prime rib, potatoes, assorted plates, glasses, silverware, serviettes, salt and pepper shakers—and a four-inch steak knife.

Sprawled face down on the floor in front of him, Kate felt the knife—heavy, hard, ready—pressing into her hip. Krasky advanced. When he fell on her, Kate rolled with the knife. The big Ukrainian's weight did the rest; the blade found its way through flesh and bone, severing his aortic arch.

She felt Krasky dying, his trembling hands still pawing at her breasts. His eyes glassed, his breath fouled, and his bladder flooded his trousers. His weight settled against her.

Kate closed her eyes against the stink and the blood.

She opened them again as the smaller man strolled past her, pausing to glance at Krasky and the Russians. Kate looked up at him, but it was as if she weren't in the room. Looking neither right nor left, he crossed the hall and pushed the elevator button.

Hector Molina had the air of a man whose work was finished.

KATE PUSHED herself out from under Krasky, then crawled back to her room. Using the side of the bed, she pulled herself upright. What had the smaller man been looking for?

She had only a brief moment to ponder the answer.

In fact, she had no time at all.

Novyck stood at the door.

Chapter 63

His gaze swept from her disheveled hair to her toes, with a long pause in between. Still trembling from her encounter with Krasky, Kate pulled her coat closer. Abruptly, Novyvck returned to the foyer and stood over his two fallen henchmen. Through the open bedroom door, Kate saw him tear the duct tape from the mouth of the one named Andre.

"Aaaghhh!"

She heard a sharp cry as the tape peeled off, then their voices.

"Who's this?" Novyck gestured toward the heaping mound that had been Vulcan Krasky.

"He-he came in with another, smaller g-guy, a Latin." Vodka blurred the henchman's words. "The woman k-killed him."

"What Latin guy? Where's this Latin?"

"Gone. He l-left." Andre burped. A thin wave of froth broke over his lip and ran in a stream down his chin.

Novyck sneered. "You dumb fucks! Two guys jump you, tape you up like mummies. Then a hundred-pound woman kills the biggest one, and the little one gets away. And you're still sitting here like mummies. You're pathetic."

He paused, his tone less sarcastic, but more menacing. "The one who left. Was he carrying anything?"

"I don't think so, Excellency."

"You don't think? You don't know? You fool." He walked to the suite's still open entry door, shut and locked it.

Kate heard a sound like a butcher cutting meat.

"Please," Novyck's henchman groaned in pain.

Novyck re-entered the bedroom, bolted the door behind him, crossed the short distance to the bed and slapped Kate full in the face.

The blow stung from her temple to her jawbone.

"You bitch! You'll find me more of a challenge than that stupid Slav you killed. I'll deal with you momentarily."

With the door closed, the air seemed stale. Novyck strode to the closet and pulled back the carpet. Kate heard him tapping the buttons on the safe, saw his shoulder dip as he dropped his hand inside. Then he rose.

The alexandrite glowed in his palm like a late afternoon sun.

He turned back to her, suddenly calm, assured. "Now, my dear," he said, "we are about to begin the last steps in our journey. The bank expects to see us this afternoon. I must prepare you for our appearance."

Kate's gaze followed him as he drew closer.

Despite his average size, the bed groaned with his weight as Novyck sat down beside her. He took her hand, looking deeply into her eyes.

"You really are a fine subject," Novyck mused, as if talking to himself. "At least a Grade Four virtuoso, perhaps higher. We really won't need our little medicines anymore. That is your gift, Katya, your gift to me. It means everything I have been working for is now within reach. I've been very patient with you, but now you must perform for me at your highest level, as I know you will." He patted her hand.

Kate nodded. "I will," she said aloud.

Even the most skilled hypnotherapist, Kate knew, could only tap a capacity in his or her subject that already existed. She also knew she must stop that from happening. She must create her own inner space, a self-trance so profound it barred penetration, even by a master mesmerist. Yet she must also convince Imre Novyck that she remained under his spell. At stake were her life and everything she hoped for. Indeed, if Novyck prevailed, within the next twenty-four hours, Kate knew, she could count on two things: First, the stone and money would be gone; and, second, so would she.

"Now, I am going to employ a special technique whereby you will rapidly enter a deep trance." He moved closer to her. The smell of the city came off his clothes, mixed with the scent of his own body—an acrid odor that told her his nervous energy was high.

With the door closed, the room had fallen quiet.

In spite of herself, Kate began to relax. Like an X-ray, his power seemed to painlessly pierce her skull. She could almost feel him reaching inside, grasping for her brain's frontal lobes—the circuits that control thoughts and behavior.

Dr. Borshel's words came back to her. What was each dive but a trance, a frozen moment in which the athlete erects a barricade against every distraction, and strives to express physical perfection?

Kate reached deep into her own subconscious, turning her mind into itself. Shutting Novyck out, she imagined perfection.

For the first time in a long time, she knew exactly what to do.

"Katya," Novyck commanded, "roll your eyes upward."

Kate appeared to comply. In truth, as if she were "spotting" for a dive, she fixed her vision on the valance high above the room's only window. She pictured a perfect forward dive with three and a half somersaults, and a single half twist—the one dive she'd never fully mastered.

"Marvelous roll," Novyck commented approvingly.

She stands on the board, feeling every muscle and fiber in her body take on a separate life, preparing itself for what will follow.

"Breathe deeply," Novyck continued. "Imagine cool, pure oxygen filling your lungs, streaming into your blood vessels and capillaries, reaching into every part of your being, relaxing you, gently sweeping over you. Your arms and legs are as light as down . . ."

He smiled, and continued. "Now, Katya, I am going to take you to Harrods so you can choose some fresh clothes—what you have on is a bit worse for wear. Then, my dear, we will make our visit to the Bank of England."

A Time Traveler

KATE WAS standing in the spacious but dimly lit Harrods dressing room when she heard the persistent double-buzzing sound. It drilled through her lingering disorientation like a dentist's tool. Who knew this room had its own phone? She followed the sound to its source in a cupboard below the clothes rack. Opening the door, she removed a vintage, cradle-style telephone.

She lifted the receiver and heard crackly static, like a long ago radio broadcast from the European front.

Turning back toward the room, Kate realized she was not alone. Taking care not to hang up, she put down the telephone, and peered more closely at her surroundings.

Rectangular, with a chair and dressing table at one end and a floor-to-ceiling mirror at the other, the room was illuminated by a single overhead light, which cast a weak yellow glow over the faded, cream-colored walls. A figure stood near the door. Was this one of Novyck's people? A sales clerk? The invader remained motionless and silent. Adjusting to the poor light, Kate's eyes made out the form. It was a young girl wearing an old-fashioned white tunic that stopped at mid-thigh and buttoned up the front from neck to hem. Standing before the dressing table, the girl faced her. But her image was semi-transparent—Kate could see the furniture through her clothing.

Her lips moved, but she made no sound.

It was only after Kate again picked up the telephone receiver that she could hear the girl's voice. At once Kate knew her identity.

"Katya," said Anya Putyatin, "I wanted you to see what we wore when I first began dancing." The crackling sound rose and fell behind her words like an electrical storm. Bowing gracefully, the young ballerina extended her arms toward her legs, as if to commence a movement or series of steps.

"We weren't allowed to fully uncover our legs until the early Twentieth Century," she continued. "That shouldn't seem surprising. After all, women dancers were forbidden to perform ballet until the middle of the 17th Century."

Anya tossed her head, stirring that signature auburn whirlpool. "I wanted you to see what I overcame," she said. "Even as a child, and years before I met Nicky. Before I fled Russia with Lydia. Before your mother, and before all the rest too. Before the Romanov Stone."

Anya's voice seemed to grow weaker. Kate pressed the telephone receiver closer to her ear. "Granmama, why are you here?" she blurted.

"Because, child, you are my last surviving flesh and blood. Because I want you to know how much I love you. And because now that dear Irina is gone, you—and I—are the only ones to escape the Romanov assassins. Why do you suppose I watch over you, *Katinka*? Whose voice do you suppose you hear when you face danger, when you make an important decision, when you begin a dive?"

Kate shook her head. She must be dreaming. Was this an apparition, the result of the drugs Novyck had given her? She felt drowsy again, and the phone seemed heavy. Was the young Anya fading away? Before Kate's eyes, her great-grandmother's form seemed to grow decades older. Now she was the woman Kate had known as a child. This Anya wore a high-necked dress and wire-rimmed spectacles that glinted in the low light. She moved to the chair, sat, and stared fiercely at Kate.

"You chose not to listen to your inner voice in college, Katya. Listen to it now." She paused, then spoke again.

"You must succeed. It is not just a matter of honoring my memory or Irina's memory. It is not even a matter of righting past personal wrongs. You have a rare chance to balance the scales of justice and to help our world in an important way. Many people will be affected by whether you succeed, people you do not know and probably never will."

"Grandmama, am I really seeing you? Are you really here?"

"Dreams are our destiny, child," the old woman replied. "You must dance with your dreams, not with your doubts. Do you remember what I told you when you were little, about putting the things you care for at the center of your life? Where your attention goes, Katya, your energy will flow.

"Focus that attention, use your energy to defeat our enemy, Imre Novyck."

The crackling sound intensified and Anya's voice receded, though her image remained. Kate put down the receiver. *Dance with your dreams, not your doubts.* What did Anya mean? How had she come to her?

Nearly a quarter century had passed since she'd last seen her cherished childhood companion and ally. But never in her life had Kate Gavrill more desperately needed her relative than now. Crossing the room, she knelt and put her head in the old woman's lap. Wordlessly, Anya Putyatin stroked her hair.

Chapter 64

SIMON BLAKE paused at the Langley suite doorway. Four, five, six and finally eight Metropolitan Police followed, their uniforms swirling into a dark blue pool in the foyer. Inspector Hudson stood on the outer edge, staring at the hulk of Vulcan Krasky and, a few feet away, the freshly slaughtered corpse of one of Novyck's guards. The man's throat had been slit, and the wound gaped at Blake like a foolish smile.

Blake's eyes went to Hudson, who peered into the bedroom that had been Kate's brief prison.

When the inspector turned back, his face held only questions; Blake knew at once that Kate was gone and Novyck had escaped.

He pushed his way through the police, following Hudson into the bedroom.

Andre, Novyck's other guard, sat at the foot of the bed in a small lake of his own blood.

"This one must have worked his way out of the tape, then died in here." Hudson said. "Novyck probably killed them both with the knife used on Krasky."

A few feet away, the floor safe stood open.

"He took the stone," Blake said numbly. "He's got Kate."

Hudson stepped toward him, putting out his hand.

"Mr. Blake, I assure you we will make every attempt to prevent this man from leaving the country. He'll be charged with murder, of course."

A police officer wearing rubber gloves and carrying a large wooden case stepped between them. He knelt beside the dead man and peeled up his eyelids, then pulled them down.

"But we must be realistic," Hudson continued. "He has resources. The stone is worth millions. And, as we know too well, Novyck is damnably clever."

Blake rubbed his chin. "Yes," he said. "But not so clever that he can avoid a return visit to the Bank of England."

★ ★ ★

PETER CUSHING stood at the top of the Bank of England's steep main staircase.

"Hello Kate, Mr. Novyck," Cushing greeted them. His eyes told Kate what he saw: Despite the trim black Harrods pantsuit and body-hugging navy top, the young woman Cushing first met in New York had become a sallow-cheeked zombie who stared blankly ahead, her gaze fixed on a point beyond him. Given his generation, Cushing probably thought, like so many people he met nowadays, that Kate Gavril was medicated. Or perhaps she'd been drugged by the aphrodisiac of all that Romanov money.

But Kate showed Cushing exactly what she wanted him to see. She was about to dive—not dance—with her dreams.

They adjourned to the same room where the bank's officials had met with Novyck earlier in the day. This late afternoon, however, Cushing arrived unaccompanied, as did Frederick Carlyle, the bank's attorney. Carlyle sat opposite them at the conference table in the same seat previously occupied by Sir Reginald, the bank's director.

After a quick exchange of pleasantries and his introduction to Kate, Carlyle moved quickly to the point.

"Let's proceed, shall we?" the solicitor asked briskly. Kate marveled at the speed with which the bank's officials were moving, but she understood why. Settling this well-documented case as quickly and quietly as possible could only be in the Old Lady of Threadneedle Street's supreme self-interest. The last thing the bank wanted was a flood of copycat czarist claimants hectoring them in the courts and the press.

Cushing bent to his briefcase and removed a white cardboard box. He opened the lid and withdrew the alexandrite's gleaming, egg-shaped carriage.

As if on cue, Novyck placed the stone itself on the table. Under the conference room's diffused light, the alexandrite glittered a dark green.

Kate had not uttered a word. She looked at the treasures on the table, set before Carlyle like offerings to a king. The green stone and its golden container spun in a Dali-like daydream. She again thought of Anya dangling the frog before her eyes as a child. *Go girl!* As she had so often before, Kate heard the words in her head. But she now knew their source.

She begins her hurdle, stepping forward, springing from one leg at the end of the board.

"Mmm, lovely," mused Carlyle. He gave the fabulous display a passing glance, then pushed a sheaf of documents toward them. "These are non-disclosure agreements, drawn especially to cover this, er, matter," he said. "Their terms are quite straightforward: Not a word of this settlement must reach the public. Ever. You are not to speak to the press, or even to discuss this in private correspondence. You may not reveal this document's existence to family members, immediate or otherwise, and they too are bound to silence by its provisions.

"We have no wish, nor intent, to engage in pettifoggery," Carlyle continued in a monotone. "But for reasons that should be obvious, the bank is unwilling to create an electronic record of this transaction with an account-to-account transfer of funds. Upon Miss Gavrill's signature, we will issue a hand-signed certified cheque in her name." He cleared his throat and reached for a water pitcher on the credenza behind him. The tumbling ice cubes made a crashing sound in his glass. "The cheque"—he cleared his throat again—" is for 42 million pounds, the amount of Nicholas Romanov's initial deposit plus accrued interest.

"By your signature," he continued, "you will, of course, relinquish any and all future claims upon the bank, its subsidiaries and affiliates." Carlyle surveyed the table. His mouth turned slightly down in what appeared to be disgust.

"We agree—happily," gushed Novyck. His lips were wet. "And please allow me to thank the bank on behalf of myself and Miss Gavrill for your very enlightened response to our request." An almost beatified expression appeared on his face, as if, for a fleeting moment, he'd entered the portals of heaven.

Kate brings her legs up into pike position for her first somersault. She searches the room for a spot and finds a gold-leaf rosebud near the ceiling.
SPOT.
LOCK ON.
NOW!

She whirled to face Novyck. Her eyes, clear now, focused their defiance like pinpoints on a map, straight into his.

A confused expression crossed Novyck's features, as if, momentarily, he'd lost his way in a crowd.

Kate stood. In a room of powerful men, she was stronger, more powerful, an Amazon brandishing her spear. Heads moved to follow her.

Novyck's expression changed from puzzlement to amazement.

"I won't sign anything," Kate said, her voice loud. "This man"— she gestured at Novyck—"is a fraud. He kidnapped and drugged me and is trying to steal my inheritance. I demand that he be arrested."

The room and its stolid symbols of Empire collapsed in shambles. Audibly gasping, Carlyle pushed back his chair and collided with the credenza. The water pitcher wobbled, fell to the floor, and shattered, strewing bits of glass and ice across the carpet. As he tried to catch the pitcher, the Englishman's flailing arm struck the golden carriage, which rolled down and off the table, clunking loudly.

Cushing turned to Kate and started to speak, but only gaped. He stared past her to Novyck.

She saw the weapon in Novyck's hand even before he moved. In an instant his left arm crooked around her neck. His right reached for the table, and the Romanov Stone.

Kate felt his thin but powerful arm around her waist and the touch of a polycarbonate blade against her neck. The heads around the table turned again, toward them both, eyes round and astonished

Carlyle was half-standing. "See here!" he said.

But Kate and Novyck were already gone.

Chapter 65

As Hector Molina could have told Imre Novyck, the moment comes, even for the most carefully planned *crime de maitre,* when success turns on sheer fortune, when the master of determined discipline must yield to the commander of fickle fate. The doorknob that twists, but does not open. The pistol hammer that cocks, but falls on an empty chamber. The hotel detective who chooses the right floor, but the wrong corridor.

Or the empty, double-deck Routemaster bus, proud and polished for a vintage run, rumbling along King William Street on its way to Tower Hill.

Novyck's arm lashed out, long fingers grasping the upright pole at the slowly passing vehicle's rear platform. Like a spider clutching his prey, the Russian gracefully swung himself and Kate aboard. Keeping the polycarbonate knife against her throat, he pushed around the staircase that led to the ancient transport's upper deck.

Reaching for his ear, he touched the ubiquitous Bluetooth he'd slipped back into place as they left the bank. "Calling Base," Novyck yelled into the headset. His voice rose against the noise of the city and their clattering, bright red conveyance. "Change pickup location," he commanded. "Meet other side of river."

So this is it. This is how it goes down. He gives up the bank money, kills you here, then moves on, free. With the stone.

Novyck traded positions, dragging her forward, still barking into the headset.

Albert Gunter Jr. had watched in the rear view mirror as the fare jumpers boarded his bus. But since he'd not yet picked up a conductor, there was little he could do. A moment later the interloper, his hair toussled by the wind, and the woman, her jaw clenched in defiance, were beside him. A glossy black knife pressed flat against the female's glistening alabaster throat; her head jerked back and away from the weapon.

"I'll cut her unless you do exactly as I say!" His male passenger shouted above the roar of the engine and passing traffic. Gunter noted, however, that the woman's eyes held a steely presence.

Gunter had driven the 73 RM for more than 20 years. When the Royal Transport Authority decided to retire the venerable vehicles such a fuss erupted that a pair of lines were kept in service, mostly for tourists.

Gunter believed his Routemaster's open design gave it a special connection to the city. "My bus passes through London, and London passes through my bus," he'd told his wife, explaining why he opted against taking an early pension. "People, pollution, noise, and weather—they're like passengers who hop on and off."

But this passenger wasn't hopping.

"Straight over Tower Bridge," Novyck commanded. "And pick up your pace."

"You don't understand," the gray-haired driver protested. "I have a schedule and a conductor to fetch . . ." He saw cold mayhem in the hijacker's eyes and fell silent.

Carrying just a fraction of its normal human cargo, the big alloy-bodied bus rattled onward. Gunter cranked the huge mahogany wheel to make a wide left turn at Lower Thames Street, then turned left again at the Tower of London.

With each swing of the bulky vehicle, Kate felt Novyck's weight press against her. Behind the driver, the Tower's grim, 90-foot walls reflected in the window glass, their latticework of stones and mortar flicking by like cards on a pinwheel. Erected by William the Conqueror a millennium ago, the Tower had variously been a palace, a prison, several chapels, a vault for the crown jewels, and a site for high-profile executions. Here, King Henry III's pet polar bear had fished from the end of a leash in the Thames. Here too, after being lopped off by a French swordsman, Anne Boleyn's dripping, severed head had been held high by the hair, its owner's eyes wide with horror for a full eight seconds.

Kate's neck twinged at the pressure of Novyck's knife. She clenched her jaw tighter. This fake Houdini wouldn't be taking her head!

Downriver, she saw a private yacht approaching from the open sea. High above the vessel's deck, a radar dish rotated lazily in the late afternoon sun.

Kate knew now: Her time was coming.

Gunter turned right. A block ahead lay Tower Bridge Road.

Twisting Kate's arm behind her back, Novyck brought his blade close to the driver's face. "I said, Faster!" he yelled above the roar and clatter.

Kate felt the bus pick up speed as it blasted through blinking red warning lights, rolling under the first stone-covered arch that anchored the Bridge's massive steel supports.

Suddenly, Kate felt a trembling deep in the earth. The ship she'd seen had drawn closer. She was almost directly below.

The driver turned toward them, his eyes disappearing into the corners of their sockets, like a spooked horse. "Sir, this bridge is opening! I can't go on! I've got to stop!"

Fifty feet down, huge hydraulic pumps shuddered again.

"Go!" Novyck yelled again. "*FLOOR* it!"

The big Leyland diesel whinnied to the spur of Gunter's heavy workshoe. Even empty, the doughty vehicle weighed well over seven tons. The stink of hot metal and diesel fumes gusted into the open cabin. All that weight was on the hoof now, thundering forward like a bull elephant on rampage.

Kate watched the bridge heave itself into a mountain. The pavement lifted, rising to a clean edge that became the end of the world. Far below, between yawning jaws, the Thames swirled like a cauldron.

She saw the helicopter then, hovering above the river.

Novyck moved toward her, sliding like a snake to the doorway. Kate felt a sharp, stinging pain as he slipped by. The knife he'd meant to bury in her breast cut a glancing slice in her side. In pushing off, her onetime Svengali had stabbed her.

Now, like a stick toy, Novyck was falling toward the water, screaming commands into the headset as he descended.

The same slow-motion sensation that flooded Kate before a dive blocked her pain.

Her ultimate moment had come.

One.

Two.

She grabbed a leather passenger strap. Hoisting herself to the same door Novyck had used, she flexed her knees and launched.

Three!

Her body is airborne.

Kate curls, scrunches her legs against her chest, circles into herself like a seashell. One, two, three-and-a-half somersaults. As she rolls, her shoes fall away and her eyes spot on the flying bus, two-thirds through its mid-air arc.

The red behemoth thumps on the bridge's other side, squatting from the force of its own weight.

Kate's body drops through the London sky like a Nazi rocket, vertical, deadly, falling straight to target.

She spins in a triple corkscrew before sliding noiselessly into the water.

She's made a perfect entry.

For the rest of her life, Kate will remember how quiet it is below the surface.

Chapter 66

"It's too choppy," Hudson said. He looked back from the sniper's rifle, mounted on the bow of the Scotland Yard speedboat.

Minutes before, while parking on Threadneedle, the police official noticed what first appeared to be two fare fiddlers jumping on a bus.

"That's Kate! And Novyck!" Blake shouted.

Giving chase, the pair had been stuck at a red light when Hudson decided to change course. "We'll take a boat. We can pick up another car on the other side," he said, swerving down an adjoining street to the river. They'd already left the Metropolitan Police dock when Blake saw Gunter's bus take flight and Novyck make his sky bolt for freedom. Hudson immediately spun the rudder toward Tower Bridge.

"Too much risk of hitting innocents," he said now. "Including the girl."

Blake nodded. As if to underscore Hudson's assessment, the boat's flat hull slapped the water, jarring the rifle butt against the inspector's chest. They were closing fast.

★   ★   ★

Seventy-five yards away, Kate swam toward Imre Novyck in long, swift strokes. Wind from the helicopter's blades blew the tops of the waves into a creamy froth. She shrugged off her jacket. The knife wound burned at her side.

Reaching the chopper's pontoons, Novyck grabbed a line someone threw from the cabin door, and hauled himself out of the river.

In the water below, Kate flung up her right arm and grabbed the Russian's ankle.

Novyck turned. Bracing himself on the aircraft's metal frame, he stretched across the float. Breaking Kate's grip with his free foot, he pushed her back under.

Water and air swirled over Kate's head in a rush of bubbles and current. When she broke the surface, Novyck stood on the pontoon above her.

His laugh taunted her. "I've still got it!" In his left hand, high above his head, he held the Romanov Stone, glowing like an ember. In his right, he held a Walther automatic. "Stupid cow. You're going to die the same way Grigori did."

Kate heard a sharp mechanical sound as he cocked the pistol's firing mechanism.

The first slug plowed harmlessly past her, traveling about two feet before it fell straight to the bottom.

The second seared her left arm like a branding iron.

Kate flipped her legs in a dolphin kick and headed straight down. Murky and cold, the Thames molded around her like an icy gel. A third slug churned past her left ear.

On the surface, she heard the hum of the helicopter motor, gaining momentum for liftoff.

She had to get him into the water—he'd be no match for her here.

Spinning in an underwater somersault, Kate reversed direction and headed back up. The pontoons floated above her like huge gray sausages. Novyck peered over the side, his face wavering through the water. A fourth bullet went wild, boring an oxygen tunnel before dropping harmlessly to the depths.

Kate surged out of the water and onto the pontoon next to Novyck, beaching herself on her elbows. Startled, her opponent turned, but too late. Kate rolled into his calves, rose to a half-crouch and drove her weight into his mid-section. Novyck lost his footing. With a loud splash he fell backward into the water.

The Romanov Stone hung in the air like a small balloon.

Thunk!

The gem made a hollow, metallic echo as it hit the pontoon and rolled lazily down its length.

Kate stood frozen, her eyes locked on the moving treasure.

Novyck stroked frantically, racing the jewel to the end of the pontoon.

He lost.

The stone slipped over the edge and splashed into the river.

Kate dove.

For an instant, even in the tenebrous river, the jewel gleamed red. Less than a yard from Kate's outstretched fingertips, it darkened to green. Arching her back, Kate pulled her arms apart in a powerful breaststroke, and frog-kicked. She shot forward.

But the big alexandrite was falling faster than she could swim.

It turned black and vanished.

Kate pulled up, momentarily treading in place. Then she pushed her palms toward the river bottom and scissored her legs. She drifted back to the surface. Gasping, she gulped in a fresh supply of air. Her lashes squeegeed the water from her eyes.

Simon Blake leaned over the side of a Scotland Yard patrol boat.

Novyck and the helicopter were gone.

Chapter 67

"I suppose we could ask Cushing to try for an extension," she said, her voice as distant as her eyes.

"I already did," said Blake. "He commiserated, but said it was pointless. Even if we got the stone back, Parliament set the deadline; there's really nothing anyone can do."

Kate stared between the planks of teakwood decking. She could see the smooth interior of the small boat's hull. How far below was the Romanov Stone, mired for eternity in a mud and sludge strongbox? Her chest seemed to collapse around her windpipe. "I had him and I let him get away," she wheezed, speaking as if to herself. "And I lost the stone as well."

"Don't blame yourself." Blake circled her with his arm. Both the wounds Novyck had inflicted were superficial, but the stiff police bandages made her wince with movement. Her shoulders trembled.

"Novyck may have escaped for the moment," Blake said, "but he fled empty-handed. He won't last long."

"I can't believe how much power he had over me."

Blake looked down at her. "I know I may have just seemed jealous," he said, "but I wondered about that from the start. You talked about Novyck as if he were a demigod, but he just didn't add up. Something didn't ring true.

"The good news, however" he continued, "is that you stood up to him."

Kate sat very still, mulling his words. For much of her life, she'd locked her emotions behind a door. She'd created the same kind of closed house her mother had kept her in—believing it was for her own safety. And in those dark rooms her heart had grown cold.

With Anya's recent help, she'd flung open that door. She might have trouble seeing clearly at first—abruptly looking into the sun could do that to you. But at least she'd stepped out of the shadows.

"They say life is a journey," Kate said, squinting up at Simon. "But does the journey create the person, or the person create the journey?

"I suspect a bit of both," he replied.

They reached the dock.

Simon Blake leapt gracefully off the bow, then turned back to her.

"I lost everything," Kate said, taking his hand. "I lost Imre. I lost the stone. I lost the money. I let Anya down. I missed my last chance to make things right with Irina."

"You haven't lost everything," Blake countered in a measured tone, "and you haven't missed any last chances. Every day you live you make Anya and Irina proud."

"There are things about me you still don't know," Kate protested. Even in uttering the words, however, she realized how trifling a 10-year-old sports scandal seemed compared to what they'd just been through. Kate stared back at the Thames and Tower Bridge. "I owed them their dream," she said.

Blake moved closer to her. River spray slickened his face, plastering his hair to his forehead. "I know about your past, Kate. Let it be the past." He grinned. "Like I said, we'll talk about it when we're old and gray. And as a matter of fact, you're wrong about the dream. It may not be lost, at least not all of it. Cushing said the bank was highly receptive when he suggested using the account to fund a special Romanov Center for Russian scholars. It would offer grants and fellowships to strengthen cultural and commercial ties and improve understanding with the west. He wants to talk to you about the idea as soon as you're ready.

"Besides," he went on, "you still have the egg. That would be a handsome dowry for any Russian princess. You also have this." His hand opened to reveal Anya's Faberge frog, the jeweled amphibian that first brought them together. Stepping behind her, Blake kissed the back of Kate's neck as he fastened the twice-repaired necklace. "And you still have me, such as I am."

Kate finally smiled. "But Simon," she said, turning back to face him, "It's not just the Romanov stone or the money. Novyck killed my mother and escaped justice, and he almost killed me. The worst part is no-one will ever know that the tsar—my great-great grandfather—had a living heir. It's as if Anya, Lydia, Irina and I never existed. As if the past hundred years of our history never happened."

"Kate, darling Kate," Blake said, drawing her close into his arms, "Don't you see? *You* know. *We* know. It's your history. I hope it becomes our history."

She looked at him. The truth of his words slowly filled her.

She reached for his hand.

"Not Kate," she said quietly, shaking her head. "From now on, call me Katya."

Epilogue

On the other side of the city, a Daimler limousine drew up outside a neighborhood park in St. John's Wood. A slender olive-skinned man rose from a bench. He passed a caretaker kneeling in a rectangle of lavender flowers, and approached the long black car.

The rear passenger window made a scuffing sound as it slid open.

"Please join me inside," said Jacob Massad.

"Much appreciated, but I am—as you say—*pooshed* for time," the other man replied in a soft Latin accent. "One thing," he added, "you will absolve the woman and Mr. Blake of any and all obligations regarding the stone?"

"You have my word," Massad replied.

The Colombian nodded and slipped a heavily padded package, about the size and shape of a small grapefruit, through the window.

He accepted a thick manila envelope in return.

"*Vaya con dios,*" he said, smiling.

Then, with a wave, Hector Molina walked briskly up the street. He'd catch a cab on Abbey Road. With any luck, he could still make that 2:00 P.M. flight to Spain.

THE END

Historical Notes and Acknowledgements

In *The Romanov Stone*, actual and imaginary facts, characters and events mingle freely. For example, principally found in Russia, Sri Lanka and Brazil, the alexandrite is the world's rarest precious gem and changes color under illumination, from various shades of green to various shades of red. It was ostensibly discovered and named in Siberia as described, in 1830, the year Alexander II came of age, and for whom the gemstone is named. The Romanov Stone itself and the meeting between Tsar Nicholas I and his timorous lapidary are both, of course, apocryphal.

The character of Anya Putyatin is, as readers may have guessed, loosely modeled on Anna Pavlova, the greatest ballerina of her, or perhaps, any time. Russian noblemen of the period frequently drew mistresses from the Imperial Ballet and Nicholas himself had a love affair with a prominent ballerina—and the young Pavlova's contemporary—Mathilde Kschessinska. This liason, however, occurred before Nicholas' marriage to Alexandra.

It is also true that Empress Marie Feodorovna, along with a retinue of servants and relatives, escaped to Denmark aboard the HMS *Marlborough*, dispatched by England's King George V to Yalta. The empress stuffed many of the family's prized jewels into a trunk, which she kept under her bed in Copenhagen. Queen Mary subsequently obtained valuable pieces through sharp bargaining with the beleagured empress, for whom the jewels were a primary source of income. Today, the gems can be seen being worn by English royals, including Queen Elizabeth.

As described, after a hair's-breadth escape from pursuing Bolsheviks, Princess Olga Romanov married her longtime lover and lived in Denmark on a farm, becoming a prolific watercolorist whose works remain highly regarded. As related in *The Romanov Stone,* many other Russian expatriates settled in Paris, enjoying a privileged cultural and legal status until the assassination of the French president by a deranged muscovite.

The Romanov's pre-war finances came under intense scrutiny during the Anna Anderson "Anastasia" trials, which wound through international courts for decades. Reports of these proceedings, arguably the longest European civil case on record, supplied much of the detail about the tsar's Bank of England accounts in *The Romanov Stone.* Although the trials established the existence of the accounts the tsar set up for his children, bank authorities claimed the funds were withdrawn to pay for the war, a point Andersen disputed until her death. Subsequent revelations of other untouched Romanov-era bank accounts, notably at Barings Bank in England, were trumpeted by Anderson advocates to support her claims.

The technical descriptions of the Romanov alexandrite and tests used by Simon Blake and Professor Bertram to test the stone, were as accurate as Mr. Cotes and I could make them. For example, the discrepancy between modern practice and 19th century standards of weight exist as described and must be taken into account in appraising the size and value of older gems.

As trivia experts in the United Kingdom may be aware, *The Romanov Stone's* ending, in which a double-decker bus hurtles across Tower Bridge as it opens, is based upon historical fact. Indeed, in 1953, a Routemaster bus, fully loaded with passengers, jumped the gap when the bridge opened due to a malfunction. Its driver was widely hailed as a hero—had he attempted to stop the vehicle, it surely would have plunged into the Themes with resulting loss of life.

Many interview sources helped inform and authenticate this book. Dr. Peter Bancroft, of Fallbrook CA, has served as Curator of Mineralogy at the Santa Barbara Museum of Natural History and as Director of Collections at the San Diego Gem and Mineral Society. He has spent years visiting remote mineral and gem deposits around the world, including Siberia's Toyovaya mica schists, where the original alexandrite was found. His guidance, especially on the conditions and locations in which raw alexandrites are found, was appreciated.

The author is similarly grateful for two lengthy interviews with the late Dr. Herbert Spiegel, MD, of Manhattan, who died in 2009. At the age of 95. Dr. Spiegel helped establish hypnosis as a mainstream therapy. He coined the term "hypnotic virtuoso"—and defined its physical indicators—to describe the small number of subjects who are highly hypnotizable. His theories drew considerable interest from the American intelligence community. He was a proponent of "hypno-programming" in the assassination of Robert F. Kennedy by Sirhan Sirhan, whom he defined as a hypnotic virtuoso.

Others to whom the author owes thanks include Kenneth Taylor, stagecraft wizard extraordinaire for San Francisco's Bohemian Club, who provided detailed guidance on creating the illusion of a fake-looking Romanov stone. The comments of Shannon Bresnahan, faculty member of the San Francisco Ballet and a former soloist and principal dancer with companies in Europe and New York, on the technique of dance, including "spotting," as well as general observations about life *en pointe*, were especially helpful and deeply appreciated. The notes and comments of the late Jane and Don Wallace, recounting their visits to the Monastery of the Caves at St. Sophia in Kiev, were similarly valuable. *Barron's* contributor, writer and photographer Susan Neider provided helpful technical information through a series of emails.

Many writer friends and colleagues commented on *The Romanov Stone* in its various stages, including Nancy Boas, Michael Libbey, Terry Raskin, Shannen Rossmiller, Judith Egan, Racheal Yeager, Judith Leaper, Brent Barker, Lucy Sanna and members of the Gold Rush Writer's Conference, including novelist Antoinette May, the conference's founding director. Editor and writer Aviva Layton and Hollywood producer and entrepreneur Tom Colbert made notable suggestions which improved the book and their stalwart efforts to see it reach print were deeply appreciated.

Published sources include: *Anastasia: The Lost Princess*, by James Blair Lovell; *The Lost Fortune of the Tsars*, by William Clarke; *Nicholas II: The Last of the Tsars*, by Marc Ferro; *The Romanovs, Autocrats of all the Russias*, by W. Bruce Lincoln; *The Last Tsar*, by Edvard Radzinsky; *Rasputin, The Saint Who Sinned*, by Brian Moynahan; *Nicholas and Alexandra* and *The Romanov Family Album*, by Robert K. Massie; *Russian Imperial Style*, by Laura Cerwinske.

I would especially like to thank my collaborator Ben L. Cotes, for his long and dedicated participation in developing the ideas, content and events depicted in The Romanov Stone. Finally, Judi Yeager should be rewarded by the heavens for her patient and countless rereadings of the manuscript as well as her insightful comments and suggestions.

Robert C. Yeager
March, 2012
The Sea Ranch, California

CPSIA information can be obtained at www.ICGtesting.com
Printed in the USA
BVOW072247260313

316555BV00001B/20/P